SUSPECTING HER

By the Author

Forging a Desire Line

Suspecting Her

Suspecting Her

by

Mary P. Burns

2021

SUSPECTING HER

ISBN 13: 978-1-63555-960-6

This Trade Paperback Original Is Published By
Bold Strokes Books, Inc.
P.O. Box 249
Valley Falls, NY 12185

First Edition: September 2021

Credits
Editors: Victoria Villasenor and Cindy Cresap
Production Design: Susan Ramundo
Cover Design By Tammy Seidick

Acknowledgments

Many thanks to the Bold Strokes Books family for everything you do. Sandy Lowe wears so many hats and yet answers every email whether my hair is on fire or I'm just reaching out to find out if my book proposal passed muster. Cindy Cresap makes sure every comma is where it belongs and puts it there if it's missing (she does a heck of a lot more than that!). Victoria Villaseñor, my editor, keeps me grounded and in line while still giving me free rein, challenges me, goes to bat for me, and questions everything (have you watched *My Fair Lady* yet?).

Thank you to my beta readers, Gary Reed, who has an unerring eye for the forest, and Peter van Gelder, who saw all the trees and caught many small mistakes. I honestly couldn't have done it without you.

Thank you to the Monday Night Brilliant Writers Group for pushing me to be clear-eyed with the second novel.

And a special thanks to Tammy Seidick, the cover artist, who kept going back to the drawing until I had exactly what I wanted. It's beautiful.

Dedication

This novel is dedicated to the Monday Night Brilliant Writers Group—Paulette Callen, Gary Reed, Jon Fried, and Suzanne Schuckel Heath. You have been my staunch supporters since 1994, through many lean years of not writing very much, and now as a published author trying to hone my craft. You have been cheerleaders without pom-poms. You have offered the kind of constructive criticism that makes all the difference when telling me "it isn't working." You've been unstinting with suggestions for fixing things, offering scenes, phrases, and whole sentences that I'm pretty sure later on you realized could've been used in your own work. You've pulled no punches, telling me you wouldn't have read past Chapter 10, or that my main character wasn't very likable, or that I'm window-dressing or sending in a brass band. And then there was the week you told me that the novel should start with Chapter 2 when I was on Chapter 24, and you wished me luck with the rewrites as you walked out the door smiling, leaving me sitting there with the knowledge that I had to tear half the novel down to thread in all the information from Chapter 1 because you were right. You are always right. But you also always come from a place of love.

You have been the most exacting editors a person could wish for (and yes, I'm ending the sentence with a preposition). You are, in short, the reason I'm published. And I thank you for every minute of your time, your care and concern, your unwillingness to let me settle for anything less than my best, for pushing me to do better. But most of all, thank you for your years of friendship.

This is also for Greg Carstens, who invited me into the group when all he knew about me was that I was funny, I had an MFA in playwriting, and I was really good on a country/western dance floor. The world lost a very bright light when you left. I miss you. The Brilliants miss you.

Chapter One

Erin O'Connor swung her legs out of bed and right into a pile of clothes. *Damn.* She pushed back her unruly hair, rubbed the sleep grit out of her eyes, and considered kicking the clothes out of the way, but needing a clean shirt, she picked one from the jumbled mess and sniffed it. *Nope, not the clean pile.* She looked around. *Shit. I left them in the dryer in the laundry room!* She grabbed her key to go down there but knew she'd be late to meet Nat if she did that now. The clothes would have to sit until later. And it didn't matter that Nat was never on time; it was a point of pride for her that *she* was never late. Erin checked her phone for any texts from her and found one of Nat's usual shotgun-short messages, "*c u sn,*" sent minutes ago. Did that mean she was on her way or just getting out of bed? Hard to tell, and if she'd replied with that question, Erin knew the response would include any number of rude finger emojis. She sighed and opened her dresser drawer to find a clean polo shirt balled up in a corner. It was that hideous orange thing with the lime green stripes that a woman two girlfriends ago had given her. It would have to do.

She headed to the bathroom. Ten minutes later, swishing mouthwash and dripping all over the floor, she tossed her dry bath towel onto the pile of dirty clothes. It was too smelly even for her to use. She spat the mouthwash out through the screen on the open bedroom window. With any luck, it hit those stupid red bee balm flowers the landlord grew all around the backyard garden, which ran right below her windows. "Scarlet bergamot," he called them. They smelled like rotting lemons when they bloomed and looked like something Morticia Adams would wear pinned to her dress. But apparently the rats that sometimes cavorted in the garden hated the smell as much as she did, so they stayed away as long as the bergamot perfumed the place. The irony was not lost on her. She'd always wanted a New York City apartment with a garden. When the sublet had presented itself, she'd grabbed it, not knowing that the city's rat population also loved garden apartments. It was a constant battle to see if she could outlast the little gray devils for the lease. Luckily, Lincoln, her Siamese cat, was a formidable foe.

Last night's rainstorm had cooled everything down, but the air was fast getting thick again with a streak of humidity unusual for early June. She turned on the air conditioner, reluctantly removed the screen from the window, and closed it.

It had been so nice sitting on the windowsill breathing in the loamy scent of the garden and watching the moon traverse the sky as the rain tapered off. She loved that wet earth smell of spring and summer with its inherent possibilities of things growing. It was life-affirming. She also loved that the scarlet bergamot didn't smell at night. Which flowers were nocturnal perfumers and which were not had been part of her eighth grade earth science class, but Erin was too busy doodling sketches of pretty redheaded Jennifer Warner in her notes to pay that any attention when Mr. Peterson had illuminated all things floral. Anyway, flowers only mattered to her if she was drawing them. She'd left the windowsill long enough to grab a tall bottle of Coke, dropped a splash of rum into it, and enjoyed the peace and quiet of the garden, grateful for the relief not only from the monotony of the canned air but of having to fork over large sums of money she didn't have to Con Edison to keep the AC running. In fact, she'd spent half the night there after Nat called with not one, but two job offers, neither of which was more than a life preserver, but the call had brought momentary reprieve, lifting the financial burden she'd been grappling with, at least for now.

She looked at the thermometer outside her window. It was already promising the day would be a scorcher.

There was an old crumpled paper towel on her dresser, and she grabbed it to wipe the wet screen. Then she stood in the stream of cold air looking out at the garden. Anika had told Erin she wanted to learn how to draw every flower in it. Erin sighed. It had been ages since she'd even considered a flower. Or kids. She'd been surprised when Anika Jelani, the ten-year-old who lived across the hall with her mother, had approached her while she was sketching in the garden one day, watched her, and asked if she could teach her how to draw like that. Erin pushed away the melancholy thoughts and started to get ready.

A search for her bra was futile. She snapped the polo shirt out and slipped into it. Her khaki shorts were draped on the back of the chair at her desk. Siamese cat hair stuck out all over the front of them from Lincoln spending last night snoozing in her lap while she watched TV, so she gave them a brisk shake and spritzed them with her Tom Ford's Fabulous All Over Body Spray. Every time she used it, she thought fondly of the redhead who'd ambushed her with it the Christmas before last in the aisle of the men's cologne counters at Lord & Taylor, spraying it in the air as Erin passed by, forcing her to walk through the mist when she was on her way to buy her usual Bvlgari Man in Black. After the encounter, she'd taken the woman to the eighth floor ladies' room, locked the door, fucked her against it, and then bought a bottle on the way out. She liked how it smelled.

Sunlight prismed through the empty Coke bottle she'd left on the windowsill. It was an automatic reflex to reach for her colored pencils, to want to catch the rainbow splash on paper, but with the infinitesimal shift of the sun in that moment, it was gone. She looked around the room at the mess that had built up around her, and she knew that grabbing the life preserver Nat had thrown her had been the right choice. She needed to let Nat rescue her this time before something bad happened. *Or something worse than bad. It's already been bad.* It wouldn't be the first time one of them had saved the other, and probably wouldn't be the last, either.

She tossed the bottle into the empty popcorn bowl on the floor next to her bed. It rolled around among the rattling popcorn kernels that weren't stuck in the coagulated butter. Detritus littered almost every surface of the room: mugs and glasses were on the floor on both sides of the bed; there were food-stained plates on the dresser; a fork peeked out from under the pile of dirty clothes. She gathered them all, put them in the popcorn bowl, and hooked several used coffee mugs onto her fingers. She turned to take them to the kitchen, and her desk caught her eye. It was the one sacred place in the apartment, and it was in its usual pristine condition. Sketchbooks were lined up, binders labeled. The notebook of bills and expenses was next to them. The loose-leaf notebook with photos of all her canvases, sectioned into "sold" and "unsold," the latter now the much thicker one, came next. And the "BFF" mug from Nat that held her Blackwing pencils acted as a bookend to them all. She ran the fingers of her free hand over the desk blotter calendar, its big squares bereft of any activities for the last several months now, and lifted the pages to peek at September, and the star on the twenty-second. *Hm. I'll be thirty-three, same age as Jesus when he died. At least he did something with his life.* She let the calendar pages fall back into place. Once upon a time, every one of those blocks would've been filled. Hating the moment of self-pity, she headed for the kitchen.

The living room was flooded with sun. She'd forgotten to close the curtains last night, so she paused long enough to let the jackass from the building across the abutting backyards see that she was completely dressed. He turned away and walked back into the depths of his apartment.

Erin put the dirty dishes in the sink and ran hot water over them. The dish drainer was full of clean pots, plates, and silverware she had no interest in putting away. In fact, lately, she'd been leaving dishes in the sink until she needed them. After Nat's call, she'd washed them all. At least that was one step. She was keenly aware she had to get hold of herself and stop living like this.

Lincoln minced into the kitchen on black-mittened paws like a bored Vegas showgirl, his black tail fanning the air, blue eyes glittering through his black mask. He looked up at her and she stared back at him. Then she pulled one of his ceramic sushi dishes from the cupboard. She'd bought them one day a few years ago when she was in a humorous mood and thought it would be funny if the cat had his own set of sushi dishes. There was a tinfoil packet in the refrigerator with several scoops of last night's chicken and brown rice casserole, and she opened it and dumped it into the dish. She eyed the peas and carrot bits and thought momentarily about picking them out for him. He'd spit them out and try to hide them behind his plate, so it was a matter of which cleaning process was easier. Opting for sweeping them up later, she plunked the dish on his placemat as he wound his way through her legs. He poked his nose disdainfully at the offering, looked back up at her as if to ask what she was thinking. She eyed the broken coffeemaker and sighed. *Neither one of us gets the breakfast we want.* "Fine. Be a junkie." She reached into the cupboard, pulled a small bag of catnip from the highest shelf, and sprinkled a tiny pinch on the food. Lincoln hunkered down. She petted his shoulders. "Don't get too high, buddy. You need to be on your game at all times." He hadn't left a rat by the garden door in a while. She didn't know if that meant the rats were on hiatus until the bergamot finished blooming, or if they'd brokered a détente with Lincoln for the time being.

Five minutes later, Erin taped a note to Anika's apartment door across the hall; she was moving their nine o'clock drawing lesson to the late afternoon. Hopefully, the kid would be back from day camp, or whatever it was her mother sent her to, by then. Having promised to meet Nat in the pocket park across from the subway station, she walked up 72nd Street toward Broadway. Disappointing Anika wasn't something she liked to do, but Nat took precedence. In the canvas bag slung over her shoulder was the sketchbook with the unfinished drawing of the very pretty brunette she'd silently flirted with last night at the Bleecker Street Pizzeria. As she'd sat at one of the outdoor tables, she'd watched the brunette, and roughed out the planes of her face. There was another woman at the table, her wife, maybe, or at the very least, a lover. Until several months ago, Erin wouldn't have let a thing like that deter her. In that moment, though, she summoned a vestige of her old self, tucking a napkin with her phone number on it into the woman's back pocket as she moved past her and out onto the street, glancing back to make sure she'd gotten it. The woman touched her pocket as her gaze followed Erin. Of course, if the woman called, Erin wasn't sure what her next move would be. Her swashbuckling mojo had drained away as evenly as her bank account during this deep valley of unemployment and idleness. She innately knew a hot dog from a cart in Times Square wouldn't be a smooth move no matter how irresistible Erin could be. But she still hoped the woman called. That might be another step in this nascent phase of her recovery. She hadn't wished for a woman for several Christmases. And Santa hadn't left one under her tree anyway, the fat bastard.

Wanting to finish a first draft of the likeness before Nat arrived, Erin settled onto a bench, the weathered wood already warm from the sun. The sketchbook open in her lap, she jealously watched commuters coming out of the subway station head right for the Starbucks on the corner. She'd really wanted a coffee this morning, but even their short eight-ouncer was too much for her tight budget, especially after last night's splurge on two slices of veggie lover's pizza, the second one ordered so she could continue sketching the gorgeous brunette. Anyway, she thought, caffeine is bad for you in this heat.

She tilted her head back and sweat dripped down her scalp. It wasn't a sensation she cared for, so she ruffled her fingers through her hair. It had gotten so long it was grazing her collar and was thicker than she liked it. But since she couldn't even spare the twelve bucks it would cost to go down to that place in the Village where kids learning to cut hair could rent a chair for the day, she had to put up with the annoyance. The sweat dissipated and she closed her eyes as a humid breeze wafted through the stand of trees, making the leaves of the maples shiver and whisper in its wake. Erin rubbed the tip of a white rubber eraser through the sharp charcoal pencil marks and began coaxing out the hint of desire she'd seen in the woman's eyes. She loved sketching and could do it for hours. In fact, it was all she'd been doing for the last several years, although to what end she wasn't sure. What she needed to do was to get back to painting. She needed to sell something. She needed to *do* something. But nothing came to her except these sketches of women, pretty women, old women, little girls holding their mothers' hands, Goth girls downtown, Talbot's girls uptown, tourists at the Met; her pencils moved all day. But nothing translated to the canvases sitting in the corners of her bedroom and living room no matter how often she stared at them in the long dawn hours when sleep eluded her.

As she worked, her mind wandered to Nat's call last night. She'd spent the afternoon hunched over her keyboard studying her financial spreadsheet, working out how much longer she could manage before she'd have to find some place cheaper to live. Even with the unemployment checks, eleven months without a job had strained her finances, and there was nothing on the horizon. It was bleak and she didn't know what she was going to do.

Struggling wasn't new to her. It was how she'd begun her post-graduate life, hitching a ride from a classmate driving to New York City the morning after she graduated from the Rhode Island School of Design, already in debt. Her MFA degree was tucked inside her big black portfolio case, and fourteen dollars and ninety-five cents, all she had to her name, was jammed into her front jeans pocket. She trusted that she'd figure it out. And she had, staying with friends, walking the city instead of taking the subway, and waiting tables. Eventually, she landed a gig with a fine art moving company just to be near the kinds of paintings they moved from airports to museums. Shortly thereafter, she graduated to unpacking the precious cargo under a curator's eye. It was beyond thrilling to be so close to that many masterworks. A semester later, Nat had her master's degree from Columbia's School of Journalism, and they'd gotten their first apartment together. Life had been good. Poor, but good. "Money's overrated anyway," Nat had said. Erin had rolled her eyes, knowing Nat came from money but was foregoing Dad's helping hand at this juncture.

Before Nat's call last night, she'd been thinking about letting the apartment go, and that maybe Nat and Kendra would let her couch-surf for a while until she figured out a way out of this mess. Selling her furniture for some much-needed cash would be a first step. She almost wished she had a home to move back to, and parents who would give her respite. But they'd made it clear when she came out to them after college that she was no longer welcome in the home she'd grown up in. So calling them wasn't an option.

It wasn't like she'd been slacking off in the job hunt arena in the last year. She'd brought her résumé to every gallery in every borough, including Staten Island. No one was hiring assistants, and nobody wanted to see her paintings, either. Most galleries were fighting to keep their heads above water, just like the one where she'd been working until last May. She'd arrived there one bright sunny morning to see the "going out of business" sign in the window and her beautiful May day lost all its luster. By the time the owner locked the door at the end of the week and handed her an envelope of cash, she was in freefall panic mode. However, she'd pushed herself, even getting creative before Christmas and going to stores large and small all over the city selling herself as a display artist. Only one store had bitten, in the East Village, and they couldn't pay her. At least it had kept her busy, though. With a sign in the window announcing who she was, she'd picked up several more stores on the other side of the Village, including the Army Navy Military Surplus store and that small, famous apothecary shop, and those owners *could* pay her. She'd cobbled together enough to keep her from the defeat of temp or gig jobs. So, Nat's very timely call, her saving grace, was going to keep the wolves from the door, and maybe her behind off Nat's couch. If she thought Erin could pass as a "researcher" and had sold that angle to the website's publisher, Erin was going with it. Less forthcoming about the second job, Nat had glossed over something about managing a schedule for someone, and Erin hadn't pressed. A drop of sweat hit the page right where she was working. *Dammit!* She held the sheet up and fanned the wet spot.

Erin scanned the converging streets and sidewalks yet again, in case Hell *was* freezing over and Nat was somehow on time and saw a woman approaching a bench across the triangular park. Everything about her woke Erin up: the tall athlete's form in a tailored red suit, white shell, and black sling-back heels; blond hair pulled into a chic, tight bun; the long, delicate hands with red lacquered nails, bracelets on her left wrist. She was the epitome of the ice queen in this god-awful heat. Even her makeup was photo-shoot perfect, any sweat too intimidated to make an appearance on her. The woman took a large handkerchief out of her big black purse, swiped at the bench seat, sending pieces of bark and dead leaf bits flying, and primly sat down.

Erin looked at her own wrinkled ensemble and almost laughed. When she looked back up, the woman was regarding her pitifully. At least, it seemed to Erin that was what was written all over that beautiful face. Erin blinked at her, and then, neither knowing nor caring if the woman was straight or gay, but hoping she might be the latter, she turned on the high wattage smile gay women always noticed. More than one girlfriend had told her she was "Sarah Shahi handsome" and that it was that smile that took them down when she was chasing them. The blonde hesitated, seeming to reappraise her, then carefully folded the cloth back into her bag and took out what appeared to be a small leather date book with a buttoned clasp on it, glancing at Erin again. As she opened it, her cell phone rang, and she reached into her jacket pocket for it. Erin watched her perfectly arched brows knit into a frown.

"Yes, I can be there in ten minutes. Although we've shown this apartment to this guy three times already… Okay, if you think so." She wrote something in the book, slipped it into her bag, and rose, meticulously straightening her skirt. Erin searched for a wedding band, and then spotted the white Kate Spade logo between the handles of the bag. Single with money. She watched her exit the park, admiring her shapely legs and the perfectly rounded backside in the snug skirt. Just as the woman slid gracefully into a cab, Nat shot out of the subway station and zipped across 72nd Street to the park, dodging the few cars like she was still the center forward on their college soccer team. Erin chuckled at her ensemble of black shorts, an oversized white polo shirt, and the Louis Orlato Spikes silhouette high-tops that were the reason for today's color scheme. And of course, she'd changed the beads in her dreadlocks to black and white. No one could say Nat didn't cut a dash.

"Hey, great! I thought you might leave!" Nat panted.

Erin hugged her, breathing in the familiar strawberry scent, feeling the tension in Nat's body, and then feeling it drain away.

"Are you kidding? I'd have sat here till winter for you, especially since you're paying me now. Am I on the clock yet?"

Nat laughed, her locs clicking softly. "We'll work that out. It's gonna be good pay and we'll have fun." She took a black-and-white checked bandana from her back pocket, snapped it open, and dabbed at the sweat running down her neck. "Oh, damn, it is *way* too hot to run in this heat."

Erin fanned her with the big flat plastic sleeve she'd slipped her sketch back into and watched Nat's skin turn from glossy black to matte black as she cooled down. She was one of a very few people Erin loved to sketch over and over because under the right lighting, there were more shades of color than Erin thought she could ever capture, and it made her appreciate all the more the beauty and resonance of art and life.

Nat refolded the bandana and tucked it back into her pocket. "Okay, so about that second proposition…I wasn't real honest with you."

"Oh?"

"Yeah." She shifted her stance. "Um, you'd be working for me and Kendra. Well, for me, really. Kendra's dance troupe just got booked at the Joyce for the month of August to fill in for a company that cancelled."

Nat began to worry one of the shirt buttons on her collar, a sign Erin knew well. She couldn't imagine why such good news would cause Nat anxiety. "Wow! That's a huge break for them!"

"Huge, yes. Now, here's the part where I really need you. Please don't get bent. This means Kendra will be gone all day."

Crap. It started to fall into place, and she studied a half-folded leaf at her feet.

"She's gonna have rehearsals in the morning, she'll be at her gym all afternoon, and working on choreography at night. And I'm gonna have my hands full with this series of articles for the website and I only have until Labor Day to get it all researched and written. Man, this is pressure! I need another set of hands to run the apartment and another brain to help me with these articles. Because you know how I get when things are hectic."

Erin nodded. "All too well." She could still see their dorm room freshman year looking like a hurricane had hit it during midterm exams and papers, all of it a result of Nat's normally messy persona kicked into overdrive by stress, anxiety, and poor deadline planning, not to mention her devil-may-care attitude toward boundaries. Erin had no choice but to clean and straighten up if she ever wanted to see her desk and bed again. Luckily, she and Nat had bonded by then. And in return for her continued "housekeeping" that year, Nat helped her wade through Chaucer, the Middle English poets, and Shakespeare. Who knew Latin could be such a handy language? She'd taken the blue ribbon that year among art students for her canvas that mimicked an Old Masters painting, the lone figure in it comprised of Latin words or phrases.

"You want me to dust off my Alfred, don't you, Batman?"

Nat grinned. "You always get me."

Erin rolled her eyes and shook her head. Doing it meant pulling together her organizational skills, along with her patience.

"C'mon, I had you at 'I really need you,' didn't I?"

"That depends. You said there was a salary?"

"I can manage a hundred a week, and I got Red to agree to pay you four hundred, and that's something because he runs this website with a fist so tight that the buffalo farts every time he parts with a nickel. It's not much, but even I can do the math on that." Nat shifted on her feet.

Erin quickly totaled it up in her head. She would barely squeak through on that kind of money. It would be enough for rent and utilities, but sustenance was questionable. Considering that her unemployment had run out and she was approaching rock bottom on her savings, this was the gift horse she needed.

"We can mostly work out of my apartment, and if you cook us dinner every night but Monday, when the theater's closed, and stay to eat with us, that'll keep you here, won't it? Because I need you here. Your home is in this city. With me. With us." Nat worried the button again. "I know it's been a little hard for you this year. Please don't be thinkin' about bailing."

Nat knew her well. Erin was acutely aware she was under the microscope as she weighed her answer. Nat knew her body language as well as she knew Nat's. But she already had her answer. Dinners were the deciding factor. All she had left in her freezer were three chicken thighs, a box of corn, and half of a forty-ounce jar of peanut butter sitting next to twenty cans of cat food on her pantry shelf. She'd get to spend six nights a week with two people she genuinely loved, and maybe that was exactly what *she* needed. The thought of leaving Lincoln alone so long every day nagged at her, but considering that he rarely paid much attention to her when she was there, Mr. Personality would probably be fine. She could always make pit stops. Nat wouldn't mind, she loved Lincoln, and a mid-afternoon visit would be better for both of them than a coffee break. Erin nodded her assent.

"Great, you saved my life!" Nat threw her arms around Erin's shoulders.

Not half as much as you just saved mine. Erin held Nat at arm's length. "Won't Kendra wonder why I'm at dinner every night? Have you told her you hired me?"

"Had to. You're cooking. But I told her it's really because you're really depressed and you need to be with people, us in particular."

Erin nodded again. "Thanks, asshole."

"You're welcome. The job helping with the articles was actually her idea, but it's brilliant," Nat said.

"So, we're going to be stuck in your apartment all day and then I change hats and cook?"

"No. I need a partner for the series of articles I'm working on because we'll be out in the field. It's about racism and New York City landlords."

"C'mon, you're kidding. That doesn't happen here."

"You think? I mean, how would you know if Kendra and I didn't get an apartment we were looking at because we're African-American?" Nat thumped her large brown leather bag onto the bench, sat down, and took out her tablet.

"You're not apartment hunting—wait, are you? But…how would you know if you were being discriminated against?"

She patted the bench beside her. "It's always a hunch, that unspoken something. You know, like when you pick up on someone not liking you because you're gay. But that's not what this is about. Look at this."

Nat opened a file. It contained hundreds of applications for a one-bedroom apartment on East 84th Street. Erin swiped through the first few, realizing she was seeing serious personal information: salaries, birth dates, Social Security numbers. Then she saw the name of the realty company the files came from and gawked at Nat in disbelief. It was one of the best known in the city, had been for decades, and it had a sterling reputation.

"Why do you have all this?"

"Keep going. Never mind the personal stuff."

Erin paged through until she came to several with little black circles in the upper right-hand corner. Nat stopped her and silently pointed to them, then circled her hand in the air to indicate she should keep going. Pages into the file, she began seeing brown circles, then yellow and green circles. "I'm lost. What does all this mean?"

"I got this file, and two others, from Marquita Martinez. Remember her?"

"Vaguely." Erin clearly recollected the tall Latina woman with the long, curly black hair and the slow, burning smile who'd been on the periphery of their circle since Kendra had met her in a salsa class the winter before last. Erin had been attracted to her cool beauty, sensing there was something beneath that exterior that would be worth getting to know, but Marquita had a girlfriend. Then they'd run into each other last summer at Cherry's on Fire Island. No girlfriend. But she still had that smile, those dark eyes that gave up no secrets, and legs for days...she couldn't take her eyes from her every time Marquita hit the dance floor, flying through sharp turns and spins with someone else, and neither could any of the other women. And when she managed to score a dance with her, the tropical perfume she wore nearly derailed her. Erin had no idea what flowers in Puerto Rico smelled like, but she imagined they smelled like Marquita. Erin wanted to ask her out, had even bought her a drink to smooth the request. But the women swarming around her near the bar, some of whom she recognized from the city, were sweeter talkers than she was, and she knew she'd be waiting a long time for that date. So she'd retreated, despite feeling Marquita's hand in her front pocket during one slow dance.

"She works for Sumter Realty now," Nat said, "and sent these to me yesterday. Each form is a different letter of the alphabet, and the circles are an additional code. Black for African American, brown for Latinx, purple for Asians."

"Purple? And what, the green are for Martians?"

"Middle Easterners."

"Seriously?"

"Marquita overheard some really disturbing conversations when she was bringing water and coffee into a couple of meetings. So she dug through all the files a couple of nights ago and saw that they had these letters and the circles in the top corners that corresponded to people they don't want to rent to in certain neighborhoods. She brought this story to me and I brought it to my boss. We've come up with a plan for an exposé. And we've got a meeting with him in…" Nat checked her watch. "Oh, crap! Half an hour. We're almost missing it!"

"WE do?"

"Yeah. Red needs to meet you, and I have to print these files so I can work with them hands-on." Nat took a MetroCard out of her back pocket and handed it to Erin. "Fully loaded monthly. Welcome to my team. *Now* you're officially on the clock."

Erin took the card, kissed it, and grinned at Nat. Things were looking up.

CHAPTER TWO

How exactly is this going to work?" Erin asked as Nat muscled her way downstairs to the subway platform, hugging the railing against commuters surging toward them. "And why didn't you tell me I'd be meeting your boss?! I look like I'm on my way to Coney Island for Christ's sake!"

Nat grabbed the closing subway door as the *bing-bong* sounded, and Erin swung into the just-vacated seat next to it before the guy who had been standing in front of it had a chance to think about sitting. She reached for her water bottle as he scowled at her, and Nat widened her stance, effectively edging him over so she could grab the strap above Erin.

"I work for a website that covers the city, Erin. Look at me." Nat swept her hand down her body. "This is how we dress in our office."

Erin chuckled.

"What?"

"You look like Janelle Monae about to hit Rodeo Drive."

"She doesn't shop there," Nat scoffed. "Anyway, point being, most people work from home, so no one's even *in* the office most days. Even Red wears flip-flops and shorts. And occasionally some pretty cool Hawaiian shirts."

"Okay, but what do I have to do or say? I mean, I don't even have a copy of my résumé with me." Not that it would matter. It wasn't exactly corporate.

"Don't need it. I vouched for you. My articles are going to prove that these Realtors are working with landlords to keep certain 'elements,' shall we say, from renting their properties. Like me. I'm an element." Nat rolled her eyes. We're having lunch with Marquita later, so I'll let her tell you more."

Erin caught her breath at the thought of seeing Marquita again. But she didn't want Nat to see her reaction, so she quickly punted. "How big is *Street Sense's* readership now?"

"We topped a hundred thousand a month ago, after that steam pipe explosion on Lexington killed that cabbie and his passenger and we published that map of where all the really old pipes are and when they could possibly blow."

"That's some serious stuff."

"Did you even read the article?"

Erin winced and tried to look apologetic.

"You should. We started with a whole timeline of all the blasts since nineteen eighty. Then we collected info on when these pipes were laid and what they were made of. The corker was running the map of working pipes in those age and material categories against those blasts. We predicted from that what was likely to blow where over the next five years. You think the city's proactively done that? Or Con Ed? Wow, this car is cold." Nat drew her palm across her forehead. "My sweat turned to ice." She grabbed the bandana again, swiped it over her forehead, and returned it to her pocket.

"I checked out the website last night, but I didn't read many articles." In truth, she hadn't read any. She'd been looking at the photos of the New York Liberty women's basketball team.

"Read them. Especially since you're going to be working with me now. That article on the pipes will scare the daylights out of you. The city needs to dig up the really old ones and replace them before someone else gets killed. When the next pipe bursts on, say, Fifth Avenue, like, right beneath a bus, and it will happen, you could be sitting *on* that bus and be toast."

"Gee, thanks. I love thinking about all the ways I could die in this city and then being told about a new and exciting one to add to my list."

Nat shrugged. "Be informed."

"Very funny. That's *Street Sense's* motto."

Nat moved to the door as the train pulled into the 18th Street station and pushed gently on the window a number of times. Erin knew it wasn't a sign so much of her hallmark impatience as it was of her claustrophobia. "I need some strong java before we tangle with Red. You want one? There's a great deli on the corner."

"Nah, I'm okay."

"I'm buying."

Nat's sly glance wasn't lost on her. "Yeah, okay."

Moments later, they strolled down 20th Street, coffees in hand.

"You going to the beach this weekend?" Nat asked.

"Not really doing the beach this summer." She tried to sound casual, not wanting Nat to know that something as simple as Long Island Railroad fares and a beach pass were financially out of her reach.

Mid-block, Nat opened the black wrought iron gate of a mauve-colored brownstone with black shutters and held it open for Erin.

"Classy," she said, scanning the building up and down.

"It's Red's home." Nat clicked the gate shut behind them. "We heard he mortgaged it to the hilt to launch the news site when the *Times* downsized him, but he comes from money and his wife's still at CNN, so I'm sure he's still a one percenter." Nat drained her cup. "Word to the wise, it's been obvious from day one that he's out for blood." Nat paused between the wide stairs leading up to the front door and the smaller set leading to the basement. "The guy that runs the financial *Street Cents* half of the business? He hired him away from the *Wall Street Journal.* Gutsy move on both their parts that's paid off. But when we split the two sections in May, we found out his readership was bigger than ours so now Red's on the warpath to upend those figures. So *our* story could be a big key to that. C'mon, we're downstairs."

Nat bounced down the cement steps, swung open a wrought iron door and hip-checked the door behind it. "This door always sticks in the humidity." It opened with a loud crack, and they were greeted by a wall of cold air. Erin stepped in behind Nat and was surprised by the cacophony of activity: people at little round tables sharing tablet screens as they worked on stories; others walking around involved in phone conversations that grew in volume as they competed to hear themselves above the others; and at the end of the room standing behind a huge desk was a tall, almost larger-than-life bearded redhead shouting at a boy who was shouting back at him. Obviously, Erin thought, this was the infamous Red Fitzgerald.

"Jesus, what's going on?" Nat asked.

Erin heard one guy on a phone frantically ask how many people had been injured or if there were any dead as his fingers scrabbled over the tiny keyboard of his tablet. A kid who looked like he wasn't even out of high school was begging the mayor's office for a quote about the disaster with the new school chancellor. She scanned her surroundings, spotting an old Underwood typewriter on a table in the corner, then took in the worn metal filing cabinets lining the wall. Clocks set to various international time zones hung above them like newsrooms of yore, though a huge flat screen TV smack in the center brought in the modernity. The picture caught her attention even though the sound was muted. She grabbed Nat's arm.

Possible terror attack in Times Square.

They watched the report coming from *New York 1 News* and saw a banged-up car on its side in front of the Marriott Hotel, ambulances and cops everywhere, and Erin spotted a sheet-covered body on the sidewalk. The car, she noticed, didn't appear to be blown up so maybe it wasn't a terrorist attack. Maybe a drugged-out driver had lost control and sped down the sidewalk, knocking pedestrians every which way.

"Jimmy, get off the phone and go!" Red yelled.

"But my friend is right there, Red!" he yelled back, holding up his phone.

"Yeah, but he doesn't have your press pass! Go, dammit!"

The young man picked up his tablet and, cell phone still to his ear, jogged out the door.

"Nat," Red's voice boomed again. "You're gonna have to wait a few minutes. It's like the city exploded this morning. I gotta make sure all my other stringers are out there."

"Sure." She turned to Erin. "Obviously, that's Red. I gotta print out some of Marquita's files. C'mon." Nat headed for a small annex under the London and Tokyo clocks. A compact office machine sat next to a small round table and two chairs. She handed Erin her tablet. "You think you can send 'em to the printer? I need to check all my news feeds, see if there's anything to cover that Red missed." She pulled out her cell phone and perched on the chair.

Erin briefly studied the tablet, brought up the files Nat had showed her, sent them to the printer, and began running them.

A minute later, Nat laughed out loud. "Well, the mayor sure looks like a jackass! That school chancellor he lured away from San Francisco dumped us last night. Sid broke the story at three this morning," she said, turning to Erin. "A friend of his at a party in San Fran overheard the guy's wife say she was packing the house to move to Dallas to take over that school district. He never bothered to call the mayor. I love it! We scooped everyone!"

"Hey." The boy who'd been shouting at Red before leaned into the annex. "Red's calling for you."

"Grab everything and let's go," Nat said, taking the tablet back from Erin. A moment later, they were seated in front of Red's gleaming oak desk as he scowled at Erin.

"Mayor woke me up at six with a verbal Niagara Falls of bile after Sid posted his article on the chancellor in the middle of the night. That's a good way to start the day!" Red grinned at them like a kid who'd just stolen their lunch money. In the next blink, he was the perfect model of a gargoyle. "So. This is Erin O'Connor."

Erin held her breath, not daring to say a word. He held out his hand to her and she exhaled in quiet relief as she stood and shook it, noting that there was even ginger hair on his knuckles to match the thick shock on his head and his neatly trimmed beard and moustache. She detected the faintest trace of a brogue.

"Nice to meet you, sir," she said politely, even though Red didn't seem much older than her.

"What county?"

Erin blanked. *County of New York, isn't it?* She'd committed that to memory for her tax forms. "Oh! Cork, sir. My people come from Cork." *My people?* Suddenly, Erin felt as though *she* might spout an accent.

"Good working-class stock. Maids, liverymen, horse thieves, and gun runners. You come from any of those?"

"My great-grandfather ran a speakeasy here during the Depression."

"Good man!" Red nodded. "I'm a Dubliner myself, but I've been here so long you wouldn't know it anymore. All right, Ms. Robicheaux, let's break us a big fucking story on institutional racism in the biggest, most liberal city in the world! Give me an idea how quickly you and your new sidekick can get this done because I want this front and center right after Labor Day. We'll smack all those returning Hamptons summer shares in the face with the reality of what *can* go on here if the Fourth Estate doesn't do its job."

Red's righteous glee hit Erin head-on. Suddenly, she wasn't just working with Nat but helping to put a spotlight on something her fellow New Yorkers needed to know. And, thankfully, getting paid to do it. It would be a totally different canvas, and she had a feeling that not only was it going to be fun, but she might actually like the work.

Chapter Three

Erin wanted to smack Nat upside the head. "We're going to pretend to be a couple renting an apartment?!"

"Or buying. And we're married. Or not. I have to talk to Buzz about how we're going to handle that online. So, sometimes it'll be me renting, sometimes you, or I'll be your friend checking out the place with you, or vice versa. And sometimes we'll be going after the same apartment like we don't know each other. Marquita will let us know who the apartments actually get rented to."

"I don't get how this will work. They run background and financial checks." Erin suddenly felt sick. *Oh, my God, financial checks.* "They'll find out who we really are. None of them would rent to me on principle."

Nat smiled. "Let me introduce you to Buzz. She's our resident hacker." She walked toward the tiny glass-fronted office tucked next to the printer/copier annex and knocked on the door. Erin swore Nat had said "she," but the person sitting behind the bank of computer screens looked like a twelve-year-old boy. Once Nat got the "enter" high-sign, they sidled in and inserted themselves onto the folding chairs in front of the slab of wood lying on three sawhorses that supported all of Buzz's computer screens. Erin spotted several modems and routers on the floor. The wires were neatly bundled and had labeled tags sticking from them, leading her to study Buzz with admiration. She was a slight young woman with fine features, and Erin *would* have thought she was a boy if she'd passed her on the street. In fact, she reminded Erin of the little boy mannequin standing next to the dad mannequin in the current Brooks Brothers "Sunday Barbecue" window display, only instead of matching white shorts and navy polo shirts with the fat beribboned sheep logo on it, Buzz was wearing a Liz Phair T-shirt, ripped black jeans, and boat decks. With the big tortoise-shell glasses balancing on the end of her nose and her neatly combed short brown hair, she could've passed for Encyclopedia Brown. Erin studied the shelves full of coding books behind Buzz. *Be pretty funny if her dad has a matching Liz Phair T-shirt.* That *would be a completely different Brooks Brothers window display...*

"What chaos can I cause in the world for you today?" Buzz asked, regarding first Nat, and then Erin. Her voice sounded like what Erin imagined would come out of Bugs Bunny if he had that flat Long Island accent.

Nat introduced Erin, explained the story they'd be working on, and pulled out her marriage certificate.

Buzz's foot quietly tapped the floor as she squinted at the certificate. Her fingers flitted across the keyboard and she peered at the screen on the right. "All right, well, this is gonna be a little iffy. I could redo the certificate with Erin's name on it. But if anyone, you know, of import, like a bank or something, happened to be searching for you and your wife, Kendra Smalls, in real time online, seeing someone else on that doc wouldn't be good. So what if we make it disappear for a month from the city's records and wherever else I need to scrub it from while you do this story? You tell anyone who asks that your marriage," Buzz wagged her index finger between Erin and Nat before she went back to typing without looking at the screen, "is so new that you've got a paper doc, that the city didn't e-file it yet. If you need the one for you and Kendra, send a scanned copy. I'm emailing a copy to you now, so you have it while this is gone."

Nat shrugged. "Sounds good."

"Okay," Buzz said. "I'll fix up your bank accounts, Nat. Erin, I'll need your info to do the same."

Erin hesitated.

"Your address or cell phone. I can find everything about you from that."

Erin looked pointedly at Nat. "Could you please excuse us?"

Nat's head snapped back a little. "What. I already know your address and cell number. Not like I'm gonna make off with your identity."

Erin raised her eyebrow.

"Okay, I know *that* look," Nat said, collecting her bag. "Gimme the files, I'll be in the annex."

When the door shut behind Nat, Erin folded her hands in her lap and studied them. "I don't exactly know how to say any of this..."

Buzz straightened her glasses and leaned forward in her chair. "I'm like a priest. I know everything about everyone because they frequently have to confess ugly stuff to me if I'm doing bad stuff for them. Nothing that comes in here ever leaves. I don't have the little window or the collar, I can't absolve you, but when that door closes behind you, I will fix it. For the duration of the story. Then I reverse everything, and you get your shitty life back."

Erin nodded, drew a deep breath, and laid out her financial woes.

"That's it?" Buzz asked. "No exes that need to disappear or alimony payments to ex-wives in another state, no prison record, no gender stuff I need to be aware of, you're not being blackmailed, you didn't steal a dead baby's social to switch out identities? You're not illegal. Just broke. Dude, that's nothing."

"Well...yeah...eww...who steals dead babies' social security numbers?"

"My dad's in prison for it. That's how I came to do this sort of stuff for a living. Okay, I can fix the money thing by this afternoon. I'm assuming you and Nat are apartment-hunting today?"

"I don't know. We have to work out a schedule with our friend who brought her the story. How will you fix my money problems? And so fast?"

"Red has a slush fund, and I'm a magician. I'm gonna put five thousand in your savings account. Don't touch it. And twenty-five thousand in a back-dated CD in your bank in your name because you look like the kind of dork who would have that. Your bank will never know it's there but anyone doing a credit check will see it. Plus I'll lay in a ton of T-bills. That'll make you seem legit. Don't worry, I'll shield it all from Uncle Sam."

That the IRS might be interested in her sudden wealth and come sniffing hadn't occurred to her, so she was grateful for Buzz's technical sleight of hand.

"I'm disappearing your current credit cards." Buzz looked pointedly at Erin. "But keep paying them. And I'll put three new clean ones with a clean history online for you. Don't try to find them and use the numbers. I'll use them once or twice for groceries and at LL Bean." Buzz eyed the polo shirt. "What other kinds of things do you buy when you're not broke?"

"Umm…" Erin hadn't bought anything in so long, she had to think about it. "Oh, art supplies."

"Like what? Paintbrushes, pencils?"

"Yes, and oil paints. And canvases." Erin gave her the names of a couple stores.

"Okay, so we'll buy ya some of that, and I'll pay them in full so they look real. Don't look for the merch, you won't get it. Give me all your other info so I can make sure everything else about you is clean."

"How can you do all this?"

"Don't ask. Dark web stuff. What's your date of birth?" Buzz's fingers hovered over her keyboard.

On the subway ride uptown toward Marquita's office, Erin waited for what she knew was coming. Nat was making notes on her tablet and finally glanced at her. "You wanna talk?"

Erin shook her head. "Father Buzz told me she keeps all secrets."

Nat tapped her stylus against the tablet. "Not like you to have 'em."

Erin glanced sheepishly at Nat. "Thank you for leaving the room when I asked you to."

"I'm your friend. I would never pry. Okay, well, I would, but I won't right now." Nat patted Erin's thigh. "We're good to go now. We're meeting Marquita way uptown on Amsterdam so no one from her office sees us. It's a terrific barbecue restaurant. I'm expensing it."

Erin's heart rate spiked a little. She wondered if Marquita would remember her, or if she was seeing anyone now. Or how she could find that out without seeming obvious.

"I thought she liked her life at Citibank. What happened?"

"Way too dry. She's studying for her Realtor's license now, thought this gig might be a good way to get her foot in the door." After a moment, Nat looked up from her notes. "You said you didn't really remember her. How did you know she was at Citibank?"

Erin hesitated and shrugged. "I dunno. Like the answer to a *Jeopardy* clue, kinda came to me now out of the blue."

Nat returned to the tablet. "Uh-huh."

When they walked into the restaurant, Marquita was already at a table sitting behind an enormous pink daiquiri and looking sharp in a navy blue suit. She waved at Nat, and when her eyes lit on Erin, she sat back, her expression curious.

Still remote, and yet...

After Nat hugged Marquita, she turned to Erin. "You never called me."

"I what?" *Still with that mesmerizing Bronx accent with its slight upper class lilted twang.* Erin stared at her blankly, almost falling into the dark brown pools staring demandingly back at her. Like a scented halo, that perfume that had made Erin weak in the knees on the dance floor enveloped Marquita now, and she felt unsteady again.

"I slipped my number into your pocket at Cherry's that night."

Erin bit her lip. There had been no little piece of paper, no damp napkin in her pocket when she got home that night, only a folded wet dollar bill stuck to the side of her wallet. She'd spent everything else. Erin felt the flush creep up her neck to her face and slowly shut her eyes.

Marquita smiled. "Mm-hmm. On the dollar bill."

Erin had no idea what to say without sounding stupid, and pleading for the number now would look sad.

Marquita tapped Erin above her heart. "You should wear a sign. 'Cute when flustered.' So." She sat down and waved the waitress over. "I think I'll have more files for you tonight. I talked another agent into letting me do a data dump on his files to our main file storage. And I need to know your plan."

"Okay, good, and I have something for you." Nat took a cell phone from her pocket and put it on the table in front of her. "It's a burner. My cell and home numbers are on it. So's Kendra's cell, just in case. And Erin's home and cell, too."

Erin quietly thrilled at the fact that Marquita had her numbers now.

Nat turned to Erin. "You need to put that number in *your* phone. And her cell number, too."

Erin picked up the burner, opened it, transferred the number to her own cell and handed it to Marquita.

"Sure beats a dollar bill, doesn't it?"

Erin felt the flush of heat again as Marquita smirked, her fingers flying nimbly over buttons as she glanced at Erin.

"Okay, so we talked about this plan the other day," Nat said to Marquita, looking at Erin quizzically. "You'll make sure we never get the same Realtor twice, and you'll direct us to the apartments where they're likely to turn us down."

Marquita nodded. "I also know which apartments they might rent to Black tenants, which of course would blow your story to smithereens, so I'll call you when one of those comes available, too."

"You said—"

"I know what I said, mija. But you have to be fair, right? If it turns out I'm wrong, we have to know that, too."

"But we start with the different colored circles," Nat said. "And how do they come to appear on the form? You never said."

"There's just the one rental application and the one sales application on the website. The guys change it afterward for the filing system they put together, using the letter of the alphabet with the colored dot." Marquita took a sip of her drink. "Some of them now carry a blank altered version with them so they don't have to bother with changing it later. Most of the Realtors were in that first meeting, and the subsequent meetings the boss held, but the ones that weren't wouldn't have access to these files because they're on a different drive."

"That's brilliant."

"So we have the original in the files on the shared drive, and then the altered versions in a drive that's password protected, and I have access to both."

"Where would they rent to Nat, then, and not discriminate?" Erin asked.

"Way the hell uptown, they have some tiny juniors in a crappy neighborhood where they're buying up some buildings."

"Why are they buying there?"

"How do you think gentrification begins? Also, I know it's their legal out for what you're about to accuse them of. For instance, if you keep coming back to them and asking to see more places when you don't get the ones you're looking at. Three months ago, they rented a place up there to a nice buppie couple in one of the buildings they're renovating when the couple didn't get the dream apartment they were looking at down here. They told them they were getting their foot in the door of what would become a prize co-op." Marquita made air quotes when she said, "Didn't get."

"You think they'd rent one of those to me. But what about to her?" Nat hooked her thumb at Erin.

"They wouldn't even show those places to her. And this is the thing. They're practicing segregation, and no one knows it."

Nat began fiddling with the button on her shirt collar. "Then if a place opens up there, let's send Erin so we know for sure."

Erin nodded, her eye on Nat's repetitive button fretting, wanting to make sure it was impatience and not anxiety that was at the base of it.

"Okay," Marquita said. "They're gonna have another apartment ready to show up there on Tuesday. We can have her say she heard about it from a friend who decided to pass on it, so I'll put the appointment in the books for you, but we'll send her."

Sitting right here. Erin watched Marquita slip her long fingers under the bowl of her giant daiquiri glass. Granted, she wasn't part of this journalist-Realtor world, so maybe she had to earn her stripes, but they could at least talk to her, not over her.

"Perfect," Nat said, fishing a piece of cornbread out of the basket the waiter set on the table. "And you'll look for whatever color circle they put on *her* application, in case they do a reverse race thing?"

"Yes. And," Marquita took a piece of folded paper from her pocket and handed it to Nat before grabbing her own piece of cornbread and slathering it with honey butter, "here's a list of the next group of apartments showing over the next three days, which Realtor is listing which apartment, and where we're advertising them so you can tell the agent where you spotted the ad."

"We'll need to know that?" Erin asked.

"It's on the form. We want a count of eyes on our media sources, who's competing for which apartments and in what neighborhoods, and where'd they see it advertised."

"Where *do* you guys advertise?"

"Zillo, HotPads, craigslist, Apartments.com, you name it, we use it. Oh, and Facebook."

"Facebook, wow." Nat seemed to be impressed as she took notes. "Who knew people used that to find a home. So what'll happen if Erin shows up for that uptown apartment instead of me?" Nat asked as she perused the list Marquita had handed her.

"By law, we have to show it to her. But I'd bet my next month's rent they wouldn't give her the lease."

"Where do *you* live?" Erin blurted out, hoping it sounded like a casual realty question but knowing by the mild look of surprise on Marquita's face, and the hint of the smile that followed, that she'd been caught out.

"East Harlem, El Barrio. A Hundred and Fourteenth Street, and no, this company didn't rent me that apartment. They don't even know where the neighborhood is." Marquita turned back to Nat.

"Okay, why don't you put together some kind of schedule, and I'll try and get you in first or second if it's not open house."

"Give us an hour, and I'll text you on the burner."

Erin wasn't sure how often they'd be seeing or talking to Marquita, but she hoped it would be frequently. Then the uneasiness she'd felt before when Nat explained how their research was going to unfold settled on her again as Nat took a quick look at the piece of paper Marquita had given her. Her acting career had begun and ended when she was eight with the role of "Third Shepherd from the Right" in her church's Christmas pageant. She'd known then that she wasn't destined for the stage or screen. Would she be able to carry off the various roles of leading lady, wife, or faithful sidekick for Nat now? She'd never let Nat down before, but this would be a tall order.

Chapter Four

Nat sat on the wooden bench hunched over Marquita's list, pen in hand, Erin leaning over her shoulder. They'd stopped in the median on Broadway at 86th Street to work on the list, and when it became apparent to Erin that Nat had a master plan in mind and didn't need her input, her gaze wandered to the long square concrete-contained green dotted with flowers and trees behind them. She took out her sketchbook to see if she could capture the depth of shadows, complete with the cars coming down Broadway. As traffic barreled past, Erin wondered where on 114th Street Marquita lived. She knew she'd look ridiculous running for the M104 bus that was about to stop across the street, ride it uptown, and walk up and down the street east of Fifth Avenue trying to figure out which building was hers. Nat would think she'd lost her mind, like Freddy Eynsford-Hill singing "On the Street Where You Live" because he had to be near Eliza Doolittle or he'd go mad. She'd seen *My Fair Lady* a couple of nights ago on the Turner Classic Movie channel and been completely charmed, the songs still running through her mind days later. She mentally slapped herself for thinking in terms of such an old-fashioned musical. Marquita certainly didn't seem like the "bygone-era" musical type.

Looking over Nat's shoulder again at the notes that now resembled a rather complicated offensive football play with all the crosses, arrows, circles, and x's that she'd drawn on it, Erin knew they'd be busy for the foreseeable future. That meant no time to get to the Metropolitan Museum. It was her favorite place to sketch. Especially since a friend had provided her with a fake corporate ID several years ago that got her in for free. Erin wasn't interested in the art. She knew that by heart, except when a special show went up in one of the many galleries. It was the people she went to study. Well, and a handful of the Greek statues. She could sit for hours in almost any gallery and come away with a raft of sketches. But if she couldn't get there now for several days, she wouldn't see Steve, either, and that bothered her. They'd spent many a quick lunch together at his hot dog cart after she'd gotten to know him years ago. It was by default at first, since his hot dogs were all she could afford if she spent all day at the museum. She could only sneak in so many peanut butter and jelly sandwiches back in those days, before post-911 security searches of your bag, and before food trucks became a thing and nearly wedged Steve out of his spot. Then, of course, she'd spotted the "Vietnam vet" decal, and that had sealed it for her. That they actually liked each other was icing on the cake. He spent time looking at her sketches, and she was fascinated by his stories about Woodstock and the summer of love before the draft had claimed him. She didn't want him to worry, but she couldn't think of a way to let him know she was okay unless she dragged Nat to lunch there one day.

Erin looked back at Nat's notes and easily broke her code scribbled all over the list. She'd plastered *M* for *"married,"* an *N* or an *E,* for which one of them was seeing apartments separately, peppering other initials for who would be the "supportive friend." Nat grabbed her phone, took a photo of the list, and texted it to Marquita. A few minutes later, Marquita sent back dates and times of appointments, two of them for this afternoon.

"C'mon," Nat said. "Let's get the crosstown bus and go check out the neighborhood. And you can tell me what the heck was going on at lunch today."

"What do you mean?" Erin pretended innocence.

"Get out. You can't pull that on me. She gives you her number and you never call her? And then you get all goo-goo eyes at lunch and ask her *where she lives*?"

The bus pulled up, and Erin made a show of riffling through her wallet for the new MetroCard so she could avoid Nat's gaze boring into her. And her questions. But she knew Nat was not about to let it go.

"Why didn't you call her? And when did she give it to you? Where were you?" Nat began the interrogation as soon as they'd settled in seats toward the back of the bus, her knee popping up and down. "In fact, why did you tell me you hardly remembered her?"

Some of Nat's tics of impatience drove Erin crazy. She put her hand on Nat's knee to stop her.

"Oh, that is *so* your mother! She is so baked into you." Nat moved Erin's hand.

"Sorry, I know."

"You know what I told her when she did that to me at our graduation party."

Erin nodded. "Not your mother and barely mine."

"Well, she needed to hear it. And now I need to hear where you were when Marquita handed you the big invitation you forgot to RSVP to, because you told me you barely remembered her."

Erin gazed out the bus window at the familiar buildings she passed almost daily on her way to the Metropolitan Museum. "At Cherry's."

"On Fire Island? Like, last summer?"

Erin nodded again.

"Oh, you didn't just drop the ball here, you were knocked right out the game."

Erin rubbed her face and eyes with both hands. "I was not what she was looking for that night."

"That's never stopped you before."

"It did that time. She was surrounded by dykes who were all way better looking than me and who all wanted to take her home. I didn't stand a chance." Erin sighed.

"Yeah, probably neither did they. She can be pretty picky. C'mon, you made one hell of an impression on her if she put her number in your pocket."

"Yeah. On a dollar bill. I can't believe I didn't figure that out. You know what I did with it? I used it in the Coke machine at the dock before I boarded the ferry the next day. God, I am *such* an idiot."

Nat laughed. "You *are* an idiot! But you're also hot on the dance floor, you know that, don't you? You and Kendra took to those salsa classes like ducks to water."

Erin regarded her dolefully. "What's your point?"

"I'm betting she cares more about how a woman moves on the dance floor than if she's pretty. Or handsome, or whatever we're supposed to be these days. Because that says a lot about how a woman moves between the sheets. I think you could redeem yourself by asking her out. Take her to that salsa bar on Varick and charm her on their dance floor."

Erin shook her head. *Like I could afford that.*

"I'm not kidding! Get all sensuous on her on the dance floor and melt her with those big blue puppy-dog eyes. I'm gonna guess that's the other thing that hooked her that night. I've heard from more than one woman that it's what got them into trouble with you."

Erin reconsidered the proposal. She *was* a good dancer, she knew that. And she *had* seen a spark in Marquita's eyes when she pulled her close for some intricate turns on the dance floor at Cherry's that night. And she did know she was attractive; she just hated being egotistical and admitting it.

"But we're working with her. So I shouldn't be dating her. Aren't there rules about that kind of thing?"

"Gimme a break. This isn't IBM and I'm not your corporate daddy. Go get her. You need something like her right now to break you out of your rut."

The thought of Marquita in her arms again on the dance floor, that tropical scent she wore perfuming the air around them as they moved together, those dark brown eyes pulling her in, sent a shiver through her. Then she frowned. "I'm not in a rut. I'm just a little tired of dating at the moment. Anyway, she probably thinks I'm a loser for not calling her."

"Hey, she teased you in the restaurant and then said you were cute when you got flustered. That's, like, lighting a neon sign. She opened the door any wider, you could move your stuff in with a U-Haul."

Erin snorted. "Not funny."

"Call her tonight. Like, maybe you want to talk about how you should handle one of the Realtors. Then segue to some general life conversation, and then ask her out. I'm tellin' ya, she's into you."

"When did *you* get so handy with the women, Mrs. Married Eight Years?" Erin pushed Nat's shoulder.

"I was born smooth." Nat pretended to slick her hair.

"Ha. You were just lucky that Kendra was ripe for the picking."

"Luck had nothing to do with it. And you need to get back out there with your chaps and your lasso and get yourself a pretty filly. It's pathetic watching you mope."

"My chaps and my lasso?" Erin asked incredulously. "What, I'm John Wayne?

"Hey, like you used to say, ride 'em, cowgirl."

Erin laughed at the reference to the nights she and Nat tried to build each other's confidence in the campus's bars and the city's clubs when they went out girl-hunting. Erin scored each time, but Nat, painfully shy back then, walked home empty-handed almost every time. "Okay. Confession," Erin said. "I have *no* money. I'm flat broke. I couldn't take a girl to the opening of an envelope right now. In fact, Netflix is my last bastion. Without it, I'd go crazy, so anyone I dated, and I'm using the term very loosely, would have to be an inveterate cinephile who wants nothing more than to snuggle up on the couch and watch movies and share a bowl of popcorn they brought with them, because I can't afford that either."

"I knew you were holding out on me. You never skip the beach in the summer, so I figured something was up. But look, you're gonna have money soon, and everybody has to eat, babe. And we both know you've talked girls into bed after sharing a slice of pizza."

Erin made a face at her even though she knew Nat was right.

"Or find yourself a sugar mommy for God's sake. Live a life of leisure at her beck and call."

"Get out. They don't exist."

"Wealthy dykes looking for girl toys? They sure do. What do you think Kendra's friend Lila is doing with that way older CEO? She's being kept, doesn't work anymore, just travels and lives the high life with a wildly successful woman in her fifties."

"Seriously? *That's* what Lila's doing? Wow… And fifties isn't way older anymore."

"She's, like, twenty years older than us, dude. That's 'I could be your mom' older. Actually, that should be my next series of articles. 'Lesbian Sugar Mommies.'" Nat spread her hands above her head like she was highlighting a marquee. "Wouldn't that be a terrific research gig!"

"Kendra would put a leash on you so fast."

Nat laughed.

They got off the bus at Lexington Avenue and wandered around the streets checking out shop windows until it was time for their appointment. The building on 84th Street was a nicely kept six-story brownstone with a small patch of grass out front, tiny garden beds, and a wrought iron fence with a gate. It was the kind of building that was fast disappearing all over the city, being torn down, along with neighboring buildings on either side, their footprint being replaced by ugly sliver buildings of glass. Nat rang the bell for 6C and they were buzzed right in.

"Nice lobby and elevator," Erin said as they rode up.

In the apartment, the Realtor, a tall young white man with jet-black hair and dark eyes, extended his hand to Erin. He was handsome and she could tell he worked out. *If I was straight, he'd be the kind of guy I'd go for.* Then she imagined him as a woman and had to look away. She knew she was blushing, and that he'd caught her. She'd dated quite a spectrum of women but always seemed to be drawn to tall, dark, and striking. And polished. She liked a confident woman in a well-cut suit.

"Nice to meet you, Ms. Robicheaux. I'm Jack Hobbs." He took a card from his inside jacket pocket and handed it to her as he shook Erin's hand.

"Oh, no, she's Natalie Robicheaux. I'm her friend, here for moral support." Erin exchanged a quick glance with Nat, whose face had already become a guarded mask. She tried to hide her anger at the obvious snub, and now she knew why Nat had chosen to run with this story. Things like this happened to Nat more often than either one of them cared to admit. Erin only caught some of them, others being so subtle that they passed right over her head until Nat said something, which wasn't often.

"Oh!" Jack laughed and handed his card to Nat but neglected to shake her hand. "Really glad you could come see the apartment. It's a good deal, and I'm sure it'll be gone within the hour if it isn't already. Why don't you poke around? Brand new kitchen, hardwood floors recently scraped and polished, and we enlarged the closet in the bedroom." Jack walked down the hall toward the bedroom, turning around to point to the bathroom. "All new fixtures," he said, his smile announcing that this was something special indeed.

Erin peeked in; it was just another generic Home Depot bathroom, all chrome shiny and skinny tiles in ugly greens.

Jack stood in the bedroom with them. As Nat took a desultory look around, Erin pulled a notebook and a tape measure out of her bag.

"You're kidding, right?" Nat said, a goofy smile dawning on her face.

"Well, don't you want to know if all your furniture will fit?"

"You know all the rooms' measurements are online, right?" Nat asked.

"I always double-check," Erin said.

"Smart. Hey, I'll leave you to it," Jack said. "I'll be in the kitchen. Holler if you need anything."

When Jack left, Nat whispered, "What the heck are you doing?"

"Pretty sure we don't have to whisper, he's all the way down the hall. Aren't we supposed to look the part here?"

"Well, yeah, but that's a little over the top, don't you think?"

"If I thought that, I'd be standing here with my thumb up my butt. And now I'm just curious if what they say online matches what we're going to measure here. Take that and walk to that wall." Erin handed Nat the end of the tape measure. Nat dutifully pulled it to the wall, and Erin looked at the inch marker by the metal housing in her hand. She matched the measurement to a diagram she'd quickly sketched in the notebook and motioned Nat to the other wall. "What would you do if they told you the place was gone and offered to show you another smaller apartment?"

"I'd be thrilled. More ammo for my article. Anyway, I can get this information from Marquita." Nat walked back to her.

Erin opened the closet, stood inside and took the tape measure from Nat. "Don't do that to her. She's sticking her neck out for you, not working for you." She measured and made notes.

"Okay, Mom. You're right. And seriously, you carry a tape measure around?"

"You don't? Go look busy in the bathroom. I'm gonna play twenty questions with our Realtor."

"What? Don't blow this on me. What are you gonna ask him?"

"Nothing! I'll chat him up. Come out in two minutes and we'll measure the living room and kitchen, make it look like we're interested."

Erin walked into the living room and plopped down on the couch.

"Everything okay?" Jack asked.

"She's looking at the bathroom. What a nice place! I hope she takes it."

"Hey, maybe she'll get it. Quite a few people were here earlier looking at it."

"A lot of people?"

"Fair amount. And we had a barrage of online applications."

"You must see a whole cross-section of the world in this city, and everybody looking for apartments."

"That we do."

"Hard to figure out who to choose?"

"Not really. Whoever got here first with the best background and most money usually wins."

Nat walked into the living room. "Can I fill out a lease form? I like the place."

Jack took out his cell phone and tapped some keys. "What's your email address? I'll send it to you, make it easier. Then you can just send it right back to me."

A moment later, Nat had it. "Help me fill this out. Sooner I do it, the faster he gets it back."

Erin felt a gentle nudge from Nat's hip as she surreptitiously pointed to the letter A on the top line and the black dot at the top right of the form.

Erin nodded. This was one of the doctored forms Marquita had said the guys used. Halfway through the task, she corrected Nat on one of the previous addresses.

"How do you remember that?"

"Because I spent more time at *your* apartment that year than at mine. So, listen," Erin said, looking at the agent. "Jack says a lot of people looked at this place."

"Oh, dang." Nat looked up at Jack. "Does that mean I'm out of the running, too late to the party?"

"Not necessarily," he said, the smile on his face not reaching his eyes. "Maybe everyone in front of you is looking at other places and will go with something else, so you'd be at the head of the line then. You must be looking at other places, too, aren't you?"

"Yeah, of course. But this beats everything else I've seen. Kinda falling in love with it." Nat's gaze roamed the living room before settling back on the tablet screen. "Say, this black dot on the form? Like, that means I looked at the place in person or something?"

Jack chuckled. "No. That's so our girl knows you're interested and can do the financial background check."

Erin had to bite her tongue. She was mildly disturbed knowing that reference to "our girl" meant Marquita. Maybe if he'd appended "Friday" to it, it wouldn't have been so insulting. Equally insulting was the bald-faced lie about the black circle. Marquita had said the company line was that it was a "by the neighborhood" ruse.

"Okay, that's cool. But I'd have thought anyone filling out an application means they're interested, and you wouldn't have to mark them."

Erin gently kicked Nat without looking up from the application on the tablet. She was being way too obvious.

"Yeah," Nat continued, unperturbed, "one other real estate company already did a check on me today. Think I came up clean or they would've called."

"Oh? Who else are you working with?"

"Brown," Nat said quickly.

"Who'd you see over there?"

Nat looked at Erin. For a moment, she felt like a deer in the headlights. Then she flipped open her notebook. "Oh, crap. I didn't write her name down..."

"Cheryl?" Jack asked.

Erin tried to recall the faces she'd seen on the big poster in the Realtor's window at Broadway and 72nd every time she'd passed it. "Redhead?"

"Yeah, that's her. What property?"

"Eighty-fourth, West Side," Nat said as Erin slowly breathed a sigh of relief at wiggling out of Jack's question. They needed to get better at this.

"Oh, okay. Cheryl's really nice. Well, hey, you know if she doesn't come through, call me." He pointed to the pocket where Nat had put his card. "We'll get you something for sure. So send me that application. You can find your way out okay? I have another appointment in about two minutes."

Out on the sidewalk, Nat shook her head as she studied the facade of the building. "Well, that sounded like a kiss-off if ever I heard one. And I got a black dot."

"Yeah, but when I talked to him, either he's a really good liar or he's covering something up because he talked about backgrounds and bank accounts being the deciding factor, and I actually thought I heard the truth in his voice."

Nat patted her on the shoulder. "Nice white girl."

Erin was a little stunned. "No, really."

"Let's go see what you get on Seventy-Fifth," Nat said. "And then we can decide what you're making for dinner."

"Okay, but I'm going to have to stop back at my apartment."

"Yeah, Lincoln, I know."

"No, Anika's art lesson. I blew her off this morning, told her I'd see her at four o'clock instead. And I have to pick up my bathing suit. I think there's an Equinox near your apartment, so I'll use their pool after dinner."

Nat snorted. "Good thing you got a free lifetime membership pass out of Lana before you dumped her. Those gyms are mucho expensive. And how long you been teaching that kid? Is she any good, or is this just for the money?"

"She's paying me a quarter out of her allowance. Which is all of seventy-five cents, so it's a huge cut of her gross income."

"Oh." Nat sucked on her front teeth derisively. "Who can buy anything for seventy-five cents anyway? Why isn't her mother paying you a decent salary?"

"Her mom is trying to teach her fiscal responsibility. And because the contract is between Anika and me, I asked her to stay out of it for Anika's sake. And yes, she's a good artist. She's got an eye."

"You like her. Softie."

"Shut up. You can go to the market with a shopping list while we work. Then we can go down to your place."

"Good thing her mom isn't teaching *me* how to watch my money. That woman's a little strict, don't you think?"

"Anika's ten. She needs strict." They headed to the bus stop.

Erin saw Anika leaning against her apartment door as she slipped the key into the lobby door lock. She was concentrating on her cell phone screen, gently probing at one of the puff pom-poms in her hair with a small afropick. Smiling, Nat poked Erin and pointed to her sneakers, which were done in bold blocks of color that matched the shirt and shorts she was wearing. Erin chuckled. The kid definitely had style.

A plastic bag of clothes sat on the floor next to Anika. She looked at Erin and Nat disdainfully. "You. Are. Late."

"Yes. I. Am. And oh, that's my laundry!"

Anika picked it up and handed it to her. "You're welcome. Mama folded it for you. You're insane for leaving it down there." She leaned against the door again.

"What, you think old Mr. Phelps in Four-D is going to steal my panties?"

"Eeeww. And are those Louis Orlatos?" Anika pointed to Nat's sneakers.

"They are."

"Huh."

Erin unlocked the door, but Anika still didn't move. Instead, she held her hand out. "You. Owe me. An apology. For being *laaate!*" Anika drew the word out dramatically as only a ten-year-old could.

Erin bowed. "My sincerest apologies, grasshopper. I was delayed chasing the mysteries and injustices of life with my very good friend here."

"That's some bullshit. What injustices?"

"Language, young lady. Your mother would not like that. And let's hope you never have to find out," Nat said.

"You don't want me reporting you to your mother, do you?" Erin asked.

Anika frowned. "You're too cool for that."

"You got the grocery list," Erin said. "We'll be working for about half an hour."

"No, I'm staying."

"What for?" Erin asked.

"How do I know you're teaching her how to shade all skin tones properly, or draw the right consistency of hair?" Nat looked from Anika's hair, with the three pom-pom puffs, to Erin.

Erin looked at Anika, who rolled her eyes. Then Erin took her sketchbook out of her back pocket and paged through it until she found the one of Nat, showing it first to Anika and then to Nat.

Nat nodded. "Wow. Okay. Nice."

"She already explained this stuff to me. Light and shade and tone. How that affects oranges that have nubby skins and peaches that are soft and smooth."

"Are you saying you and I are oranges?" Nat asked.

Anika flicked Nat's shoulder with her middle finger and thumb. "I'm saying we're all different." Anika showed Nat her nails, each one with a different color nail polish. "Oranges are different from peaches but they're all fruit. And like the daisies are way different from those little Johnny-jump-ups in the garden but they're all flowers. I'm even different from you." She held her arm next to Nat's, her midnight black skin so much darker. "I'm from Ghana. See? Different. But the same."

Nat nodded. "Okay." She took Anika's hand and studied her fingers. "You're smart for a ten-year-old. What's with the nails?"

Anika grinned. "All the colors I want to paint with!" Then she frowned. "But we're still sketching in pencil."

"In time," Erin said.

"She says I'm still a grasshopper," Anika whispered to Nat.

"You are," Nat whispered back. "But here's a news flash. She wouldn't have taken you on as a student if you didn't show promise."

"She just wants my quarters for the washing machines," Anika whispered, holding up the coin.

Nat and Erin laughed. As she unlocked the door, Erin had to admit Nat was right. She liked this kid. Mentoring her had become the highlight of her week.

CHAPTER FIVE

The next morning, Erin got in a workout at a pool closer to her apartment, and then she met Nat to look at an Upper West Side apartment as a couple. As Nat had predicted, the Realtor sent a doctored Form A to her complete with a black circle. Erin had been asked to fill out the original form on the website the previous afternoon. They were both completely charmed by the apartment neither one of them would ever have been able to afford. "Unless I won a Pulitzer," Nat said. "That comes with fifteen thou. That'd get me….what, three months here?" She'd looked thoughtfully around. "Hey, what's *your* Pulitzer?"

"My what?" Erin asked.

"Your art world award. Don't they have some big award for painters?"

"Oh…" Erin thought for a moment. "I guess maybe the Annenberg…or the MacArthur."

"Yeah, but that's for geniuses."

Erin frowned at her. "Walking on thin ice, babe."

"You gotta prove yourself again," she said, matter-of-factly. "You never talk about it and that's not good. You threw it away."

Although it had always been Nat's way to call her on her shortcomings even though she wasn't being judgmental, Erin couldn't believe Nat had said that, and glowered at her. Of all the people in her life who knew the insurmountable wall she'd run into, Nat had always been the most sympathetic, which said a lot about her friends. But today, Nat's matter-of-factness irritated her. "Fuck you, Nat."

"Hey, I didn't mean it that way—"

"Never mind." Erin walked over to a living room window.

Nat joined her. "It was five years ago. Nobody remembers reviews."

"Everybody who attended that Biennial or read about the girl genius barely out of art school who couldn't paint a straight line will always remember that review when they see the next canvas I hang anywhere."

Nat ran her hand along the windowsill. "I think you're wrong," she said quietly, but Erin was already walking away.

After lunch they split up and Erin headed for a place on 104th Street and Riverside Drive, still angry at Nat's insensitivity, even though she knew it hadn't been her intent. She peered in the window of the ground floor studio, saw quite a number of people at the open house looking around, mentally girded herself, and walked in. She almost turned around to leave, but then she saw her. The hot blonde from the park yesterday morning. And she looked magnificent in a striped navy and white shirt-waist dress, a navy blue belt cinching her waist, and red heels; a thin red headband held back her shoulder-length blond hair, the waves running through it in gentle slopes. Erin wanted to run her hand over them.

She tucked her madras camp shirt into her khaki shorts, ran her fingers through her hair, and went in. The woman, talking animatedly with a young couple, reached into her pocket and handed them a business card. Erin recalled the snippet of phone conversation she'd heard. *Of course, she's a Realtor.* Erin watched her for a few minutes as she moved around the apartment talking with people, noticing that she didn't exclude anyone. She took the woman in, from the red heels up her curved calves, and slowly up all the rest of her curves, and when she alighted on her face, the woman was studying her with an amused smile that quirked up on one side. It was a smile that reached her eyes. Caught, Erin felt the blush rising, and crossed the room.

"Hi. I'm Erin O'Connor. Should I leave? It's a bit crowded." She tilted her head at all the other people, and then proceeded to get lost in the deeply set bright blue eyes. There were crinkles at the corners, and a quick glance at her hands told Erin the woman was older than she'd thought, maybe in her mid-forties Her hands were the long, graceful kind that gave Erin goose bumps. Women with those kinds of hands were always such good caressers. She hoped the vibe she was picking up from that smile was right. It didn't *seem* to be a sales smile. Despite Nat warning her not to do anything stupid, maybe a night with this woman could be that lift she needed.

"Depends on what you came for." The woman sucked in her lower lip.

Erin chuckled quietly. "Well, I thought I came for the apartment."

"Uh-huh." She nodded, quickly smiling at someone walking past.

"But it looks like I'm too late. There must be two dozen other people here now. Not to mention the hundreds you've probably already seen. And I so hate to leave empty-handed." Erin widened her eyes a little, hoping that at thirty-two, she could still carry off the ingenue's innocent deception.

The woman's smile broke out completely and she handed Erin her business card. "You can find our form online at this address." A perfectly manicured apple red nail tapped the website listing at the bottom of the card. "Let me know if you need any help filling it out," she said, arching an eyebrow before turning back to talk with other potential customers.

Crestfallen, Erin put her phone on a corner of the kitchen counter and watched the agent walk away. Then she looked at her business card.

Catherine Williams

Commercial / Residential Broker

Licensed in the State of New York

Erin glanced back up at her, now ensconced in conversation with another young couple. *She looks like a Catherine.* A few minutes later, Erin was completely focused on the form on her phone when

Catherine slid a white card in front of her with an address written on it. Erin caught the expensive watch on her wrist as she looked up.

"There are other places I can show you. Because you're right, you probably won't get this one. Too many other people got here ahead of you today."

"Thank you." Erin was genuinely surprised at her willingness to be helpful.

"Would you be free in about an hour?"

"I would be." She'd miss out on getting winning lotto numbers for a chance with this one.

Catherine pointed to the address on West 92nd Street written on it. "Meet me there."

"Would this be a private showing?" She looked pointedly at Catherine.

"It would be."

That settled it. She'd be there.

An hour later, Erin stood in front of the brownstone. She hunkered down on the steps, against the wall, in the one slice of shade provided by the slant of the three o'clock sun and took out the small sketch pad she always carried with her. Moments later, she was engrossed in shading the shoulder area around a likeness of Catherine, wondering if she'd flirted at the studio apartment as a matter of business or if she'd sensed Erin was gay and offered her this showing for a reason other than business. She had seen her flirt with a number of men at the apartment, had even watched her become a little playful with one of the young couples she'd been talking with. If this was part of her sales pitch, Erin wanted to find a way around it. She'd sensed something grounded and down-to-earth in Catherine despite their mutual teasing. Maybe she was that one-in-a-million who really wanted to help. And maybe Erin was drawn to that after so many years of dating unfocused women. Maybe there was more to Catherine, maybe that thought made her a little nervous. And maybe, she thought, shaking her head, she was getting way ahead of herself. Her thought process was interrupted by a high-heeled foot hitting the step right below where she sat.

"Well, well, well. Eager beaver, aren't you?"

A wry smile crossed Catherine's face when Erin looked up at her, and she quickly flipped the sketch pad closed and smiled back. "You have no idea."

"Oh, I think I might. Shall we go upstairs?" Catherine retrieved a set of keys from her pocket and opened both the front door and the inner vestibule door. "Hold on a minute," she said, and headed toward the mailboxes in a small anteroom on the left. Erin watched as she opened and cleaned out a box, quickly sorting through and winnowing out junk mail to a trash can. Then she headed to the stairs. "It's the fifth floor, so nice sun on all sides."

Erin followed her up the wide gray-green granite stairs, her eyes glued to those lovely long legs in the red heels, and the calf muscles she'd admired flexing and relaxing hypnotically. "That's a nice service you provide."

"What?" Catherine glanced over her shoulder.

"Picking up your client's mail?"

Catherine laughed. "Well, I guess you could say she's my client. I *am* selling her apartment."

Erin realized almost too late that Catherine had stopped and turned around.

"It belongs to my ex."

Erin tripped on the step and felt Catherine's hand on her elbow. Oh good. Exes were always a good indicator of fun.

"I'm not showing it to just anyone. At least not yet. It's a beautiful apartment. I want to make sure it goes to the right person."

A mild wave of guilt swept through Erin at the possibility that she was misleading Catherine into thinking she might be that person. On the other hand, if she had the bedroom in mind…

At the top of the stairs, Catherine unlocked both the top and bottom locks of 5R and swung the door open onto a sun-filled oasis of carved oak walls and floors the color of autumn acorns. Erin felt an immediate peace as she stepped in, thinking the cozy yet stately living room looked staged except that the furniture was too nice, not the big-box chain store stuff one saw in most of the "nobody really lives here but we're pretending they do" apartments for sale in Manhattan.

"Wow." Erin turned to look at the whole room and the adjoining open kitchen, noting the hallway she was sure led to a bedroom, and then ran her hand along the back of the navy blue couch. Several red pillows sat on the couch, each with a different landmarked building done in needlepoint: the Empire State Building on one, the Chrysler Building on another, and Radio City Music Hall featured on the third pillow. Two wingback chairs upholstered in a smart regimental stripe sat opposite the couch, a walnut butler's table between them.

"This isn't a usual apartment staging," Erin said. She looked at Catherine, who very neatly fit into the decor in her own navy and red.

Catherine nodded. "They're from my apartment."

"Oh. Is there anything *left* in your apartment?"

Catherine laughed again. Erin liked the quiet depth of it.

"I wanted it to look nicer than usual, so it goes quickly. Too many painful memories here for me. Now that Susan's decided to sell it, I don't want it on my hands for a long time."

"I certainly understand that."

"Been there, done that?" Catherine asked.

"Yes." Erin thought briefly of Adele, who had breezed into her life right after college, swept her off her feet, and then made her life a living hell five years later when she had an affair with her boss, who ultimately won the battle for Adele right when Erin needed her most. After she'd recovered, it had been one ultra-short relationship after another so she wouldn't get burned again. For the first time, Erin realized, standing in the middle of someone else's home, even if it *was* for sale, that she wanted something more.

"Erin?"

Erin snapped back and knew from the look on Catherine's face that she'd wandered far away for a second. "Sorry, took a train I shouldn't have gotten on."

"And apparently got off at the wrong stop. She did a number on you, didn't she?"

"No…Yes…I don't know. Or maybe I didn't see that it was over. My mistake."

"Never a mistake if you learn from it."

Erin regarded her and then looked out the window. Only a flippant response came to her, and it didn't feel right to say it out loud.

"Did you?"

Erin looked back at her questioningly.

"Learn from your mistake?"

"I think I took the wrong lesson away from it. And I'm only realizing that now."

"Why don't you have dinner with me tomorrow night and we can discuss whether or not it's too late? To learn."

Erin felt the pulse in her neck gently pounding. She could hardly take her eyes off Catherine, but she was pretty certain dinner with her wasn't a good idea on a number of levels. Her thought about a one-night stand vanished into her promise to Nat not to screw anything up with this story. Catherine would definitely complicate things.

"You're not in the market to buy an apartment, are you?" Catherine asked.

"No. But I bet you knew that when you invited me to see this place."

"Mmm. I think I did, and I'd love to know why. Maybe we can also discuss what you *are* in the market for over a nice plate of Thai food? Or Mongolian barbecue?"

"I kind of like the diner on the corner at Broadway. Unless you have agonizing memories from a past relationship there." So much for not allowing things to be complicated.

Catherine snorted. "Susan would never have been caught dead in a diner. And I do like a good bacon cheeseburger now and then. Seven thirty tomorrow night?" She picked up the set of keys from the small silver plate she'd dropped them in by the door.

"You work late hours," Erin said, taking one last look around before walking to the door.

"Apartments don't sell themselves." She opened the door.

"But they do, don't they? Either you fall in love with a place, or you don't." Erin followed her out.

Catherine considered the remark, then fit the key into the top lock. “You have a point.”

“I know I’m right. Tell me one thing you’ve said to a prospective buyer that made a difference and got them to buy a place they were iffy about liking.”

“The gold standard in a New York City apartment, of course.” Catherine pointed down the hall. “Washer and dryer in a separate little laundry room.”

Erin paused on the top step and looked at her, a smile breaking slowly.

“I win,” Catherine said, a teasing smirk challenging Erin.

She knew immediately that she liked sparring with this woman. Catherine wielded a sharp sword and Erin liked the challenge she presented. As they walked down the stairs, she banished the image of Nat admonishing her.

CHAPTER SIX

"Listen, I didn't get to the market so there's nothing to eat," Kendra called from the bathroom.

"Don't worry," Nat called back. "I'll take care of it." She leaned over and whispered to Erin, "Can you order from our market and get them to deliver it?"

Erin nodded.

Kendra trotted into the living room looking for all the world like a tall, thin marathon runner in loose track shorts, a sleeveless T-shirt. and a sweatband pushing up the shock of Odell Beckham Jr. blond curls she'd adopted, her wide brown eyes focused on Erin.

"I'm really glad you'll be having dinner with us while you and Nat work on the articles," Kendra said, shouldering the enormous gym bag she'd hauled out of the bedroom.

"Shouldn't you be putting that on one of those luggage wheelies?" Erin asked. "You don't want to pull something before you get to your first rehearsal."

"Oh, this is all going into the dressing rooms they're giving us at the theater, so I won't have to lug it anywhere again. Besides, this has to be my workout today since I can't get to the gym." She kissed Nat. "Later, doll."

Not wanting to lose any time, Erin turned to Nat. "What am I ordering at the grocery store?"

Nat looked at her blankly. "I don't know. What are you cooking us this week?"

"What do you two usually eat?"

"Oh, crap." Nat put her head in her hands. "I don't pay attention to that."

"Seriously? Well, what did you have last night?"

Notepad in hand, Erin opened the refrigerator and started poking around in bins and on shelves as Nat pulled the last few dinners from her memory. Within an hour, they had cobbled together several menus, called the supermarket, gotten groceries and breakfast delivered, and made notes for the next few days' worth of apartment visits before heading uptown to a place on West 94th Street.

"Hey, you didn't give me yesterday's report on that studio apartment."

"Yeah, about that…" Erin hesitated.

"What, you didn't go?"

"I went." Erin picked at one of her cuticles. "Ton of people there. Filled out the application anyway so Marquita can flag us."

"Okay, good. You know I don't care about the particulars. I just want those circles. Or not."

"Yeah, I know, but…" The subway pulled into the 96th Street station and they got off and joined the other commuters slogging up the stairs in the wet June heat.

"But what? You killed the Realtor because he was a jackass? Can't say I'd blame you."

"No. I have a date with her." She glanced at Nat who had stopped dead on the steps. The look of anger on her face was apparent. The guy behind her tried to elbow past and pushed his way around her. So did everyone behind him. "Way to bury the lede, Clark Kent. A date! You're kidding me! You know you can't meet her. You can't jeopardize this story, Erin."

Surprise and anger flooded her, even though she'd known full well she shouldn't do it in the first place. "You can't tell me not to see Catherine."

Several commuters grumbled loudly as they pushed past, and Erin grabbed Nat's wrist, but she pulled it away.

"You *can't* blow this story on me."

"I won't. It's one date, Nat. I'm not an idiot. C'mon, before somebody shoots us for blocking the stairs." When they reached the corner outside, Erin confronted Nat. "She's gorgeous. I want to see her. And anyway, it'll probably be a one-off. She's way out of my league."

"Seems to be your MO these days, hotshot." Nat crossed the street, not waiting for Erin.

"What, you think Marquita is out of my league?" But her further entreaties fell on deaf ears as they made their way to the showing. In the apartment, Nat stalked from room to room as Erin chatted up the Realtor, and when he gave her his business card and told her to log on to their site to fill out the application, Nat approached.

"I'm not acquiescing, so don't even ask," Erin said, not looking up. Nat angrily turned and left. She was going to have to ask Marquita later if a dot appeared on this application because Nat was walking around in such a snit the Realtor might not know they were there together. By the time Erin emailed the application to the Realtor and ran to catch up with Nat, she was almost ten blocks away. They walked in silence, Erin catching her breath after the run, Nat pointedly looking straight ahead, stone-faced.

"It was the original application, no circle," Erin said, once she could talk. "He didn't know you were with me."

Nat didn't register that she'd heard her.

"So I called Marquita. He wasn't in the meeting that day. But she's going to look at his files." Erin had been tempted to ask her to look at Catherine Williams's files, but an idea had begun percolating instead: what if, over dinner tonight, she convinced Catherine to show her ex's apartment to Nat? If Catherine reacted negatively to Nat, it would be one more piece of ammunition for the articles, and she'd never go out with her again. She hoped Nat wouldn't be hurt in the face-to-face moment if Catherine did react negatively.

Silence enshrouded them at the next apartment, Erin again playing the possible tenant, Nat the helpful friend, though being less than helpful at the moment. Finally, when no one was around them in the living room, she hissed at Nat, "Come on, act the part! Don't blow our cover!"

"I'm not the one asking Realtors out on dates," Nat snapped.

"Well, this one's really not our type. He's got the wrong parts," Erin shot back.

Nat folded her arms over her chest.

Erin confronted her. "Why don't you trust me?"

"Because you're a goddam Casanova and you'll be confessing everything while you lie in her arms. When are you seeing her anyway?"

"I don't know," Erin lied. "And I don't confess everything to the women I sleep with. I barely tell them my name."

"No, you just steal them."

"Oh, my God, that's *nine years ago*. I didn't steal Yvonne from you, for the hundredth time. You walked away from her. And I don't need Catherine to know a damn thing."

"Except that you want to get into her panties."

"Pretty sure she already knows that."

"Everything okay here?" The Realtor approached them with a clipboard, a look of confusion on his face.

"Yup, terrific," Erin said, shifting gears to sunny, eager apartment hunter. "I fill out your application online, right?"

"Yes, right. And is it just you or are you renting together?" The Realtor indicated Nat.

"Nope, just her," Nat said. "I don't think I could live with her if you paid me."

"Oh, okay." The Realtor nodded and laughed a little nervously. "Well, then, fill out the application on our site and email it to me." He handed Erin a business card. She and Nat looked at each other.

"It's actually already on your site's files. I looked at another apartment this morning."

"Oh, well, hold on and I'll chat with you in just a second." He shook her hand. "I'll be right back."

Erin turned to Nat. "Why don't you wait for me downstairs? This won't take long. And maybe," she growled as Nat swung her canvas bag onto her shoulder, "you can cool off a little bit."

Nat glared at her and strode out of the apartment.

After she and Realtor found her form on his tablet, Erin raced down the stairs expecting to sprint another several blocks to catch Nat again but found her sitting on the bottom step of the brownstone stoop twirling several dreadlocks together as she read an ebook on her phone. She settled next to her.

"You're gonna have a twisted mess on your hands if you keep that up."

"Kendra's good at untangling."

"She'd have to be to put up with you."

Nat looked at her. "Sometimes I hate you."

"Sometimes I hate you, too, dear."

Nat sighed. "Look, I'm worried, and deservedly so. Ninety-nine percent of the time, you can handle yourself. But that one percent, you fuck up really good."

Erin threw her hands up. "You know I thought you were done with Yvonne or I never would've stepped in! Can you stop reloading your gun with something a decade old?"

"I almost don't even care that you slept with her," Nat said. "It's that you did it before I got the chance. After that she didn't want to sleep with me. I don't know what you do to them in bed, but they can't walk straight for days afterward and they don't want anybody else for weeks." Nat stretched her legs out, shielded her eyes, and looked skyward.

"Anyway, she was a lousy lay," Erin said.

"Mm-hmm. Waitin' for you to say that. 'Cause you always do."

Erin flinched and looked away.

"Like it was scripted. Thing is, I'll never know."

Erin shook her head. "I'll remind you, that's the night you met Kendra."

"I know. I reload the gun so you don't forget in situations when I need you to remember." Nat put her hand on Erin's thigh. "Like now. Don't blow it with this woman. Because this time, it's my job, not my emotions, and somehow, that's more valuable to me. But beyond that, it's our friendship."

Erin nodded. She'd originally thought of Catherine as a potential one-night stand. Then, her next-level flirting had led Erin to reevaluate the possibilities. And as usual, she didn't want to wait to find out if there was something greater at hand. Of course Nat knew how she operated. But Erin suspected this situation was different. She was only beginning to sense Catherine's depth, and instinctively knew she needed to pursue her, at least for now, which was why she'd pushed the boundary Nat had set. Nat would have to trust her.

As they walked to the subway, Nat slung her arm around Erin's shoulder, the sign of peace one always offered the other after an argument.

"I can chop vegetables, you know. And make a pot of rice. I am by no means a good cook, but if I know what you're doing, I can be a really good sous chef. I'm not totally clueless."

"I've never ever said you were," Erin said. "I've always been on your side."

"Yeah. Mostly, you have." Nat sighed.

"We'll get dinner going so you can finish it, and then I have to leave. My date's tonight."

Nat laughed and pushed Erin away. "You bitch! You held out on me!"

Erin nodded. "Yup."

When Erin got back to her apartment, she riffled through her emergency money envelope and put a twenty-dollar bill on the dresser. That should cover the cost of a hamburger and fries at the diner. Then, she did something she hadn't done in a long time. She tore apart her drawers, her closet, and the armoire looking for the perfect outfit for the date, throwing clothes every which way. Lincoln appeared in the bedroom door to survey the scene, and as Erin pulled more things from drawers, he jumped up onto the bed and burrowed into the clothes she'd piled there.

It's a diner, for God's sake. But she wanted to look... What? Like the twenty-five-year-old babe in the woods she was when she first hit this city? The one who attracted all kinds of women with her innocence? She was long gone. What she was, though, and what she was pretty sure had caught Catherine's attention, was younger. And maybe Catherine was into someone younger.

Erin was well acquainted with the pursuit of younger lovers. The year she turned thirty, she dated a string of girls right out of college. It was flattering to be worshipped by a young acolyte. It was also a good recipe for dismissing out of hand that you were getting older if you could still attract pretty, young girls. Was Catherine looking for some sort of validation along those lines?

Erin surveyed all the discarded clothing on the floor and thought she might be the biggest fool ever. It was stupidly hard work trying to be someone she wasn't. She realized with a jolt that she didn't want to do it anymore. Catherine would have to accept her and like her for who she was on this date.

After a cool shower, Erin began to hang everything back up, folding it back to drawers and the armoire, when she spotted a paw stealing out from under the pile of clothes, patting the bed, searching for something. She grabbed at it and Lincoln pulled it back in. Then she poked at the pile and it jumped. She quietly chuckled and tickled both ends of the pile until Lincoln's head popped up and he launched himself off the bed, shooting down the hallway like he was on fire, leaving Erin laughing in a heap.

She returned the rest of the clothes to their drawers and put on a pair of red shorts and a sleeveless plaid camp shirt, snapping the collar up, leaving several buttons undone. She found the paintbrush necklace Nat had given her when she finished her MFA at RISD. It nestled right at the top of her cleavage, and Erin could always see when a woman stole a look.

As she was leaving the apartment, her phone dinged with a text message. Hoping it wasn't Catherine canceling, she clicked on the icon and Marquita's number came up. She was surprised but couldn't help but smile.

Marquita: *At a movie. Needed their overpowering refrigeration tonight. U gonna be home later?*

Erin looked down the hall. Her bed was invitingly framed in the bedroom doorway. *Yes. Not sure what time. Having dinner w/a friend.*

Marquita: *Kk. U owe me a call. Collecting tonite.*

Erin suddenly felt warm. *Got the # on something more solid than a dollar bill.*

A moment later, a winking emoji appeared on her text screen. Erin wondered at the exchange. Nat had been right the other day. Marquita was flirting. She wasn't sure how she was going to handle this. Marquita didn't seem the type to want to date someone a little down on her luck and unable to afford the things she was used to, but then again, Erin had no idea what those things might be. So, maybe one date to find out wouldn't hurt. She'd have to figure out where she could afford to take her that would make her look good. Then again, she realized, if Marquita had called her, maybe Marquita would be the one taking. She smiled, slipped the phone into her pocket, and headed out to walk the twenty-three blocks uptown. A good stretch of the legs was just what she needed to put herself in the mental state to parry with Catherine over dinner. Besides, she didn't think she could use Nat's MetroCard for a date.

Chapter Seven

Erin hung back across the street from the diner until Catherine arrived, took a table by the window, and began perusing the menu the waiter handed her. She didn't want to seem like the eager beaver she'd been yesterday, arriving early. Of course, Catherine was right on time. She crossed the street and stood on the corner several feet away watching Catherine and traced the planes of her face with her artist's eye. She had one of those high Medici foreheads with its prominent widow's peak that highlighted her aquiline nose, almost wing-like cheek bones, and cherry red lips, the color Catherine seemed to favor. Erin couldn't help dropping her gaze to that lovely sweet spot at the base of her neck, and then, of course, a little lower. Catherine's eyes were downcast as she read the menu, but Erin already knew they were the color of the Mediterranean Sea on a sunny day. She could even see those fine lines at the corner of her eyes that crinkled when she smiled, lending her that air of gravitas. She was heart-stoppingly beautiful.

When she joined Catherine at the table, two things occurred to her: she could spend hours looking into those eyes, and Catherine was wearing perfume. It was a scent Erin was familiar with if only because over the years in this city, she'd passed maybe a dozen other women wearing the subtle cherry scent that trailed a hint of vanilla. She didn't know what it was, but she wanted to lie in Catherine's arms surrounded by it.

"Hmmm..." Erin said, sliding into the banquette. "Eager beaver."

Catherine gently sucked in her bottom lip and looked at her watch. "And you're late."

For an instant, Erin panicked. She hated being late as much as she hated people who thought it was okay to *be* late. Out of the corner of her eye, she caught the time on the clock above the cash register by the door. "Five minutes?" Then she saw the sly smile appear on Catherine's face.

"I do like teasing you. You're so transparent. It's refreshing."

Erin took a sip from the glass of water already at her place. "Transparent, huh?" She breathed a little more easily. "I'm not sure I should like the sound of that."

"It's a compliment. I like that you don't play games."

The saleswoman persona fell away, and Erin saw the woman she'd been with in her ex's apartment yesterday, a vulnerable woman with a touch of sadness and the small light of hope now evident. This was the woman she liked.

"So…I wasn't playing games when I was flirting with you?"

Catherine laughed. "That. That was cute."

"Thanks. Now I feel like Hello Kitty."

"Well, Kitty, tell me something about yourself that I don't know." Catherine squeezed a lemon slice into her glass of water. "For instance, why are you looking for an apartment that you aren't actually looking for?" She sat back, an expectant look on her face.

Erin froze for half a second. She'd never been good at storytelling or lying. She preferred instead being the appreciative audience of said stories. And the ignorer of lies or anyone perpetrating them. She could hear Nat yelling, *"Don't blow this on me!"* "Um…I have a roommate, and we sort of got sick of the whole setup. So we tossed a coin for the apartment and she won." Dammit. Lying wasn't how this should start. "But I can't really afford to move right now, so this is really research."

"You must be looking for a place with studio space."

Erin looked at her blankly.

"All right, confession, I ran the background check on you. You had two gallery shows several years ago. Impressive. Do you work out of your apartment? I know studio space can be expensive."

Catherine reached across the table and delicately slipped her fingers under the gold paintbrush on Erin's necklace, running her thumb over it for a moment, her fingers grazing the skin where it sat. "So can art supplies."

Feeling the heat rising in her face, Erin didn't know where to look. And she was doubly confused. There had been no shows since the explosive *Times* review five years ago had sent her into a tailspin. She'd been one of the youngest artists to crack the show. But the disastrous review had driven her to take a knife to most of her canvases, and she'd gone into seclusion. It was Nat who'd talked a friend of theirs into offering her a job in his tiny Soho gallery, afraid Erin would starve to death in her apartment otherwise.

Then she understood. Buzz must've created a whole online life for her since she didn't have one beyond that horrific crash-and-burn moment. She quickly collected herself, and figured she'd better google herself to see what was out there now. She couldn't blow this research for Nat. And maybe this was the door opening to find out where Catherine stood in this landlord's scheme. "I…uh…I use a small room in a friend's apartment. In fact, I was going to talk to you about her tonight. She's looking to buy an apartment and I wondered if you might want to show her Susan's place? I think it might be perfect." Erin had pulled the trigger without consulting Nat. *Well, she's going to have to trust me.*

"Where is she now?"

"Home."

"No, I mean what neighborhood?"

"Oh." Erin realized how stupid her answer must've sounded. "Is that real estate jargon for how much is she worth and what can she afford?"

"Yes." Catherine smiled. "You catch on fast."

Erin looked down at her placemat, disappointed that the saleswoman persona had reappeared so quickly. "The Village. She's been down there since we got out of college."

"That's a long time to be in one place. Why did she stay there?"

"She liked it. Plus, she could save up her money if she stayed in the smaller place."

"Yet large enough to have a room for you to work in."

"Well, yeah. But it's a really small room. Like a closet, really." Erin made a tiny box with her hands. "But it's got terrific light."

"That means your apartment doesn't."

"The shared spaces do. But I can't set up my paints and canvases there. I need a space where I can leave everything, come back to it and pick up a brush without worrying about infringing on anyone."

"And your friend doesn't mind."

"She doesn't mind the rent she charges me, no."

"Well, if she buys Susan's place, your rent will go up for sure. But yes, if she wants to see it, I'd be happy to show it to her."

"Do you need to do a background check first?" This was promising. Maybe her instincts had been right about Catherine after all.

"No. If she's a friend of yours, that's good enough. For now. Call me tomorrow to set the appointment."

"Don't you want Nat to call you?"

"No, I want you to call me so I can ask you out on another date."

The waiter interrupted before Erin could say anything. When he left, still jotting down their order on his pad, Catherine folded her hands on her arms.

"So. Tell me about painting."

Erin stopped stirring the coffee she'd poured a healthy dollop of milk into and looked at Catherine. She felt handicapped not knowing what Buzz had put out there about her. Or if the *Times* review had also been there for Catherine to read. Could Buzz erase something like that?

Catherine cocked her head. "Don't tell me you're one of those artists who can't talk about her work. Or was it that nasty review I read about the Whitney Biennial? *Times* critics can be so provincial, can't they?"

Erin closed her eyes. There was her answer.

"It must've hurt."

"You have no idea."

"You seem to have disappeared for a few years after that. Where did you go?"

Nowhere. I went nowhere and I stayed there. "I needed to keep to myself for a while."

"There weren't very many photos of your current work. But you obviously continued painting eventually."

Erin was sure her face must be as blank as her brain. What the hell had Buzz posted? How had she found any vestige of her work? "I had some shows, but they were too small for anyone to care about. And I didn't allow media at them." What a simple lie. How easy to tell.

"Understandable." Catherine nodded thoughtfully. "Tell me about the process, your inspirations. How do ideas come to you? I've always been fascinated by creative minds and how they work since I'm not remotely creative."

Erin looked out the window over Catherine's shoulder, searching for a way to put those answers into words, wondering what it was about Catherine that even made her want to. The saleswoman was gone again, her eyes holding a child-like attention instead. Ideas *did* come to her, and she executed them. She thought of the canvasses sitting in the corners of her living room, executed, photos taken of them, and then executed again, literally quashing them, if she painted a white base over them. Which she'd been doing to many of them after taking those photos. There were a couple dozen sitting there now, watching her while she watched television, mutely mocking her in tones of blacks and browns, dirty yellows and deep brick reds, colors that were almost not colors. "Ideas come to me all the time. On the subway. On the street. Standing at my kitchen window."

"And then what?"

"I write them down." She thought of the list in the back of her sketchbook. "Maybe I'll rough something out. If I like it, I start a canvas."

"Start?"

Erin frowned. "I don't always finish it. Or I paint over it."

"I've often wondered about that, you know, when you hear about someone discovering a master work beneath someone else's painting, or they find out that Rembrandt had painted what we now consider a masterpiece over something he'd already painted, but it's too hard to figure out what it was."

"Pentimento."

"That's the word. But don't you think that sort of describes people, too? How we cover up who we are and no one knows what's really underneath?"

"You could also call that a patina, the appearance of something, the thing you think you see but maybe isn't really there. That's how curators discovered some of those paintings. They thought they saw something leaking through the paint on the canvas."

"I thought a patina meant something that was buffed to a high shine, really polished."

"Key word, polished. So if Rembrandt didn't like what he'd created the first time, he painted a new picture over it, and that one was really good, a much better version of what he wanted, so, a polished piece."

"I get it. So, after all these years, *you* must have some pretty polished pieces. Do I rate a private showing?"

"Oh, I…" Erin absently shook her head.

"I'd even settle for seeing one of those sketches you talked about. Isn't that what you were doing on the stoop the other day?"

She caught a spark of genuine curiosity in Catherine's eyes, so she took the little book out of her back pocket and flipped the pages open to the impression of Nat she'd made on the subway the other afternoon. "That's my friend Nat, the one I think would like your apartment."

Catherine studied the small drawing, nodding. "That's good."

Erin was relieved, and curious that Catherine had no other visible reaction. She made a mental note to ask Marquita if Catherine had been in any of those meetings. Thinking she would hand the sketchbook right back to her, Erin was surprised when Catherine flipped through the pages. She reached to take the book back from her, annoyed that she'd overstepped her bounds, when Catherine stopped and sat back, looking mesmerized by what was on the page. Erin knew it was the sketch of her from the other day.

Catherine looked up at Erin. "When did you do this?"

"When I was sitting on the steps waiting for you."

"So, from memory. But you'd only seen me once."

"Everything is from memory."

"This is a lovely portrait and not because it's me, that's not what I mean. But if you can do this kind of portraiture, why does your website say you're an abstract expressionist?"

Erin wanted to slip her cell phone out of her pocket and search for this website right now while Catherine gazed at her likeness.

"I was experimenting for a while. And these." Erin pointed to the sketchbook. "These are the equivalent of batting practice."

Catherine nodded. "I see." She deliberately paged through the book, studying each drawing. "When you're ready, I want to see something you've painted. And if you don't want to show me the abstract work, then why don't you let me see a piece that has meaning for you?"

Vulnerability peeked through Catherine's exterior again. Erin sensed there was no pretense in this moment and, if only for a fleeting second, that she could trust her to look at one of the completed canvases and understand that there was more than paint at stake. "Maybe. I'll think about it." Erin studied those blue eyes. "And maybe you could tell me a little bit about Catherine Williams when she's not selling apartments."

Catherine closed the sketchbook and handed it back to Erin. "There's not a lot to tell since that's what I spend all of my time doing." A veil seemed to have dropped over her countenance.

Erin decided to challenge it. "Really? Huh. I wouldn't have guessed that about you. No hobbies, no friends, no family, you don't take vacations to favorite or far-off places, you never go to a movie or read a book or go bowling or go to a museum—"

By now, Catherine was laughing. "Bowling?"

"Those shoes are sexy. Tell me why I should go out with you?"

Catherine's laugh dwindled and she looked at Erin contemplatively.

"You're the saleswoman. What was it you said yesterday that could change the mind of someone not quite sold on taking an apartment? 'Washer and dryer in the next room?' What is *your* washer-dryer? What about *you* would make me want to be with you?" Erin had never taken a step like this before with anyone. She almost felt like she was shaming Catherine, but she wasn't. She wanted to fracture that veneer, see more of what was underneath it. Because she was beginning to think she really liked the woman beneath it. Instead, she saw Catherine's smile disappear, and her eyes lose their luster.

"You mean, if I was an apartment?"

"If that's the way you need to do it, but no, I mean you." Erin rested her elbow on the table, her chin in her hand. "I really like what I see. The building sure is nice. But what would make me want to live there? What's the neighborhood like?"

Catherine drew idle circles in the condensation left from her glass. "You want to know what makes the neighborhood a fun place to be." She looked back up at Erin. "Okay, well, it hasn't been a very fun neighborhood for a while now. There used to be a movie theater, and a bookstore. There was a nice park to walk in, but it doesn't get used much anymore. There are lots of restaurants that deliver, of course."

Erin nodded. It was a version of her own neighborhood lately.

"There's not really a lot to tell. The truth is, I haven't gone anywhere or done anything in months. I haven't wanted to. I keep winning our Realtor of the Month award because I all but live at the office since Susan left, and I spend so much time with my clients that I'm now going to their baby showers and weddings."

"Oh, that's just sad." Erin smiled to take the sting out of it.

"Yes, it is. For them, too. Can you imagine?" Catherine's eyebrows arched up as she challenged Erin. "But I'm not sure it's any sadder than disappearing for several years after a single bad review of your work."

Catherine's look was challenging and as scorching as her words. Erin winced. "Okay, ouch, that kind of hurt."

"Look, something about you hit me, made me sit up and pay attention. That hasn't happened to me in a long time."

"You said I was cute."

Catherine smiled. "You were. You are." She played with the spoon next to her plate. "I thought what I felt was reciprocated. Either that, or you're just a flirt."

"I *am* a flirt. But for me, it's a contact sport."

Catherine regarded her, a smile playing at the corners of her mouth. "Is that so?"

"And I play to win."

"I see. Well, then, I've got my work cut out for me. Because I figured we'd get to know each other as we dated."

Erin rolled her eyes. "If we're going to do that, then it would follow that you have to give up some information."

Catherine cocked her head questioningly.

"How can there not be a lot to tell? You're a what, forty-year-old woman with a successful career and one smashed relationship behind you? Of course there's something to tell."

"Then why did you ask me why I think you should go out with me?"

Erin hesitated, taken aback. "Because I want to know what *you* think makes you special, what makes you that apartment that's perfect for me?"

Catherine nodded and sat back. "You tell me. What made you flirt with me in the park by the subway that morning last week?"

Erin's eyebrows shot up and her mouth dropped. Busted.

"Oh, yes, I noticed you checking me out. And what made you walk right up to me at the showing and very boldly tell me you hated leaving places empty-handed? Or compelled you to say yes to meeting me at Susan's apartment?" Catherine cocked her head, a small seductive smile appearing, and Erin's stomach plummeted several stories.

"Your physical beauty." Erin licked her suddenly parched lips.

"Hmmm. Honesty. What else?"

With that one simple question, Erin knew Catherine had completely turned the tables on her, and she had to meet the provocation.

"Your intelligence and sense of humor."

"Ah! The washer and dryer you were seeking, perhaps?"

Erin snorted. "Okay, yes, smart, funny women do it for me. But..." She hesitated, not wanting to drive Catherine away in this delicate moment. "Inside that sharp saleswoman is, I think, someone charming and witty and vulnerable, and I want to get to know *her.*"

Catherine's eyelids narrowed as she studied her. "And what about you? What's that cute bold exterior masking? Strength or fragility? You stopped painting, didn't you, when that review came out. And what about that mistake of a relationship you mentioned? I'd be taking quite a chance on you, wouldn't I? But then, I don't seem to have much of a life, so I suppose you'd be taking quite a chance on me."

"Then what are we doing here?" This wasn't the easy hookup she'd planned on using to get out of her rut. This was more in the moving on territory of something serious, and now that it was in front of her, she was terrified.

"I'd like to take the chance. If you would."

"Why?"

"Because you look at me like I'm possible."

Erin was stunned by the remark. The exterior of the beauty she had been so attracted to was pierced by the foundation she'd been trying to find. "You are very possible. That's why I'm sitting here."

Catherine looked down and smiled. When she looked back up, her eyelids half closed, her eyes seeming darker blue, everything in Erin heated up. "So, how about we see each other again soon, and begin looking into each other's washers and dryers."

Erin bit her bottom lip. "That sounds so dirty when you say it that way."

Catherine laughed out loud. "By the way, forty years old? Try forty-five. I thought you were at least as smart as I am."

"Oh, but I am..."

"Ah. Touché."

Erin wanted to know how Catherine had gotten into real estate and was surprised to hear her story of having moved from social work to real estate to find answers to the city's ever-changing homeless crisis. She was now on the boards of organizations that worked to create housing for homeless LGBT youth and veterans. Their conversation turned to the many things the city could be better at, as well as the reasons they loved it. Afterward, outside the diner, Erin felt self-conscious, shy even, despite how much more she'd gotten to know about Catherine. She wanted to kiss her when they said good-bye. Would Catherine think it was too soon? She opened her mouth to speak and suddenly Catherine was there, her arm around Erin's waist. She hesitated for a moment, as if seeking permission and, finding it, her lips were on Erin's. She took Catherine's hand in hers and pressed against her, that surge of electricity when you first feel a lover's body against yours coursing through her, and she put her other hand on the back of Catherine's neck, wanting more of those soft lips. The moment she thought of yielding to her, Catherine broke the kiss and put her finger on Erin's lips, her arm still around Erin's waist. Those bright blue eyes seemed luminous. Erin realized they were both breathing hard, and her legs weren't quite solid beneath her.

"Thank you for coming to dinner with me. You'll call me to let me know when Nat can see the apartment?"

Erin nodded.

"And I'll let you know when I can see you again."

Erin nodded again and Catherine turned to walk uptown. She watched her go, admiring yet again all the curves. She touched her lips. The kiss, unexpected, had been serious. She liked it. A lot. But she hadn't told Catherine the truth, and that worried her. At some point, sooner rather than later if she wanted this to be something serious, she'd have to come clean.

She pulled out Nat's MetroCard. She'd use it to get home. After all, Catherine had said she should make an appointment for Nat to see Susan's apartment, so the night had really been research. Hadn't it?

Chapter Eight

When Erin got home, she went right to the internet, typing her name into the search engine to find whatever Buzz had created online about her. Several listings popped up. One was about the nonexistent shows Catherine had mentioned, one was a personal website for "Erin O'Connor, Artist" that hadn't existed before yesterday, and of course, there were the articles from five years ago. She clicked on her website, and a second later, gasped at what she saw. Buzz had found a college yearbook picture of her in the large, airy student art studio, arms folded across her chest, leaning up against an enormous canvas, all confidence and promise, fresh from her stint at the Yaddo colony that summer. Scanning the page, she was floored by the information Buzz had amassed from everywhere on the web, things about her she'd forgotten were ever online.

Then she quickly perused the two new articles in which Buzz had managed to manufacture the shows Catherine had read about. They were at galleries apparently long out of business, one in Seattle and another in Chicago, which would make either show hard to refute. Of the two canvases shown in the articles, Buzz had somehow picked one up off the floor of her studio and enhanced it; the other she'd swiped from a Facebook posting years ago, that account deleted after the debacle at the Biennial. She clicked back into her website and spotted the notation that many of her current paintings were now in the homes of "discerning collectors." As she studied the screen, marveling at everything Buzz had done to make her look and sound like a living, breathing, and working artist, she began to understand why Catherine was intrigued. Buzz had quoted things in those articles from that same deleted Facebook page, things she'd said about art and life that seemed arrogant then but simply true now, things she couldn't imagine thinking or saying today, like her insistence that, for her, creating art allowed for redemption. And that she'd seen the beauty of that same redemption dawning on the faces of people as they contemplated her paintings and perhaps saw themselves in them.

Or, after she'd won her coveted spot in the Biennial, that there was nothing new in art except the people with money who made it so because they wouldn't know talent if they tripped over it. She wondered what Catherine had thought of that remark. Life had a cruel way of slapping you in the face sometimes. She knew that artist was long gone. The one struggling to replace her was still down on her knees with no redemptions in sight. And she fervently hoped she'd get up before the bell counted her down for good.

Her pocket vibrated. She fished the phone out of it and saw the text from Nat, a conga line of question marks.

"I'm home, Torquemada. Harmless dinner, no state secrets tortured out of me. I will find out if she's part of the cabal, I promise. Done, going to bed."

Erin waited a few moments for a reply, but there was none. Sometimes Nat respected the boundaries Erin rarely put up. But she wasn't going to bed. Instead, she grabbed a fruit punch Gatorade from the fridge and stretched out on the couch. She found Marquita's number in her contacts and pressed it, wondering how much trouble she was about to get herself into.

"I was almost gonna text you a picture of a dollar bill," Marquita said when she answered on the second ring.

Erin chuckled. "Good thing you didn't. I probably would've deleted it by accident."

"So how is the apartment search going? You and Nat haven't said much."

That wasn't the reaction Erin had been expecting, but she decided to follow Marquita's lead to see where this might go. "Not much to say yet. We're still collecting data."

"I'm so worried, Erin. The guys keep filing more color-coded forms every day. I really want you two to get this story right. But then I think if you do, it's gonna be bad for me."

"What do you mean?"

"I left banking when my career was about to take off because I hated it. I like the real estate business, but I'm less than halfway through the coursework for my license. This story breaking could ruin me."

"It *will* break, Marquita, right after Labor Day." Erin had never thought of this as a problem for her since she was the one who'd approached Nat, not vice versa.

"I know. And it could derail my career before it ever gets off the ground if I'm found out. I think Jack Hobbs saw me talking to Nat the other day outside the office. I was giving her actual hard copies of stuff." Marquita sighed. "I'm not sure where else I'd turn at this point."

"Well, maybe be more careful about where you see Nat or hand stuff off to her? And don't you have the whistleblower laws behind you?"

"No, cariña," Marquita said softly. "Those laws are for federal employees. So this company would simply wait until all this had blown over, and several months down the line, when my first few sales fall through, that'd be it."

"I don't understand."

Marquita gave Erin a quick tutorial in the ins and outs of the real estate business, and it became clear to her that Marquita was, indeed, in a tight spot. Sumter Realty could easily bury firing her under a performance review if they found out she was the source of Nat's articles, and no one would be the wiser. "Now I'm not sure I can ask any of these agents to mentor me," Marquita fretted.

"Seems to me you should still ask them. Wouldn't that be the perfect cover?" She wondered if Marquita had heard her in the next moment of silence that followed.

"Yes, it would. And I might be able to help you nail them if I played stupid and got them to put into words what's going on, wouldn't I?"

Erin chuckled. Marquita had gone from poor me to Jessica Jones in the space of one sentence.

Marquita sighed, and it came through the receiver loud and clear. "Wow, I just never envisioned becoming part of this mess. Thanks for listening, Erin. I know I might sound a little crazy, but this is a lot I put on the line without really realizing it, I guess. You're easy to talk with, though. I like that."

For a moment, Erin felt like a bowl of melting ice cream in the warmth in Marquita's voice. "Well, I know what it's like to implode your life. Who were you going to approach? Among the agents."

Marquita ran through a short list. Many of the company's agents were full-time, and even more were part-time and worked from their homes. Erin and Nat had seen all the agents who'd sat in on that meeting, and a few who hadn't, including one part-timer they considered the double-blind part of the study. He'd been on the Polycom for part of the meeting. Marquita thought the agents had hung up on the guy partway through the meeting, but she couldn't be sure.

"You wouldn't ask Catherine Williams?"

"She can be ruthless."

Not exactly what she wanted to hear. She waited for more. "Hard and cold, for sure. I could never be like her, just to make a sale."

"She wasn't hard or cold when I saw her." Erin imagined Catherine's hand with the perfectly manicured apple red nails pushing that card with the address on it into her line of vision, the way her striped dress and red heels accented everything about her figure. And her teasing smiles as they traded mischievous repartee in Susan's apartment. Then there was the kiss.

"Of course not. You were prospective money in her pocket. Everyone is cash to her."

Erin was a little horrified and a lot intrigued and wanted to hear more but didn't dare ask for specifics.

"She's a phony, gilt-edged machine," Marquita continued. "*That* I definitely don't want to learn."

Erin took the last remark like a personal blow, wincing at the mean nature of it. Had Catherine simply been playing her? Or maybe

Marquita only saw the saleswoman persona, and nothing else. She also wondered if she should reevaluate Marquita.

"I could sell as well as she does, maybe better. People seem to flock to me, and I wouldn't have to be ruthless like she is."

Erin knew she was right, since she was one of that flock. But before she could form other questions to dig into both that aspect of her *and* into further insights about Catherine, Marquita had switched gears.

"Look, could we have dinner tomorrow night? I have some real concerns about this series of articles and Nat isn't as easy to talk to as you are."

"Well, yeah, sure."

"We could just get a slice of pizza somewhere on Broadway and sit and talk."

How different from a year ago, Erin thought, when she could hardly get near this beauty for longer than three minutes at a time on a dance floor. A date with Marquita… But was it a date? Or would it be more hand-holding, like this phone conversation had been? She definitely didn't want that. And now she was torn. Catherine was very much on her mind. What she might've felt about Marquita had shifted in the space of the time she'd sat across the table from Catherine in the diner. And she wasn't sure what to do about that. Then again, Marquita seemed interested in her at the moment only for her connection with Nat. So maybe there would be nothing further to think about or do. Erin didn't want to admit it, but she was relieved.

The next night at five thirty, Erin loitered outside Sumter Realty until Marquita appeared. Despite the third day of this preposterous heat wave, she kept her suit jacket on, and didn't trade her black heels for sneakers. She looked stunning. Erin wasn't the only person staring. Marquita hoisted a black leather bag over shoulder and kissed her on the cheek.

"Thanks for saying yes to this dinner. I probably just need you to hold my hand, but when I get like this, I spin, and it's nice if someone can anchor me."

Inwardly, Erin rolled her eyes at the reference to hand-holding, but she was also only too happy to anchor. "There's an Original Ray's Pizza at Eighty-Eighth Street."

"Not an original. Just the Ray's chain."

"No, I know. Well, none of them are. I mean, only the one in the Village is. The original, I mean."

"Everyone knows that." Marquita gave her a teasing smile and turned in the direction of the pizza place.

They wove the few blocks through rush hour sidewalk traffic, with Marquita blowing off steam about some of the things that had happened at her office that day. As she listened, Erin was grateful she'd never suffered such a fate except for the one time she'd taken a temp job in an advertising agency and barely made it through the two-week contract. When they were finally perched at one of the high-top tables on the sidewalk outside Ray's, Marquita removed her jacket, hung it on the back of the chair, and delicately picked up her slice. Erin stared at her figure in the loose white tank top. Marquita clearly worked out, her sculpted arms being what were referred to in the vernacular as "guns." Erin hadn't remembered such definition last summer on the dance floor. For a second, she imagined being held by those arms. She cleared her throat, took her bottle of water from her canvas bag, and sucked down a huge gulp. "So. Concerns?"

Marquita put the pizza down. "I'm redoing my résumé because I can sense the handwriting on the wall. If something bad happens here, and I know that's not Nat's intent, but I just know something is going to backfire horribly because, doesn't it always? Then I need to be ready to get out of there, but it won't look good on my résumé."

"Nat will protect you as much as she can, you know that. And maybe things won't go horribly wrong. What are you thinking those things could be?"

"She's intimated she wants to talk to some of the guys in the office, but I don't know how she can do that without blowing my cover."

Erin laughed. "She talked to over half the upper management of Con Ed without them knowing they were giving her all the ammunition she needed for that article on the cab that got blown to smithereens on Lexington last winter."

"She did?"

"She's an incredibly good investigative journalist. You're going to have to trust her. And not go there yet. Let's see what happens. And I'll talk to her, but, you know, not so she thinks it's coming from you. I'll sound her out and see if I can steer her away from the interviews for now, if only to give you some breathing room."

Marquita reached for Erin's hand. "Thank you. I knew I could count on you."

They made short work of the rest of their pizza and Marquita pulled out her cell phone. Erin wondered if she was suddenly boring her, or if Marquita had gotten what she wanted and was now moving on. It had been whispered among their friends that she could be like that.

"Look, we're just a few blocks from the movie theater at Eighty-Fourth Street. And they're playing some really good stuff. Wanna check it out?"

Erin was game. She hadn't been to the movies in a while. It was hardly a memorable picture, but by the time they left, they'd set up a real dinner date for the weekend at a restaurant in Marquita's neighborhood, with the promise of the dinner after that being at a restaurant of Erin's choice. She might as well find out how Marquita measured up to Catherine. She'd waited at the bus stop with her, and gotten an unexpectedly hot kiss as the bus came. When she got home, she told Lincoln all about the evening as he kneaded her lap, climbed onto it, made several tight circles, and dropped into a little ball. He sighed and looked up at her.

"You really couldn't care less about all this, could you? The drought is over, I'm dating two women, and you're just in this conversation for the comfy landing spot, aren't you? Fine. I'll be happy for myself."

And for half a second, she was. Until, that is, it occurred to her that Marquita and Catherine worked at the same company.

CHAPTER NINE

Erin wondered how much longer Nat would punish her with silence as the No. 2 train raced up the West Side. Plus she'd been playing with the button on the collar of her white button-down, which always drove Erin nuts. She was blown away that Nat had worn her khaki suit and a pink tie with khaki polka dots loosely knotted below the open top buttons of the shirt. Erin, in the black shorts and red polo she'd put on that morning, hadn't even thought to dress up. She continued to play Monster Busters on her cell phone, glancing at her from time to time, but Nat sat stone-faced as the doors opened and closed at stop after stop. Finally above ground at 96th Street, they stood looking in the window of a tiny ice cream storefront.

"We've got twenty minutes. You want to get an ice cream cone?" Erin asked. The need for an olive branch was paramount before she introduced Nat to Catherine. Equally as important to Erin's peace of mind was to stop Nat's button-worrying, since she was pretty sure it was a sign of her anger and not the usual flag of her impatience.

"Yeah. Okay."

A few minutes later, they headed toward 92nd Street, Erin with her chocolate cone, Nat with a vanilla.

"Ironic, huh?" Erin said, pointing her cone at Nat's.

Nat chuckled. "Asshole."

"Well, that's better than silence." She poked her finger at Nat's ice cream and was batted away.

"I'm just not sure what we're doing. And I feel kinda ambushed."

And there it was, the edge to Nat's voice. "I told you. Catherine wasn't on Marquita's list. What easier way to find out than to have the two of you meet at a property?"

"So, what, you think if she blows me off as a possible buyer, it'll prove she's in on it and you'll stop seeing her?"

"Maybe. Probably. Yes." Erin wasn't sure she believed herself. "And Marquita will see the dot on your application."

"What if it's as simple as she doesn't like my financial background?"

"I thought Buzz made yours look like you could afford to buy?"

"She did. But have you seen what she's asking for the place?"

"No."

Nat pulled out her phone and brought up the listing on the apartment.

"Holy shit."

"Yeah, not exactly in my lane."

"So tell her your father said he'd be a guarantor."

"Then she'll want to check *his* background."

Erin exhaled a loud sigh. There had to be some way around this. She caught a line of chocolate dripping over the edge of the cone. "Okay, so tell her you need to talk to him first. But don't give her his info."

"Hmmm…No, she can find that out online. And then dad will call me wanting to know what the hell is going on."

"Yeah, you're probably right."

"And anyway, what happens when I walk away from it after all this? Especially if she's doing us a favor. That won't be cool."

"I don't think she'll care," Erin said. "Precisely because it's a favor."

"Yeah, well, Catherine is smart enough to figure out what might be going on. Especially if she sees my applications and all the apartments we've looked at and not taken."

"She's not going to look for your applications because she doesn't think you're actively looking for a place. Besides which, Marquita said they're on a password-secure drive she probably doesn't have access to." Erin hoped her face didn't give it away that Catherine had already figured out *she* wasn't looking for an apartment.

"We don't know that for sure." Nat had finished her cone and picked at the button on her shirt collar.

"And it had better be a world class apartment. I will remind you again that we can't blow this story."

They finished their cones and turned onto 92nd Street. A moment later, Erin spotted Catherine walking toward them and waved. She waved back.

"That's her?" Nat asked.

"Yup."

"Wow. I might need to hit you up for some flirting lessons."

"You're married, remember?"

"Doesn't mean I don't like to tease pretty women out of their clothes on Saturday night. And by 'pretty women,' I mean Kendra," Nat said, turning closer to Erin's ear as Catherine was steps away. "Man, she is one good-lookin' woman. And, she didn't blink."

Erin looked questioningly at Nat as Catherine hugged her and then introduced herself to Nat.

"We're right down here a block and a half," Catherine said. "And you'll get to see the place in the late afternoon light, when it's at its best."

"Erin told me it's a terrific apartment."

"I think it is, but I'm biased. I lived there for almost fifteen years."

Erin couldn't imagine what Catherine's current place was like if she was willing to leave such a nice apartment behind. It was an age-old story in New York City real estate, staying where your relationship crashed because by then, the square footage was worth more than your shattered emotions. Obviously for Catherine, the price of peace of mind was most valuable.

"Listen, I have to fess up," Nat said, "before I fall in love with the place and decide I have to live there or die, I can't really afford your asking price."

Catherine nodded. "Everything's negotiable." She took a set of keys out of her pocket. "I learned a long time ago to list certain properties well above what you actually want so you attract the kind of buyer you want."

Erin suddenly felt sick and looked at Nat for any sign that she was going to back out right there.

"What kind of buyer is that?" Nat asked, reaching for her collar button again.

"The kind with money. In this case, I was looking for a young couple who've been saving for their first apartment and who'd be as happy here as Susan and I were. As long as Mom and Dad can guarantee it."

"Oh." Nat looked a little uncomfortable.

"But since Erin recommended you so highly," Catherine said, walking up the brownstone's wide steps, keys in hand, "I thought neither one of us had anything to lose here." Catherine unlocked the outer and inner doors and ushered them into the lobby.

"So," Nat said, as they made their way up to the fifth floor, "if my dad had no pockets to speak of, and my wife was, say, Asian or Muslim, would I still be the buyer you want?"

Erin cringed at the obviousness of the questions. Why wasn't Nat soft-pedaling this up front and going in with those kinds of questions later? But Catherine stopped on the landing and turned to look at Nat and Erin, a little surprised. "Oh, Nat, I hope I didn't offend you. Usually that phrase means a client with deep pockets and the charisma to pass the co-op board's muster." They headed up the next flight of stairs. "You know, sometimes I meet people who can't afford a place and I like them so much that I want to negotiate with the owner on their behalf." She sighed. "But this is a business, and if we can get more for a place than it might really be worth, well, that's the name of the game. It helps our bottom line, and it pleases the board because their building's value rises. An ugly reality, I know, and I suppose I shouldn't be sharing this with you, but now you understand the room to negotiate part." Catherine continued up the last flight of stairs. "So, if your wife was a crazy *rich* Asian, or Muslim, well, rich is good. And if not, if she can charm the board like Fred Astaire—no, make that Ginger Rogers—that works for me, too." She unlocked the door and opened it. "Personally, Nat, I wouldn't care if you were purple with pink polka dots or worshipped a pine cone as the Goddess Earth. You're a friend of Erin's and that's good enough for me. So, come on in."

Once again, Erin was smitten, sunlight drenching the stately old rooms. Nat let out a low whistle and gently hit Erin's arm. "You didn't tell me she had oak floors and walls in here."

"And, the falling in love begins," Catherine said. "Go ahead, look around."

Nat walked down the hall toward the bedroom.

"I'm going to follow her for a moment," Erin said.

"Don't want to keep me company out here?" Catherine's smile went right to Erin's solar plexus.

"No. Yes, I mean yes. I just want to remind her of something we talked about last night."

Catherine cocked her head quizzically.

Erin shook her head. "About dinner. I'll explain in a minute." In the bedroom, she found Nat standing in the middle of the room. "What did you mean, she didn't blink?"

"She didn't blink." Nat shrugged. "When she saw me with you on the street. She didn't blink."

Erin was baffled.

"She didn't care that I'm African American. In fact, she said she wouldn't care if I was purple."

"She already knew that."

"What? You told her?"

"No. She saw my sketchbook."

"You showed that to her?" Nat began playing with the collar button again.

"She saw it the night we went out to dinner. I was showing her another sketch and she ended up looking through most of them before I could stop her."

"Oh, so you think… No, she would've figured out a way to say no."

"Unless she thinks she and I have something going here and she wants to preserve that, so she's seeing you to mollify me."

Nat leveled Erin with a serious gaze. "Is there? Something going there?"

Erin put her hand in her pocket.

"I see. Maybe we should talk later." Nat picked at the button again.

Half an hour later, Erin and Catherine stood on the same corner they'd stood on last night. Nat had left, saying she had another meeting. Erin knew she didn't.

"I know Nat loved it," Erin said, "but I sensed hesitation. On her part, I get that. But on yours?"

"What do you mean?"

"Well, I know the financials are iffy. But you asked her some tough questions. Is it that the board won't want an African-American female, maybe?"

"The board wants to know that whoever buys can weather any economic downturn, that they won't default and run. Because that could lead to property devaluation. And Nat is in that iffy financial category."

Erin was beyond relieved that Catherine hadn't hesitated with her answer. "But she's got a great job, a sizable bank account, some good investments—"

"And if that fashion website she works for goes belly up?" Catherine interrupted. "I did some quick research into it last night after you told me she worked there. Is it going to last? What if it goes 'poof'?" Catherine indicated an explosion with her hands. "Of course that led me to dig up her background and I saw that she's been at several fashion websites for some time now, almost all of them having disappeared over the years while she worked her way up to senior writer and editor. Would Nat land on her feet at some place like Vogue if her current website shuts down? Is she good enough to claw her way in there?"

Erin silently thanked Buzz for her deep dive that had Nat working everywhere but at *Street Sense*. "Okay, I get it—"

"No, I'm not sure you do. I have a fiduciary duty to everyone involved in a sale I make, myself included."

Erin thought of Marquita's comments in the bit of ice coming from Catherine now.

"And quite frankly, I consider myself the most important part of that sale." She looked at the ground for a moment. "Erin, I have to be *so* careful. I can't put someone who can't afford it into a place where they don't belong financially. If they wash out, everyone loses."

"Except the banks that the government bails out," Erin said curtly.

"Yes. And that was a shit show I for one don't want to see repeated. It was economically beyond horrible for everyone."

"Including you?" Erin asked. Even she heard the accusatory tone in her voice.

Catherine's expression told her she'd heard it. "Yes, even for me. Look, everyone thinks Realtors can be crooks, but not all of us are, you know."

Erin, feeling a bit like a heel, scuffed at a stone on the sidewalk. "I never thought about the repercussions to you."

"Well, forgive me for thinking this way, but I really am the one I'm most concerned with in this equation."

Was Marquita right? "Of course. You have to be."

"Especially if I want to continue taking you out. I was thinking brunch might be nice, but I can't do it until a week from Sunday. Would that be okay?"

Erin smiled. "You're sneaky, working that into this conversation."

"Oh, I'm all kinds of sneaky. There's a terrific little French place around the corner. Let me call you next week." Catherine touched her cheek and turned to walk back up Broadway.

Erin, anticipating another kiss as good as the one the other night, watched her disappear into the rush hour crowds, disappointed. Then she texted Nat. *"Don't forget. Honey mustard sauce for chicken cutlets on 2nd shelf fridge next to mac and green salads. You'll be fine tonight."*

A minute later, a middle finger emoji pinged on her screen, along with an unusual run-on text:

Nat: *remember we're not working tom'w because I hv to write and you hv to send me 50-word essay on What Catherine Means to Me, hv a nice wknd.*

She smiled. She'd have the day to herself and already knew she'd spend it at the Met.

Erin: *What did you think about Catherine?*

Nat: *like I said, she didn't blink, think we're good*

Erin waited a moment longer, and then came the question she knew Nat would ask.

Nat: *what did she think about me`*

Erin: *Not enough $$$.*

Nat: *figured & btw, yr right, she's outta yr league, sister*

Erin laughed and sent the middle finger emoji right back to Nat. But that feeling had already been eating at her. It worried her as much as the gravitational pull toward Catherine's orbit, even though they'd only had the one dinner. That kiss, with all its possibilities, still resonated. She wanted to find out so much more about her, and about what they might be like together, a thought that had terrified her that night. And still did. This was the kind of woman she'd been seeking, a smart, funny, established woman who knew exactly who she was. It was who Erin thought she'd be by now, and wasn't. Did that make her more in Marquita's league? Marquita was still searching, too, and might not find herself at this juncture, either. A slightly sick feeling took hold in the pit of her stomach. She knew Marquita didn't care for Catherine's sales tactics, but what if she remained friendly with her in the office for the sake of politics? Was it somehow going to come out that they both knew her? Really knew her? Now Nat's warning about not screwing up this series of articles took on a different, and much more dangerous meaning. If Marquita and Catherine put two and two together, she and Nat were toast. And Erin would lose the possibility of something she was only beginning to realize she wanted.

CHAPTER TEN

Erin sat on one of the few benches in one of the rooms of the Costume Institute of the Metropolitan Museum casually looking around at all the dandies, peacocks, and petrified women who hung out there wanting more to be seen than to see. This imitation cakewalk always amused her, but after a few minutes of studying the crowd, she zeroed in on a garishly dressed young man with a large pad resting on his lap as he, too, studied the crowds.

From her bag, Erin pulled a sketchbook much larger than the one she kept in her back pocket and folded it open. Making it look like she was fiddling with her cell phone, she took a quick picture of the young man for later reference, along with several surreptitious shots of other people who had caught her attention, and began to work. Not wanting the man to figure out what she was doing, she kept the book tilted up toward her and pretended to be sketching one of the costumes in front of her. As she worked, the guilt she felt at taking photos of unwitting people dissipated, but it always made her wonder how Diane Arbus had gotten away with it.

Because she could never really take people like this guy seriously, she was frequently tempted to do caricatures of them. Today, she had a sense that maybe she needed to give in to that temptation and see what came of it. As she began roughing out an oversized form of this other artist, she wondered how long it would take to develop a style of her own in the cartoonish genre. She'd entertained the idea before but had never taken it any more seriously than she took her subjects here. But today, sitting in this space that she knew as well as she knew her own apartment, the thought of her immediate future nagged at her. The reality that after her stint with Nat's work ended, and she wasn't doing the cooking for Nat and Kendra anymore, she'd be staring right back down the black hole of her future again began to galvanize her. She needed to consider these drawings and what they could do for her more seriously. Could she stop turning her nose up at the genre and turn it into her future? Because right now, the books she'd filled with such drawings over the last year were all she had. What would make them different enough, what would it take to turn them into skillful works of art that would catch the eye of a gallery owner? And then the public? Erin sighed. She had maybe two more months to figure that out. That had always been the hard part for her, though. Selling herself was awkward and weird.

Now, however, the uncomfortable feeling that she was going to have to embrace that, and work to make it into positive action settled heavily on her. She pushed it off as she concentrated on what she wanted to bring out in this young man. Exaggerating his wild mass of hair made her smile. He looked like Einstein on a windy day. Then she honed in on his tiny, close-set eyes, bringing a laser-like focus to them. His nose reminded her of a jumbo jet, high and prominent, but his lips were hardly there. She gave his large Adam's apple a life of its own before moving on to the spaghetti-thin arms protruding from the sleeveless buffalo-checked shirt. The knobby hand poised above the pad holding a Lilliputian pencil as he concentrated on the distance reminded her of all those drawings of Abraham Lincoln's hands she'd seen over the years, rough-hewn. Looking it over when she was done, she recognized a spark of something different in this sketch, actual life in his countenance and bearing, and something else she couldn't put her finger on, so she decided to take a break and see if Steve's hot dog cart had joined the exotic food trucks that began taking up residence on the plaza around ten o'clock. Her rumbling stomach told her it was well past noon.

The little silver cart was tucked in its place among the bigger food trucks in front of the museum, and Erin breathed a sigh of relief. She hadn't done anything in the last week, like she'd promised herself, to let him know she wouldn't be here, more off than on, and felt a smidge guilty. But there he was, sitting in the webbed chair tucked next to the cart, waiting for customers.

"Judy Chicago!" Steve stood to greet her. "I was on the brink of trying to figure out how to track you down."

"I'm so sorry! I got a semi-job and couldn't get here to tell you."

"Maybe we should get smart and fix that, don't you think?"

"For sure," Erin replied. "Let's exchange numbers before I go."

"Good idea." Steve set up the spare chair for her, sat down, and they traded phones. "This feels like the Treaty of the Met, huh? Like something formal, and maybe I should have my Marine dress blues on."

Erin laughed. "Kinda does, yeah."

"Okay, we got numbers," he said, getting up from his chair with a groan. "Lemme burn a couple dogs for ya. What's this job?"

Erin angled her chair so she could see him behind the cart and filled him in. After she'd eaten her lunch and they'd caught up on each other's lives, she took out her sketch of the artist in the Costume Institute and showed it to him. Steve studied it for a minute.

"Huh. Not like anything you've ever done before. And I know you've done hundreds of sketches here over the years. Kind of a haunted, hunted look in his eyes. And unusual lines. Actually one line, really, yeah? Brings it to life like you've never done before." He looked at it a little longer, and slowly nodded. "I like it."

For all they'd talked about over the years, a lot of it about art, she knew Steve had an informed eye. He'd dreamed of being an artist until the realization that he had no talent hit him, so he'd visited museums in Europe after he'd served in 'Nam just to see all the great works, and sometimes he talked about the vast numbers of collections he'd seen when he'd taken a motorcycle trip across America after he'd gotten back. So to hear this kind of critique coming from him really meant something.

"I need to work on this some more," Erin said, and she gave Steve a hug.

"You come next Saturday, okay? I want to know that you're okay. And you didn't tell me about any girlfriends, huh? You're not losing your touch, are you?"

Erin opened her pocket and mimed a moth flying out.

"Oh. Got it." He cocked his head toward the museum. "Gotta be some wealthy gal in there who'd look at you with as much interest as she's lookin' at the art."

Erin laughed. "Not you, too? Nat proposed that last week."

"Smart girl, our Nat."

Erin turned to look at the museum's facade. "You realize you have one of the greatest office views anywhere in New York?"

"Every day."

Erin headed to the sidewalk by the 79th Street side of the park to find a place to work along the walk leading to the Great Lawn. Just beyond the underpass, she spotted an empty bench beneath a low overhang of branches. It was a quiet nook where no one would bother her and would afford her the privacy to people watch as she concentrated on some of the other recent sketches she'd done. Maybe she could transform them with the same kind of style she'd infused in this morning's young man. Maybe lightning would strike twice. Or ten times.

She set her things on the bench, sat back, and looked up at the museum. She loved its beautiful solid Beaux-Arts architecture. From this vantage point, she could barely see the cheneau on the top of the main hall. It held the carved faces of Bramante, Michelangelo, Raphael, Rembrandt, Velazquez, Durer, and the four caryatids that represented painting, music, sculpture, and architecture. She quietly called upon them now to infuse her with a spark of whatever she needed to bring these drawings to life. Then she sat back, opened up her sketchbook, picked up a pencil and, with the whole afternoon before her, got to work.

❖

Erin sat on her bed Saturday evening trying to decide what to wear to dinner with Marquita as she brushed her wet hair. The cool shower had made her feel much better after a day spent traipsing to four different apartments with Nat and getting four different receptions from four different agents. Erin understood Nat's need for research, but some days it was all she could do to maintain the ruse. She tried not to let Nat see that, though.

On one of the subway rides, they had composed the simple email to Catherine saying that Nat had decided that as beautiful as Susan's apartment was, it wasn't the right fit for her. It was the right thing to do, a polite email thanking her for the favor. Of course Nat also continued to intimate she wanted Erin to stop seeing Catherine, and Erin pretended to be oblivious. Instead, she'd let it out of the bag that she was having dinner with Marquita tonight, hoping it would distract Nat. It had.

Erin finally pulled her khaki slacks and black sleeveless shirt out of the closet. It was one of her better outfits, classified as such because it needed ironing after laundering. Then she slipped her black tooled leather concho belt off the rack and tossed it on the bed. She wanted to look sharp for Marquita. Earlier in the day, she'd googled La Fonda, the restaurant she'd said was her neighborhood favorite. It looked like a simple storefront, but she had a feeling that once those doors opened, she'd be inside a completely different world. The online photos showed it was anything but simple with its five-piece house band.

A quick perusal of the menu online told Erin this was going to be an adventure in taste. She already knew she could order one of just about everything, although she didn't like plantains. Hopefully, Marquita might be the kind who didn't mind splitting dishes so she really could partake. She got dressed, gave Lincoln half an uninspiring can of chicken liver, threw a handful of kibble into his other dish, and escaped before he could complain about needing a hit of catnip.

Even though Marquita had been working all day, she told Erin to meet her at the restaurant instead of picking her up at her apartment. She probably wanted to go home first and shower, so Erin headed for the bus up Broadway. If she took the 96th Street crosstown to 3rd Avenue, she could walk the ten blocks to 106th

Street and see what that part of the city looked like these days. The subway would've been faster even with the transfer at Times Square, but it also would've been hotter. Watching the city pass by her bus window in all its architectural grandeur was perhaps Erin's favorite thing to do, next only to visiting its museums. She loved observing the people on the sidewalks and inside restaurants when the bus was stopped at a light. She could get consumed studying the faces of people waiting at the crosswalks whenever the bus was caught in traffic.

And of course she loved looking at store window displays, thinking about what she might've done differently with the products in the window. If she knew the store, she'd daydream about what other, better merchandise she would've pulled to spark the kind of presentation that would've caught the attention of pedestrians. New Yorkers were famous for stopping for nothing, but she'd stuck around long enough after her windows went live to see that they stopped to look. It made her want to run up to them and high-five them.

Saturday night traffic at this hour was just as bad as rush hour traffic, everyone making their way to restaurants, theaters, movies, concerts. She was glad to get off the bus and walk, finding that not a lot had changed since she'd last been here. Pharmacies, McDonald's, Popeye's Chicken, and small supermarkets still abounded. Now there were urgent care centers where dress shops used to be, an Islamic cultural center had sprung up near the school, and Cherry Tree Park was still there. And flags of Puerto Rico and the Dominican Republic adorned balconies and windows of several of the walk-ups that she passed. Her calculation was right as she walked into La Fonda at seven thirty. It had taken her just under an hour even with the ten-block walk. Marquita was already there, seated at a table near the front door, talking to a waiter. She stood to hug Erin.

"I just ordered a pitcher of sangria. I hope you like it."

"I haven't had it since college, but I liked it then."

"Oh, this will be much better than that."

They sat down across from each other and Erin's eyes were pulled to the shirred top of Marquita's short blue seersucker dress. For a moment, she felt like one of those pudgy pop-eyed bespectacled characters in a *New Yorker* cartoon captioned, *"My eyes are up here, buddy!"* She shook herself out of her quick stupor when the waiter set the pitcher and the menus on the table. Luckily, Marquita hadn't seemed to notice. She poured Erin a glass of the blood-red liquid, spilling some of the fruit into her glass, and poured another for herself.

Marquita held up her glass. "A los buenos tiempos."

"To good times," Erin said, and touched her glass to Marquita's, grateful that her high school Spanish was coming in handy.

"I thought we might get a couple of appetizers and then split a dish?" Marquita suggested.

"Terrific," Erin said. "I looked at the menu online and there are so many things I want to try." She perused the page.

"Do you want me to tell you about anything?"

"Yes," Erin said, looking up at her. "Tell me about passion fruit."

"Ahh, on the salmon." Marquita's gaze lasted a little longer than it needed to.

Erin nodded, and Marquita gave her a quick history of the fruit.

"But what does it taste like?"

"You know what? My mom was Irish and she used to call it a strawberry pear, but let's order the fish so you can find out."

"But did you want that? I don't want you to not get what you wanted tonight."

"I'm here all the time. We should order for you tonight."

"Okay, then I have a confession, before I disappoint you when you order something with plantains."

"You don't like 'em."

Erin shrugged.

"You've had them?"

"Yes, a long time ago, admittedly."

"All right, well, I'm going to get the tostones anyway, so why don't you pick out two other dishes, but promise me you'll try them. Maybe your taste buds have grown up."

Erin figured her taste buds were her taste buds and weren't going to change after all this time, but she agreed, and ordered the codfish-stuffed empanadas because she definitely wanted to try the criolla dipping sauce. She added the carne frita with mofongo so she could find out what escabeche dipping sauce was. Marquita seemed pleased. When the waiter came back to the table, she conversed with him in Spanish as she ordered. Erin tried to keep up but was woefully left in the dust. If this thing went anywhere with Marquita, she might have to get serious about learning more Spanish. Would any of the local high schools offer night courses, or someplace like the New School?

"So, what happened today? With the apartments you guys saw?"

Marquita's questions popped the bubble of Erin's language dilemma.

"Everything's turning out just like you said. She gets the dot applications, and I get the original."

"All right, next week, I'm sending you to the agents I don't think are involved. And Tuesday, you're going uptown, right? To that building we just bought to begin gentrifying that neighborhood?"

"Can we not talk about this?" Erin asked. "I've had Nat all day in my ear about it."

"Oh." Marquita bit her lip, then took a sip of her drink.

"Nat's sure you're right, and it's all happening like you said it would, so the info from you has been invaluable," Erin said, making the "okay" sign with her fingers. "It's going to be a really good story. I think Nat is going to blow the roof off it, and that's because of you."

Marquita's brows quirked down toward her nose, and she looked a little lost. "But?"

"I need a break. I'm living, breathing, and even eating this stuff with Nat." Well, at least tonight she didn't need to be talking about it over dinner. Nat had decided she and Kendra could order out so Erin could be sitting here.

"Oh."

Marquita looked uncomfortable, and Erin wondered if it really had been the only reason she'd asked her to dinner tonight. Maybe she'd read it totally wrong. "I know you're worried and you want to talk about all this. But what if we maybe tabled it for now and just enjoyed our dinner. Maybe later we can get an ice cream cone after dinner and talk then?"

Their waiter arrived bearing three dishes and Erin was relieved to be saved by the appetizers.

"I am worried, you're right. And I know it's not your problem, or Nat's." Marquita dipped a plantain into the garlic mojito sauce and brought it to Erin's mouth.

She took a bite. A promise was a promise. It wasn't half bad, but she still wasn't wild about the taste, so she took a forkful of the roasted pork, dunked it into the escabeche sauce and popped it into her mouth.

"No, huh?' Marquita asked.

"Maybe. So, if your mother's Irish, how did your parents meet?"

Marquita rolled her eyes and shook her head, and they spent the next couple of hours talking about families, food, cooking, and how much of Marquita's life revolved around all three since she had four brothers and three sisters. Being an only child, Erin was always fascinated by the dynamics of large families.

"Oh, please, you can have a couple of mine," Marquita said when Erin told her she thought brothers were a good idea in the general scheme of things. "They are royal pains. Before I came out to my family, when I was dating boys and trying to figure things out, all of my brothers had to check these guys out after my father did. And the questions they would ask them! Ay, Dios mío!"

"Okay, well, maybe that's not so cool."

"Didn't you ever get lonely?"

"Growing up? No. It never occurred to me. In fact, my mom used to tell me I was lucky, having everything to myself."

"Dinners must have been a little quiet."

"Well, I'd help my mom make dinner and we'd clown around in the kitchen a little, but yeah, my dad wasn't exactly around a lot." Erin was caught short thinking about how cold her father had been the night she left for her senior year of college and he told her not to come back.

"La vida del partido."

Erin looked up at her, hoping her face didn't betray the escaping emotion. Marquita's expectant expression caught her doubly off guard, those dark eyes so warm and enveloping.

"The life of the party," Marquita said.

"Oh, right. Not my dad, nope."

Marquita ate another plantain, looking thoughtful. "You should come to family dinner one Sunday evening soon at my house."

"Where does your family live?"

"My dad is just up the block from me. And some of my siblings are over on a Hundred and Eighteenth Street. But some moved out to Long Island. We all come home on Sundays for dinner, though." Marquita devoured several plantains, emptying the plate, much to Erin's relief.

"Wow. And if you bring me home?"

"What?"

"Are your brothers going to grill me?"

Marquita put it together and laughed, her face lighting up. "No! It's the women I *don't* bring home that make them nervous."

"Who don't you bring home?" Erin was intrigued. And then of course she was concerned, having just gotten the invitation.

"I bring the friends home. The women I'm serious about, no. My brothers don't get to meet them. I'm going to go pay the bill and then we can go get that ice cream."

"No, wait," Erin said, taking a small wad of cash out of her pocket.

"I asked you out, remember?"

"Well, yeah, but..."

"And I volunteered you to take me out next." Marquita winked at her and was gone in search of the waiter.

Erin didn't know whether to laugh or cry. How had she ended up in the "friend" category with the invitation to Sunday family dinner? Part of her wanted to pursue Marquita. It was just the sort of thing she would've done in the last five years with little regard for anyone else who might be involved in the equation. But Catherine's arrival in her sphere had changed things. Her life had taken on a new perspective. She had a hunch that Catherine would be a greater presence than she'd originally bargained for when that business card had slid into view, and for the first time since Adele, she welcomed the "intrusion." That also obviously meant that sleeping with the tall dark Latina beauty wouldn't be the wisest choice. Marquita's disdain for Catherine had surprised her, too. Beyond that, mixing business with pleasure with Marquita when Erin was already bucking Nat on seeing Catherine would be the kind of mistake she couldn't come back from if it all backfired. Especially if Catherine and Marquita found out about each other. That would surely torpedo Nat's articles. And it would just as surely have grave consequences for her friendship with Nat.

So, maybe, for once, the friend zone was exactly where she needed to be.

Chapter Eleven

At nine o'clock the next morning, Erin's doorbell rang. She was sure it was Anika, and she left her sketch pad on the kitchen counter to let her in. She checked the peephole and chuckled. The kid was decked out in pink and white to match her pink high-tops. At the sound of the peephole clicking open, she smiled, and then stuck out her tongue. Erin laughed and opened the door.

"Grasshopper here for her lesson, oh wonderful teacher." She had her big sketch pad and pencil box under her arm. "And I brought my colored pencils. I want to draw one thing in color today, or I'm not going to pay you."

Erin steepled her fingers under her chin. "So, what, this is a strike? The student is rebelling?"

"Yes, ma'am."

Erin put her hands on her hips, tried her best to look serious and tapped her foot. "Hmmm…most rebellions don't start with the words 'yes, ma'am.'"

"My mother told me to be polite about it. But you're right. Most rebellions start with the word no." Anika suddenly shrieked and jumped back.

Erin didn't have time to be surprised as Lincoln went flying out the still-open door after a little fluffy gray blur. "Shit!" Erin snapped the deadbolt open and ran after the cat, the door banging on its bolt behind her. She pulled up short when the cat slammed into the corner of the back hall and stopped still. She waited for him to fall over like Wile E. Coyote did when he ran full tilt into a rock outcropping chasing the Road Runner. Instead, he backed up and shook his head violently. Had she not seen this once before, Erin might've been afraid he was having a seizure. But a moment later, he turned, shoulders thrown back, head held high, standing proudly with the now limp and slightly bloody mouse in his teeth. Anika had been plastered up against the wall next to Erin's door, and as the cat advanced toward it, she dashed across the hall and hugged that wall instead. When he reached the door, Lincoln deposited the mouse in front of it and looked at Erin.

"Good boy!" She patted him on the head, and he sat down, looking every inch the self-important hunter. "Anika, wait here a minute. Good boy, let's go get a treat!" She opened the door and the cat sauntered in, tail high. Several soft chewy treats later, and with two pieces of cardboard in her hand, Erin held the door open with one foot and proffered a piece of cardboard to Anika. "Want to help me sweep this guy up and dump him in the garden?"

"Eeewww! Nooo!"

"Oh. Yeah, I guess he's kind of gross."

"You have mice?"

"The garden has mice, so, yeah. Occasionally I do."

"Does my mother know this?"

"Your mother wasn't born yesterday, Anika." Erin quickly swept up the mouse. "Come on inside, bolt the door, and let's get to work."

Erin quickly dumped the mouse in the back of the garden, washed her hands, and set up a blue bowl with three pears in it for Anika, placing it in the sunshine on her counter. She'd dashed into Fairway last night to buy them for today's lesson. They looked so good she hoped she didn't bite into one while they were working. "Okay, so here's our still life subject, and let's do it in color."

Anika perked right up. "Yes!"

"A tight frame on the bowl and pears."

Erin was watching Anika's work, coaching at certain intervals when her phone rang.

She glanced at the screen before she answered. "We're not seeing apartments today, are we, because I have Anika here."

"No, you keep teaching, Professor, only tell me about your date with Marquita while you do," Nat said.

"Oh, for Pete's sake." Erin sat down at the counter. "It was a dinner date. We had dinner and ice cream cones, and then went our separate ways."

"Ice cream is always a good sign. Did you get coffee ice cream, and did she get vanilla?" Nat chuckled.

"You're an idiot. Look, I'll call you later."

"But it went well."

"Yes." Erin reached in toward Anika's pad with her own pencil and made several swipes.

"And you're seeing her again."

"No, the pear is much rounder there, see? Yes."

"Okay, later, but just give me one detail."

"She has a huge family."

"Oooh. Big families make me nervous. I liked being an only kid. No sharing. Okay, but call me. I know there was a lot more than that. And you're still on for Tuesday at that apartment way uptown that Marquita's sending you to instead of me?"

"Yes, but I wish you'd at least come with me." Erin didn't want to admit she'd be uncomfortable in Inwood, and it would be nice to have Nat along for the ride. She could sit on the front stoop of the building while Erin looked at the place.

"Can't. I need to be writing. Text me afterward so I know what they make you fill out. Later, babe."

Erin put the phone down.

"You seein' someone?" Anika asked, glancing up slyly.

"I don't know, maybe," Erin said, irritated at Nat's poking around in her business.

"Well, you don't have to be grouchy about it."

"I wasn't. No, more roundness here with the pear. Should look a little like a pregnant woman, you see that?"

Anika bugged her eyes out and grimaced. "I don't know, maybe."

Erin laughed at the kid's imitation of her grouchiness. "I'm pissed off at Nat, not you. She's being nosy." Erin flipped a page in her notebook and quickly sketched a pear for Anika. "It flows like that. Watch the way the tip of my pencil moves."

"Oh, I get it." Anika quickly followed suit.

Erin glanced at the clock on her kitchen wall. They'd lost a bit of time with the disruption of Lincoln's mouse-catching escapade, and their hour was almost up, but she wanted to give full attention to Anika's developing artistry. Truth to tell, she liked her, liked how honest the kid kept her. And that sense of giving the next generation a leg up fed something in her that was missing when she was only paying attention to her own world and her own work. Back when she actually painted, she thought. "Okay, now, let's look at that bowl."

"My hour's up."

"I don't care. If you want to keep working, we can."

Anika hesitated.

"No quarters needed. Just call your mom." Erin pointed to her cell phone on the counter.

Anika smiled and picked up Erin's phone.

Erin had never been to Inwood and was a little apprehensive when she stepped off the bus with the address in her hand. Not wanting to look lost or touristy, she walked slowly as she glanced at the buildings. It reminded her a bit of parts of both Brooklyn and Queens, taller buildings mixed in with old walk-ups, many with storefronts and restaurants, everything feeling a bit as if time hadn't passed much here in the last forty years. She looked down various streets. Some appeared considerably better than others, better buildings sporting more shrubbery, newer cars, nicer trees. Those others were a little frightening in their dinginess. It was one of those streets that Erin turned onto. She knew better than to assume broad daylight would protect her, so she casually looked up and down the block, but there was only one man walking a dog several buildings away, so she went into the lobby of the walk-up and rang the bell to 5C. A brand new intercom system purred, the Realtor's voice coming over it loud and clear, and she was buzzed up.

She made her way up the flights of stairs, noting that not only was the building clean, but that the "clean" seemed newly painted. The windowsills had no dirt on them, and even the window frames, usually dotted with the black specks of the city's general pollution, were spotless. She sniffed a wall and detected the smell of paint.

When she rang the bell to 5C, the Black woman who opened the door seemed surprised to see her.

"Hi. I'm Erin O'Connor." She held out her hand and the woman shook it.

"Well, hello, come on in, I'm Jane Thomas. But you're not Nat Robicheaux."

"No, she actually couldn't make it, but she thought I might like the apartment, so I came to check it out."

"Oh. Nat is a 'she'?"

Now Erin was confused. Had Jane looked at her oddly at first because she was expecting Nat to be a man, or had she been surprised to see a white woman? Marquita had said Jane wasn't involved with the group of Realtors she and Nat had met so far. So how was she going to figure this out for Nat, or what did it mean if Jane was expecting a man? "Yes, Nat's short for Natalie."

"Of course!"

Erin nodded. "So, the neighborhood is nice."

"Oh, yes, it is, lot of nice restaurants, shops. Is your friend Dominican?"

"Nat? No, she's Darien."

"Excuse me?"

"Connecticut. She grew up in Darien, Connecticut."

"Uh-huh, I see." Jane looked a little perturbed. "Well, let's take a look around."

Everything was exactly as the website detailed, and precisely as Marquita told her it would be. And when Erin told her she had already seen a few Sumter apartments and had an application online, Jane pulled it up on her tablet.

"Well, you seem to have a couple of different applications here. Are you and Nat renting an apartment together?"

Erin wondered if she'd made some kind of mistake as the Realtor toggled between applications. The original was there in her name only, alphabet-free and without a dot. But somehow, an application had appeared with both their names on it, and the telltale black dot. Why wasn't it in the locked drive? That was odd. She mentally kicked herself. She should have told Jane she wanted to put in an application so she could see what Jane presented her with just in case Marquita had been wrong. Now she'd muddied the research. "You know, we haven't decided. We've looked at some places together, but unless it's a two-bedroom, we're kind of over having roommates at this point in our lives. It's just a matter of what's affordable."

"Well, I've been told to use the application that's exclusively for this building, the Ludwig, but I'll just copy and paste your information into it, so, not to worry. But honestly, you'd think between the two of you, you could buy a place. You know, we've just bought a building down the block that we're renovating for a co-op and I bet it would be just right for the two of you. Nice big airy apartments, two- and three-bedrooms, amenities. We've already got a website set up for it. I'll send you the info. Maybe you gals rent a place downtown and wait for this other building."

Marquita hadn't mentioned exclusive applications before. And Erin's ears pricked up at the word "downtown." She was sure it was key somehow. Yet Jane was encouraging her *and* Nat to buy in this neighborhood. Marquita was going to have some explaining to do.

On the bus back downtown, Erin shot both Nat and Marquita quick texts. Marquita got back to her almost immediately.

Marquita: *Let's have dinner tomorrow night to discuss.*

Erin: *Can Nat make that?*

Marquita: *Only inviting you, chica.* That was followed by a winking emoji.

Erin texted Nat with the change in plans.

Nat: *yeah, I know she asked you to dinner, I'm on the phone w/ her now about this Ludwig thing. But it's a date, dope. GO*

Erin thought she just might be the stupidest woman on the planet She also thought their second date was supposed to be on her dime. And could it even be called a date when Marquita had clearly sent her to friend territory? As she weighed these conflicting problems, Catherine's kiss came crashing into her thoughts, muddling everything. She sat back, unsure where to put her feelings about that kiss, still with her several days later, and then she let it sit with her for several stops.

Somewhere around 86th Street, Erin realized she probably didn't have enough disposable cash to take Marquita out, but she could certainly cook an inexpensive dinner that would rival a lot of restaurants, so she texted Marquita her address with the invitation to come to her place tomorrow night. She got off the bus a stop early and headed to the Fairway market. Thank God the heat spell had broken, she thought, so she could clean the apartment in relative comfort this afternoon.

CHAPTER TWELVE

Wednesday afternoon, Erin left Nat early to tie up loose ends for tonight's dinner with Marquita. Of course Nat had given her grief about pretending dinner at her place was all about her wallet until Erin had shut her down, telling her she had no intention of sleeping with Marquita. What she didn't tell her was that Catherine was likely the reason she wasn't going there.

Of course then had come last night's conference call with Nat and Marquita where sparks had flown between those two, and not in a good way. Nat was mad that Marquita had neglected to tell her about the special application for the apartment building in Inwood. Marquita claimed she hadn't known about it and became indignant that Nat couldn't cut her a break, considering everything she was doing for her. Erin was sure Marquita would have a few things to say to her this evening about Nat's attitude.

As Erin chopped vegetables, Lincoln sat next to her patiently waiting for shrimp to appear. He'd smelled it the minute she'd walked in with the groceries. It was probably why he'd sat in front of the refrigerator half the night. She glanced at the clock. In a matter of minutes, Marquita would be here, so she put the cheese and crudité platter on the coffee table, tossed a couple of coasters beside it, and returned to the kitchen to break up a piece of shrimp for him. He stretched with excited anticipation. When she put the plate on the floor, he vacuumed the shrimp morsels in seconds and looked at her for more. "Fat chance, buddy. You're lucky I could afford the extra piece for you."

She was shaking the mustard vinaigrette dressing when her buzzer sounded. Erin pressed the intercom button to let Marquita in and opened her apartment door.

"Oh, my God, what a shitty day!" Marquita kissed Erin on the cheek and handed her a cold bottle of white wine. "Here. Thanks for thinking of dinner here. So much more relaxing. And is there anywhere I can hang this?" Marquita had a dry-cleaning bag over her shoulder.

"Oh, sure." Erin opened the junior coat closet by the front door and hung the bag inside. She was able to make out a navy pinstriped suit and what looked like a little black cocktail dress that shimmered in the light. Closer inspection told Erin there were some sort of spangles on it. She wondered where Marquita wore it.

"Sorry I had to pick this up tonight. I need the suit tomorrow. Your place is so nice." Marquita walked right in, looked around, and went into the living room.

Erin put the bottle of wine on the kitchen counter and fished the corkscrew out of the utensil drawer, letting her explore on her own. Marquita walked down the short hall to her bedroom. Erin watched her, captivated by the sleeveless color block dress and black peep toe heels. The dress's primary colors looked smashing against the deep summer tan of her already dark olive skin, and Erin felt the blush of lust rise. Marquita went into the bedroom, reappearing a moment later.

"Erin, this place is adorable. How long have you been here?"

"Almost eight years."

"How much is your rent? Can I ask?"

You just did, Erin thought, a little surprised, although she should have seen the question coming, considering where Marquita worked now. "I sublet from a friend who grandfathered this place from, well, her grandfather, so it's rent-controlled."

Marquita looked at her expectantly. "Wow. Rent controls never make it to market anymore. So, cheap?"

"A little over a thousand a month."

Marquita whistled. "Must be a pretty hard secret to keep."

"The super gets a very generous Christmas tip."

Marquita nodded. "Of course. If you ever move, please call me first."

Erin considered her curiously. She was beginning to feel Marquita was all business and no play. "So, why the shitty day?"

"Oh, I need a big glass of that wine before I unload." Marquita made herself at home on the sofa.

Erin opened the bottle, filled a goblet, and brought it to her, a much smaller glass in her other hand for herself. "Spill. You should clear all the toxins before dinner."

"Which, by the way, smells pretty damn good!" Marquita ran her hands through her hair. "There was a huge brownout in our neighborhood this afternoon for starters. The AC powered down to almost nothing for three hours. That made everyone cranky, and then the boss chose this afternoon to hold an impromptu bottom-line meeting."

"What's that?" Erin asked.

"It's his big sales chart shamer. Who's selling, who's brought in the most, who's not producing. He fired Jack Hobbs."

Erin was shocked. "The guy we saw last week? But he seemed like a well-oiled machine."

"His numbers were way down. And something tells me he was so desperate he sold a place uptown to a Muslim couple the other day. I think this really proves something is going on. Even though he couched the firing in Jack's poor numbers."

Erin wanted to ask her how Catherine had fared at the meeting but refrained. She had a feeling Catherine's sales numbers were never down.

Marquita went to her briefcase by the front door and took a folded document out of it. "I managed to photocopy this this morning when it crossed my desk."

Erin unfolded it and riffled through the papers. "Hashir Faraj. Is this the signed agreement of sale that got Jack fired?" She looked at Marquita, whose exhale told her everything. "Thank you for getting this."

Marquita nodded, and Erin made a mental note to take pictures of it later and send them to Nat.

"Now, tell me what I smell that's so goddam good?" Marquita asked, taking a huge swallow from her wine glass.

Erin looked toward the kitchen, shifting gears. "Shrimp stir-fry with a touch of bacon."

"Smells divine. And you used a lot of garlic, yes?"

"Sautéed with the shrimp. *And* in the vegetable gratin currently simmering in the oven."

Marquita pointed at Erin. "That's a lot of garlic."

Erin nodded. "It's in the vinaigrette dressing, too, that's going on the endive salad."

"This sounds like a high-end restaurant menu. You're either out to spoil me or you think I'm a vampire."

Erin laughed. "I don't have a stake to put through your heart, so you're safe."

Marquita looked at her over the rim of her glass as she took a sip. "Spoiling me, then." She laughed softly. "You bad girl."

Maybe she wasn't all business after all, Erin thought, as the mood shift set off another blush of heat. "I'm atoning for spending the dollar you put in my pocket last summer. And teasing me won't sit well with your girlfriend." Erin was fishing, but she couldn't help herself.

Surprise registered on Marquita's face. "My who?"

"I thought last summer…" Erin hesitated. "Aren't you seeing someone?"

Marquita shook her head. "Past tense."

"Oh, I'm sorry."

"I'm not. It was never right, not from the start. And right now, I'd rather not be tied down." Marquita dragged a cherry tomato through the hummus and popped it into her mouth. "Mm, I'm starving."

Erin rose reluctantly. "Then let me get the stir-fry up. We'll be good to go in about ten minutes."

Marquita followed her into the kitchen and put her wine glass on the counter. "Anything I can do to help?"

Erin was already tossing the vegetables into the sauté pan. "I was thinking we could dine al fresco." She indicated the door to the garden, and then pulled out a drawer with silverware in it. "There are placemats in the drawer underneath this one. Can you set the table? You'll need to bring some wet paper towels out with you to wipe down the table and chairs. I meant to do that earlier."

Marquita looked out the multi-paned window in the door. "What a beautiful garden! You didn't tell me about this when I was looking around. What I could get for this place."

Erin looked at her, taken aback. "I have no intention of leaving."

"No one ever does. Oh, hello!"

Lincoln was kissing Marquita's shin.

"Oops! Forgot to warn you about His Majesty, the King of Siam."

"He's gorgeous."

"And he knows it."

"Can I pet him?"

"I'm afraid he won't leave you alone until you give him his due."

Marquita squatted down to pet Lincoln and coo sweet nothings at him as he brushed his cheek and whiskers on her fingers, and Erin wondered what would be revealed if her short dress rode up any higher.

"All right," Marquita said, scratching Lincoln's back, "we have a dinner to get ready, you cutie patootie. More loving later." She reached for the paper towel roll and turned on the hot water. "Will he try to get out when I go outside?"

"Definitely. He's like Houdini, only low to the ground." Erin scooped him up, took him down to her bedroom, and shut the door. She brought him his litter box from the bathroom and went back to the kitchen for his food and water bowls.

"Are you sure he'll be okay in there?"

Erin picked up his bowls. "He'll be fine. Without TV, he'll have to sit on the windowsill and watch squirrels instead." She headed back down the hall and teased the bedroom door open a hair. Lincoln was standing several feet away, so she squeezed in and put the bowls down. He looked at her, at once expectant and indignant. "Yeah, I know, it's a travesty." She picked him up, hugged him and set him down on the windowsill. "Here, watch TV."

When she got back to the kitchen, Marquita was wetting down several paper towels. "Poor guy. I hope he doesn't hate me." She held up the paper towels. "And so much for spoiling me! Now I feel more like Cinderella."

Erin picked a piece of shrimp out of the sauté pan and put it in Marquita's mouth. "Think of it more as a Beauty and the Beast thing."

Marquita looked her up and down. "Well, that just might be promising." She winked at Erin and bounced down the two wide concrete steps to the backyard.

Erin fanned herself as she watched her go and then pulled a large serving tray from beside her refrigerator, took two bowls from her cupboard, plated the stir-fry, and added the gratin ramekin to the tray from the oven. Then she retrieved two bowls of salad from the fridge.

"That's a lovely fairy land out there." Marquita tossed the wad of dirty paper towels into the trash and picked up the placemats and silver. "Who takes care of it?"

"The super." Erin hoisted the tray to her shoulder, a trick left over from her waitressing days in college, and Marquita opened the door.

"I'll come back for the wine in a minute but let me help you set up."

A few minutes later, Erin topped off Marquita's glass, and broached the topic she'd wanted to earlier, hoping it wasn't forbidden territory. "So, tell me about this relationship that went south?"

Marquita dropped her eyes. "Really?" She looked back up at Erin, who shrugged. "That will require the rest of that bottle of wine in my glass, please."

Marquita told her the whole story from start to finish. There wasn't much Erin could say. It sounded like so many of her own past relationships. Things were good, then they grew apart, and then they weren't together. So they moved on to other topics. But Marquita kept circling back to Nat's article, and to what was going on at the office. So Erin finally took the bull by the horns and patiently answered all of her questions and addressed all of her fears, and they began to bond over some of their exasperations with Nat. It was a bit of a relief to poke fun at Nat with someone who understood where she was coming from, although it felt a little disloyal once or twice in the course of the conversation. As they talked, the bright blue sky faded into rose pinks and yellows. Soon, it blazed a fiery red shot through with fingers of orange, finally fading to the dusky gray of an early summer night. Somewhere in the reds and oranges phase, Erin lit the candle she'd brought out.

"How are you friends with her so long? She is way too intense for me," Marquita said.

"That's exactly what I like about her. She's there and focused one hundred percent of the time."

"But she expects so much! I see her do that to you, too."

"But she gives a lot, too." Erin picked at the leftover vegetables in the gratin that had now congealed in the warmth of the setting sun.

Marquita shook her head. "You must be a really good friend, then."

"I like to think so."

"Well, then, friend, why don't we clear these dishes and go out dancing."

"Really? Now? It's after ten. And don't you work tomorrow?"

"Nope. Thursday and Friday are my Saturday and Sunday this week. And I know for a fact that Nat has no apartments on the docket for tomorrow, which means you're not working, either. So we should go out. I haven't had a good dance partner in a while, and you're good."

That was exactly what Nat had said. Why hadn't she listened to her? Marquita began clearing the table to the tray, and Erin followed suit, blowing out the candle and grabbing the wine bottle and glasses, and opening the door for Marquita.

"Where do you want to go?"

"The salsa place on Varick Street. I love it there."

Erin could hear Nat cheering all the way from downtown.

It didn't take them long to clean up the kitchen.

"I have a dress with that dry cleaning that I brought in. Do you mind if I use your bathroom to change?"

Erin had seen it but was a bit surprised, and curious. "You just happen to have a dress with you?"

Marquita pushed her shoulder playfully. "I wore it this past weekend, so I had it cleaned with the navy suit." She went to the closet for her dress.

Erin went to her bedroom for the one outfit that would complement Marquita's little black dress. Lincoln looked up at her from where he'd sprawled on her pillow, and then surveyed the room, the very essence of a monarch appraising his lands. The mess of clothes on her floor was gone, cleaned up like the rest of the apartment for tonight's dinner. She hadn't anticipated needing anything to wear to go out dancing tonight, but it was the one outfit she kept at the ready in her closet, always cleaned and ironed. *You're an idiot,* she said to herself as she quickly traded her shorts and polo shirt for her Tom Ford body spray, the black dress slacks, the black blouse with the gauzy sleeves, and the low patent leather shoes that so easily glided over the dance floor. She checked herself in the mirror. It felt good to be back in these clothes. For half a second, she flashed on Nat's text that Marquita was considering this evening a date, but how could she when she'd relegated Erin to the friend zone? And then there'd been the hour spent talking about the articles, and the real estate business in general that had almost put her to sleep. No, Marquita just wanted to go out dancing. It didn't matter with whom.

Lincoln was already asleep on her pillow when she slipped back out the door. She leaned against the hallway wall and waited for Marquita to come out of the bathroom so she could brush her teeth and put on a little makeup, but when the door swung open, Erin wasn't prepared for the vision that greeted her. She registered the little black dress that hinted at all of Marquita's curves. The spangles made it sparkle with her every move. It was held up by a single knot at the back of her neck, leaving her shoulders bare. But it was her long black eyelashes and the dark eyes beneath them that rendered Erin unable to move. The eyelashes, which hadn't been there earlier in the evening, were false, she knew that, but the danger those eyes held was very real, and Erin felt everything between her and Marquita shift, felt her pulse pounding in places she didn't know it could. She dropped her gaze, suddenly feeling vulnerable, and wondered how Marquita would be able to navigate dance moves in those peep toe heels. Erin swallowed. Hard.

"Are you ready?" Marquita asked.

Such a loaded question. Erin wasn't sure where to look, but finally met those dark eyes again. "Teeth." She pointed to her mouth. *Who does that, four-year-olds?* "Have to brush them."

Marquita smiled indulgently, stepped out of the doorway and Erin slid through it into an invisible cloud of that exotic perfume that had already begun to make inroads into the rest of the apartment. Erin inhaled as she shut the door and the scent filled her senses. She turned on the tap so it would drown out the sound of the groan that felt like it was coming from deep between her legs and shoved the toothbrush into her mouth.

Marquita insisted on taking a cab downtown, and Erin didn't fight her. She had robbed all her cash from the emergency envelope she kept in her desk drawer so she could keep them both in drinks all night and was sure she'd need it all.

The club was busy for a Wednesday night. Erin hadn't been there in quite some time. She usually came on Saturdays along with the crowd. She'd never considered that Wednesday night might be an interesting option. Obviously, Marquita knew.

On the weekends, there were far more men on the floor. Tonight, the floor was full of women, but Erin concentrated on Marquita. After their fourth dance together, they returned to the table they'd staked out when they'd arrived, and Marquita ordered another round of drinks. It turned out she was paying for those, too, to thank Erin for dinner.

"Where did you learn to dance?" Marquita asked her. "You're really good."

"One of my first girlfriends out of college was a dance teacher, and she loved salsa. But then Kendra and I took those salsa classes last spring when you were doing ballroom, remember?"

Marquita nodded and raised an eyebrow. "Oh, right. And you lead, no less."

"Oh, I can follow, too."

Marquita laughed. A young Latina woman approached the table and asked Erin if she would dance with her. Erin looked at Marquita, who nodded. They weren't out on the dance floor long when Erin watched a man approach Marquita, and soon she was on his arm. A little niggly worm of jealousy poked its head up through her sensibilities.

They stayed for several hours, the heat growing between them with every dance, and connecting them even when they were on the floor with other partners. Erin always kept her eyes on Marquita when she was dancing with someone else, especially after she caught Marquita looking at her as she sat simply watching, as though she wanted Erin to know that no matter whose arms she was in, Erin was hers tonight. She wasn't sure what to think now. Was Marquita teasing her or leading her on? And if so, to what end? When they finally left the club, Erin was wonderfully exhausted, and she knew by the way Marquita leaned her head on her shoulder in the cab that she was, too.

"Thank you for tonight. I needed it." Marquita looked at Erin.

"I think I did, too," Erin replied. Marquita's perfume mixed with the light salt scent of her sweat created a haven that Erin didn't want to leave when the cab arrived at her door. She wanted to kiss her good night, but before she could decide how to handle the situation, Marquita paid the driver and pushed open the door.

"I have to get my dry cleaning."

"Oh, of course."

They walked up the steps of the brownstone, and when Erin unlocked the lobby door, she felt Marquita's hand on her back guiding her inside, and then right up against the wall of mailboxes.

"I was hoping to get something more than my dry cleaning, though."

Erin felt a lump in her throat and swallowed hard to get rid of it. "I—"

Marquita began to unbutton Erin's shirt. "You set me on fire on the dance floor tonight."

Erin looked down at her nimble fingers and saw the twin manifestations of Marquita's arousal poking at the fabric of her dress and put a thumb on each one, a knee-jerk reaction. Marquita leaned in to kiss her, and the second those full lips touched hers, the sound of traffic beyond the door faded, her world shrank to encompass only this woman, and Erin put her arms around her and kissed back.

"You set me on fire last summer."

"Oh, pobre bebé," Marquita whispered. "You should've called me."

"I couldn't." She kissed Marquita again. "I was out of work and I couldn't have afforded to take you anywhere."

Marquita kissed her back. "I wouldn't have cared." She put her finger on Erin's lips. "Kiss me."

Erin did, softly at first, but then need overtook her and she thrust her pelvis forward, hugged Marquita to her, clenching a handful of her hair, another handful of that luscious bottom, and pressed her lips into hers. Marquita pulled the tails of Erin's shirt out of her slacks, all the buttons open now, her hands on the lace of her bra, pressing on her breasts as Erin pushed her tongue deep into Marquita's mouth in response. When Marquita slid Erin's shirt off her shoulder and pulled her bra strap down, her hand moving inside it to capture her breast and rub her hard nipple, Erin stopped her.

"Not here," she panted, looking outside to see if anyone was watching, hoping they hadn't attracted any attention. She fumbled with her keys, unlocked the inner door and swung it wide, scanning the lobby and stairs to make sure no one was there, and then propelling Marquita into the foyer. She turned to make sure the door clicked shut, and Marquita pinned her up against the wall and kissed her. She was surprisingly strong, which Erin hadn't expected. She liked it. But beyond that, an alarm sounded in her head. What if a neighbor came out? The thought was jarred loose by Marquita's knee bumping up between her legs and setting off a tiny earthquake, and, back on autopilot, she found the hem of Marquita's dress and grabbed her high up on her thigh, the side of her thumb pushing against Marquita's now-wet panties. Just as abruptly, she broke the kiss and pulled Marquita by her wrist the twelve short steps to her apartment door.

That neighbor thing nagged at her, but Erin dropped her keys before she could voice her concern, and Marquita turned her around and kissed her hard, her tongue demanding entrance. Against her better judgment, she untied the dress's knot and it came right down to Marquita's waist, revealing beautiful breasts with chocolate-drop nipples. Marquita was already pulling at her belt. When they heard someone's door lock flip, Erin quickly pivoted Marquita against the door to protect her. They listened, breathing hard, for a second lock, a door, footsteps. Erin's lips brushed the line of sweat descending along Marquita's temple as she quietly moaned. When no other sounds followed, Erin whispered, "What are we doing?"

"I don't know but I can't help myself."

And they were at each other again, the kisses noisier, wetter, Marquita finding the belt buckle, pulling it open, Erin suddenly going down on one knee, taking Marquita's panties down, lifting one of her ankles so she had no choice but to step out of them. Erin's hearing like radar as she listened for anything from behind the closed doors all around them. She stuffed the panties in her pocket, shot back up and kissed Marquita's breasts, then made an inroad into her velvety wet pussy with her finger. Marquita inhaled and let out a deep groan, arching against Erin's mouth.

"Take me inside!"

Erin stopped. "That's what I'm doing."

"No." Marquita looked at her, melting Erin with the dark desire she saw there. Then, she laughed, startling her. "Inside your apartment because if you don't, I'll be fucking you right on this floor in half a second, right after I come! And we really don't want your neighbors seeing that, do we?"

Erin swiped her wet fingers on her pants, picked up her keys, and opened the door.

Marquita's dress and heels were on the floor before Erin had flipped the locks closed. "Take your clothes off," she demanded, trying to pull everything off Erin as quickly as she was trying to get out of it. Finally naked, she took Marquita's hand and walked quickly across the dark living room, glancing at her neighbor's window across the yard. Thankfully, he wasn't there. She'd have to remember to come pull down the shade before sunlight so he couldn't see anything in the morning.

Erin opened the bedroom door ajar. Lincoln was curled up on her shorts on the chair. She led Marquita in and turned to her. "Please trust me when I tell you I have to move Lincoln's stuff out of here."

"I can help you."

"No." Erin held up her hand. If the neighbor came to the window, that could ruin the night. Erin pulled the covers down on the bed. "You just get comfy. I'll be back in two minutes." She hurriedly picked up the cat's litter box and took it down the hall to the bathroom, returning for his food dishes. On her way back, she could see Marquita stretched out invitingly on her bed, but she stopped long enough to take care of the living room shade.

Back in the bedroom, Erin wasted no time putting the blinds down, and then she slid into bed next to Marquita. Here, it didn't matter that Marquita was taller than she was. It really hadn't mattered on the dance floor, either. Marquita pulled her on top of her.

"I have heard so much about what you can do in bed."

Erin feigned surprise but was quietly pleased. Nothing wrong with having a reputation as a stud, right? Marquita's scent overtook her, and Erin gently moved her hair back, caressed her face and neck, and ghosted her lips over the rise of Marquita's breasts. She was rewarded with a deep sigh. She inched back up to her face and began a series of soft kisses, running her fingers through her hair. She slid to Marquita's side so she had the whole of her body to play with, her hand like a paintbrush covering every surface. Marquita moved beneath her, turning to wrap her leg over Erin's hip, so her hand found new surfaces to paint, and she traced Marquita's lips with her thumb as she kissed Marquita's breasts. She teased her nipples and Marquita groaned. By then, she had found her way between Marquita's legs with her hand and found her open and wet.

But she didn't want it to be that simple, that perfunctory; she wanted to tease her more, make her writhe and moan and whimper. And she wanted to taste her perfume. So she pushed Marquita onto her back, straddled her, and started kissing and licking her way down her body, continuing caresses where she would least expect them. She kissed her neck, stroked the inside of her arm, nipped at her earlobe. Marquita exhaled. She filled her mouth with Marquita's breast, traced her finger over her groin muscle, and gently bit her nipple. Marquita moaned. She kissed her way from one shoulder to the other, licking the hollow of her neck, and traced the back of her hand between Marquita's breasts and down her stomach. Marquita whimpered, caught her hand, and pressed it downward toward her pussy. Erin let her, for just a moment, before she followed her kisses with her hand down the same trail.

"Please," Marquita whispered.

"So soon? I'm hardly getting started." Erin rolled her onto her stomach, making sure her legs were wide apart, and followed the same map from her scalp down to her calves, kissing, touching, licking, nipping. Marquita went from contented sighs to moans to a writhing mess under her hands and lips, and finally rolled over, hooking her legs behind Erin's and pulling her down on top of her.

"Now, please. Don't make me beg."

Erin smiled wickedly. "I believe you just did."

Marquita swatted at her and she dipped between her legs. A moment later, she felt Lincoln jump up on the bed, heard his little snuffling, and reached out to push him into a prone position. *Don't you wreck this for me, buddy.* She ran her tongue through Marquita's wetness, prodding her clit with the tip of it, and Marquita moaned. Erin ran her finger around the slick slit several times, Marquita opening her legs wider, pushing her hips up toward Erin's mouth, allowing her to slide two fingers inside her. Lincoln poked his head closer, his whiskers brushing Marquita's legs.

"Is that your cat?"

Erin glared at him. "Don't pay any attention. He's feeling left out."

Marquita giggled. "Don't stop now!"

Erin picked up where she'd left off, her mouth tight on Marquita's smooth pussy, plunging her tongue in and out of her as rapidly as she could, and holding her bottom up with both hands, knowing what was about to come screaming up her body. Suddenly, she felt soft fur on the backs of her hands. Lincoln had scooted into the tent-like space beneath Marquita. A moment later, she had dropped Marquita to the bed, the moment undeniably broken, and they were both laughing. Lincoln barely escaped getting squashed and fled the bed for the security of the chair.

With him out of the way, Erin turned Marquita's laughter into a series of breathy cries as she came. And with one light touch between her own legs, she quickly climaxed. Marquita reached for Erin, and Erin wrapped her in her arms.

"I just need to lie here for a moment. You lived up to your billing."

"Where did you hear about me?" Erin only knew Marquita through Kendra. She didn't think she knew anyone else that Marquita knew.

"You dated Eva Diaz a couple of years ago."

Erin remembered Eva immediately. She was a firecracker of a woman Erin had met on the pier at the gay pride parade dance. Their brief affair had burned bright and short, and then the dark beauty with the red hair was gone. Erin hadn't been sure if it was something she'd said or done until one of Kendra's friends told her no, Erin had just met her match in the "love them and leave them" set.

"You don't remember Eva, do you?"

"Oh, no, I remember her." Erin thought that Eva might have broken her heart if she'd let herself get closer or convinced her to stay longer. "I remember all the women I've been with."

Marquita turned to look at her. "That's a lot of women, mija."

"What can I say? I like women." Erin didn't want to get into the mess her life had become when her wife had cheated on her, and the resulting bitterness that followed. Easier to chalk up her affairs to insouciance. "All kinds of women."

"So I hear." Marquita regarded her. "You're only the second white woman I've been to bed with."

Erin wasn't sure she'd classify tonight as "having been to bed with" on Marquita's part yet. "I'm not sure I've kept a statistical count. But I'm not picky. Long legs, sultry eyes, nice tits…" Erin ran her hand over Marquita's breasts. She caught it and held it.

"My family has certain expectations for who I bring home for them to meet. That's why I only bring home friends."

Erin hadn't forgotten their conversation the previous weekend when Marquita invited her to dinner. "Then you should have as much fun as you can with as many women as you can before you bring that right one home."

"Oh, I do," Marquita said. "Just not as much fun as you do."

"Meaning?"

"You date quite a wide swath of women."

Something about the statement irked her, but she couldn't put her finger on what. It wasn't like it wasn't true. "If you're worried about anything, I do get tested regularly."

"Funny, that didn't occur to me. I completely trusted you."

"Sometimes I don't even think about it. It's just a part of life now. I suppose," Erin mused, "if I ever do find someone, there won't be a need for that anymore. But I have no desire to settle down."

Marquita lay back against her again. "I don't either. And I want to sleep with a lot more of them before I do, too"

A moment later, Erin realized she'd fallen asleep, so she made herself comfortable, and drifted off herself. She'd think about what tonight had meant tomorrow.

Chapter Thirteen

When the phone rang at eight thirty, Erin's first thought was that she was dreaming. When she figured out that she wasn't, she wanted to hurl the thing out the window. Then she realized that with such a short drop, it would just keep on ringing. And then she remembered Marquita and sat up in the bed. But Marquita was nowhere in sight. If she hadn't still smelled her perfume all around her, she might've thought she *had* been dreaming. She spotted the note on her night table, grabbed it, and answered the phone.

"Hey, bright-eyed and bushy-tailed. Last night good?" Nat asked.

Erin barely functioned enough to amble to the kitchen to feed Lincoln. "Yes. Quite."

"Good. But you don't sound like you're making her breakfast. Or did I call too early?"

"Way. Too. Early. But no, she's gone. No need for breakfast."

"Wait. You said it was good."

"Sort of. I mean, yes. But she's still not here."

"Okay, you're not making sense and I need your help. I've got a ton of data here and I think I have most of it sorted out but I'm not really sure and I think you may see something else in it that I'm missing. So why don't you shower and get down here and cook breakfast for us and you can tell me what happened while we look at this stuff."

"Data?" Erin had opened the note and stared at the contents. Marquita wanted to be fuck buddies? She set the note aside and grabbed a can of cat food.

Lincoln jumped up on the counter when she slapped the can of beef morsels in gravy into his sushi dish, and she left him there slurping noisily, happily spraying gravy everywhere.

"On our apartment search. The story! Hellllooo. I put everything together into some Excel charts Thursday night, and I worked on the story all day yesterday but something's missing. I keep looking at the data, but it's not right. Can you come over? How was the Met, by the way?"

"Good. You want me to come over now?" Erin didn't really want to have to power up and go downtown to Nat's, not after last night. She was still half asleep and processing what happened with Marquita. Or hadn't.

"Yeah. You're not doin' anything if she's gone."

She was right. Erin sighed. "Okay. But you know I'm no good at data."

"Don't give me that. Your data tracking saved the student board elections senior year."

"That was then. I don't speak Excel."

"Yeah, but I do, and you still have eyes, so I'll translate, you look. I put the data into a bunch of different charts. I know you're gonna see what I can't."

Erin sighed. "Be there in an hour."

Her doorbell rang while she was shoving her sketchbook and pencil case into her bag. Who the hell could that be? She knew most of the people in the building, mostly by sight, but she wasn't on a doorbell-ringing-basis with any of them except Anika and her mom. *Oh, crap!* She dashed to the door and checked the peephole. Anika's quarter was pressed right up against it. She could actually read the raised year next to Washington's neck. "Dammit!"

"I heard that."

Erin laughed and opened the door. "Did we have a lesson this morning?"

Anika snapped her head back and opened her eyes wide. "You think I just hand out quarters to anybody? You forgot I didn't have camp today, didn't you, and you promised to work with me."

Erin hung her head, her hands on her hips. "I have to go down to Nat's."

"So?"

"So? I have to reschedule."

"You told me she's always late."

As Erin considered this, Anika walked into the apartment and plunked her quarter on the kitchen counter. "So today, we're gonna sketch something in your apartment. Only I'll cut you a break." Anika walked into the living room and looked around. "Let me pick out something to work on, I'll take a photo of it, and you can go. Then I'll work on it today and tomorrow and you have to give me the other half hour on Saturday to look at it with me. Or I get my quarter back."

She was a hell of a negotiator. "Deal."

"Whose is this?" Anika asked, looking at the painting hanging in a corner of the living room. "You said you didn't have anyone else's paintings but yours."

"I don't. It's my biggest mistake."

They stood looking at the abstract painting with the thick splotches of blue splashed across it.

"It's cool." Anika took her phone out of her pocket and snapped a picture of it. "I'm gonna post it to Instagram so everyone knows I'm studying with a real artist." She pressed several buttons.

"I wouldn't if I were you. You might end up being a laughingstock." Erin reached for her phone.

"Too late." Anika showed Erin the post. "I am so gonna rock when everyone sees this. What is a laughingstock?"

"Someone everyone laughs at."

"Why would everyone laugh at me for posting this?"

"I'm not a real artist. Long, boring story."

"Then don't bore me with it. Anyway, Mom says you are. A real artist."

Erin envied Anika her certainty in her mother's knowledge. She hoped it lasted her lifetime. She didn't have the heart to advise her to take the post down. Who was going to see it anyway but a bunch of tweens? "Okay, grasshopper, pick out something from my artist's garret to sketch."

"Your what?"

She opened her arms in mock exasperation. "Choose a still life subject!"

❖

"All right, so I don't get this." Erin shoved the empty plate aside and peered at Nat's figures on the screen. She had pulled all the numbers into multiple charts so that a big tapestry might emerge. That way, little threads would show themselves to anyone who knew what they were looking at and wanted to pull them to see what would unravel.

They had carefully looked at all seven charts on the screen. Nat explained that this bar chart was by neighborhood, that one was by race. One of the pie charts was divided into triangles according to apartments she'd seen alone, that Erin had seen alone, that they'd seen as a married couple, and as supportive friends. She crossed that one with another pie chart of which apartments had been shown by which brokers and a third one that broke down the dots, or lack thereof, on the applications. Nat had also put together a table of which apartments they were offered. It was a short table: Erin had qualified for two apartments for which she'd turned down the leases, including that one way uptown that Marquita was sure they wouldn't rent to her. Nat hadn't been offered even one lease. Erin's mind was a jumble of columns, lines, pie triangles, and bars.

"Wait." Erin pointed to Jack Hobbs's name. "Is he in all of the charts?"

"Yes, all the agents are, here, in this chart. But look. Not everyone is guilty all the time, even when they should be, even when they were at first, and there aren't dots or circles where they should be," Nat said, scrolling to the pie chart with the dot breakdown.

"Okay, could you speak English, not data, please?"

"I didn't get circles where I should have on the forms I was given to fill out." Nat brought up another pie chart.

"Yeah, you did. I didn't get any except when you were with me and we were renting together, see?" Erin pointed at one triangle with both their names on it. "Minimize this, and bring up the other so we compare."

"No, I didn't." Nat clicked on the other chart. "Realtors who should've marked my application didn't. This guy we saw on day one—"

"Jack Hobbs."

"Yeah. Black circle. But he saw me again a week later, alone. No dot, no alphabet letter." She pointed at the screen.

"Wait a minute." Erin studied the chart.

"And here. And here. And here with that other guy."

Erin actually touched the screen with her fingertip, following Nat's supposition across the columns.

"After the first dot, neither of these guys gave me a second one when I saw them alone." Nat rolled her neck and rubbed at her eyes. "They just had me fill out the original lease application online. Marquita found them in the accessible drive."

"That makes no sense."

"Right?"

They looked at each other. "Did Marquita send you all the info from the applications you put in? And you never told me you saw some of the other Realtors more than once."

"She said she did. And I had to know for certain if these guys were really in on this a hundred percent. Plus now we have that sale contract Jack got fired for. We need Marquita," Nat said, picking up her cell phone. "Or wait—maybe we should leave her alone today. How did it go anyway?" Nat sat back.

"It was…none of your business." For some reason, she couldn't bring herself to talk about the complicated emotions running through her after their encounter. "Move over, I want to check something on Facebook."

"Why?" Nat said as she rolled her chair away.

Erin minimized all the charts on the screen and opened Facebook, checking Marquita's page after logging into her own.

"Oh, my God. You want to see if she changed her relationship status."

"No, I don't." Erin searched her page, but didn't find anything, and let out the breath she'd quietly been holding. "Yes, I do."

"It was that good?" Nat asked. "So good you think she'd change her status after a single night?"

"I don't know. She left this morning while I was asleep." Erin fished Marquita's note out of her pocket and handed it to Nat. She was minimally embarrassed by its contents, although it wasn't as if Nat didn't know her dating history.

"Oh," Nat said after reading it. "Well, okay, so you're both on the same page. No relationship, just fuck buddies."

"Yeah, I don't know if I want that anymore. With anyone. And anyway, she didn't fuck me. She fell asleep."

"Oops."

Erin looked back at the screen and reached to close the application but stopped. The right side of the page caught her eye: it was a scrolling ad for several local Realtors, all of them recommending actual apartments, with online viewing and applications. "Hey, look at this."

"You're changing the subject."

"Yeah, but to one that's of way more concern."

Nat rolled her chair back over to the table and looked at the screen. "What the heck?"

"Remember Marquita said they advertised here? Open *your* page. Let's see if they're on your page and who targeted you if they are."

Nat quickly opened her page. They toggled back and forth, clicking in and out of real estate ads on both their pages.

"Will ya look at that?" Erin said in disbelief.

"Son of a bitch," Nat whispered.

Erin leaned on the desk. "None of the neighborhoods Sumter Realty showed me are on your page. And vice versa. Everyone else is showing both of us apartments in all their neighborhoods. They're all using social media to target us, but only Sumter is doing it by neighborhoods, effectively segregating them, don't you think?"

"I think it's why no apartment is 'available' for me. This story just got way bigger," Nat said.

"Are we sure it's that you weren't first in line for any of the apartments?"

"Marquita made sure I was shown these three apartments first." Nat pointed to one chart Erin had overlooked when they'd been clicking through them, probably because it pertained to only the apartments Nat had seen. Not that she'd paid any more attention to the one Nat had done for the apartments only Erin had been shown. "Two might've been questionable, but three is evidence."

Erin wasn't sure she'd ever seen such unmitigated anger on Nat's face before and thought for the first time she was seeing what Nat was up against on a daily basis. "What are we gonna do? I mean, this is Facebook. With a zillion dollars behind it and laws that protect social media on a ton of fronts."

Nat tapped Erin to scoot over, and she closed the Facebook page, bringing her email page up. "Yeah, but it's all ads, and who buys them. And we know who bought these. But I'll ask Buzz to find out for sure. So first, let's sift the data and mine it for what we can. Then, we're ordering lunch. We have to find an answer we can weaponize in print."

Erin was sitting at the fountain at Lincoln Center on a cool Friday morning capturing quick sketches of passersby when her phone rang. She reached for it thinking it might be Marquita. She couldn't decide if she was happy about that or not, still not having completely sifted through how she felt about their night together. The morning after had left her feeling like a cast aside piece of lettuce, and she hadn't heard a peep from her since.

Her mood took a different turn when she saw Catherine's name.

"Hi there," Catherine said.

"Hey, how are you?"

"Well, I didn't fall off the face of the earth, in case you thought I had. But you might think so when I tell you I can't see you this weekend because I have to go out of town."

"Oh. Okay, that's fine."

"How about brunch next Sunday?"

"You'll be gone that long?" Erin felt a little sad at the prospect of not seeing Catherine. She was keenly aware she didn't feel the same about Marquita.

"Well, no, just a couple of days, but I have a full schedule next week and I won't be much good until I get a day off to catch my breath."

"Okay. Sure."

"Good. I'll call you next week."

After Erin hung up, her phone pinged with a text message. She wondered what Nat needed, but was surprised by the messenger.

Catherine: *And maybe I'll text you in between just to stay in touch.*

Erin quickly found a close-up of the Michelangelo painting with God's finger reaching out to Adam's and texted it to Catherine. A moment later, she had a reply.

Catherine: *Of course. You're an artist, you text in images.*

Erin sent back a smiley face, and realized she was smiling when she slipped her phone back into her pocket. And it wasn't only because of the call and text message. Catherine had called her an artist. Suddenly, she felt possible. A moment later, she went back to her sketches.

The week dragged as she and Nat continued their research. It didn't help that the heat was creeping back up as June was about to give way to July, and they were in and out of hot subways and cold apartments. What did help were Catherine's many texts. They kept her from thinking too much that Marquita might call. She almost hoped she didn't. She felt a little guilty for not calling Marquita. It was a point of pride for her to be in touch on an almost daily basis with women she was seeing, even if it was only to text a rose emoticon. But considering Marquita's note, which had said she'd be fine with a "friends with benefits" relationship, the radio silence didn't bother her.

On Friday she'd gone back to the Met and sat in the Impressionism gallery to find an unwitting model. So many tourists flocked to this wing, and so many people seemed to stand in front of a painting for minutes at a time, allowing Erin to rough out a study. The ballerinas Degas painted were like a magnet, and she could always count on lots of mothers and little girls to stop at those canvasses. She could also count on a fair amount of men there, too. They certainly knew why Degas had brought the girls to life. And of course, the couple of canvasses the Met had from Monet's *Houses of Parliament* series were a big draw. Today, though, she sat near Childe Hassam's 1910 oil painting of the *Rue Daunou on the Fourteenth of July*, the French flags waving in the breeze down the avenue. While it didn't carry the same brilliance as his paintings of American flags snapping in the wind on Fifth Avenue, it always attracted a certain older viewership, usually European, and that was what she was after today, that kind of older, gentler life image that evoked a long-past era.

Several hours and three sketches later, Erin stopped for lunch at Steve's hot dog cart, showed him the new work, and then made her way to the same little bench she'd adopted the last few weeks to solidify what she'd done. It was a cool, quiet nook, no one bothered her, and she could people-watch with impunity.

It could have been a minute or hours might've passed when she became aware that someone was saying her name and looked up to see Catherine standing in front of her. She didn't realize she'd so tuned out the world.

"You seem to be in all the same parks I am," she said, an amused smile lighting up her blue eyes.

"What are you doing here?"

"I'd ask the same of you, but I think I know the answer." She glanced up at the museum. "I'm walking over to a property on Central Park West."

"In this heat?"

"Summer, winter, I don't care. I like to walk."

Erin looked down and saw sneakers where she was used to seeing high heels.

"Well, I can't walk that kind of mileage in heels."

Erin chuckled. "I suppose not." She gazed at Catherine in her crisp linen suit, and then Catherine cleared her throat, looking from Erin to the bench. Erin followed her eyes. "Oh!" She grabbed the pencil case sitting on top of her bag and stuffed the bag on the other side of her. "Won't you have a seat in my impromptu studio?"

"Why, thank you. I believe I can visit and look around for a few minutes." She sat and leaned toward Erin's open pad. "What are you working on?"

"Something new. I think." She turned the pad so Catherine could see the stooped, mustachioed man in front of the Childe Hassam painting, Erin studied her for her reaction.

"Oh. That's different from the sketches you showed me the other night."

Erin nodded. "And? But?"

"Erin, I don't know anything about art. I don't even remember the last time I walked into that building." She nodded toward the Met.

"Really?" Erin tried to hide her incredulity. "What do you hang on your walls?"

"Photographs, mostly. I find them at craft shows from local amateur photographers."

Erin wanted to see the photographs and knew she'd have to wrangle an invitation to Catherine's apartment somehow.

"I like what I like, but that doesn't mean I know anything at all."

"But that means you at least have an opinion."

"Well, yes, but doesn't everyone?"

"So, opine."

Catherine pulled back and settled into the corner of the bench.

Erin studied her face. "You don't want to say anything, do you?"

Catherine looked down at her hands on her lap. "I don't want to say anything wrong or anything that would jeopardize what we've maybe begun here."

"It's a drawing. It would be your opinion, completely subjective. And there couldn't be anything wrong with your opinion."

Catherine laughed. "Oh, it *has* been a long time since you've been in a serious relationship, hasn't it?"

Erin stayed silent, looking from Catherine to her drawing and back again. "If we don't feel free enough to say what we really think to each other, I'm not sure we *have* begun anything here."

Catherine's face fell.

"The funny thing is," Erin continued, "I probably haven't been honest with any of the women I've had relationships with, either, over the last several years, because we weren't together long enough for me to care."

Catherine's expression changed. Erin couldn't read it.

"But with you, I knew I wanted more after we had dinner the other night." Erin looked at the pencil still in her hand, suddenly feeling more exposed than she had in years. She panicked, but then quickly shook it off when an idea dawned on her. "So. You may not want to tell me what you make of this sketch, but you *are* going to meet me here Sunday morning before we go to brunch and we're going to take a walk through the photography wing. And you're going to tell me what you think about what we see there. Because I want to know."

"But—"

"No buts. Ten o'clock. And then we'll go to brunch."

Catherine's expression relaxed. "Yes, ma'am." A late afternoon breeze had blown Erin's hair around, and Catherine gently moved the strands that blocked one of her eyes, tucking them behind her ear. The sensation it generated on Erin's skin traveled all over her body.

"See you Sunday, then." Catherine rose and walked off.

Erin watched her go.

So little had happened between her and Catherine yet, just that kiss, these conversations, and yet her touch held so much promise.

The night with Marquita had left her empty-handed, unfulfilled on so many levels. She'd thought there might be something there, and then she'd found out she wasn't even worthy of a short relationship. That had stung.

This was unfamiliar territory. She might've entertained Marquita's proposal even a month ago. But now, as she watched Catherine blend into the crowd, she knew it wasn't possible. And she hoped Marquita didn't call. Nat would want to keep her happy, but Erin was pretty sure that wasn't part of her job description. On the other hand, she wanted to do her best work at Nat's side, and any involvement with Catherine wouldn't qualify as 'her best.'" Either way, she was courting trouble on all sides.

❖

The humidity had broken Sunday morning, and Erin waited at the bench where she and Catherine had talked Friday afternoon, a cool breeze stirring the branches of the trees. She'd texted her last night to meet her there, and then spent most of the rest of the night trying to come up with questions for her that might reveal what had drawn her to the photos she'd collected, but she realized around three a.m. how futile that would be until they were standing in front of a photograph she liked. Her imagination was still running wild, hoping Catherine wasn't the flowers-and-puppies kind of art "appreciator," when she saw her coming down the sidewalk from the west side of the park. Erin took a moment to appreciate all her curves in red shorts with a white polo shirt tucked tightly into them, and a pair of cute black canvas wedges on her feet that matched the thin black belt at her waist.

"I have a confession to make," Catherine said, looking up at the Met. "I was up half the night trying to figure out how to put into words what I like about the photographs on *my* walls, never mind what I'm going to see on the walls in here."

Erin laughed. "Seems like we both lost a little sleep over this, then. Let's go in and look around."

"You didn't sleep, either?"

"I'm not confessing a thing." Erin crooked her arm and Catherine linked hers in it.

After passing through security, they headed to the entry desk to pay, and when Catherine pulled out her wallet, Erin stopped her, about to insist on using the pass her friend had given her, when Catherine stopped her.

"My company has a free pass to most of the museums in the city. I checked on Friday when I got back to the office. Apparently, we donate so much it's one of the perks."

Erin slid her wallet back into her pocket, glad she hadn't pulled her pass out. She wasn't sure it covered guests.

Catherine showed her ID to the woman behind the desk and took the two paper buttons from her, peeling one off and pressing it onto the breast pocket of Erin's shirt, her eyes searching Erin's as she ran her hand over it. Erin knew the blush was rising, and Catherine smiled at its appearance. They headed up the wide marble stairway to the second floor.

"Thank you for getting us in, then," Erin said.

"Let's see if you're still thanking me in an hour, when I can't form a coherent idea about what we're looking at."

"Oh, come on, it's all about what you like, not about right or wrong."

"And you couldn't sleep last night because you're afraid my taste is pedestrian, or perhaps worse, or that we won't like the same things."

"Still not confessing. But is that what you think?"

"I'll plead the Fifth." They had reached the photography wing and stood inside the main entry. Erin stole a glance at Catherine as she looked around in awe. Then she followed her over to a portrait of Georgia O'Keeffe. The little plate affixed to the wall at the right of the photo identified it as a 1918 shot by Alfred Steiglitz.

"She was fascinating," Catherine said. "I find her work incandescent. It draws me right in, but I'm still not sure I like it."

"Really?" Puppies and flowers went right out the window; Erin knew Catherine had been hiding her critic's eye. What she needed to find out was why. "Where have you seen it if you don't come here?"

"I was in Taos once. And I spent a whole day at her museum in Santa Fe and then of course made the pilgrimage to Abiquiú. But her work's online, too, and there are marvelous art books in all the city's libraries. I suspect you knew that, though."

"I did."

"Of course you did." She glanced at Erin. "Needn't have pointed that out to you."

"Again, nothing we say within these walls is wrong or right. And how come you turn to books instead of coming here to look at the real thing?" Erin was intrigued that Catherine might actually be an art aficionado, even if by proxy.

"The library's three blocks from my apartment. And I know, before you say it, books can't replace the real thing. But when I finally get home, I like to snuggle in, and books are conducive to that."

Erin nodded, imagining snuggling in with Catherine, turning the pages of oversized art books to marvel at Degas or Dorothea Lange.

"Besides, I haven't had anyone to go to the museum with in a long time."

"Maybe we can remedy that."

"Twist my arm. I'm sure I'll learn a thing or two from you."

"And maybe I'll learn things from you. Where to first?"

There weren't very many people in the wing yet and, enveloped in silence, they moved from one photograph to another, Erin making mental notes about which ones Catherine stopped in front of and studied. Eventually, she began pointing things out to Erin about how each photographer worked and what strides were being made during the years a particular photographer was on the rise. Erin knew some things about the history of the medium. She'd studied the science behind it in art school. But she was spellbound hearing it from someone who didn't consider herself remotely creative, getting a lesson in silver negatives, laced with biographical bits, and how certain shots came to be.

"How do you know all this?"

"Well, in addition to the art books, I read biographies."

Erin tried to stifle a smile.

"What? I like to learn everything I can if something interests me, especially if I'm a neophyte."

"So you know your art."

"I know this," she said, her hand making a sweeping arc around the room. "Painting, drawing, what you do, I'm not so sure about."

"But it's the same form. Lines and planes, light and shadow."

"And shading, and vanishing points, and don't even get me started on Cubism. It's not the same, Erin. Painting deals with an artist's *interpretation* of reality. Photography deals with reality."

"Except when it doesn't. Like those superimposed things."

"Touché."

"Is that why you were afraid to say anything about my illustrations on Friday?"

Catherine sighed. "I'm not on solid footing with that. And I really *didn't* want to say anything wrong, for lack of a better word. I like line drawings, but if all I could say was, 'I like it' without a reason why? Something told me you were shooting for more."

"Well, I suppose if you were the critic for the *New York Times*, I would be. But I just wanted to know what *you* thought."

Catherine took Erin's hand and smiled. "I like line drawings. And I like your ability to distill a line."

"You are a piece of work." Erin shook her head. "The last time I heard anyone talk about distilling lines was in *ARTnews* several years ago."

"You can learn a lot from an artist's biography."

They headed to the next room.

"So who is your favorite photographer?" Erin asked. She understood now that Catherine might downplay her knowledge, but it was there, just under the surface.

"Irving Penn."

No hesitation. Erin liked that.

"His portraits are mesmerizing, all smoky grays, a moment of vulnerability in someone's eyes. He must have had to wait a long time for just the right second, though, and all the while probably taking shot after shot. But his fashion photos have those deep blacks, brilliant whites, and clean sharp lines. And he leaves the story he's telling up to his viewer to interpret."

Her answer opened the window a little wider. Those clean sharp lines extended to the way Catherine dressed, and Erin surmised they extended to how she led her life. But the urge to tease hit her. "But he's not your favorite because he did fashion photography and you're a clothes horse."

Catherine's surprise was evident.

"No? You don't think you look like you stepped off the cover of Vogue every time you walk out your door?" Erin's gaze traveled down Catherine's body, again taking in the immaculate white polo shirt with the upturned black striped collar, the pressed red shorts, the black belt and espadrilles. "See? I rest my case."

"Okay, smarty-pants. I also really like Margaret Bourke-White, the war photojournalist. And Gordon Parks the documentary photojournalist. So what does *that* say about me? And I would love to own one of Berenice Abbot's photos," she said, looking over at a small frame containing a 1930 shot of cars under the el at the Battery. "But I'll never live long enough to earn that kind of money."

"Or me a Monet."

They had reached the end of the third room they'd walked through, and Catherine wrapped her arms around herself in a hug. "I'd say you have a better chance. At least you're in a business where you could sell something for millions."

"So are you."

"Yeah, but I only get a percentage of what I sell."

"But you're always making money of some kind. It's not really a business for me. It's what I am. I don't paint because I could possibly make millions, and I can barely make the rent sometimes."

"I know that." Catherine leaned against her and they looked around, the crowds having grown quite large since they'd first entered the galleries.

Erin felt like they were in a bubble of their own making.

Catherine sighed. "I feel like that little boy in *The Goldfinch*. I've always wanted to pluck one of these off the wall, slip it into my bag, and casually walk out."

Erin nodded. "Kind of how I feel every time I'm standing in front of Monet's *Houses of Parliament*."

"I never would've taken you for a fan of the Impressionists."

Erin smiled. "Something very romantic about them."

"Yes, there is." She glanced at Erin. "What does that say about you?"

Erin looked at her quizzically, but she'd gone back to studying the crowds. "You tell me."

Catherine gently pushed away from her and sat on the maroon velvet banquette nearby. "That you're a realist and a romantic."

She looked up at Erin. "Maybe? But then again, I'm not sure." She cocked her head. "Like I said before, I like to learn everything I can if something interests me. I haven't had enough time to do that yet."

Erin eyed her. The words had the same effect on her that Catherine's touch had two days ago, soft, promising.

"Either way, it's a deadly combination, being a romantic in a realist world." Catherine stood. "Okay, enough dreaming about things I'll never own. I came to the Met for you, now I need brunch. And a couple mimosas."

Several hours later, a waiter put a check on the table. "I'm having too good a time. I don't want this brunch to end," Erin said, gazing at Catherine as she signed the credit card receipt.

She glanced up at her, amused. "It doesn't have to."

"How many appointments did you move around? We've spent almost the whole day together."

"Complaining?"

Erin smiled and shook her head.

Catherine handed the waiter the leather billfold and sat back. "I have four weeks of vacation a year and I haven't taken any of them for the last five years. Technically, I could take half a year right now if I chose to, but I'm only taking today off so I can spend it with you."

Erin bit the inside of her cheek to keep the blush she felt rising at bay. "So, where should we go now? What should we do?"

"I thought we could walk to the boat basin. I know a nice quiet bench there by the last pier where we could continue our conversation because I don't want it to end, either."

"Good. I didn't want to think it was just me feeling…" Erin hesitated, not wanting to show her entire hand of cards.

Catherine cocked her head. "Like?"

"Like I could spend the rest of the day and night talking with you."

Catherine's half-smile teased Erin's next breath and it caught in her throat.

"Well, then. Let's get out of here."

The Hudson River was a deep blue in the late afternoon sunlight as they settled on a bench that Erin calculated was down by 70th Street, the last bench in a long row of them that stretched many blocks north. It was almost hidden by an enormous oak tree that provided shade at this hour that, combined with the breeze coming off the water, was akin to air conditioning. Erin noticed Catherine casually putting her arm across the back of the bench behind her and almost laughed. It was a rookie move that Erin used all the time. She leaned back and a moment later felt Catherine's finger tracing a small circle between her shoulder blades. She closed her eyes, pleasure sweeping over her. "Where were we?"

"Really? You want to talk?" Catherine asked.

"I always want to talk. Didn't we start a conversation in the restaurant about the state of cinema today, why Hollywood is so out of touch, and how that's given birth to this new golden age of television?"

Catherine chuckled. "We were talking about really good shows on TV."

Erin sighed. "Oh. I thought we were being much more erudite than that." Catherine's fingers moved from the circle they'd been tracing into a line up to the nape of Erin's neck and back down again, and she began to feel like a pat of butter melting into a yellow-dotted puddle in the bottom of a pot.

Catherine leaned close to her. "*You* were on a tear about several shows you couldn't believe I'm not watching. And I'm not sure I want to be erudite right now." She began stroking the side of Erin's neck with the back of her hand. "However, if you insist, we also compared notes on books we've read lately, and we seemed to have picked up several of the same authors."

"We did?"

"Indeed. We've read many of the same books in the last couple of years."

Erin wanted to put her head on Catherine's shoulder because the sensations coursing through her were overwhelming. Every cell of skin felt like it was purring under touch. Her heartbeat seemed to have accelerated. She felt light-headed and elated and sad all at once. Being here with her, talking, felt so right, and she already knew the absence she'd feel tonight alone again in her apartment. "We did, right." She studied the clouds to keep from doing that.

Catherine turned Erin's head toward her. "You made some astute observations about them."

"I did?" She looked back at the clouds and pointed to the bank of them over New Jersey. "Look, clouds like Pissarro painted them."

Catherine looked in the direction Erin was pointing. "You do like to talk, don't you?" Then she kissed Erin, gently, softly, running the back of her hand from Erin's cheek down her throat and lightly holding it. Then she deepened the kiss, her hand moving down Erin's shirt to settle under her arm, her palm on Erin's breast, pressing tenderly, moving back and forth, the pulsing raising Erin's nipples. She moaned quietly.

"I'm finding out from my study that except when you see something impressionistic, you're a very logical, linear thinker." Catherine's lips brushed Erin's.

"Nat says that about me, too."

"She does? I knew there was a reason I liked her."

Erin pulled Catherine toward her, her hand on the back of her neck, and kissed her hard. She hoped there was no one around to see this display, but she couldn't help herself. She was hungry for Catherine, who seemed to be able to read her and still come back for more. Who could talk to her, touch her like she meant it, open her, make her feel like there was no one else she cared about in the world but her. When Erin let go, they sat holding each other, but Erin couldn't look at her, afraid of… What? What she might see in Catherine's eyes? What if it wasn't a reflection of what she was feeling for Catherine?

"I'd like to take you to bed right now," Catherine said, nuzzling Erin's hair. "But I won't rush this."

"No," Erin replied, even though her hormones were telling her to rip the covers off the nearest bed regardless of who it belonged to and push Catherine onto it. "We shouldn't."

Neither of them moved.

"What are you doing two weekends from now?"

"I'm not sure. If Nat doesn't need me..." Erin hesitated, and Catherine pulled back to look at her. "She's writing an article and I sometimes help her with online research and overviews so she can concentrate on the writing." Erin heard Nat's admonishment in her head, *"Don't blow this for me!"*

"Okay, well when would you know?"

"I'm talking to her tonight. I'll ask her. Why?"

Catherine sat back. "This is kind of...crazy, but I don't know, would you like to come to a wedding with me?"

"A what?" Erin almost laughed.

"Yeah, a wedding. I know. It's a bizarre date request."

"Well, maybe not. Tell me about it."

"I sold him his first apartment, he's become a good friend, and now he's looking at his second marriage. And I really like his fiancée. We actually do things together when we have the time. In fact, that's where I was last weekend. Nikki needed some help ironing things out with the venue, so we drove to the Cape." Catherine brushed Erin's neck again, and she sighed. "It's going to be a good party, that much I know."

"Who doesn't love a good party? Wait, what Cape?"

"Cape Cod. That's where they're getting married."

"Oh, that changes things."

"We can drive up Wednesday to avoid the weekend traffic. That way, we'd have a whole day to ourselves before any of the festivities and dinners. And if we drive back late Sunday, we'll avoid that traffic, too."

Erin looked down at her hands. She knew that even the money in her paintbrush can coupled with the money in her emergency envelope would never be enough to cover whatever this trip would require. Could she borrow money from Nat against future earnings?

"And I have a suite with two queen beds, so nothing to worry about there."

Erin looked at her, unsure how to say no without disappointing her.

"And because I'm asking you, the weekend is on me. You can leave your wallet at home. But bring your driver's license in case I need you to take the wheel for an hour to give me a break."

"You can't do that." It was an automatic response.

"Ask you to drive? You *do* have a license, don't you?"

"Yes, of course, but you can't pay for me."

"Erin, it's *my* friend's wedding. I'd be out of line if I didn't. I'm asking you to join me on a weekend away in a hotel you didn't have any choice about booking to attend an event with a hundred people you don't even know."

"Smooth sales pitch, Dale Carnegie."

Catherine grinned and looked like she'd won.

"Yes." Erin kissed her. "I would love to come."

"Don't you need to speak to Nat first?"

"No, I'll just tell her. I'm a fool. Considering I want to spend all night talking with you right now, I shouldn't have even had a second thought about a weekend with you, and some lobster."

Catherine laughed softly. "Oh, now because it's Cape Cod, you're all in."

"I think I'd go to Siberia with you." Erin caressed Catherine's cheek.

"With me and some caviar." Catherine caught her hand and kissed her fingers.

"Gross. I don't like caviar. But for some blini with raspberry jam, you could easily have your way with me."

"I'll remember that."

"So. What do I need to know about this weekend? If I'm coming as your date, I want to crush it and make you look like a superstar." Erin tried to contain her excitement as Catherine began to talk about Nikki and Daniel and the festivities they'd lined up for their guests.

CHAPTER FOURTEEN

Nat and Erin stood beside Red's chair Monday morning looking at the computer screen with him. "Okay? That's Erin's page. Now..." Nat reached for the keyboard and hit a button that brought up another screen. "Here's *my* Facebook page."

"Okay, so, what am I missing?"

"Look at the Sumter Realty ads versus everyone else's."

Red toggled back and forth between the two pages studying the border ads, watching the filters change.

"You see?" Erin said, pointing. "All the other companies sent us both all their ads, regardless of where the apartments were. But Sumter, only certain neighborhoods sent to her, certain ones only to me."

"Oh, hell, no," Red said. "That's not marketing. That's redlining. All right, we got ourselves a problem. *If* it's driven solely by your realty company. There's other engines involved."

"I already spoke to Buzz. She's looking into it," Nat said.

"You focus on your story. I'll work with Buzz to see if this is extensive or local," Red said. Nat nodded and Red spread her charts across his desk. "I'm gonna find that thread. It's in here somewhere, you're right. Like it's just out of focus. But you're gonna visit some of these Realtors a second and third time alone as a yardstick, right?"

"Yup. Already have stuff scheduled."

"Okay, I'll look at the rough draft of your first article later."

Nat hoisted her leather bag onto her shoulder. "Thanks."

"Hey," Erin said as they walked through the gates of Red's brownstone. "Let's get breakfast at that diner on Fourteenth Street."

"That Mexican one?"

"Yeah, I like their huevos rancheros."

"That place is spicy."

"They have avocado toast."

"Oh. Okay, then."

After several blocks walked in silence, Nat stopped. "Why do I suddenly feel like Father Thomas in the confessional back at college? Only I didn't do any sinning this weekend."

"Man, I'm just an open book to you, aren't I?" Erin sighed. "Because maybe I transgressed yesterday. But you'll think I sinned."

Nat folded her arms across her chest. "What did you do? Do I have to worry? Is this a colossal blunder or a hiccup?"

"Let's go to the restaurant first." Erin turned and walked in the direction of the diner, but several steps out, knew that Nat wasn't following her.

"Tell me." Nat cocked her head, the expression on her face one Erin knew from many a confrontation. "Don't ruin my breakfast."

"Fine. I think I'm in love."

"What? I thought Marquita hadn't called you."

"She hasn't."

"So you called her. And what?"

"Not Marquita. With Catherine."

"Uh-huh. You don't say." Nat held up her finger in front of Erin's face. "No."

Erin held up her hand against the retort that might come her way. "Hear me out. I spent all day yesterday with her."

Nat fixed her with that look again, arms folded across her chest. "Define all day."

"The Met in the morning, brunch, the afternoon in Riverside Park, dinner, then a long walk around the Upper West Side."

Nat leaned forward and studied her Louboutin high-tops that looked like a Jackson Pollock drip painting to Erin. They complemented her gray shorts and red polo shirt. "And you're in love. After one day with someone."

"We've already had dinner together, too. She's really different, Nat. So, okay, maybe not in love, but I want to spend time with her, talk with her, find out all about her."

"You've obsessed before, you know. How different?"

"I spent twelve hours with her, and we didn't sleep together. And I can't wait to see her again. I've never done that before."

"Correction," Nat shot back. "You haven't spent twelve hours with another woman since Adele left you."

Erin's hands went to her hips, her stance a challenge to Nat's stare.

"No." Nat put her hands on her hips, mirroring Erin, and shook her head. "You are not gonna screw this up for us."

"I won't, I promise. If anything, I'll get every bit of information on her that there is to get." Erin watched Nat's face for clues that she was winning her over. Sometimes she could be so hard to read.

"How are you gonna do that? Search her purse next time you're in a restaurant with her and she goes to the bathroom? Rifle through her online files if she has her laptop with her, after you get out of bed?"

"No. When I go away to a wedding with her in two weeks."

"She invited you to a wedding? Like, on a date?"

Erin nodded.

"And you said yes?"

Erin nodded again.

"Jesus. You *are* in love, or at the very least, obsessing way beyond your usual self." Nat shifted. "So why do you look so sad?"

"Because I knew you'd react like this, trying to stop me. And," Erin ran her hands through her hair, "I promised myself I'd never get like this about a woman again."

Nat let out a dramatic sigh. "Fool. Let's go. I need that toast for sure now." They walked a block and Nat stopped again. "Wait, did I hear you right? This wedding is an away game?"

"Yeah. Cape Cod."

"What if I need you?"

"Boss, can I have five days off week after next?"

Nat shoved her and started walking again.

The breakfast rush was over so there were plenty of tables in the window, prime seating for almost any New Yorker. Nat slid into the booth, assessed the flatware, and began aligning it more precisely with the lettering that framed the placemat. It was another of Nat's tics that sometimes drove Erin crazy.

"So I don't understand. How did this happen? You're a walkaway Joe. Did she cast a spell on you?"

"Maybe. I don't know. Yes."

"But what about Marquita?"

Erin snorted. "Talk about a walkaway Joe."

"What, because she didn't do you?"

"No, it's not that. I'm so tired of hook-ups and short relationships that are hardly a blip and women who want you to hang out with their posse. And I guess now I know how women might have felt after being with me. Marquita just showed me that. But I don't think I knew I might be ready to even think about settling down again until I met Catherine. Which is, you're right, totally fast because we've only seen each other a couple of times."

"I did not see this coming."

The waiter brought glasses of ice water to the table. Nat drank the whole thing right down while Erin put in their order.

"Besides, Marquita didn't call me."

"Did you call her?'

Erin studied her fingernails.

"I see. So lemme ask you again. How did this happen?" Nat caught the waiter's attention and held up her glass for a refill.

"It happened because she's smart. And funny. No, not just funny. Witty. She's clever and classy."

"So, Cole Porter and Scott Fitzgerald all in one, am I right? Your favorite era for the urbane."

"Pardon me for wanting some sophistication in my life." She was annoyed at Nat. And grateful that she'd always understood how very last century she was, and could read and decipher her mental hieroglyphs.

"Ouch. Okay, I'm not criticizing. I'm trying to understand."

"She's got her shit together, Nat. She's confident, she knows who she is and what she wants—"

"And apparently she wants you."

"I kind of hope so, yeah."

"You want her. Don't you?"

"Yeah." Now it was Erin's turn to fiddle with the silverware. "But if I go there, I want to get it right."

"So is this wedding a really good friend of hers?"

"Yeah, a client-turned-close-friend. A guy, actually. But she's good friends with his fiancée. I get the sense Catherine lost a lot of friends in the divorce. They defected to her ex."

"That sucks."

"Yeah. I think she's been doing some slow world-building since then. But really slow."

The waiter brought their food to the table and Nat leaned down into her plate and inhaled. "Life is good."

Erin cut up her omelet, potatoes, and bacon, and mixed them all together on her plate into one big stew.

"You know that hurts me," Nat said.

"These things can all touch each other in my world."

"Potatoes are a free agent, yes. But I can't have my bacon touch anything else, not even my toast, especially if it's buttered. I can't look at that plate. It's revolting." Nat took a big bite of her toast and concentrated on the view outside the window.

"Sorry. I know you have food sensory issues, but a girl's gotta do what a girl's gotta do."

"Fine. Just stick a knife in me. Let's figure out how we're gonna handle these next apartment visits."

"Why don't I pretend I'm someone who wandered in off the same elevator as you, but I don't have an appointment. Then I can keep an eye on how the Realtor works with you."

"We can give it a try. But we really have to work this thing out about Catherine. 'Cause you know I'm worried. I don't trust that you won't either let it slip along the way if you keep seeing her or out-and-out tell her if you sleep with her. And if she's in on it, that will blow my series."

"I'm not going to sleep with her."

"So you're just gonna lie to the woman you're now having all kinds of feelings for."

"I'm compartmentalizing. I'll share it with her when it's safe."

"And what if it's never safe? What if you get really involved and she turns out to be a racist bigot who's actually contributing to this scheme? Are you going to set up house with her anyway?"

"I would never." Erin was hurt that Nat would even think that.

"There's a lot we think we would never do until we fall in love," Nat said.

"Can we talk about that later over dinner?"

"Oh, sure, when Kendra is there to referee."

"She seems to be the only one who can yellow card us when we have these matches."

Nat eyed her and then seemed mollified, returning the conversation to their approach with the next few Realtors whom Nat had seen before. But Erin's mind was on Nat's doubting her. They'd never been here before. Then again, who Erin dated and slept with and dropped had never mattered to them like it did now. Well, except for that one-night stand with Yvonne back in college when she had no idea Nat had a thing for her.

How could Nat think she would choose Catherine over her? How could she think she'd ever spend time with anyone who wouldn't welcome Nat into her world with open arms? She loved Nat unconditionally, warts and all, and had never doubted that it was returned. They knew each other as well as it was possible to know a best friend. So Nat's doubting her was troublesome. She knew she was going to have to call her on it sooner or later.

Erin lay on the bed, the cell phone cradled in the crook of her shoulder, her ear as close to it as she could get it. She hoped she wouldn't accidentally hang up on Catherine in this position, but she was feeling particularly lazy.

"So what did you do today?" Catherine asked.

They'd never talked on the phone before. Erin suddenly went from feeling like a teenager to feeling trapped. "Some cleaning and laundry." Telling her she'd been at three apartment showings with Nat was out of the question. But lying to her gave her a sick feeling in the pit of her stomach. She envisioned a little model of herself pushing the lie out of her mind like it was a giant canvas.

Catherine sighed. "Sometimes I wish I had a whole day to do that."

"I've decided you work too hard. Or maybe it's too much."

"I do. But it's what keeps me going. I told you that."

"You did." Erin cleared her throat. "What if I was to find something else to keep you going?"

"What did you have in mind?"

"Movie night."

"I don't really go out to the movies anymore."

"I didn't say we were going out." Erin liked teasing Catherine this way. It was so easy to get under her skin.

"Oh?"

"I will make the best popcorn you've ever had, and we'll watch something you choose, at your place or mine."

"That could be a bigger decision than the movie."

"So could the popcorn. If you're adventurous, I make a terrific curry popcorn. I also make cheddar." Erin was met by silence. "Are you still there or did the thought of curry popcorn send you fleeing into the night?"

"No, actually, I'm intrigued. That *is* adventurous."

"Mmmm. None of my friends ever accused me of being dull."

"All right, let me think about the popcorn, but come over tomorrow night. Let me give you my address."

Erin had to put the phone down to grab a piece of paper and a pencil off her desk.

"Any flavor popcorn your heart desires," she said, once she'd scooped the phone back up and written the information down. "But I bring the pot. It's a special copper-bottomed pot."

"Okay, that has my attention, too."

"I like having your attention."

"Do you?"

"Mm-hmm." Lincoln jumped up on the bed and sniffed at the phone. Erin put her arm around him and pulled him down next to her to pet him.

"Well, you're very good at diverting it. I don't remember the last time I was out of the office for a whole day. Or had so much fun."

"Good. Because I intend to keep luring you out."

"Or in. As in movie night."

"I think 'luring' is the operative word."

"You're very good at that, too."

"So are you."

"Me? Oh, I'm afraid I don't do that, no."

Erin laughed. "It was your opening salvo! The private showing?"

"Oh, that." Catherine sighed. "You were too adorable, telling me you hated to leave empty-handed and batting those big blue eyes at me. You've been luring me from the start."

"That was the plan, yes."

"Oh, you had a plan?"

"Of course I did. That red suit you were wearing in the park rocked my world."

"You flirted with me even then. But you had no idea who I was or how to find out."

"I want to touch you right now," Erin interrupted. She was met with silence but sensed this one was different.

"You make me think and do things I shouldn't." Catherine's voice, barely above a whisper, wavered.

"Like?"

"Like taking off my T-shirt here in bed."

A wave of desire passed over Erin. She'd pictured Catherine naked so many times she'd wanted to re-create her on paper, and after spending almost two hours with her in the park on Sunday talking and kissing, she could almost smell her perfume now. "And like?"

"You tell me."

Erin collected her thoughts, which had scattered like marbles at Catherine's sultry tone. She slid her hand over her breast. "Run the back of your hand down the side of your neck. I love when you do that to me." Erin waited. She heard a little sound. "Put your hand on your breast. Your nipples are hard, aren't they?"

"Yes."

"Play with them." Upending the cat from his warm nest, Erin moved the phone long enough to pull off her own T-shirt and panties and lie back down. She set the phone back in the crook of her shoulder and then touched both of her breasts, gently rolling her nipples with her fingers, listening to Catherine's breath grow quicker. "Brush them with the palm of your hand."

"I'm using both hands." Catherine was almost breathless now.

"So am I."

"I wish I was there. Tell me what to do. They're aching."

"Pull them. A little bit at a time. Think of my mouth on them."

Catherine moaned quietly. "Can I touch myself somewhere else that's begging for it?'

"Where else?"

"You know where."

Erin wanted to transport herself through the phone. Everything on her body seemed to be pulsing at once.

"And you…must need…"

"Yes," Erin whispered. "Very much."

"What would I feel if I put my hand there right now?"

Erin had decided not to shave last week. "It's downy soft at the moment, and open."

"And?"

"You tell me." It was a small intake of breath, but Erin heard it, loud and clear.

"You're wet. Are you big and hard? Or is it round and soft?"

"You've made it very big. And very hard."

Catherine's moan immediately changed the landscape.

"Oh, crap…" Erin was on the verge of an orgasm.

"Did you lose it?"

"No. That beautiful moan. I'm going to come!"

Catherine's breathing became deeper, faster. "Do you know what I'd do if I was there right now?"

Erin ran her fingers through her folds, the wet silkiness reacting immediately. "The same thing I'd do if I was there."

"You know where my tongue—"

"Yes!" Erin interrupted her. "Oh, God!" As she came in a series of gasps, she was certain she'd heard the most alluring cries from Catherine. In the long moment of silence that followed, she pulled the sheet up and rolled onto her side, squeezing her thighs tightly together before completely relaxing.

"I wish I was there to hold you."

"I wish you were, too." Erin curled up. "Did you?"

"Yes." Catherine sighed. "Hearing you pushed me right over the edge. I'm thinking about what you must look like when you come."

Erin sighed, sated, but strangely bereft, too.

"You know," Catherine said hesitantly, "I've never done that before."

"No phone sex?" Erin chuckled. "Was it as good for you as it was for me?" The cheesy line made her giggle and Catherine laughed.

"I'm not your first, am I? You're a little bit naughty, aren't you?"

Erin let the question hang. She liked the deliciousness of it, and of not giving Catherine the answer they both knew anyway.

"So, curry popcorn, huh?" Catherine asked.

"I don't want to hang up yet, either. Let's talk about what movies we could watch."

"I could talk to you all night."

"Okay, then let's start with movies that begin with the letter A."

CHAPTER FIFTEEN

Erin wandered around the apartment keeping as close to Nat as she could without seeming as though she was with her. The Realtor had approached her shortly after she'd walked in behind Nat, but after almost half an hour, he was still busy talking to other people and hadn't so much as nodded at Nat, who had already glanced at Erin several times, her jaw clenching and her eyes tight. They'd expected this. It was the whole reason they were doing the article in the first place. But knowing it and experiencing it firsthand were different things.

The Realtor finally approached Erin, but she told him she wasn't sure she was interested after all. Nat walked right over to him.

"I am. I'm interested."

"Have I seen you before?" he asked.

"Yeah. I looked at a place on West Eighty-Second that you were showing."

"Right."

"But you haven't talked to me here."

"Oh, I—"

"Talked to her twice, but not to me."

"Well, I—"

"My money's green, too." Nat sucked her teeth, looking at him.

"Yeah, sure, of course, but why aren't you working directly with one of our Realtors?"

"Didn't want to. I'd rather see the apartments I want to see, not the ones a Realtor thinks I should see." She wrote her name on a 3x5 card and handed it to him. "Here, since you already have my information in your files, all you need is my name."

He smiled at her again, took a pen out of his suit jacket pocket, and put a black "X" in the upper right-hand corner of the card.

"What's that?" Nat asked, poking her chin toward it.

"To remind me that you're in the files."

"Why didn't you just write that note, then?"

"The x is my shorthand for that." He gave her a slight smile.

Nat gave him the once-over and then turned toward another room.

Erin hadn't moved during this exchange, but now she slowly walked away, no longer worried that Nat was going to deck him.

A moment after seeing that Nat had left, Erin joined her at the elevator as the door opened. "I wanted to punch him right in his smug kisser," Nat said as she banged her hand on the button for the lobby.

"And blow the story?"

"I know, I know, I'm just so…" Nat's hands were in fists, and she jammed them into her pockets.

"But you need to maintain objectivity so you can't go there."

"Yeah, I can!" Nat exploded. "Don't you see? Don't you see what he did to me? Like it was nothing! Like they all do and like it's always nothing. I'm getting redlined, they're redlining *people* now instead of neighborhoods. It might as well be nineteen thirty-five."

The elevator door opened, and Nat charged off, Erin right behind her. "But don't you have to be clear-eyed and detached? So you can report on it without prejudice?" As soon as it was out of her mouth, Erin realized she'd released a swarm of hornets unintentionally aimed right at Nat, who whirled around, tears in her eyes.

Dammit! Erin braced her hand against the wall, tears coming to her own eyes because she knew she'd hurt her.

"Why?" Nat's voice caromed around the large old marble lobby as she turned on Erin. "They don't *rent* without prejudice! Why do *I* need to be the one to hold back? Why can't *I* sock them in the jaw and wake them up? You think I can't report a story of massive injustice fairly? There *is* no fair here, Erin!"

"We," Erin said.

"We *what*?" Nat spat back.

"Do I think *we* can't report a story."

"What the heck?" Nat finally slowed down and her shoulders dropped a fraction.

"It's our story, Nat. You brought me in on it. You did that because you know I'm broke and struggling and that's what best friends do. Color never entered into that decision. It never has for us. And that's also *our* story. Has been since we met."

"Is it? Just because I brought you in, you think you know all about it?"

"I didn't say that. You know full well I know better."

"Good. Because you don't. You don't know what it's like to get looked at and treated the way he looked at me, like I wasn't good enough or worse, like I shouldn't exist. I'm extra work, something he has to put an 'x' on and make go away."

Nat sneered as she spoke, and Erin wanted to look away, but she didn't. "He was an asshole."

"Damn right he was! But he wouldn't have acted that way if we'd come in together. He would've deferred to you and not even looked at me, like he wasn't looking at me when you came in right after me."

"So, *our* story.

"*I'm* the story Erin, not us. You can help me report it, but I live it. My dad's money might've protected me for a long time, but I always knew that whatever happened to anyone of my race happened to me, too. Just like if anyone gets gay-bashed, it's hatred on all of us. He just demeaned all Black people up there. And if you're not pissed off, with or without me as your friend, then you're not looking at this story hard enough, or at anything around you."

"Of course I'm pissed! You're my friend."

"Are you pissed for me as your friend? Or are you pissed for me as a Black woman?"

"Both! I—"

Nat took a step toward her. "You know how it is for you right now? So squeezed for money that you can't go to restaurants or clubs unless someone takes you, and you sure couldn't afford to move right now. You're not even going to the beach, your favorite place on earth, and you can't even afford a haircut."

Erin nodded, chagrined.

"Well, what if poor was the color of your skin and people could see it? What if they didn't want you in their establishment because you make people nervous, not having money but walking around Duane Reade anyway? Or they don't want to hire you because they already got three poor people on their staff. Or a gallery owner won't show your work because the guy down the street had a show of poor art last month and ya know what? It didn't sell well because the rich clientele that buys art doesn't want to buy poor art unless someone in the art world anoints you a genius of it."

They looked at each other. Erin felt like she was seeing Nat for the first time.

"Feelin' how hard it is being poor now?"

"I was before." Erin was hurt, but she knew Nat wasn't being mean on purpose. It made her feel like she was only beginning to understand, though, what Nat was driving at. She knew that microaggressions and marginalization happened to Nat even if she didn't see them happening when they were somewhere together. But now, seeing how it was for Nat during this apartment hunt alarmed and sickened her. And she couldn't imagine how she'd feel in her place.

"Yeah, but before I put you in this scenario, you could go anywhere and do anything you wanted without people looking at you sideways. Now, your poor skin color changes that. Everyone sees who you are, and a lot of people don't like that stank even if you're wearing the same Brooks Brothers clothes they are. So they shut doors and avenues, hell, they shut whole neighborhoods and all kinds of opportunities to you. Only because you and I both had those opportunities, we know what they are, we know what we'd be losing. What if you were born and grew up with poor skin color? You'd need some kind of battering ram to get doors open."

"Like daddy's money."

"Yes, I had that advantage. Please tell me you're not using that against me now."

Erin shook her head, her eyes downcast. "I would never. You know that."

"But you just did. Did that make a difference to you when I sat down next to you in the cafeteria that first night at school? That I looked like I maybe came from money because I dressed the part?"

Erin looked at her again. "I didn't know you had money."

"No, you didn't know because I looked just like you. I looked just like you, same clothes, from Bean. Sounded just like you, same educated accent, from prep school. Just Black."

"Everybody at that school looked like everybody else, whatever the financial background."

"I coulda been a savvy scholarship kid. You didn't know."

"And I didn't care. You were funny. I almost spit out my water when you introduced yourself as Nat Robicheaux, illegitimate daughter of Bumblebee."

Nat hiccupped a laugh and brushed angrily at the tears welling in her eyes. "I had to break the tension somehow. And Bumblebee's weapon *is* her superior education."

"Why didn't you just point out to everybody sitting at the table that night that you chose our table because you saw I didn't put my ice cream on my pie, just like you? Hating pie a la mode was how we found each other."

"Stop it," Nat said quietly. She opened the heavy wrought iron door of the lobby, but Erin put a hand on her shoulder to stop her.

"You're right. I don't know what it's like to be you. And I never will. But I love you. I would do anything for you. I'll stand beside you and help you write all the articles in the world to show people how fucked up things are."

"I know that. But it's not enough. Nothing changes, nothing moves the needle, it's the same stories, just different centuries. We're still getting lied to and cheated out of property and paid less and appropriated from. And we're still being hunted and killed." Nat opened the front door and walked down two of the three wide marble steps toward the sidewalk. "I know you mean well, but even people who mean well do just as much damage. You can be our friends or even marry us, but you still live your lives largely unaware or say dumb shit like 'it's *our* story' because your privilege is so deeply ingrained you can't even see it. Even your privilege is different from mine, you know?"

"I always thought I was a pretty good friend, though." Erin walked down the steps to Nat, who threw her arm around her shoulder.

"You are. You're my second-best friend."

"What?"

"Kendra."

"Oh. Right." She bumped her shoulder. "I guess you have to say that." It elicited a tiny smile, which was something.

They walked down the last step and turned toward Broadway. Nat sighed. "I got a lot of work to do. I'm gonna call Marquita, see if she has anything new for us. We could meet her at the diner near her office."

"Yeah, I didn't think that was a smart move the first time we did that, and now I really can't be seen in that neighborhood in case Catherine is there."

"Probably not a good idea, you're right." Nat studied Erin. "Wait. Did it occur to you that the two women you're involved with work at the same company?"

Erin looked at Nat and rolled her eyes. "Obviously. But Marquita said she doesn't like her, so it's not like they'll be sharing dating gossip over cocktails."

"Oh, you are so screwed, sister. What are we having for dinner tonight?"

"Leftovers from last night, remember? Plus you'll make a salad. You don't need me for leftovers. Tomorrow we'll pick up some sole at Citarella and have a really good dinner before Kendra goes to the theater."

"Damn, you do a lot of leftovers, girl. Should I be saving some of your salary and paying myself to steam leftovers?"

"Very funny. And what would you even be eating tonight if I hadn't cooked it the other night? Chef Boyardee SpaghettiOs?"

"Fine, I hear ya."

Nat talked about the article as they walked toward Broadway, but Erin's mind was on people in the Duane Reade drugstore hating her because the color of her skin was "poor," as Nat put it. She'd never been hated just for walking into a store or restaurant. Or the wrong neighborhood. The thought frightened her, and she wondered what Nat did every day just to get out of bed and face a world like that.

Cinnamon toast popcorn was what Catherine had chosen, and she'd said she'd have the ingredients ready. Erin had almost put the spices for her curry popcorn into her bag just in case. The heat of the day had finally broken, and a cool evening breeze rustled the leaves of the trees as she walked up West End Avenue to Catherine's apartment. Along the way, she indulged in one of her favorite secret pastimes: looking in people's apartment windows. She loved seeing how other people lived, with their shelves full of books or huge flat screen TVs that seemed almost as big as movie theater screens. What could be so enthralling, she'd often wondered, that it had to be seen in such epic size? The apartments that had artwork on the walls she found the most interesting bellwethers of what type of person inhabited them. Once she saw a Picasso in a second floor window, but decided it couldn't be real. No New Yorker would be that stupid. She loved glimpsing these lives lived, if only in passing.

The undercurrent hit her again, as it had last night after she'd hung up with Catherine, that she'd finally be seeing her apartment, and it was as delicious as she hoped the popcorn would be. That Sherlock Holmes sense she got when first seeing someone's place kicked in. Her curiosity about the many clues she'd be able to pick up about who Catherine was, and about her inner life, blossomed. She'd finally be inside her haven. Erin's excitement had been building at the prospect of seeing the collection of her photographs, too. After observing what she'd gravitated to at the Met, she'd tried to imagine what they might be like. Catherine's taste couldn't be quantified because she'd stopped in front of and admired so many different images.

In fact, Catherine herself couldn't be quantified. Many things Erin had guessed at or assumed about her had all gone out the window one by one as she got to know her. It proved that old adage about thinking you could know a book by its cover. Or maybe this time, Erin had taken that step back and let things unfold without meddling. The sign at the crosswalk turned to the solid little white "safe to cross" person, but she didn't move.

The parting shot Adele had hit her with still played in her head. "You're selfish," she'd said. "You always want people to be some artistic version of themselves, never just who they are."

Had she been right? Was the evidence looking her in the face again? Was she slotting Catherine in where she wanted her instead of seeing the whole woman for who she was? The thought that she might possibly repeat her history with Adele shook her. The little crosswalk man turned red as the light turned green. *No. I won't be selfish again. I can't do that to Catherine. Or to me.* When the light changed again, she continued walking up the avenue, putting that moment away and focusing on the movie Catherine had chosen, *The Handmaiden*. She'd looked up all the reviews online, especially since she knew from reading the book that there was a bit of hot Victorian-era sex. The director had changed the time and place. But he hadn't changed the sex scene. The online conjecture ran the gamut from "perfunctory" to "steamy."

What the reviews couldn't tell her was how Catherine would react. Or how *she'd* handle it, or deal with Catherine's reaction. It had been less than twenty-four hours since their phone sex, and Erin was still trying to wade through how she felt. Unable to sleep after they'd hung up, it had occurred to her as she watched the sun rise that she hadn't cared about such things for years because she hadn't been invested in how she felt when it came to women she'd slept with since Adele. Catherine had begun to change all that.

When Erin turned onto Catherine's block, her eye was immediately drawn by the visual plane of brownstones as she looked up the street. These were the stately old six-story Gothic

Revival buildings of the mid-to-late-nineteenth century that, but for their facades of oriel windows and differently decorative porticos, looked like regal cookie-cutter cut-outs attached to each other. They had all been that universal deep mauve color once, but over time, some had been painted white or light brown, and many had faded to a lighter shade of lilac or thistle.

The trees on the street were abundant, each in their little fenced-in square of earth, and every building had a little garden contained by a short brownstone-and-granite wall topped with an equally short but ornate wrought iron fence. As she walked up the street, she saw all manner of summer flowers in them from Johnny-jump-ups to impatiens, petunias, zinnias, even roses beginning to work their way around the wrought iron spikes. It was charming. And spoke of money.

Erin found herself standing in front of the one building on the block that was painted a dark royal blue. This was Catherine's place. She climbed the wide steps and rang the lobby buzzer to 5RL. She had no idea what to expect of this evening, but she hoped for two things: that she liked Catherine's collection of photographs, and that the cinnamon popcorn turned out to be really good. She also fervently hoped that Adele had been wrong.

The buzzer sounded, unlocking the door, and Erin made her way up the stairs. She was always curious about interiors, from an artist's point of view, and when she got to the second landing, she was met with a visual treat: there was a stunning tiled floor of large alternating black-and-white squares. On either side of the hallway, a black and a white table sat on opposing-colored squares, each holding large vases of bright red carnations. The effect was startling. Anticipating different but equally bright flowers on the next floor, she found an unexpectedly different décor: the hall was carpeted in a dusty French blue, with photographs on the cream walls.

Peeking over the railing at the next landing, she saw a natural plank floor polished to a high gloss, small pieces of Americana art on each door. It occurred to her as she ascended that her interest in interiors hadn't always extended to people. Maybe, she thought, it was because interiors were as you saw them, and if you didn't like a room, you could repaint, redecorate. People, not so much. People were complicated. And Erin wasn't sure she trusted herself with complications or feelings. Funny, then, that as an artist, she was supposed to trade in feelings, in paint. Funnier that she'd spent the last couple of years sketching people, trying to capture those very emotions she considered messy and maybe a little unwanted.

She reached the fifth-floor landing and stopped in her tracks. Catherine's floor had been painted by a trompe l'oeil artist who had crafted windows between the doors. Erin moved slowly from one painting to the other studying the workmanship. The window between the first two doors looked out on Paris rooftops, the Eiffel Tower in the near distance. Around the actual window at the end of the hall that looked out onto the real New York City, he'd painted beautiful floor-to-ceiling library shelves, a bench beneath the window that she was sure she could sit on to read one of the real-looking books. She was tempted to look at all the titles, sure the painter had hidden surprises on every shelf. But it was the window by Catherine's door that mesmerized her.

Pink beach roses caught in the bright sunlight draped themselves over the windowsill, and just beyond, tall wisps of light green dune grass sprouted out of sandy hillocks, the sea shimmering a deep blue in the near distance. She wanted to step right through the window. Instead, she touched one of the roses, half-expecting to feel the waxy smoothness of its petals. The door opened and Catherine stood there in a pair of small black mesh shorts and a white tank top, pulling Erin's attention from her reverie.

"I thought you'd gotten lost on the way up."

"Sort of," Erin said. "I've never seen a building like this. And then I got waylaid here." She stepped back to take in the painting. "This is breathtaking. Every floor is beautiful." She glanced around at the other walls.

"Our neighbor Damian is a painter."

"Oh, no, not even close. Your neighbor Damian is an artist." Erin experienced what she thought might be a pang of jealousy. "Do you know how hard this is to do?"

"I think I have an idea. Each one took him ages to execute."

"So you start and end each of your days with extraordinary artwork right here in your hallway."

"I do, yes. And it's very soothing. Just one of the reasons I love this building." Catherine hooked her fingers into the front of Erin's polo shirt and tugged her in for a slow kiss, brushing her lips with hers as softly and lightly as a feather. "Come on in." She said nothing about last night.

Trying to figure out exactly what it was about Catherine's kisses that made her feel like a wobbly toddler even as she shakily propelled herself forward, Erin followed her in. The cool of the air-conditioned room enveloped her, and she started to take in her surroundings, or tried to, but Catherine had other ideas.

"I was in the kitchen when you buzzed." She disappeared around the corner.

Erin put her bag down on a chair by the front door, glanced around at all the bookcases, took out the pot and trailed after her, but was caught by the photo of an ancient, rusted ring driven into the side of some old crumbling steps on a beach, a chunk of old broken rope tied on the ring.

Catherine reappeared a moment later. "The beach at Plymouth Rock."

"Really?" Erin was a little in awe. She'd never seen the historic rock. Not even in history books. Nor had she ever wondered about the beach where the Mayflower had landed.

Catherine chuckled. "No one really has any idea. That's a beach not far from the supposed site of the landing. Obviously, there were no stairs there then, so I don't believe that's the original rope from the deck of the Mayflower, either, if that's where you were going with this."

Erin snorted.

"Well, it seemed like that's what you were thinking." Catherine kissed her again. "*So* transparent." She went back into the kitchen.

Erin looked around at the other photos, wanting desperately to spend time with them, and to read the titles of the books in her collection, and then joined her. Hopefully, she'd find time to do both later.

The counter was set up with all the ingredients for the popcorn. Erin surveyed the room, impressed. The kitchen was bigger than almost any she'd ever seen, and with its white and navy blue tile pattern, it gleamed like a showroom model in the overhead light. The stainless steel KitchenAid mixer on the counter told her Catherine was into cooking, or maybe it was baking. Erin set her pot on the stove.

"So that's the magic copper-bottomed pot."

Erin nodded. "Yes."

Catherine peered into it and made a face.

"Don't do that! It's been making perfect popcorn for fifteen years. I will admit that I have occasionally burned some, and it's hard to scour that out of the bottom of that kind of pot. Consider it seasoning," Erin said, making air quotes.

Catherine looked unconvinced. "I understand seasoning, but I'm not really sure that's it." She opened a drawer and pulled a piece of tape from a dispenser. "I printed off a recipe from a gourmet popcorn site. Who knew they even existed? Shall we?" She taped the recipe to the tile wall, and they read it, heads close together.

A subtle perfume of cherry and vanilla was completely distracting. Erin stole glances at her breasts, unfettered by a bra. When she put the gas burner on under the pot, dropped in a large dollop of oil and put three kernels into it, she had to will herself to concentrate. "You should put the oven on now," Erin said, placing the lid on the pot.

"Three kernels?"

"When they pop, the oil is ready. It only takes a few minutes after that."

Five minutes later, the furiously clattering kernels slowed down, and as Erin moved the pot around above the flame, she glanced at Catherine, wondering how much she'd thought about last night since they'd hung up. She shook the pot and, hearing no kernels clinking on the bottom, Erin poured it all into the bowl, and plopped a generous chunk of butter into the pot. Catherine added the sugar they'd measured. She gently whisked the hot, sweet bubbling mixture as Catherine stood right next to her watching, leaning on the counter. Erin stole a quick look at her, and Catherine glanced away, but Erin knew from her flushed face that she was feeling more than the heat coming off the stove, too. Erin drizzled the butter mixture onto the popcorn and carefully moved a slim wooden spoon through it as Catherine sprinkled the salt and then the cinnamon onto it, like a scientist in her lab willing the experiment toward its "Eureka!" moment.

Their shoulders touched as they worked, and the sensation flowed through Erin in ways it couldn't last night. She saw Catherine flush again. Was the same thing happening to her? Erin spread the popcorn out on the baking sheet, slid it into the hot oven and set the timer on her cell phone. Then she popped the tab on one of the cold cans of seltzer Catherine had set out on the counter and took a long guzzle. She was parched. "Cinnamon?"

"Isn't it an aphrodisiac?" Catherine smiled wryly and Erin laughed.

"Seriously? That's why you chose it?"

"I wanted the curry, but I wasn't sure I could be that adventurous just yet. Let's go set up the movie."

The navy blue sectional sofa that was the centerpiece of Catherine's living room had caught Erin's attention when she first walked in, and she'd immediately imagined her stretched out on the long open chaise part of it. Naked. Erin put the thought from her mind as Catherine perched on the edge of the couch and opened her laptop.

She walked over to a grouping of photos on the wall by the door. They were all color shots of well-known, long-established storefronts in the Village, some of them gone now. There was Vesuvio Bakery with its signature Kelly green front. And the black-and-white storefront of Three Lives & Company bookstore. And a sepia-toned shot of McNulty's Tea and Coffee Company. They were charming, a throwback to post-war New York, and there was something forlorn about them, about the way they'd been captured by the photographers. What this meant as a clue, Erin wasn't sure. She turned and watched Catherine fiddle with the laptop, idly picking up the *New Yorker* magazine from her coffee table and hoping they weren't going to be watching this movie on that screen. The irony was that she wanted intimacy with Catherine, but not the kind that meant eye-strain.

"I love the cartoons in this magazine," Erin said.

"Of course you would," Catherine said, continuing to tap keys.

"I read the articles, too, when I'm in the library."

"I figured you did." Catherine picked up her remote, turned on the large flat screen TV, and the movie was there.

"Your TV is wired to your laptop?"

"Seemed like a good idea. That way I can choose whatever I want to watch, wherever I am, and have it ready when I am."

The scent of cinnamon had been pervading the living room and Erin sniffed. "It's beginning to smell good in here." Her cell phone's timer went off in her pocket and she jumped.

"Seems like *you're* wired to the oven," Catherine said.

"Very funny. That tickled!"

"I bet it did. Let's go see what we got ourselves into."

Erin gently scooped the hot soft popcorn off the baking sheet with a large flat metal spatula, so it didn't break into pieces, returning it to its bowl as Catherine put some ice in glasses. "I really couldn't think of a wine that would go well with this."

"What about that stuff that comes in a box?" Erin smirked.

"Oh please." Catherine rolled her eyes.

They settled on the couch and Catherine started the movie. "Did you read anything about this?"

Erin glanced at her, trying to gauge the question. "I did."

"So did I." She looked at the popcorn and then at Erin.

"Oh, no, it was your idea. You try it first."

As producer credits filled the screen, she put several pieces into her mouth. She smiled and picked up several more, holding them up for Erin. It hit her tongue like a sweet warm cinnamon roll, only crunchy.

"We should've put crushed toasted candied pecans in with this," Catherine said.

"Oh, my God, we should have, but that would've been totally decadent."

"There's nothing wrong with a little decadence." Catherine put several more pieces of popcorn into Erin's mouth and sat back.

Erin closed her eyes, savoring the salty sweetness and the wonderful intimacy of the moment.

She wasn't sure which was better, the movie or the popcorn. Neither one of them touched what was still left in the bowl during the infamous sex scene, but the moment it was over, they both reached for the bowl, their fingers touching, and Erin pulled away like she'd been burned.

"No, go ahead," Catherine whispered, tilting the bowl for her. She paused the movie.

This time, Erin put several pieces into Catherine's mouth one by one, and gently kissed her, wanting to take more but not daring to unleash herself, and Catherine started the movie again. When it was over, they stared at the blank screen, Erin wondering if Catherine had gotten as hot and bothered as she had when the two women made love. She'd stolen a brief sidelong glance at her then, but Catherine had sat as still as a statue.

"That was good," Catherine finally said.

"Completely different from the book, but similar enough." Erin didn't move. She didn't want to.

"That's it? No diatribe? Or deconstruction?"

Erin sighed. "I have to think about it for a few days before I can critique."

"Well, then maybe that can be our conversation on the way to the Cape next Wednesday. Should we talk about the wedding now, though?"

Erin breathed a muted sigh of relief. Any excuse to stay.

Catherine told her all about her friend Daniel, who was an editor at a major publishing house. When she went on to talk about his fiancée, Nikki St. Cyr, Erin recognized her name. She was a well-known entrepreneur with her fingers in various creative businesses, including the art world. Catherine also filled her in on some of their friends, many of whom were A-listers who frequently made the news. They hadn't even left New York City and Erin already felt out of her depth. Then Catherine Googled the Wequasset Resort on

Cape Cod and they sat close together on the couch to look at the website, taking all the virtual tours.

"So…friends with the groom?" Erin asked as they paged through the photos of the grounds, beautiful gardens everywhere. Was there a failed romance somewhere in the genesis of their friendship?

"He wanted to date me after I sold him the first apartment. When I told him I was gay, he didn't go running in the opposite direction. In fact, he wanted to meet Susan. We just hit it off." Catherine pointed at the screen. "Oh, look, this is where the wedding will be taking place, right on the water."

"Wow. Fairy-tale setting."

"It is." Catherine sighed. "Daniel became a very good friend over the years. I think he found it was easier to confide things in me than in his male friends. And he could certainly ask me questions he couldn't ask them."

"Like?"

"Like how best to go down on a woman. Here are the rooms. Let's look at the one I got." Catherine clicked on a suite as Erin stared at her incredulously.

"He did not."

"Why not? He came to the source," she replied matter-of-factly. "And I think I made his first wife a very happy woman as a result. But clearly not for long."

"Now how am I gonna look this guy in the eye? Ohhh…that's the room?" Erin feigned the need for a closer look and leaned over, her arm on Catherine's thigh, pulled in by the smell of cherries and the desire to touch her, and Catherine absently caressed her back, sending sensations spilling through her. "Tell me about the dinners and parties," Erin said, needing to concentrate on what was in front of her and not lose herself to Catherine's touch.

What she really needed to figure out was the clothing factor, because now, seeing the hotel, she knew the wedding was a high-end affair. She was going to have to comb through her closet to see what pieces she might be able to pull together that would make her look at least seaside fashionable. She'd also have to consult Nat and Kendra. Kendra was a clothes horse and a magician who could make a scarecrow look like a runway model with five pieces of clothing. As Catherine laid out the events from the Thursday night clambake to the Sunday brunch, Erin made a list in her head of what she owned that would work, and of course, what she didn't have. "And what are you wearing?"

"To which one?"

"To all of them," Erin said.

Catherine laughed. "Well, I'm not a hundred percent sure yet."

That didn't help. "What about to the wedding? What are you wearing to that?" Erin was sure she'd have had a dress picked out months ago for that.

"It's a below-the-knee strapless fuchsia dress with a belted waist. I wanted something conservative because it's an evening wedding."

Erin giggled. "Fuchsia is conservative?"

"Oh, cut it out, I'm single, not dead. I thought I might meet someone." She stopped short. "Well, I already met someone, so I suppose I could change the dress." She ran her fingers through Erin's hair and Erin wanted to purr.

"You never know what'll happen at a wedding, but don't change it on my account. Can I see the dress?" She usually couldn't have cared less what anyone wore to any event, but now she needed to know what she was trying to match.

Catherine disappeared down the hall, returning a moment later with a fitted dress in a classic cut that was going to hug her every curve, with a solid wide belt of the same material cinched at the waist. Erin's first thought was tuxedo, followed by the immediate knowledge she'd want to take that dress off her the first moment she was in it.

"Had you thought about what to wear?" Catherine asked.

Normally, Erin hated conversations about clothes. If she could spend her life in her old polo shirts and cutoffs, she would. But here was the perfect chance to get some ideas from a woman who knew a thing or two about fashion, and who had a vested interest in Erin's appearance over the wedding weekend, especially since

Erin had promised her that she'd look like a million bucks and raise Catherine's cachet. This conversation could, on the other hand, leave her looking incredibly uninformed, a potential pitfall this early in the relationship. Another reason she needed Kendra. She needed not only advice, but maybe Kendra's closet, since they were pretty close in size and Erin's coffers were empty at the moment.

Catherine must've sensed her dilemma. "I see maybe the tables are turned here, so let me just say, nothing wrong or right since you're at a complete disadvantage not knowing the lay of the land or anyone in it."

"Except you. And you just showed me the land, so to speak." Erin looked down at her hands. Catherine had stepped up to her challenge meeting her at the Met. Now she had to do the same and come clean about *her* shortcoming. "Blank. I've got nothing. I thought knowing what you'd be wearing would help, but…it hasn't." She sighed, a little defeated. "I hate dresses. I can't wear 'em. Honestly, my first thought is to wear a tuxedo. But I wasn't sure how you'd—what?"

Catherine's smile had grown slowly. "I was going to ask you how you might feel about wearing one."

"Oh."

"I think you'd look really handsome in it."

"Ohhh, you *like* the soft butch look." Erin had never seen Catherine blush. Seeing it now made her fall a little harder.

"Look, I'll even rent it for you. It's an expense I'm sure you didn't anticipate."

"Well, hold on, I might have one."

Catherine looked at her quizzically. "It's not one of those things that 'might' be in your closet. You either have it or you don't."

"I have a friend who owns one. We're about the same size."

"It's the classic black?"

"I think so. Why don't I talk to her before we rent one?"

"Let me know as soon as you can. We've got about a week to find one if hers doesn't work."

Erin nodded and they looked at each other, neither of them moving. "You're really pretty when you blush." The minute it was out of her mouth, she felt like a clumsy fourteen-year-old boy trying to talk to the pretty girl in the class, his cracking voice undermining him.

"That won't gain you instant access to any other room in this apartment tonight." Catherine looked at her with a mischievous smile on her lips. "Although I thought long and hard about this decision after last night." She sighed. "So I'm throwing you out now. I have a showing at seven thirty in the morning." Catherine checked her watch, put their glasses into the empty popcorn bowl, and rose.

"I wasn't looking for anything else tonight," Erin said. "We're not rushing, remember?" Wondering if Catherine had scheduled something so early as insurance against being tempted to let Erin stay, she dropped the thought just as quickly. She followed Catherine to the kitchen with their cinnamon-stained napkins, wishing they *were* rushing, and grabbed a dishtowel to dry her pot that Catherine had soaked in the sink.

At the door a few minutes later, she dropped the pot into her canvas bag. "I lied," she said, turning to Catherine. "I was looking for one other thing tonight." She took Catherine into her arms and kissed her, a kiss full of desire, passion, and meaning, and felt her lean into her. She tightened her embrace, her hand moving down to those little black shorts. When she was about to run out of air, she pulled back and looked at her, but didn't let her go. "Okay, leaving now."

"No you're not. Your hand is still firmly attached to my butt."

Erin peeked around her. "Oh. I believe you're right." She made a popping sound as she disengaged her hand and Catherine laughed, shaking her head as she flipped the locks on the door, opened it and gently pushed Erin out. "Go, before I do something bad."

Erin blew her a kiss and headed for the stairs.

"And call me tomorrow about the tuxedo!"

She would, and then she'd figure out ways to keep her on the phone as long as possible so she could bask in the sound of her voice.

Chapter Sixteen

Marquita put three sets of paper applications in front of Nat. "You were right. Some are actively defying the boss."

The waiter came to the table with the check and Nat took it. "Thanks for printing these out for me. I make fewer mistakes when I work with paper. Anyone catch you?"

Marquita shook her head.

Nat paged through them quickly. "Huh."

"What?" Erin asked.

"These are from the three agents who gave Nat black dots the first time they saw her," Marquita said, "but not any of the other times after that. Looks like they did it with other potential clients, too."

Nat said, "Here's an Asian couple who got dinged once and then the agent didn't note it again. And same with this guy. Green dot here with this other agent, but when this guy looked at two other places with the same agent, nothing."

"And I took the liberty of asking this one if he'd missed something on these applications," she said, pointing to the one with the green dot, "and he said not to worry."

"Did you ask him why not, push him a little?"

Marquita shook her head. "I didn't want to seem nosy or suspicious."

"What do we do?" Erin wasn't sure how this would become part of Nat's narrative.

"I want to talk to them right before we go to press to hear from them what's going on and why they didn't go along with it, or take a stand, if that's what's going on. I want these applications in my hand when I do."

"I can tell you why," Marquita said. "They didn't want to lose their jobs. And talking to them could be risky."

Nat took out her wallet, put cash on the bill, and slid it to the edge of the table for the waiter. "My risk. And I won't involve you. I already told you I'd keep your name out of it."

The relief on Marquita's face was evident.

"I'll just need you to tell me if they're going away for Labor Day so I can catch them. I think Red's decided to hold off posting until the week after, so people are settled, kids are back in school, and it doesn't get lost in any of that 'back to life' mayhem. He wants it front and center. How are your licensing classes going? You getting close enough to any of these guys to talk to them?"

"It's hard, but a couple of our agents are helping me with a lot of things. And yes, this guy," Marquita pointed to one of the applications, "is going to let me shadow him when I'm not officially at my desk when he shows his next couple of apartments, so I'll see if I can somehow get him to give up any information."

"You be careful," Nat said.

"Don't worry about me, mija. I'm good at playing dumb."

Nat stowed the folder of applications in her bag. Marquita gave Erin an appraising look before turning away and making plans with Nat for the next meeting.

Out on the street, they watched Marquita walk away.

"So. Nothing." Nat popped a piece of gum into her mouth and offered a stick to Erin.

Erin shook her head. "No."

"Neither one of you called the other. And she has no idea you're seeing Catherine. Wow. This is turning into a real soap opera."

Erin didn't say anything. Marquita had been cool and professional, like nothing had ever happened between them. So she played her part, but inside, it irked a little. They walked to the light.

"Are you ready for this wedding?"

"No. And I need your help, or Kendra's."

"Daddy always said get bath towels. Everyone needs them, and no one remembers to get them."

"That's not it. Besides, I don't know their bathroom color scheme."

"White. Free agent in any bathroom."

Erin nodded. "Of course. How could I not know that? No, clothes. I need Kendra's tuxedo."

"Ah! Shopping at my house. Smart move, very frugal. What are you making for dinner tonight? Let's talk to Kendra while you work."

Erin stood on a chair, Kendra on her knees in front of her, half a dozen straight pins sticking out from between her lips. She folded a side of the tuxedo pant leg up, removed a pin, deftly worked it through the material, and reached for another.

"Are you sure?" Erin asked. "I don't want to ruin your tux."

"I'm only whip-stitching them," Kendra said around the pins. "It'll come out easily and then I can get the hem marks out with my steam iron. Not to worry. Besides, this is my old tuxedo. I upgraded last year before the Bessie Awards."

"They missed the boat not giving you Best Choreography," Erin said. "Your show was outstanding."

Kendra shrugged and placed one more pin in the hem, then put the rest of the pins into the little peach-shaped pin cushion on her wrist. "My time will come. Or not. Listen, I have three different styles of shirts, but I think you should wear the classic placket front." She disappeared down the hall.

"Good thing I got a stylin' wife," Nat said, grinning.

Kendra returned with the shirt. "Put this on, let's see how it fits." Kendra brushed the shoulders and pulled down on the cuffs after Erin had it buttoned. "Nice. Perfect. And you need to get a haircut, okay? Look smart for her. I'm going to send you to my hairdresser." Kendra scribbled a note on a piece of paper she pulled from the scrap pile she kept next to the pencil jar that acted as a bookend to the cookbooks on the countertop.

Erin nodded, looking at the Harlem address. This would cost her. She thought again about asking Nat for an advance on her pay.

Nat knew her straits were still pretty dire, but that didn't mean it wouldn't be hard asking for the money. She'd toyed last night with knocking on her upstairs neighbor's door with the canvas he'd seen her painting in the garden several months ago. She'd captured the back of the building, trees in full bud in early May with flowers just appearing in their branches. Daffodils and tulips bloomed at full strength in the garden. The sun, the symmetry of it all and the pastels of the flowers had pulled at her the morning she'd been working with Anika showing her how to draw the elaborate daffodil. So she'd grabbed her last blank canvas and painted without thinking. Considering it as worthless as the others sitting on her living room floor, she was going to cover it in primer later.

But her neighbor had watched her as he pretended to read, and then offered her a ridiculous amount of money for it because he'd lived in the building for thirty years and it spoke to him. Maybe it wouldn't kill her to part with it. Especially if what he'd offered could cover all the expenses she'd need for this wedding weekend.

"Now, tomorrow is matinee day which means I can't go downtown and do this for you," Kendra said, "so you'll have to hit the fabric stores and find two yards of silk that's a conservative black and fuchsia or white and fuchsia print of some kind for the bow tie and the cummerbund. I'll make those on the weekend. And I'm going to suggest you don't wear the jacket at all. You'll look much sexier that way."

"Silk?"

"Take Nat with you. She can pay, you can pay her back."

"Oh, I don't know, she can find her way—" Nat said.

"I realize it's like sending two of the three stooges on an errand, but it'll have to do."

Erin and Nat looked at each other, non-plussed.

"She did not just say that," Nat said.

"Illegitimate daughter of Bumblebee, I think we're pickin' up the gauntlet."

Kendra laughed. "What, and you're Wonder Woman? Well, it's sure gonna take superpowers for you two to accomplish this. Now, what is for dessert? I need a little sugar high."

❖

After several phone calls the next morning, they were on their way to the Brooklyn General Store, which Erin had scoped out online when Googling "yard goods" and found out they had an enormous selection. The proprietor had been kind enough to text them several close-up photos of what she thought they were looking for, and an hour after walking in the door, and much grumbling from Nat about why the color fuchsia even existed, they were on their way home with their bounty, including a spool of thread the store owner insisted they needed. Nat tried to tell her Kendra had every color under the sun, but finally Erin whispered, "It's five bucks, can we just take it and get out of here?"

"It was the principle of the thing," Nat said as the subway train made its way over the Manhattan Bridge.

"I know, but she wasn't letting go. It's five bucks. I'll pay you back."

"Fine." Nat called Kendra to tell her about the thread debacle and hung up chagrined. "It's spun silk. Why didn't the proprietor just tell us that? Kendra does need it. She forgot she didn't have any." She made a face, put her phone back in her pocket and reached into the bag for a corner of the silk. "You are gonna look snatched when Kendra gets done with you."

"I hope so. I need to look like I belong at this wedding, and on Catherine's arm."

"Shoes! We forgot about shoes!"

"I have those tasseled velvet loafers, remember?"

"The ones you bought for the Biennial?"

"What's wrong with them? I like the way the tassels move when I walk."

"That's a bad idea on so many levels," Nat said. "But mostly because it's August. No velvet in summer, that's a glamour don't. You need patent leather. I think Kendra has those in her closet and you're close enough in size to make it work. What about your hotel room? Did she get two or are you gonna be in her bed?"

"Pardon me?"

"You would've told me if you'd slept with her yet, so this could be a mine field, right? I mean, weddings are bacchanals. Just want to make sure you'll be on your game is all. Because you're playing with fire. We still don't know where she stands. You need to use this weekend to find that out."

Erin was certain she wouldn't have told Nat if she'd slept with Catherine. "What do you think would happen to us if she found out I'm working on an investigative story possibly involving her?"

"Maybe definitely involving her by virtue of the fact she works there, if nothing else. And us, as in you and me, or us, as in you and her?"

"Catherine and me. It would be over between us before it began. And since we know where *I* stand, maybe you could give me a break here?" Erin didn't often get upset at Nat, but with this line of questioning, she was beginning to understand just how vested in Catherine she'd become.

"I'm sorry." Nat put her hand on her arm. "This is killing you, isn't it? But we both know if she stands on the wrong side of this, it could be bad."

Nat was good at tough love. It usually brought Erin a modicum of peace because it was so black-and-white. But now, it drove her crazy for that very reason. "It's two queen beds in one room." Erin glanced at Nat. "But you know she got that room well before I walked into her life."

Nat nodded.

"And we talked a couple of weeks ago. She wants to take it slow. Neither one of us wants to screw this up."

Nat nodded again.

"That buys me time. And it's a good sign, right?"

The train pulled into their stop. "Drunken bacchanal," Nat said gently. "Just sayin'." She rose and held the door for Erin. "Other thing I'm sayin'. And I mean it. Use this weekend to find out. When you come back, I want that answer."

The subway door bing-bonged a second time as the door tried to close, and the conductor's warning came over the loudspeaker. But it wasn't as loud as the warning in Nat's eyes.

After making a Taiwanese vegetable dish for dinner that night that really pleased Kendra, Erin made her way home with one thing on her mind. In her living room, she picked up the painting her neighbor had said he'd buy from her and set it on the kitchen counter. She knew she should've gone right back out the door and up the stairs, she knew she shouldn't have stopped here at the counter, shouldn't have hesitated. But her hands were sweating. And her stomach was roiling a little. And there was a buzzing in her ears. She walked around the kitchen, then the living room. She even walked out into the garden hoping to get rid of this feeling.

It was a beautiful night, the half-moon crescent hanging in the sky looking like a coaster someone had put a drink on, blotting part of it from view. Several green lacewings flittered around her for a moment and then were gone. She took a deep breath. What is wrong with you, she thought. It's just a painting. She put her hands on her knees. In truth, none of them were "just" paintings. But Erin had intuited that her neighbor's immediate kinship to this scene he'd inhabited most of his life meant he would value and protect it.

She went back inside, picked up the painting, took the steps two at a time to his apartment and rang the bell. When she heard the peephole open, she held the painting up close to it like Anika did with her quarters each week. The locks snapped out of their deadbolts and he opened the door, a grin on his face.

"Yeah? I can have it?"

"All yours." Erin handed it toward him and then drew it back. "You'll take good care of it, right?"

"I love this painting. Of course I will. Come on in, let me get my money and maybe you can help me figure out where to hang it."

As she followed him in, that rush she'd gotten the first time she'd sold a painting hit her. It was incomprehensible, a lightness of being. Then that sense of security settled on her, the knowing that she'd have more than enough cash in her pocket for the weekend with Catherine. It dawned on her that, depending on how things went next weekend, there might be other such sacrifices she'd make for Catherine. And that came with a different sense of security.

Chapter Seventeen

August days like this were rare. Sunny, breezy, eighty-one degrees, no humidity. And then there was that 9/11 sky, as Erin still called them, cerulean blue with not a cloud in sight. She stood on the lip of the Avis garage looking out at it. Such a sky could still shake her. That ill-fated morning, she'd skipped school because one of her friends was a newly minted driver and wanted to take them to Long Beach on Long Island. When the news swept down the beach, panic ensued, everyone racing to pack up their things. Her hands had shaken as she called her mother to tell her what she'd done because they didn't know what the drive home would be like, because no one knew what was really happening, or how much the world had changed. She stepped into the sun and let the strength of it burn off the chill that had seeped into her bones.

"Top down," Catherine said to the Avis car jockey, and he sat in the front seat to show her how to open and close the convertible's top. She asked him a few more questions which Erin should have been paying attention to, but she was suddenly too happy to want to be so responsible and competent in this moment. Then the shadow of what she had to do this weekend for Nat's article stole over her, marring that happiness. She quickly pushed it aside and gazed at Catherine. Her hair was in a ponytail, curled in the blond question mark that Erin always wanted to reach out and touch. She wore navy shorts and sneakers with a red tank top. Erin pulled the sunscreen out of the bag she'd slung into the back seat. She had a base for the tan that had become darker over the weeks because she was outside a lot, but Catherine had none. She'd get burned if they drove all the way to the Cape with the top down.

Before they headed out, Catherine ruffled Erin's short hair one more time. "I love this haircut. You look so sexy." Catherine planted a quick kiss on her lips and then looked at her as if she was someone she'd just met. In the car, Catherine turned off her phone, put it in her pocket.

"I know the way by heart," she said, "You can download Waze if you want to see the route. I don't use my cell phone at all when I'm driving. Too distracting." She turned on the radio, found the city's twenty-four-hour news and traffic station and joined the stream of cars and trucks making their way along 86th Street toward Central Park. When they crossed the Yonkers city limits nearly an hour later, Catherine turned to a classical music station instead. Erin sat back, her face to the sun and the wind. Maybe she wouldn't have to think about her duplicitousness for a while.

"Do you like classical?" Catherine had been concentrating on the road, so there had been little conversation as the radio kept them abreast of traffic problems and news. Now, heading onto the Hutchinson River Parkway, conversation became possible again.

"I used to listen to it sometimes when I painted. It depended on what I was working on."

"Used to?" Catherine glanced at her. "What do you paint to now? We can listen to whatever you like."

"I don't. Listen, that is." Erin looked at her. "I don't paint anymore, either." She surprised herself with the admission. "I haven't in a long time." She couldn't walk it back now. Nor did she want to, since something in her was weighing being honest about everything, maybe even coming clean with Catherine so she didn't have to carry this awful burden around. Nat would kill her if she did that.

"But the article said—"

"I have a very good PR person. I haven't really painted since the Biennial. I've tried, but…" Erin stared at the road ahead and screwed up her courage. "I only seem to be capable of sketching, and even those aren't great. There's nothing left, no confidence."

She watched the mile markers fly past. "I walked out on my life. I gave up because someone on a really public stage questioned everything I was." Mile marker twenty-two, mile marker twenty-three. Was Catherine going to say anything? Three more miles of markers went by; Erin wondered if she'd made a mistake.

"I had an affair. That's why Susan left."

Erin looked at her, shocked, and then the nervous reaction of laughter hit her, but Catherine's face was a mask of pain and contrition. "I'm sorry. It just surprised me. Sharing is so much fun, isn't it?" She smiled in apology.

"Well, we've certainly got a long road ahead of us to do that, don't we?" Catherine said, pointing her finger at it from the steering wheel. "But I need some coffee first." She put the blinker on for the next exit and soon they were parked in front of a diner. "Come on, let's stretch our legs." Catherine reached for the button to move the convertible top into place.

"I'll buy something I shouldn't,' Erin said.

"I think we're both going to do things we shouldn't this weekend," Catherine replied. "It's called life."

In the diner, Erin spotted the most beautiful doughnut she'd ever seen, a large round sour cream with a coffee cake crumble on top, and tapped Catherine on the shoulder, pointing at it wordlessly.

"Oh, we absolutely have to," Catherine said.

Back in the car, Erin split the donut between them, and Catherine put on the air conditioning. She lifted the lid of her cup and blew on the hot coffee. Then, she looked at Erin. "Who goes first?"

Erin shrugged. "I'll go. I'm working on the confidence thing. As for what's out there on the internet, a friend of mine felt I should look as though I was still relevant."

"So, the shows?"

"A long time ago." True honesty was going to be hard no matter what she was talking about.

"And the discerning collectors?" Catherine started the car but didn't put it in reverse.

"I had some real success right out of grad school. It's why I was invited to the Biennial. And I did sell some works there. How 'discerning' those collectors feel now, though, is anyone's guess." The car suddenly felt cold so Erin adjusted the air conditioning. "It was a body blow, that review. I went from rising young star to yesterday's news in the space of twenty-four hours. I didn't know how to survive that. So I didn't." Feeling the forlornness again, she looked out the window. "Do you know what it's like when your world goes from living color to black?"

Catherine put her doughnut down.

"It's not fun," Erin admitted. "When nothing works, and you lose your true north…" She couldn't finish the sentence.

Catherine rubbed Erin's arm.

Erin sighed. "I'm sorry. 'O'Connor, pity party of one, right this way to your table for one next to the kitchen door, your server is Typhoid Mary.'"

"You're allowed."

"Not really. Not anymore. For the last five years, I've been piecing together a living. I do some window dressing, I give art lessons. And I help Nat whenever she needs me. But I really don't paint."

"She pays you when you do the research and editing?"

"Yes, of course."

"Art lessons, huh?"

"I'm working with a neighbor kid who saw me drawing in our garden one day. I like it. It's made me wonder if I should advertise and expand."

"I would never have suspected." Catherine smiled at her.

"Yeah, it's not the warm and fuzzy you think it is. This kid happens to be way cooler than anyone I know. Nat said if you've got a gift, you need to share it. So I do."

"I think I need to get to know Nat," Catherine said.

Erin wasn't sure that "getting to know you" phase would happen the way either of them thought it would. "Now. You stepped out on your wife."

Catherine finally headed out of the parking lot, her hands gripping the wheel.

"Or we could save this for later," Erin said.

"No, we might as well do this now. This next leg is an easy drive." She began telling Erin about her relationship with Susan, the affair, and the other woman. As Erin listened, questions she wasn't sure she had any right to ask kept occurring to her. How intimate did you have to be with someone you'd just begun dating before asking why they'd broken their vows? In the silence that followed, she weighed those questions against the possibility they'd undermine the foundation she felt they were building.

"Aren't you curious about why I did it?" Catherine asked.

"Do you want to tell me?"

"Only if you want to know at this point."

Erin seriously considered the question. Of course she wanted to know, didn't she? Would this be an exercise in futility once Catherine found out the real reason they'd met? Would today's vulnerability be tomorrow's regret?

"Let me put it to you this way. Would you want to become any further involved with me if you didn't know the answer? I mean, would you trust me not to do it to you?"

"Once doesn't mean you'll do it twice, any more than my flitting from woman to woman for the last five years means I can't be a Steady Eddie. And maybe we communicate better than you and Susan did." The irony of the statement wasn't lost on her.

Catherine nodded thoughtfully as she watched the road. "I have wondered about that flitting of yours."

"I got hurt, so I decided I didn't want to play in the sandbox anymore."

"Ah, so we both pulled out of the game. Maybe that makes us the perfect couple."

Erin winced. And as muted as it was, she heard the pain in Catherine's voice before she heard the hope. "Or maybe Susan simply wasn't right for you." She suddenly felt horribly guilty, turncoat guilty. But could she possibly ruin Nat's article?

Catherine scrutinized her. "After all those years together, and the investment we put into it?" The edge to her voice was knife sharp.

"Sometimes the market crashes." Erin looked out the window at the river they were crossing as the car sped over the bridge. The water looked inviting, as in she'd rather jump off the bridge than deal with any of this. "And sometimes you sell short." Erin glanced at her and thought she might've seen tears in Catherine's eyes. "It wasn't a good investment," Erin said quietly.

"I wanted more than she could give. Instead of leaving graciously I hurt her very badly and I keep wondering if I should've stayed to work things out. Maybe I should've given us the benefit of the doubt."

"You would've stayed in a relationship that wasn't working for you when you were the one who had the affair? Maybe I overestimated you. This seat belt is getting very tight." Erin unbuckled the belt, let it slam into its housing and clicked it back into place before the dashboard alarm sounded.

"Is it the seat belt?" Catherine asked, her eyes still on the road.

"I think I'm angry." Suddenly Adele, and being cheated on, were front and center in her emotional field. Catherine's cheating was an important factor she hadn't weighed enough.

"I think you are, too." Catherine spotted a picnic area and headed for the exit.

"What are you doing?"

"I need a break."

They sat on the picnic table in silence. Finally, Catherine opened the bottle of seltzer she'd taken from the little cooler in the back seat, poured some into a cup and handed it to Erin. She took a long drink from the bottle, watching Erin swirl the seltzer in the cup.

"I couldn't leave, and I couldn't stay," Catherine finally said. "And I was pretty sure counseling wasn't going to work. So I had the affair. I knew it would push her to leave me."

Erin nodded. "Okay." She was still fuming.

"Horrible?"

"Yes."

"Well, I've clearly hit a nerve with you. So, talk to me."

"I didn't know Adele was having an affair with her boss. I was too caught up in my work. She wasn't even background noise at that point because I'd been getting ready for the Biennial for months." Erin's voice shook a little as the memory overtook her. "When I realized it the first evening of the show, nothing else mattered except getting her back."

Catherine looked up at the sky and sighed. "Of course I hit a nerve. You were Susan. Wait, is that when things went south for you? *That's* when you blew that interview with the *New York Times* critic, isn't it?"

Erin saw the light dawning for Catherine. "Yes. I saw Adele standing there with her boss and I knew. It was crystal clear from their body language. And I had to get rid of the critic and do something. Only it turns out squirting acrylic paint all over your rival and your paintings isn't the 'enfant terrible' gesture it used to be."

"I did marvel that you did that. It seemed out of place, but bold."

Erin rubbed her temple. "Should we get back on the road again?" She was having second thoughts, and tension was giving her a headache.

"Not yet. Let's get this out."

Catherine made it sound like a deep splinter, and maybe it was.

Erin leaned forward, her elbows on her knees. It was easier to talk to the dirt patches beneath the table than to Catherine. "No one knew about the affair. But my behavior was just as much under the magnifying glass as my paintings, and the crash-and-burn review was on its way to social media before I could get hold of the critic to explain that the tube of paint was in my pocket to touch up a painting, not to make some silly gesture at one of the most prestigious shows in the art world." Erin wiped at something that had caught in her eyelashes. "And anyway, I couldn't have done that to Adele, plastered our marital woes all over the internet."

She slid off the table, picked up a pine cone lying in the dirt and hurled it toward a bank of trees. "So I turned my back on the show and fought to keep her. That's when the other critics moved in to savage what was left of my work. Adele was already out the door, though. She stayed long enough to bandage my wounds and tell me that in case I thought she was the only one cheating, I had a mistress, too. My art. She said she couldn't compete." Erin drank the seltzer and tossed the cup into the recycle bin nearby. "She chose that moment to tell me I was selfish. And distant. And that I essentially expect too much from people."

"And you accepted that, without questioning her about her support for you at a critical moment in your career?" Catherine shook her head. "You know that people wreck their marriages all the time. This is nothing new," she said softly.

Erin wasn't sure what she saw reflected in Catherine's eyes. "Apparently they do." There were no mile markers flying past in the silence that followed. "I was lost after she left. She was my family."

A deer had walked out of the woods, stopping to stare at them. Erin stared back, and out of the corner of her eye she saw Catherine wrap her arms around herself.

"And Nat?"

"She and Kendra are all the family I really have since my parents made it clear my 'lifestyle,'" Erin made air quotes with her fingers. "Did not align with theirs."

Catherine rested her chin on her arms, a miserable look passing over her face.

"Do you want me to drive now for a while?" Erin asked.

Catherine stood up and hugged her, whispered, "I'm sorry," and handed her the keys. "That might be a good idea for both of us." She put her arm around Erin's shoulder as they walked back to the car. "If you don't mind, I have to call the office and get a little work done. We can think about stopping for lunch in a bit, though."

They got into the car, Catherine took her phone out of her pocket and put her hand on the back of Erin's neck to caress it. "I know a really terrific dive in Tiverton with great lobster rolls, but we'll have to get off the highway. It's about an hour away, in Rhode Island. Sound good?" Erin nodded and set off. It would be a straight shot on I-95, according to the new app she'd downloaded.

Catherine pressed a button on the phone. "Hey, Marquita, how are you? Yeah, listen, can I get you to send me some of Jack Hobbs's files?

The anticipated taste of those lobster rolls turned to ash in Erin's mouth.

CHAPTER EIGHTEEN

I'll check us in. You wait here." Catherine got out of the car and walked into the big white clapboard captain's house.

After lunch, things had returned mostly to normal. They'd switched the radio station and sung along to various songs and chatted about mundane things. There was plenty under the surface, but they seemed in silent agreement to let them stay there for now. Erin sat a moment, inhaling the salt air mingled with the unmistakable scent of cedar. She looked at the charming inn, the square additions on either side of it like bookends holding it in place. Her eye was drawn up to the tall white center chimney, so New England. In the wintertime, the place must look like a Currier and Ives Christmas card, smoke pluming above it from what she imagined was a large brick fireplace.

The sun that had been playing hide-and-seek since they'd driven over the Bourne Bridge suddenly poured through a break in the puffy white clouds, and Erin felt like Dorothy stepping out of her house in Oz as the light splashed across garden after garden of stunning flowers, lifting them from muted shade into a riot of Technicolor. The artist in her knew that there was no coincidence to the palette: hydrangeas in ascending shades of purples and blues abounded against walls of lilac-hued rhododendron bushes. Dark pink begonias waved in abundance, flocked at just the right height around the hydrangeas. Beach roses in reds, pinks, and whites seemed to climb everywhere, their sweet smell floating above all the other scents emanating from the grounds. They were meant to look as though they bloomed anywhere and everywhere, these little gardens, despite being hemmed in with brick edgings draped with dusky green lamb's ears plantings that provided a beautiful ground cover. The symmetry pulled at Erin's soul, telling her they'd been carefully laid out across the lawns that gently sloped down to the water, winding their way around stately old trees on the way.

She got out of the car, almost stupefied by the beauty surrounding her, and wandered onto one of the brick paths leading toward the lawn. Wooden signs were tucked among the flora, their hand-carved white lettering bordered in gold announcing the way to the pool, golf course, tennis courts, and restaurants. *Don't need signs for the ocean. Just follow your nose.* A large brittle leaf falling from above bounced off her cheek, startling her. It landed on the ground at her feet. She looked up at the enormous tree, its branches forming a near canopy of shade with the many others standing guard all around the grounds. Bits of crisp dead leaves littered the lawns, attesting to the waning days of summer. Each breeze that wafted through the treetops brought more handfuls of crumbly ones tumbling down and Erin briefly mourned the passing season as she watched them scatter across the grass. She didn't hear Catherine until she was standing right beside her.

"Hey, you." She put her arm around Erin's waist and kissed her behind her ear. "Our room's around back, on the water. The car stays here, though, so someone's coming for our things."

"'Kay." Erin didn't move, mesmerized by the ocean glittering in the distance, the breeze moving through the leaves sounding like a gentle waterfall, and the scents of the gardens all around her.

"Penny for your thoughts," Catherine said.

"Paradise. This is Paradise." She shook off the spell and followed Catherine around back.

The suite, on the second floor of a small separate building with weathered gray shingles, had a magnificent view. Erin made her way out to the deck as Catherine tipped the young man who brought them their bags. The tide was receding, the waves slipping out farther with each ebb and flow. She watched the seagulls dive into the shallows to pull clams out of the sand, double back to drop them on the jetties to break them open, and then squabble over the morsels. A pitched battle was ensuing between two large gulls when Catherine joined her at the railing.

Erin pointed to the jetty. “Major clam kerfuffle at three o’clock.”

Catherine shaded her brow and peered at the fight. “So I see. Well, luckily we won’t have to go that route for our dinner tonight.”

“I hoped you weren’t going to make me dig for my dinner. Which restaurant do we want to try tonight?”

“Oh, we’re not staying here. I have something else in mind. But why don’t we take a walk on the beach first?” Catherine nuzzled her neck, brushing her with a few kisses. “I just need to hit the bathroom.”

Erin sat on one of the queen beds and ran her hand over the quilted spread. She looked around. The intimate living room was tucked in front of a black wrought iron fireplace, the dining nook was cozy, the small kitchen was utilitarian but welcoming, and all of it was decorated in sand, white, and ocean blue tones. It was peaceful. The soft bed looked and felt inviting with its regimented pile of big fat pillows, and for a moment, she imagined herself there tangled up with Catherine. Nat’s warning words, “drunken bacchanal,” echoed in her mind. That counsel was the basis for Erin’s decision not to drink this weekend. She didn’t want to make a fool of herself, not that she couldn’t hold her liquor. More than that, she wanted to be fully aware of anything that might unfold between them, cognizant of any sign from Catherine that the door was opening even further. Or not. She also needed to be on her game if Catherine was going to fit work in during the weekend. She had to find an opening, glean information, get some kind of evidence for Nat. *Or not. Not if I say something.* She was still hanging on to the hope that Catherine wasn’t involved. But how could their top salesperson not be?

Erin was a little baffled that Catherine didn’t want to try any of the inn’s restaurants for dinner until they were sitting at a table on the deck of the Northside Marina overlooking the serene Sesuit Harbor cove. The walk on the beach had been long and relaxing, putting them at the restaurant late enough that most families with children given to running rampant at outdoor restaurants were gone.

Boats of all sizes were still coming in to dock, and Erin felt like she was watching a piece of nautical theater. She sat close to Catherine and from time to time, touched her hand, her arm, or caressed her cheek. They had devoured a basket of fat, full-bellied fried clams, another of French fries sprinkled with ketchup, and Erin had ordered a second helping of the coleslaw, crisp, just the way she liked it, with barely a hint of dressing.

They sat back watching the sun slip below the horizon, Erin sipping a lemonade as Catherine poured a splash more wine into her glass from the bottle she'd brought with her.

"You know I'm driving us back to the inn, don't you?" Erin had watched the wine level in the bottle sink over the hour and a half they'd been there. It had never been a problem in the city where they walked everywhere when they were together, but a car ride was different.

"Yes, I do." She reached into her pocket and handed Erin the keys.

Erin was relieved that it had been that simple, and she dropped them on the table and took Catherine's hand. "I'm very happy we did this."

"We're tied to being at the inn for just about everything else this weekend. But tonight, and most of tomorrow, we can do whatever we want."

"What did you have in mind?" Erin asked playfully.

An hour later, they were standing at the sixth hole of the Harbor Lights miniature golf course, Erin laughing at Catherine's fifth attempt to tee off, the ball having rolled right back to her the four previous attempts.

"Shut. Up." Catherine frowned, and then she burst out laughing. "I am such a loser here."

"Angle your left shoulder more sharply to the right. And hit it hard enough to bank off the wall."

"I had no idea I was challenging the Michele Wie of miniature golf." The ball went cleanly around the corner this time and ricocheted into the little cup. The crowd behind them waiting to play the hole cheered.

"That is painfully embarrassing," Catherine said as she bent over to retrieve the ball. "Can we leave?"

"Absolutely not. I didn't peg you for a quitter in the face of adversity."

Catherine bit her lip and sighed. "You like to see me suffer."

"Mmm, no." Erin shook her head. "You've got a great butt. I like walking around the course behind you." Catherine's mouth fell open in mock astonishment and Erin shrugged. "It's true."

When they got back to the room, Catherine announced that she needed a shower to soothe her bruised ego. The thought of joining her under the hot water, not rushing things be damned, passed through Erin's mind, but instead she grabbed a bottle of lemonade they'd picked up at a local store and went out to the deck. Knowing she was tempting fate, she settled into the double chaise lounge. The sound of the waves washing quietly on the beach was mesmerizing; she looked up at the full moon, and felt her eyelids closing. The next thing she was aware of was Catherine running her fingers through her hair as she lay next to her on the chaise. Reluctantly, Erin opened her eyes and couldn't help but focus on Catherine's breasts, inches from her face and barely contained in a blue pin-striped robe. Her hair was still damp. She picked up a glass of red wine from the table next to her and took a sip. She must've opened one of the bottles she'd picked up at the same local store. Then, she leaned over Erin to put it on the table next to her lemonade.

Erin breathed in the scent of cherries and vanilla, felt the weight of Catherine's body on hers, her breasts pressing into her. This was such a cruel temptation. She wanted to take her into her arms but felt paralyzed. A wet tendril of hair tumbled off Catherine's shoulder and Erin gently brushed it back. "How's your ego? Feeling pliant again?"

"Don't even." Catherine kissed her, and Erin slid an arm around her waist. She looked at Erin for a moment, as if seeking permission, and then the kisses continued, languidly at first, with Erin caressing what she could reach of Catherine's back, wanting to find the belt of the robe and loosen it. Just as she did, Catherine caught her hand and stopped her, but the kisses came harder, more insistently, and when she felt the moan on her lips, she realized it was her own, that she'd grabbed a handful of Catherine's hair and opened her mouth to Catherine's assertive overture. The red wine tasted good on her tongue. She put a hand on the soft rise of her breasts, then moved it down to cup the fullness of one of them, and that's when Catherine broke the kiss.

"Whoa, tiger," she quietly chided her.

Even in the shadows from the light spilling out of the room, Erin could see the look in her eyes and knew it was a warning. This wasn't the first time Catherine had started something and then put the brakes on, and it frustrated Erin. "You're torturing me. I know we're taking things slow," she whispered. "But I want you, I want to touch you, to feel your skin on mine, and your eyes on my body."

"Oh, believe me, they are," Catherine whispered back. She pushed herself away from Erin, out of her arms, and lay back on the chaise.

Erin propped herself up on one elbow. "Then what?"

"I'm not ready for that step."

Erin shifted, puzzled. "But we've just made out." She touched Catherine's lips, and her hand fell to her stomach, where she nestled it just below one of her breasts.

"I know. And I'm very happy with just that right now." Catherine didn't move Erin's hand. "And I know you'll think I'm being, I don't know, overly cautious or silly, even." She ran her thumb over Erin's lips. "Look, this goes back to Susan. I jumped into bed with her too soon, and then—"

"*That's* a very fatalistic outlook. And it was a lifetime ago." Erin leaned over and kissed her. "I'm not Susan. And I don't think you're who you were then." She ran her fingers through Catherine's damp hair, shaking it to dry it. "If we don't mesh, will it be a crime that we had fun together?"

"Are you hearing yourself?" Catherine's frown was deep. "You said you were tired of short relationships. And I don't want to be one."

Erin fell back on the chaise and found the moon. It was now directly overhead.

"But I want you, too. Come here." She opened her arms and Erin moved into them, Catherine guiding her head to her shoulder. Erin nuzzled her neck and sighed. A moment later, she felt Catherine's hand between her shoulder blades and settled into her as the sensation washed through her. *Paradise.*

"Erin?"

"Mmm?"

"Are you at all bothered by our age difference? I'm forty-five, you know."

"I do know. You wear it well." Erin peered up at her. "I'm thirty-two, you know. Should the age difference bother me?"

"It might in a few years, when you're about to cross that line into your forties."

Erin chuckled. "A minute ago we were talking about not sleeping with each other. Now you're planning for eight years from now?"

"It's a reality check. And that fortieth birthday can be a harsh line to cross."

"So I've heard."

Catherine riffled her fingertips through Erin's hair, gently hugged her and began humming softly. She kissed her on the forehead, and the sound of the waves drifted over her as she fell asleep.

Sometime before dawn, Catherine woke her up and they made their way toward their separate beds. Erin was almost too tired to pull up her covers, climbing into the bed with her clothes on, but Catherine snugged the quilt around her, kissed her briefly, and turned off the light. Then with her back to Erin, she took off her robe and laid it across the bottom of her bed. The pre-dawn light from the east caught her like the Greek marble statues Erin was so drawn to sketching at the Met, all planes and muscles, the rise of her rounded buttocks in lit relief, her long legs disappearing into the shadows. Erin held her breath, her senses inflamed, as she watched her slip under the covers. She wanted to move, she wanted to make her way to that bed, but if Catherine wasn't ready, there was nothing to be done about her own desires. Instead, she lay there and listened to Catherine fall asleep.

CHAPTER NINETEEN

Catherine was sound asleep when Erin pulled on her bathing suit and made her way out of the room to go to the pool. She left a note on the nightstand. After her laps, she showered and, in the small women's dressing room, changed into the clothes she'd brought down with her. Following the signs in the little gardens, she found one of the restaurants open for breakfast, and put together a tray for the room from the buffet.

Catherine was sitting at the dining table, her laptop open, a list in her hand, when Erin came in.

"Oh, that's a lifesaver. I was just about to try and figure out how that coffee pot worked."

Erin put the food on the table and Catherine reached for a croissant, breaking it apart and dunking a piece in her coffee.

"No, no, there will be no working of coffee pots this weekend." Erin took some packets of sugar out of her pocket and picked up Catherine's list. What she saw made her stop; she put on her best poker face.

"No, that's work," Catherine said, taking the list back and handing her another. She reluctantly let go of what she was sure was a roster of clients and took what was clearly a to-do list from her. She went to get a knife from the kitchen, then walked behind her chair on her way back to the table and recognized a Sumter lease application on the screen. "So, really? We're running errands today?"

"No! I want to show you Provincetown, and yes, I need to stop along the way."

"Because we had no CVS drugstores in New York," she said from the kitchen, studying the list.

"I forgot a few things."

"And am I going to want to come back from the gay mecca to attend tonight's clambake?"

"No. So it'll give me an excuse to bring you back here for Women's Week in October." Catherine pulled Erin onto her lap as she passed back by with the knife.

Erin stuck the knife in the pot of jam that sat on the plate of croissants and raised an eyebrow. Would they still be together then? "I like the sound of that. Would I be luring you away?"

"Yes, you most certainly would. You're a very bad girl that way."

Erin wrapped her arms around Catherine's neck and kissed her. "That's me. Devil incarnate. So tell me," she asked, casting an eye toward the screen, "why do you really have work with you this weekend? Do I need to be worried that you're a workaholic?"

"I only became one after Susan left." Catherine rubbed her temple. "No, someone just left, and I had to take over his clients. So I'm trying to familiarize myself with his files because unfortunately, I need to reach out to some of them later today, talk to them and set up appointments for them to look at places on Monday. I promise I'll keep it unobtrusive, though. How was your swim?"

Was she changing the subject on purpose? And interesting that she referred to Jack, because Erin was certain that's who it was, as someone who 'left,' and not as someone who was fired. "It was really good. You should come tomorrow morning."

"Maybe I will. Let's look at this list and figure out how we can get everything done and be in P'town for lunch. I'll be right back."

Catherine headed for the bathroom and Erin turned to the laptop. The open file was labeled "Jack Hobbs." She felt like a cheap thief as she shrunk it down, scanned the screen, and clicked on the "Sumter" file she spotted. It opened to another list of files that looked like property addresses. She clicked on one of those, and it opened to one more set of files that appeared to be last names. When she opened a random one with an asterisk next to it in the middle of the list, she found a black dot on the application. Erin was devastated until she scrolled to the bottom and saw Jack Hobbs's name. How was an application from the password-protected drive in her files? Unless she had the password? The worm of doubt became a snake in the pit of her stomach. The sound of the toilet flushing prompted her to close the files and she maximized Jack's file.

"I think I know the best route for us to take," Catherine said as she picked up the errand list. She quickly made notations. "And we're going to need your sunscreen."

"You can only have it if I can put it on you," Erin said, the teasing note in her voice clear.

When they were finally on the road, the worry and suspicion crept back into her mind. Now she knew she had to figure out a way to get back into Catherine's laptop. How much time would it take her to find out if the files with asterisks were all Jack's? What if they weren't? And what if those had the dots, too? When Catherine asked her what was wrong, Erin realized she was fretting the button on her shirt just like Nat did when she was overwhelmed. But she made up an excuse and a moment later, Catherine pulled into a CVS in Orleans and Erin stayed in the car. She quickly texted Nat. *One black dot, but it's Jack's. She's got his files on her laptop but I don't know how, need to dig more.* She got a one-word reply back: *Monday.* Even though it was a beautiful day out, beads of sweat collected on her brow.

A couple of hours later, they were stretched out on the beach at Race Point after picking up lunch at the Portuguese Bakery on Commercial Street. She lay on her towel, pulled a ball cap over her eyes, and reached for Catherine's hand hoping it would anchor her, keep her from thinking about what she had to do. "I don't ever want to leave."

"I don't either. Paint some masterpieces and we won't have to."

The remark hurt at first. And then it didn't. Because then it felt like a call to arms, like Catherine believed in her, and that was a challenge she wanted to meet. She hadn't felt that way about her art for a long time. She thought of her recent canvas hanging in her neighbor's living room, right above the desk where he worked. Maybe she believed in herself again a little, too. Erin let go of Catherine's hand and tentatively moved it toward her bag. She wanted her sketchbook.

"Look, you know I didn't mean it that way." Catherine shaded her eyes and looked over at Erin. "I do understand what happened—"

"No. Yes. I know." Erin sat up and pulled out her book, snagging out the pencil tucked in the spine. "I want to draw you."

Catherine hesitated. "We have to leave soon."

"Preliminary sketch. Won't take long. Just lie like you were before." Erin worked with bold efficient strokes. "Raise one leg, you know, bent at the knee, the leg away from me." Catherine complied and Erin looked from her to the page and back again as she worked. When she had what she wanted, she surreptitiously skipped ahead several pages and began rendering her as she'd seen her last night, standing by the bed, bending to drape her robe on it, a graceful alabaster statue come to life in the first flush of dawn. On the opposing page, she roughed out the glimpse she'd seen as Catherine got into bed, that moment of repose when she had one foot on the floor, one hand on the covers, a Greek goddess reclining, a faint iridescence falling on her face, her shoulders, her breasts. *One shade the more, one ray the less...* She tried to translate that delicate light through her pencil now, Byron's poem nudging her mind as she worked.

"I think we need to get ready to drive back or we'll be late for tonight's festivities."

Catherine's directive broke her concentration. She closed the book and slid the pencil down the spine, hoping she could get back to it later in the same frame of mind.

"You look terrific! Who knew you wore seersucker? I've only ever seen you in khaki shorts," Catherine said as she straightened the white sweater Erin had tied around her shoulders. "You're nervous."

"I think I am." The shorts, a last-minute purchase from Bean, passed muster with Catherine. She was certain she looked like she belonged now, and belonged with Catherine.

"You and Daniel are going to love each other, don't worry."

"Well, we both love you, so we have that in common." Erin realized a second too late that she'd let slip what she'd been grappling with since before they set out on this trip.

Catherine's lips parted ever so slightly in that moment of micro-recognition. The blue of her irises seemed to take on a brighter light.

Erin cleared her throat, hoping the moment would just go away. "Am I going to like the bride?"

Catherine continued to stare at her for a moment before she said, "Nikki. I think so."

"Okay, well, let's go," Erin said. "I need to cash in on that lobster."

Catherine laughed. "Mercenary."

There were over a hundred people on the beach, many of them milling by the bar and the tables of hors d'oeuvres. Erin mentally prepared herself to meet and catalogue people for Catherine's sake since she knew a lot of the guests. Even as they were coming down the stairs, a handsome older couple was waving to Catherine, and she made her way toward them. "This is the writer Charley Owens and her wife, Joanna Caden," she said to Erin. "Daniel is her publisher, and I sold them a lovely Central Park West penthouse a couple of years ago. I see them a lot, actually. I think you'll like them."

Erin had read one of Charley's books, the one that was short-listed for the Pulitzer, and was enchanted by the easygoing couple. She and Charley got lost in a conversation about the creative processes that plagued them both. But she was equally distracted by what was going on at the clambake pits, and eventually made her excuses to go see how they worked. This was an opportunity she couldn't let escape, so far out of the purview of anything she knew. She cut a path to the chefs standing over the pits so she could watch them work. There was just enough daylight left to take photos with her cell phone for possible sketches later.

A young woman who looked like wait staff passed by and Erin stopped her, pointed out Catherine, and asked her if she could bring her a glass of chardonnay. The girl tripped on the words *open bar* that were forming on her lips when Erin held out a ten-dollar bill. She nodded and headed across the lawn. Four years of waiting tables and working parties during college and grad school had garnered Erin all the tricks of the trade. She knew how to get the best service no matter what sort of establishment she was in. She watched, pleased, as the girl delivered the drink and pointed in Erin's direction. Catherine raised her glass. Erin nodded and turned back to the chefs, eager to find out how a clambake was put together. By the time she rejoined Catherine, she was well versed in pit digging, fire-building techniques, whether it's better to have two or three inches of seaweed over the hot rocks, and if canvas is a better steaming bet than burlap. The chefs had even offered her a beer from their stash. When she told them she was strictly a scotch drinker, a shot of Macallan eighteen-year-old had appeared from the depths of a box labeled "live lobsters." Erin was certain there was no such bottle at the open bar.

She found Catherine with a tall handsome raven-haired man, his arm around her shoulder as he regaled the circle of people surrounding them with the tale of meeting her when she sold him his first apartment, and thought she was a sign from above that he could fall in love again after his messy divorce, only to find out she didn't play for his team. Here, then, was Daniel McKinley. There was an echo of John Kennedy Jr. about him. He had the dark good looks of the Auchincloss side of that family that she'd seen in hundreds of old photos that surfaced in magazines and online stories whenever another tragedy hit the Kennedy clan, and she wondered if this is what John would have looked like if he'd lived to be fifty. Daniel inhabited a graceful athletic beauty, commanded the crowd's attention, laughed easily. And it was clear by the way he looked at Catherine that they were close friends. And that maybe he was still a little bit in love with her.

Then, he held out his hand to his bride. The woman who stepped out from the circle of bridesmaids was the tall, gorgeous African

American woman Erin remembered seeing in photographs from the *New York Times's* society pages. The radiant smile of happiness on Catherine's face seemed to speak volumes. Couldn't this be proof enough for Nat if she was good friends with Nikki? She innately knew it wouldn't be, that she'd still have to get into Catherine's files.

There wasn't any time to talk to Daniel or to Nikki during the tightly scripted dinner.

"We'll get a chance to be with them tomorrow at lunch, when we're sitting at their table," Catherine whispered as Daniel's sister delivered a roast of him over the blueberry pie à la mode. Erin watched a little finger of the vanilla ice cream run across the golden crust. It drew her right back into her anxiety. No one else but Nat had ever found it as gross as she did, soggy pie, and ice cream all gluey from thick hot fresh fruit juices. Ordinarily, she would've texted a picture of it to Nat, with the accompanying gagging emoji, and they both would've laughed. Not tonight. She drained her water glass, scraped the ice cream off the pie and dumped it into the empty glass.

Erin's attention was caught by several bonfires being lit on the beach for the party, and she tapped Catherine's leg.

"Oh, good." Catherine shivered.

The night had become cool, but Erin welcomed it. She took off her sweater, drew it around Catherine's shoulders and leaned against her. "I did say you should've brought your jacket," she whispered in her ear, relishing the intimacy, her scent, and the glance that came her way.

"Maybe I wanted an excuse for you to have to warm me up."

Erin pulled her in, and they listened to Nikki's mother talk about what a headstrong girl she'd been, and still was. When the laughter died down, Daniel invited everyone to warm themselves at the bonfires and enjoy the fireworks that were about to light up the sky. Erin made Catherine put the sweater on, sat behind her on one of the blankets that had been laid out for the guests, and enfolded her in her arms. Catherine sank back against her, and with the first burst of pinwheels in the sky, she put her head back on Erin's shoulder. Erin buried her nose in Catherine's hair and kissed her neck, moving from the crook up to her ear. When she reached her earlobe, Catherine turned her head and kissed Erin, setting off fireworks inside her that rivaled the ones bursting in the skies. In the flickering shadows of the bonfire, Erin moved her hand under the sweater, settled on her breasts, and moved over them unimpeded as she returned the kiss, feeling her nipples become hard under her shirt. Claiming one, she pressed her thumb around it just as three enormous pink chrysanthemums banged into the black sky one after the other, and Catherine's groan was lost in the noise.

She could feel the explosion as they kissed. Erin opened several buttons of her shirt and slipped her hand inside, the smooth cotton of her bra warm under her palm. Catherine's lips parted and Erin's tongue sought hers as brilliant white comets split the night. She could see them against her closed eyelids. Catherine turned toward her, pulled a corner of the blanket over their laps, and her hand traveled up Erin's thigh and under her shorts. Erin held her breath and didn't move until Catherine's fingers, subtly brushing in several directions, snugged right between her legs. She gasped at the hint of pressure.

A bright yellow fountain splashed above the applauding crowd. She saw the question in Catherine's eyes and answered it by tweaking the nipple that was poking at the cloth covering it, and Catherine dropped her head to Erin's shoulder. When an orange waterfall cascaded across the sky spilling long tails of stars, Erin lifted Catherine's head and kissed her. She wanted to shift and give her more access, but she was afraid light from the bottle rockets now exploding overhead would give them away and she wouldn't risk that. Catherine drew her fingers up and down several times and Erin slid her hand into Catherine's bra, pressing her face to Catherine's neck to stifle her moans, but they were drowned out by the barrage of shells, rockets, and confetti that suddenly filled the sky in an unending battery of noise and light.

"I want you," she said to Catherine, "and I know you want me." Catherine's brow furrowed. "Yes, you do, you've been teasing me for weeks." Catherine started to say something, but Erin put her finger to her lips. "I'm going to go up to the room." She took her hand out of Catherine's shirt as couples drifted past them, the fireworks over. "I think Daniel wants to talk to you because he keeps looking over here." She removed Catherine's hand from her shorts. "When you come up to the room, I'll be waiting."

The gift shop was just about to close when Erin got there. As she pulled a small wad of big bills out of her pocket, she was glad she'd sold that painting. She bought three small bayberry candles and headed for the bar in the restaurant down the hall. She bought a cold bottle of Taittinger champagne and asked the bartender if he could give her enough ice to put around it in the ice bucket in the room. Nat had been right. With any luck, tonight would be, well, at least a tipsy bacchanal.

In the room, she lit the candles and put them on the little coffee table in the living room next to the ice bucket and two glasses. Then she put the champagne in the bucket and poured the ice around it from the small bag the bartender had given her. She dimmed the lights and put on the white silk teddy and lace robe she'd folded into her suitcase at the last moment. She'd forgotten which girlfriend had given them to her several Christmases ago. She'd never worn them for her. Then she pulled the covers down on the bed nearer the deck and went outside to wait. Silver moonlight revealed everything: the jetty, the waves washing on shore, and most of the deck itself. Hugging her shoulders against the cool air, she hoped she was making the right move. Every instinct told her she was, but there was always that little voice of warning. She wasn't sure how she would feel if Catherine put the brakes on now.

A few minutes later, she heard her come into the room. Every part of Erin ached for Catherine's touch as she watched the dune grass bending to the breeze. I have no plan beyond this, she thought, and held her breath for a moment. When she stepped through the door into the bedroom, she couldn't tell what Catherine was thinking as she looked from the candles to the bed to Erin. Erin walked over to her and reached for the hem of the sweater. Catherine let her undress her piece by piece. And moment by moment, Erin felt and saw her guard coming down until the mask was gone, and there was only pure desire in its place.

Standing behind her, hardly believing it was happening, Erin unhooked her bra and tossed it on the chair with the rest of her things. And then, in the soft light of the flickering candles, she ran her hands over Catherine's back, over the planes and the muscles, her own artist's Braille. Gently squeezing that perfectly rounded bottom elicited a sound from deep within Catherine and her head fell back onto Erin's shoulder. This was no marble statue. She took Catherine's hair down and kissed her neck, her shoulders, moved her hands to her breasts and embraced her. When she turned her around, her breath was stolen yet again by the beautiful figure in front of her and the utter need in her eyes. Catherine reached for the lace robe, took it from Erin's shoulders and lay it across the bottom of the bed like she had her own last night. She slid the teddy off, leaving it pooled at her feet. For a moment, Catherine's face was inscrutable again.

"You were right. I do want you." She pulled Erin to her and kissed her, and Erin reveled in the soft feel of her, the heat coming from her body. "I have wanted the touch of your skin on mine for weeks. I've thought of almost nothing else," she whispered. She kissed Erin again, her tongue probing gently, her hand seeking Erin's. Then she took her to the bed. She lay down, one arm draped over her head, and Erin looked at her, unable to move.

"You can't have your sketchbook. Not yet, anyway."

"I don't want it." *My hands will commit you to memory.* In the slow vein in which she'd started, Erin bent over and ran her hand from Catherine's toes to her hair, down the back of her head to her neck, and she could see the charcoal sketch spinning out in front of her. Catherine lay still, her eyes closed. "You're like a Greek goddess," Erin slipped onto the bed and leaned in to kiss her, moving her knee between Catherine's legs where her hand had already lingered. It was much wetter there now. Erin's own desire had caused the same reaction in her, and she moved on Catherine's thigh, painting it with a slick patch.

Although it wasn't possible to pull her closer, Catherine tried, locking her arm around Erin's waist as she slipped her other hand between her legs. Erin laid her head on Catherine's breast and let the rhythm of Catherine's fingers pass through her, like one bright color after another saturating her body. She picked up the rhythm, playing with one of Catherine's nipples, watching it rise and harden, feeling her breath quicken, her own coming faster in response. Turning her head an inch, her lips were on Catherine's other nipple, and her whole body stirred beneath Erin, shifting, then squirming as Erin picked up the pace with both her lips and her fingers, pushing her knee into Catherine's wet center. When Catherine parted her and slipped a finger inside her, Erin caught her wrist and pulled her hand out. "No," she whispered.

"But—"

Erin put a finger on her lips. "Not yet." She began alternating the pace with her knee, from slow to fast and back again, mimicking the changing rhythm of the waves washing up on shore. It was forcing Catherine open wider as she ground against her, as she got slippery, and then threw her arm over her eyes. Erin reveled in the moans, knowing she was the reason behind them.

"You're driving me crazy."

"That's my intention," Erin said. She kissed Catherine, demanding entrance. Her fingers replaced her knee and she traced patterns around her sex, dipping in and out. Her thumb on her clitoris, out. Several soft circles, in. Her thumb returning to her clitoris, out. Catherine arched, moaned, grabbed Erin's short hair, and kissed her hard, and still she traced the patterns until she felt Catherine tremble and move her hips toward her. Then she broke the kiss and quickly moved down between her legs to kiss her there, her tongue tracing the patterns. A figure eight, then in, then out. Circles, in, out. Flicking her clitoris, delving in as deeply as she could and moving in every direction…fast flicks, slow drawn-out licks, until Catherine was whimpering. And then her body went completely still. Trusting that she was on the verge of her orgasm, Erin took her all in, her tongue hard on her clitoris, and the uncontrollable spasms rolled through Catherine. She reached for Erin's head, and Erin caught her hands in hers, clasping them tightly as Catherine came in waves, Erin's tongue still engaged with the soft button of nerves.

"Stop…you have to stop before I break in two.'

Erin moved up beside her and Catherine hugged her. Before she could settle into her arms, Catherine was inside her and she arched against her, surprised at how close to the edge she was. Then Catherine's lips were on hers and she shattered, pushing against her, opening up to her, consuming her, hugging her like a drowning woman as she thrust against her again and again. Catherine's lips were on her neck, her breasts, as she held her, pressing back against her until there was nothing left and Erin lay beside her, spent. Her senses returned slowly, and she heard crickets singing above the sound of the waves. Whole choirs of them out in the gardens, singing one-note oratorios in bass, tenor, and soprano tones. She sighed and relaxed into Catherine. *Paradise.* But she was oddly wide awake. She caressed Catherine as she felt her falling asleep. Her mind wandered to the day she saw her in the little park while she waited for Nat. If anyone had told her she'd be here with her now in this big soft bed after several weeks of the first real romance she'd experienced in years, she would have thought they'd taken leave of their senses. She sighed. For a moment, she felt a completeness she hadn't known in a long time, and she basked in the warmth of the moment and the comfort of Catherine's arms. But then, reality butted her with its ugly head, and that feeling broke into little pieces as she contemplated the possibility of the betrayal she was about to unleash.

Chapter Twenty

"Crap. I forgot to plug my phone in last night," Erin said, pulling it out of the charger before Catherine saw her do it. "Can I check my email on your laptop while you're in the shower?" She tried to push away the feeling of duplicity that wormed its way into her gut.

"Sure."

"Do I need a password to open it?"

Catherine smiled. "It's your name, capital E and capital O, followed by the pound sign and the number one."

"Really?" Erin suddenly felt like a grilled cheese sandwich, all melty inside.

Catherine walked over, her robe falling open, and gave her a kiss that was almost more searing than any they'd had over the course of the night's lovemaking. "Really."

She disappeared into the bathroom, and nausea washed over Erin. And then she hated Nat for a second. Deeply hated her. But that was all she had time for if she was going to get into the files, so she grabbed her cell phone. She'd hidden it out of view on its charger at dawn knowing it would be her excuse to access Catherine's laptop. She looked at the password on the screen for a moment and wanted to cry. But there was no time for that, either. Scrolling through files, with one ear on the bathroom shower, she checked the applications with asterisks. They were all Jack Hobbs's, some with dots, some without. And again she wondered how that was.

Then she began randomly clicking on files whose last names were obviously of Middle Eastern origin. Many applications were clean, no dots. The fourth and tenth ones she looked at were not, and had green dots in the upper right corners. And Catherine's name the listed Realtor. She sat back, sick with this new knowledge. And then wondered why only a few had them. Quickly, she got back to work, taking pictures of each screen with her cell phone. She didn't care if she hadn't spoken to her in over two weeks now, Marquita was going to have to help her figure this out. She sent the photos to her email, opened that, and forwarded them all to Marquita with a plea to find out if these were clients original to Catherine and how many others she might have with dots. *Electronic or hard copy—can you find out? I only have so much time here with her laptop.* This couldn't be right. Something had to be wrong. Marquita had to have the answers. Then she deleted the emails from Catherine's sent file to cover her tracks.

A moment later, her text message dinged. It was Marquita: *Where are you that you have her laptop??*

Erin hadn't thought that move through. *I'll explain Mon. Pls, can u check her files?*

The shower stopped. Erin closed all Catherine's files and checked her email, just as she'd said she was going to do. There was one from Anika.

"I know you're away and we don't meet until Monday, but I had a fight with my best friend, and I don't know what to do and mom says I'm being silly but I'm not. What happens when you and Nat fight? Love, Anika. P.S. I'm getting a gazillion likes and comments about your painting. Who is Jasper Johns? He liked it and my Instagram blew up. Studying with a master is cool."

Erin stared at the screen. Then she grabbed her phone and opened Instagram, searching Anika's account. It *had* blown up. She had thousands of comments after the artist posted *"Interesting."* If it really *was* Johns. The sink had been running and now that water was turned off. Erin put her phone in her pocket and turned back to the email. The kid was asking her advice, and it made her feel ten feet tall and really small. And considering what was going on between her and Nat right now, she wasn't sure how to answer. She felt Catherine's arm around her shoulder.

"That's sweet. This is the young girl you're giving lessons to, isn't it? She obviously looks up to you."

Erin nodded and closed out the email.

"No, you can stay with it. I have to dress."

Erin looked at her, saw the robe cinched at her waist, the long damp hair, and was out of her chair in an instant, her mouth on Catherine's as she guided her to the bed, opened her robe and brought her to an orgasm so fast they both looked surprised.

"What was that?" Catherine asked, gasping for air.

"I needed you."

Catherine pushed Erin onto her back. "Well, now I need you."

Erin came just as quickly. They both lay on the bed, their breathing finally slowing down.

"I don't know what you do to me, but I like it," Catherine said. "All of it."

Already feeling the depth of her betrayal, and then needing her so badly, Erin had no rejoinder. "We're going to be late to lunch if we don't get dressed."

"You're right." Catherine headed for the closet.

Erin exhaled. How had things gotten so messy?

When she and Catherine walked into the restaurant, all the floor-to-ceiling windows that faced the ocean were open, and Erin immediately felt lighter. She spotted Daniel waving to them and took Catherine's hand, weaving through the tables. As she'd promised, Catherine sat next to Nikki so Erin could sit next to Daniel and get to know him. He was an adept conversationalist, and Erin found herself drawn to him as they talked about life and politics in New York City. She kept her eye on Nikki and Catherine, whose heads were close together in conversation punctuated by easy laughter. Needing to know more about Nikki, Erin steered the conversation toward how Daniel met his soon-to-be-wife, and his friendship with Catherine. When the raspberry gelato dessert arrived at the table, Daniel insisted he and Nikki switch seats so that she and Erin could talk.

"After all, I think we could be seeing a fair amount of each other in the city," Daniel said. He leaned closer. "I haven't seen Catherine this happy in a long time, so thank you for that."

Erin smiled, but she was cringing inside, and couldn't look at Catherine.

"So," Nikki said, "I'm going to skip a lot of the small talk because I feel like I already know you." She poured a large splash of white wine into the empty glass at Erin's place.

"Oh, no, not drinking." Erin held up her hand.

"It's a wedding! You have to," Nikki said, smiling.

Erin let it go but moved the glass a little farther away.

"Catherine tells me you're a painter. She showed me your website. I'm a collector, so we need to talk. I'd love to see your current work."

"She showed you my website?"

"I must admit, there wasn't a lot of work on it, so I wondered what you're hiding in the way of canvasses. Are you getting ready for a show, maybe?"

Erin hesitated. She heard Catherine's voice whispering in her ear before they'd fallen asleep in each other's arms at dawn. *"You need to start painting again, darling. Anyone who has as much passion as you do in bed must be brilliant on canvas."*

"No, I'm working on a new project. It's a series of…I guess you could call it illustrated portraits."

"But you must have something in your studio. All artists hold back on their canvases, I know that."

One look at Nikki's face and Erin saw the seriousness behind the question. Thinking she might be insane, she opened her Instagram account and found Anika's post of the ruined canvas on her living room wall. She opened and enlarged the photo and handed the phone to Nikki. She was suddenly aware that both Catherine and Daniel were leaning over them, looking at the screen.

"My student took that photo when she was in my apartment recently and saw this on my wall. She thought it was cool and posted it to her Instagram account. But she's ten years old. Everything's cool when you're ten. It's the only remaining canvas from my debut at the Whitney Biennial five years ago."

Nikki nodded. "I remember that. Quite an entrance into the art world." She stared at the screen, then looked at Erin. "And I got an alert yesterday when a certain someone spotted it and weighed in. You saw that, I'm sure."

Erin nodded, barely.

"You sold the rest after all?"

"No. I destroyed them all." She heard the small noise of surprise that came from Daniel.

"All of them but this one?"

"Yes."

"And what do you want for this one?"

"I'm not sure…" Erin didn't finish the sentence "it's for sale" because she felt Catherine's hand on her shoulder.

"You'd have to check with your dealer, wouldn't you? Before you could say for sure?' Catherine said.

Erin looked up at her. Catherine was obviously trying to buy her time to figure out a good price for the painting, but she didn't have a dealer. Or an agent. And she wasn't sure she could go along with the ruse. Or that she could let the woman she might be about to destroy help her make her first big sale in years.

"Well, maybe you could call him, or her, today or tomorrow, and find out?" Daniel asked. "We could come see it when we get back from the honeymoon. Now, who wants to join me on the beach?"

Back in the room, Erin quietly changed into her suit as Catherine went on about how Nikki's interest in the painting could change Erin's future.

"I don't want to sell it." The declaration was a near-whisper, but it stopped Catherine. "It's a very important reminder of how I can screw up my life."

Catherine sat on the bed. "Maybe this is the universe telling you it's time to let that go."

"Catherine, I…" She was about to come clean to her about Nat's story, but her phone rang. The name on the screen made her blanch. "I have to get this." Catherine nodded and Erin went out onto the deck. "Hey."

"There are more," Marquita said. "Not a lot, but enough. And that's only one filing drawer. She has three credenzas in here, but I can't stay because if the other Realtors see me spending so much time in her office, they'll wonder. So I'll check her online files now."

"Okay, I just need proof and that sounds like it. Were they always her clients?"

"I'm not sure how to figure that out."

"Ask someone. This is really important."

"Okay, but look, why don't you come over here Monday night after everyone leaves? If you can help me, we can find them all."

"What time?"

"Do I hear the ocean? Are you at the beach?"

"Yeah, I'm on Cape Cod. So, like, eight o'clock?"

"Yes."

"Okay. And could you let Nat know? She wanted proof by Monday." She knew she couldn't make that call and that bothered her. When Erin stepped back into the room, Catherine was brushing her hair. She swept it into the ponytail and Erin swallowed at the sight, guilt and desire colliding with a bang like last night's fireworks, and still she wanted to peel that bathing suit right off her.

"Is everything okay?" Catherine asked.

Erin could barely look at her. "Sure. You go down to the beach, I'll be there soon. I just need to take care of a couple of things." She sat on the bed after Catherine left. This was one of those times she really needed advice from her best friend. But she couldn't turn to her.

Erin pulled up Anika's email on her cell phone and hit reply. *Call her. Tell her you need to talk to her because nothing should come between best friends*. She sent it. Her phone showed it was just three o'clock. Kendra would either be at the gym or rehearsal. Erin dialed her number.

Of course Daniel and Nikki wanted close friends at the rehearsal dinner to keep the mood light. But Erin was distracted and had to work hard to be social. She found herself on the patio more than once taking a moment to herself to think about Kendra's advice that if Catherine was involved, Nat was saving her from heartbreak. "But I'm already falling for her, Ken. Nat can't be right."

"Then disprove it. Or confront her."

"But I can't blow the story."

"What's more important? Catherine, or the story?"

That shook Erin. Was her best friend's wife suggesting she cross her best friend?

When Saturday morning dawned, Erin was exhausted from their second night of lovemaking, but more than that, she was frayed from the thoughts chasing around the hamster wheel in her mind after Catherine had fallen asleep. She caressed her cheek, her face peaceful, impassive, like a statue. Quietly, she moved out of the bed, found her shorts and a T-shirt, picked up her sketch pad and pencils, and went down to the beach. Before the sun had cleared another inch on the horizon, she crashed on a chaise lounge, the sketch pad on the ground beside her.

What seemed like a moment later, Catherine was shaking her awake, a look of worry on her face. "Are you okay?"

"I'm fine." Erin pulled herself together as people around her settled onto other beach chairs in their bathing suits, looking crisp and summer-morning-like. She felt like crap.

"When did you come out here?"

"Around sunup."

"Why?"

"I don't know. A lot on my mind."

"Come back up to the room. You need some real sleep."

Erin stood up. Catherine picked up her pad and guided her back up to the room and onto the bed.

"You sleep. I've got work to do. Maybe we can talk about what's bothering you when you wake up"

Erin pulled the comforter up to her chin and fell asleep, but her dreams were chaotic and desolate.

CHAPTER TWENTY-ONE

Erin felt so much better after Catherine woke her with lunch, she showered, and then they'd gone to the beach for a couple of hours.

She leaned on the deck railing, careful not to get anything on her tux shirt or pants. People had begun gathering on the lawn for the wedding, finding their way to one of the sturdy white folding chairs that sat in tight rows on either side of the brick walk facing the small altar and the ocean beyond. Erin watched with curiosity the delicate dance taking place as some people sought out others while other people politely passed up rows with groups of people already seated. She hadn't noticed cliques on Thursday, but maybe she'd been oblivious. Some guests were already perusing the program handed to them by one of the tuxedoed ushers. Still others were gawking, checking out what everyone was wearing.

Erin's eye was drawn to the trellis that stood at the stone wall by the stairs leading to the beach. It was woven with more beach roses than she'd seen in one place at one time, and she wanted to get her sketchbook to capture it. Instead, she took pictures with her cell phone, hoping that would suffice when she re-created it later. Several rows of chairs were still empty, so she photographed them as well. It must've come to her when she was sleeping, but she'd had the idea to put together a sketchbook of the wedding for Daniel and Nikki, and now she began taking pictures of several of the groups of people gathering in pockets in various rows.

"We'll have to put our phones on silent for the wedding."

"Of course," she said, turning to greet Catherine, stopping when she saw her in the doorway. Everything but her eyes seemed to shut down for a moment. The fuchsia dress came to life on her even beyond Erin's imagination, the cinched belt creating an hourglass effect. The top hugged Catherine's breasts, beckoning Erin like a magnet. She wanted to touch the strand of pearls at her neck, run her hand over the soft skin. She managed to stay still, though, knowing that if she gave in to that urge, they'd miss the wedding, hearing it instead from the bed.

A fuchsia shawl was draped over Catherine's arm, a black patent leather clutch in her hand that matched her heels. Erin shoved the phone and her hands into her pockets. "Yes, of course, we'll silence our phones."

"You look…wow." Catherine walked over to Erin, straightened her bow tie, and ran her hand over the tuxedo shirt placket, causing a chain reaction in her that cascaded from her nipples down through her stomach and right to headquarters in her clitoris. "I'd kiss you but I know everyone can see us and I'm afraid we wouldn't make it to the wedding and everyone would know why," Catherine whispered.

Erin closed her eyes. "If you touch me again, we *won't* make it to the wedding. I'm not sure I can control myself, either." When she opened her eyes, she saw the amused smile that always thrilled her, those perfect red bow lips quirking up at one corner.

"Well, that's going to make this evening very hard for both of us. Because I'm going to want to dance at the reception."

Erin groaned. "Of course you will. And I will oblige." She held out her arm for Catherine.

The ushers seated them on Daniel's side of the walkway right on the aisle, a sotto voce request from Erin. Envisioning the whole layout of the book she wanted to put together for Daniel and Nikki, she wanted a clear shot of Nikki coming down the aisle. Throughout the ceremony and afterward at the reception, she quietly and carefully took photos, often standing near the official photographer and taking her shots from a different angle, out of the field of vision of the guests he was shooting. Catherine finally asked her what she was doing when Erin slipped away from the dinner table for the third time.

She nodded when Erin revealed her plan. "I like that idea very much." She traced Erin's lips with her fingers. "Put that phone away and dance with me."

The orchestra played well into the night, and they spent most of it on the dance floor. Finally, a single violin signaled a slow number, and Erin held Catherine so close, her elbow crooked on her shoulder so that her hand rested on the rise of Catherine's breasts. "I think I need to take you upstairs," she whispered as she kissed Catherine behind the ear.

"When this dance is over. I like having you here like this, in my arms. I like declaring that you're mine this way."

Erin felt the involuntary pulse between her legs. She liked being someone's "mine," liked being in Catherine's arms, in her bed, in her life.

Everything moved as slowly as it had the first night as they stood by the bed. Erin unzipped Catherine's dress and lowered it, steadying her arm to help her step out of it. She lay the dress on the other bed.

"We should have bought more candles," Catherine whispered.

"We have the moonlight," Erin whispered back, kissing the nape of her neck.

Catherine turned around to embrace her, and Erin saw the thong, a strand of pearls between her legs, attached by a silver ring to two ribbons of black silk held in place by her hips. The pearls were nestled deep in her pussy, six of them leading out from the top of that lovely smooth cleft, and for Erin, it was like Christmas morning, discovering something under the tree that she hadn't asked for and didn't know she wanted. And then the wrapping paper came off and she was overcome with the need for it.

Erin unbuttoned her shirt, Catherine's eyes following each button coming undone. She lay the shirt next to the dress and unhooked her bra. Catherine pulled it off and tossed it on top of the shirt. Her hands on Catherine's shoulders, she sat her on the bed, her heels still on. Then she went to her knees and draped Catherine's legs over her back, feeling the hard spines of the heels on her skin, and Catherine lay back. Settling in, she visited each individual pearl with her tongue, delighting in the sound and feel of Catherine's increasingly more ragged breathing. As the coming orgasm built, and the arch of her back became more prominent, Catherine lifted her hips toward Erin, and her heels dug deeper into Erin's back. The heel caps would soon leave deep impressions in her skin.

She pushed the strand of pearls aside with her tongue and moved as far inside Catherine as she could until she heard her whimpering, felt her tremble. This is the real Paradise, she thought, being here, with her, inside her. The gathering storm ripped right up Catherine's body, eliciting those audible intakes of breath that Erin loved to hear. She trapped her legs open and continued as Catherine grabbed handfuls of the quilt and pulled, shaking uncontrollably.

"Please," Catherine gasped.

"Please what?" Erin clamped her mouth back in place, reveling in the feel of the clitoris pulsing against the flat of her tongue.

"Please, come up here."

Finally, Erin stood and shed the rest of her clothes, stretching the length of Catherine, sighing at the feel of her skin on hers, finding her hands and trapping them over her head. She gently bucked against Erin. "My God."

Erin kissed all around the strand of pearls at her neck. "You are a Naughty Nell with your pearls."

"Oh, I think you're the naughty one with that tongue of yours."

Erin moved down so she could play with Catherine's nipples. "Oh, no you don't," Catherine said, rolling Erin onto her back.

Dawn was breaking again when they finally decided they were sated and fell asleep in each other's arms.

When she said good-bye to Daniel and Nikki after brunch, she was a little sad. Would she see them again? Or would her duplicity, however unintended, ruin everything? She'd know after Monday night.

❖

Erin was surprised to find Nat in her apartment when she got home Sunday night, watching a pre-season football game on TV. Lincoln was curled up in her lap. "Except for his love of the Green Bay Packers, apparently you and I are interchangeable," she said. "He was good all weekend, but he definitely missed you. So I stayed with him tonight. Wanted to see how you are. Oh, and that stupid Peeping Tom of yours came out when he saw your light on."

A bad feeling hovered in the air. "Yeah, he's annoying." She sighed. "I'm okay." She turned and looked at the ruined painting. It had taken on a new life with one snapshot from a ten-year-old kid. Suddenly, she felt old and burdened. "I don't like this, Nat. I don't like what I'm doing to Catherine."

"Not 'our story' anymore, huh?" Nat lifted Lincoln to the ground, and he sat still, looking up at the two of them.

"I didn't say that."

"It's not personal, Erin. It's business."

"I really hate that, too."

"Then quit. I'll find another route."

"No. I don't quit on friends. And this *is* personal. It's very personal for you. And what hurts you hurts me. But I'm going to hurt her and that's going to kill me."

"You're going to her office Monday night to sleuth around with Marquita. She told me. So disprove it, like Kendra said. Find the proof that she doesn't know."

"Kendra talked to you?"

"We tell each other everything," Nat said. "Please, don't make me the bad guy. I'm not the bad guy in any of this. You knew it was a bad idea to get involved with Catherine. You could have waited until this was all over. *You* decided not to, and now things are complicated. That's not on me."

Erin looked at the floor. She knew that. Lincoln meowed and she picked him up.

"Even the brown boy knows I'm not the bad guy," Nat said.

Erin buried her face in his fur and inhaled his cat smell. It always made her feel better, like the teddy bears of yore she used to hug in bed at night for their security against the frightening darkness of her room.

Nat walked to the door. "You know, for what it's worth, if she's their top saleswoman, wouldn't there be a whole lot of dots on a whole lot of her applications if she was part of it?"

Erin didn't reply.

"And you didn't find that, right? Just something to hang on to. I don't know." She twisted a couple of her dreadlocks together, then let them drop. "Okay, I'm interviewing Jack Hobbs tomorrow. If you want to come, let me know." She opened the door. "And, Erin?"

Erin and Lincoln looked at her.

"Thank you for doing this article with me. I needed you. You always know what to say in situations when I don't. And you're my best friend. Whatever happens."

Erin nodded.

"Oh, by the way, you have a ton of messages on your landline. Someone called while I was sitting here, some dealer, about that painting." She nodded toward it. "Why the heck would anyone be interested in that?" Nat shut the door after giving her a quick wink and a wave.

Erin was alone with her thoughts, thoughts she didn't want to have, so she carried Lincoln into the bedroom, set him on the bed, and lay down. She took out her cell phone and opened her Kindle to the Georgia O'Keefe biography Catherine had recommended. She'd unpack her suitcase tomorrow.

CHAPTER TWENTY-TWO

Monday, Erin stayed home. Nat didn't need her at the interview. She was writing her article. Lincoln didn't need her. He was curled up in his bed. She wanted to call Catherine, tell her the drive home had been wonderful as they flew over the dark roads that led off the Cape, top down, the smell of salt water, pine, cedar chips and the end of summer enveloping them. Catherine's phone was plugged in, playing an old David Sanborn album, the mellow, sensual jazz leaving Erin wanting Catherine all the more. But if she called her now, the sound of the guilt in her voice about what she was going to do tonight with Marquita would come through, so she sat on the windowsill waiting for the evening, waiting to walk uptown to betray her.

At four o'clock, her doorbell rang. She was confused for a minute. And then it occurred to her. Anika. She peered out her peephole to make sure, and saw the kid standing far enough away so Erin could see the drawing of the vase of slightly wilted flowers that had been sitting on her coffee table last week. She smiled and opened the door. "C'mon in, Van Gogh."

"Okay, him I know. I got both my ears, ya know."

"Let's take a look at this."

They sat down at the counter and Erin considered the drawing, a pencil in her hand. "Hey, how'd it go with your best friend? You guys talking again?"

"Yeah." Anika's smile lit up the already sunny room. "But..." Her face clouded. "We got a question for you."

"Okay. Not like I'm an expert in anything."

"But you are. Tiff said you were smart to tell me to call. So we figured you'd know. How do you keep your best friend you love, you know, like, forever? How do you not have fights and stuff?"

Erin sat back. "That's a really hard question."

"But you love Nat, right?"

"Yes, I do. But we fight. We're sort of fighting right now."

"About what?"

"She asked me to do something that is hard, that could hurt me."

"Tell her."

"I did. It's kind of complicated. If I don't do this for her, it could hurt her."

"Why would she ask you to do something that could hurt you?"

"She didn't. We didn't know it would happen like that. It involves someone else. But we didn't know that then. And, well, Nat's my friend. I'd do anything for her."

"I would have to tell Tiff no. Even if we didn't find out until after she asked me. She would understand. Nat should understand."

Erin looked at the peaceful certainty on Anika's face. *I hope you never have to test that theory.*

Eight o'clock on the nose. Erin looked around, feeling like Humphrey Bogart as she stood in front of the storefront door to Sumter Realty, only it was ninety degrees, so, no trench coat collar to pull around her face, or a fedora to pull down over her eyes. The setting sun threw harsh fingers of light across Broadway. Marquita assured her everyone on staff was long gone, but she was still uncomfortable. Then she was there, unlocking the door. Erin hoped it wouldn't be awkward as they worked. She had no interest in Marquita, and was glad nothing had come of that one night between them.

"Hey, c'mon in. I turned all the lights off, but we can close Catherine's door and turn the light on in there."

Marquita locked the door behind her and they made their way to Catherine's office. "Thanks for doing all this," Erin said.

"Well, I'm the one who blew the whistle."

And changed my life, and now we'll possibly ruin it together, Erin thought.

She looked around quickly. Catherine's office was spare. Two plants on the windowsill. Then she spotted the small conch shell she'd picked up on the first beach walk with her this past weekend sitting on her desk. Catherine had pulled her in for one of many beach kisses when she'd handed it to her like a treasure. Obviously, she'd put it there this morning, a sign of how much the weekend had meant. Reluctantly, Erin got to work opening the drawers of different credenzas, pulling out files.

She contemplated asking Marquita what had happened that she'd never called. Instead, a quite different question came out. "Did you find a lot in her electronic files?" Erin asked.

"A fair amount. But here's the funny thing. When I asked him, Billy said he and the guys traded clients interested in sales to Catherine in exchange for her renters."

"What did he mean?"

"Dunno. He wouldn't say any more than that. But it's gotta have some financial meaning, right? Sales mean bigger commissions. Maybe they gave her the dots."

"They did give her the dots. You said they were in a protected drive, though."

"They were. I don't know why she'd have them."

"Does that mean she's not part of this?"

"I don't know. Maybe the guys told her. Maybe she is."

Erin thought she heard a sharp note in Marquita's voice. "Then she'd have files in the other drive. And you said she didn't."

"Maybe she keeps hers separately, like she keeps everything here. Erin, she doesn't like me, so she doesn't tell me anything."

This time Erin couldn't miss the bite in Marquita's tone. They continued pulling files in silence.

"Did you have dinner yet?" Marquita finally asked.

"Yeah. I ate at Nat's."

"Oh, okay. I might have to order something."

"Sure." Erin got out her phone and took pictures of several applications she'd laid out on top of the open drawer. "These are recent."

Marquita looked at them. "Oh, I recognize those. They were Billy's first. Why does she even print these out?"

Erin studied them, black circles in the top right corners. "She's old school." Erin flipped through several more pages. "Look. Alphabet letters and dots."

"I don't know what to tell you."

Erin's shoulders slumped.

"I'm gonna go order something. The menus are all in my desk. I'll be right back. You sure you don't want anything?"

Erin shook her head.

When Marquita returned, she left the door ajar. "Hey, you said you were on Cape Cod this weekend?"

"Um…yeah." Erin pulled a thick stack of files out of the drawer so she could avoid looking at her.

"Catherine told me this morning she was there this weekend for a wedding."

"Oh."

"Don't 'oh' me," Marquita said quietly. "You were with her. Why else did you have her laptop?"

Erin paged through the files, the light dawning on Marquita's attitude. Ironic that Nat thought she knew what to say in certain situations. Words escaped her entirely now.

"Are you seeing her? Are you sleeping with her?"

Erin felt like a trapped rat even as she wondered how this was Marquita's business or concern, considering neither one of them had called the other after their night in bed together. "It's complicated."

"No, it's not. You never called me."

"I didn't owe you a phone call. And you could've called me. You just left. And your note said we should do it again 'some time.' What is that?"

"We both talked about not wanting relationships right now in our lives. So why were you with Catherine? And does Nat know?"

"Of course she does. She stayed out of my way."

"Are you saying it's for the story? What, you're fucking Catherine as part of your research? So I'm yesterday's news?"

"What research? What are you doing here, Erin?"

Erin's head snapped up. Catherine stood in the open doorway, a legal portfolio under her arm. Erin's stomach took that now-familiar elevator ride it always did when she saw her. She looked magnificent in a black poplin suit and white shirt, the red tie tabs just beneath the collar matching her red heels. And then she felt Catherine's black heels digging into her back Saturday night.

"The door was locked." Marquita's complexion suddenly drained of its olive hue.

Catherine held up a key. "What research? What is going on here? And what are you doing with my files?"

"You said you weren't coming back." Marquita was now shaking.

"I sold the apartment. I came back to start the paperwork and saw my light on. What. Research?"

Erin slowly rose. "I can explain—"

"Those files are private. What on earth are you doing with them?"

"I can't—"

"You can't what?"

"I'm working on a story with Nat." It was barely a whisper and Erin suddenly understood how Alice in Wonderland felt when she was Too Small.

"For her blog?"

"For the website she works with."

"About what? What could you possibly be looking into that you need *my* files? And behind my back. After we just spent a weekend—" Catherine's voice hitched. "Is Marquita right? Are you fucking me as part of your story? And you don't want a relationship right now?"

"No, I—"

"What story, Erin?"

Erin felt a pain across the bridge of her nose that quickly flowed up her temples and began to pound. She couldn't breathe. "A series of articles about racism in real estate. Here, in your company."

"Racism. That's a ridiculous accusation. And you thought you'd find the answer by rifling my files instead of coming to me?"

"Your computer files, too," Marquita volunteered.

Catherine froze and Erin's mouth fell open in surprised horror. She turned to Marquita with murder on her mind, but the fire about to erupt in front of her was more important to prevent.

"I needed to be wrong about your being part of this. But if I'd come to you, I could've blown Nat's story. Tell her, Marquita."

"How could you…" Catherine had gone pale. "I trusted you!" She braced herself on the doorjamb, her hand at her mouth. "And are you involved with her?" She pointed to Marquita, not taking her eyes off Erin, eyes that were suddenly a very dark blue in a hard-set face.

"Look, I—"

"Is she?" Catherine demanded of Marquita.

"Once. Just once."

"Oh, my God." Catherine's eyes filled with tears. "You had the *nerve* to tell me you love me. What a fool I've been. What an *utter* fool. I knew you weren't renting an apartment, but I never suspected something like this." Catherine threw the portfolio she'd been carrying at her desk. It landed on the chair and bounced onto the floor. "Get. Out! Both of you! Get out of here right now."

Erin took a step toward Catherine. "I *do* love—"

"Don't take another step. Get out." Catherine cut her off, her voice low and filled with rage.

Erin saw everything running through her fingers like so much sand, and opened her mouth, but walked out behind Marquita instead, who was now softly crying. Erin glanced back and saw Catherine's head in her hands. She felt sick to her stomach.

Marquita grabbed her bag and let them out the front door. "Shit. I'm gonna lose my job."

Erin didn't care. She'd just lost the most important woman in her life.

"How could you sleep with her!" Marquita was furiously wiping her tears away. "*And* tell her you love her?"

Erin was astonished. "Really, Marquita? Really? You imbecile! Telling her about the computer files? You just wrecked my life!" Erin turned and walked away. She didn't care what Marquita was yelling after her. It was in Spanish anyway. She took her phone out of her pocket and dialed Catherine's number. Of course, there was no answer. "Please," she said when she heard the message, "please let me explain. I have so much to tell you. And I *do* love you. I'm in love with you."

She hit the "end call" button and stopped dead on the sidewalk. It shouldn't have surprised her to say those words. After all, they'd been chasing through her waking thoughts for days now. But voicing them somehow made them real, changed the game. A game she might've just lost. *I do love you.* She leaned against the building on the corner, her hands on her knees, out of breath. She'd never run a marathon, or had a panic attack, but this felt like both of those wrapped in one. She realized she was shaking. *What should I do? I don't know what to do.* This couldn't be happening, none of this could be happening. The M104 came into view around the bend on Broadway, and she walked toward the bus stop. There was only one place to go.

"I don't want a cold compress!" Erin swatted Nat's hand away and let her head fall onto the back of the couch. It seemed there shouldn't be any more tears left in her, but still they came.

"Your eyes are a mess. This will help."

Kendra took the wet cloth and shooed Nat away, sitting down next to Erin and gently applying it to her eyes. "Hush, baby. Just sit here quietly, please, for a few minutes."

"I don't sit quietly."

"She doesn't," Nat said.

Erin took her phone out of her pocket without moving the cloth from her eyes or Kendra's hand from rubbing her arm and handed it to Nat. "Look at the photo gallery. I got a lot of shots of paper applications from her files, although who knows why they still use those."

Nat took the phone and moved uneasily in her chair. "Thing is, she may not be involved."

Erin jerked her head up, and the cloth went flying into her lap. "What?"

"You know that interview I had today with Jack?"

Erin just stared at her, and Nat fiddled with Erin's phone. "He said they all passed clients to her. To get them off their desk. You know, right after this began. The junior guys gave her the dot clients looking to buy and took rentals off her hands because they all knew she hated rentals. They don't amount to enough money for her. And they all just let her continue using the original lease application. None of them told her about form A gets the black dot, form B gets the brown dot."

"Marquita said the same thing. But she had forms with dots. I don't understand."

"Yeah, some of the guys goofed and didn't clean up their files before giving them to her, including Jack, and when she asked him about the code, he told her the different letters and dots were how the junior guys kept track of their financials. She bought it." Nat twisted some of her dreadlocks around her fingers. "They didn't tell the boss they gave them to her because he didn't want her in on this. He figured she wouldn't go along. The guys were trying to get her fired because her numbers were always awesome, and she made them look bad. Although how they thought that would work is beyond me. Meanwhile they could legitimately keep people like me out if even one white person saw the apartment ahead of me, and not lose their jobs." Nat handed Erin's phone back to her. "When Jack realized his numbers were that low, he panicked and sold to the Muslim couple and got fired. The boss hung it on a complaint from a prospective buyer to cover it up."

"That's wrong. That should be part of the story."

"It will be. But there's more. Jack was right. Catherine sold an apartment to a dot couple in a seriously upscale building on Riverside. Today."

"So that's good! She's *not* involved."

Nat nodded. "She could get fired and not know why."

"No!"

"I don't know," Nat said. "I'm waiting for Marquita to let me know what happens tomorrow."

"God. What if I cost her the career she loves?" Erin sobbed and let her head fall back onto the couch.

"Look, I want you to stay here tonight," Kendra said, putting the cold cloth over her eyes.

Erin batted the cloth away. "I can't. Lincoln. Plus, I have to finish listening to all my messages."

"What's goin' on with that?"

"Anika posted that stupid canvas of mine from the Biennial to her Instagram."

"So?"

Erin took the tissue Kendra offered and blew her nose. "Somehow, Jasper Johns found it and liked it."

"Are you kidding me?" Kendra asked.

Erin shook her head. "Galleries and people I never heard of, and some I *have* heard of, are calling me."

"This is great!" Nat said. "You have to do something about this!"

Erin looked at her. "I just lost Catherine." She stood up and picked up her bag. "I just screwed up the best thing that might ever have happened to me. The only thing I *have* to do is figure out how to get her back." Erin walked out of their apartment and took the bus back uptown past her stop, past the dark windows of Sumter Realty, and got off at Ninety-Sixth Street to walk the several blocks to Catherine's apartment. She wanted to ring her bell but settled on the steps of a brownstone across the street instead.

Everything inside her felt empty. Why hadn't she quit the story? *I couldn't quit something so important to Nat, so fundamentally wrong.* So why hadn't she waited to start something with Catherine? Because, as usual, she'd seen something she'd wanted and gone ahead, damn the consequences. She had no one to blame but herself, and she knew it. She pulled out her cell phone and scrolled through all the photos of Catherine that she'd taken over the weekend. Would they be all she had left of her? She grabbed at the collar of her shirt and wiped at the tears that started to come again. Crap, how many tears could one human body make at one time?

She called Catherine and spoke to her voice mail again. "I need to talk to you. Please. Please let me in. I'm across the street. Just give me another—" Before she could say the word "chance," Catherine's phone cut her off. Or had she answered and hung up? She called right back but got the "you have been forwarded" recording. Catherine had turned off her phone, not something she did lightly considering it was her lifeline to her clients. Erin took out her sketchbook and settled back against the step. There was enough light from the bulb over the front door. She could wait.

At around three in the morning, she went to the bodega on the corner for a cup of coffee and ended up getting one of those horrible pastries in plastic factory wrappers of indeterminate identification that no New Yorker ever buys. She'd never eaten cardboard before, but aside from the splotch of red goo in the center, that's what she imagined cardboard tasted like. By ten o'clock, there was still no sign of Catherine. Erin couldn't imagine that she wouldn't go to her office, but she had to go home and feed Lincoln. Returning at four o'clock, she decided, would be a pretty safe bet.

Nat wasn't happy that Erin wasn't coming over to make dinner.

"Use leftovers. Besides, you're writing the article now. My work is done, isn't it?"

"I need your help editing."

"Tomorrow at eleven." She listened half-heartedly to the rest of the messages, unable to get excited about the surreal turn with her art when her love life had gone down the drain. She made a list, though, of people to call back eventually.

It went on that way for several more days. Erin even stood across Broadway watching Sumter Realty several times during the day, going back downtown to work with Nat and coming back uptown again. No sign of Catherine anywhere. Not at six a.m. Not at eleven p.m. Nor at seven thirty in the morning or anywhere between six and nine at night. Or, quite frankly, ever. Oddly, she didn't see

Marquita at Sumter, either, although she cared less about that. But Marquita hadn't been in touch with Nat, either, which was strange.

At night, she lay in bed looking up at the ceiling, reliving almost every minute of the last two months, of falling in love when she hadn't expected to with someone she shouldn't have. Lincoln curled up beside her, his protective paw on her arm. Her only small solace: with the arrival of September, she could turn off the air conditioner at night and open the windows. She felt like she was adrift in a dinghy in the middle of a big ocean with no North Star visible.

Finally, one morning she picked up her sketchbook and went to the Met. Steve's cart was already snugged in between the taco truck and the gelato guy. The roller bars held a full count of fragrant roasting hot dogs, and Steve had stacked buttered rolls beside the grill, waiting to be toasted.

"Long time no see, working girl!"

"Hey, Steve."

"Whoa, you don't sound too happy."

Erin sat in Steve's folding chair, her head falling to the back of it, and looked at the bright September sky.

"So, what do you need, a priest, a hitman or Dear Abby?"

"All three?"

"Oh, that's bad." He brought a thermos and a mug out of his cart and sat down beside her. "I got French roast. You want some?"

Erin held out her hand. Steve twisted open the handled cup thermos cap, poured the steaming coffee into the mug, and handed it to her. He poured a splash into the thermos cup.

"Who's first?" he asked.

"Dear Abby."

Steve nodded and Erin took him through the whole story of how Nat's articles brought her together with Catherine, even admitting that she'd fallen in love. Several times she had to stop while he attended to customers. Then, he was back in the chair, listening intently, sometimes nodding. When she finished, she sighed, looked at him, and said, "Sincerely, Lost in New York."

Steve rubbed his chin for a moment. "Dear Lost, unless you want him to take you out for being a bone-headed idiot, you don't want the hitman. As for the priest, I absolve you of being said bone-headed idiot. We all do stupid stuff in life. But rule of thumb, always trust your gut. You should've told her."

Erin nodded. "I know."

"But, in the 'Barn Door Open, Cow Gone' department, not sure what to tell ya, kid. I'm real sorry how this played out. I know that's not helpful."

Erin sat back and looked at the sky again.

"Listen, I got friends in the NYPD. I could ask about tracking her phone so you could find out where she is."

The sun now nearly overhead, Erin squinted at him. "Pretty sure we need probable cause for something like that."

Steve nodded. "Yeah, and I guess, a broken heart doesn't constitute breaking and entering."

"No," Erin said, watching an enormous fluffy white cloud way up above move slowly across the sky like a huge float in a parade.

"It should, though. Woman breaks your heart, there should be some jail time involved. You want a couple dogs and a Coke?"

"Yeah, I guess. Can I sit here and work?" Erin took out her sketchbook. She'd spotted a little girl sitting on the steps of the museum, involved in an animated discussion with her teddy bear, as her mother sat beside her talking on her cell phone. Even in her misery she found a moment of beauty.

"Yeah, sure. Stick around a while, we'll talk some more."

On the bus ride home that afternoon, it suddenly occurred to her. Catherine could've gone to Susan's apartment. So after she fed Lincoln, she took up a vigil across the street from that building, returning for several mornings and nights. Nothing.

Almost every day, Erin called and left Catherine a message. Always, it was almost the same message: "I *was* working for Nat. But I fell in love with you long before I told you I had. I need to talk to you. *We* need to talk. *Before* this story hits the internet." She began to feel like a stalker. How would she explain it to the police? *I broke her heart, so she broke mine, and now I'm just trying to pick up all the little pieces for both of us, and it's a time-consuming, hands-on job, as you can see.*

Throughout the insane vigil, Nat texted her constantly. But the article had been with Red for several days now, so there was no need for her to be anywhere with or for Nat. And she certainly didn't want her sympathy, her warnings, or her advice.

Then late one afternoon, Nat stepped off the bus on the corner of Broadway right where Erin was leaning against the building, her eye on Sumter Realty. Erin was beyond annoyed.

"C'mon. When's the last time you ate? I'm takin' you to the diner."

"No. I had a date there with her."

"I know. Let's go. I need to tell you something."

"Tell me here."

Nat eyed her. "She's not in the city. Let's go." Nat walked toward the diner.

"Wait, what? How do you know?" Erin followed her.

"I need a bacon cheeseburger. No one's been cooking at my house like they were hired to do."

"You can't just walk away!"

"Bacon cheeseburger."

Erin followed her, angry, peppering her with questions that Nat wouldn't answer until they were seated in the booth in the window. The exact same booth she'd sat in with Catherine.

"Look, I'm sorry about how angry and hurt you are."

"It's my own damn fault," Erin said quietly.

"That doesn't mean I can't help you figure things out, and that's what I came to do. To tell you I called Catherine. The second time, she called me back."

"When? Where is she?"

"She asked me not to tell you."

"Why?"

"Would you just zip it and listen? God, you're worse than me."

Erin sat back. The waiter appeared and Nat ordered two bacon cheeseburgers for them.

"After you left last Monday night, she went through her computer files to figure out what you and Marquita had been looking for. Plus, Marquita left open files on her credenza. She put it together and called Jack Hobbes. He told her everything. Alphabet letters, colored dots, everything. Then she called the two other top sales guys and they snowballed her. That was the tell. So she called her boss and quit."

"She what?"

"And she packed her bags and took off."

"But you won't tell me where? Or you don't know?"

"A little of both. I know where she's been but she's moving around." Nat shrugged. "She spends a couple days in one place, then goes somewhere else. And your calls are killing her."

"No." Erin didn't want to hear that.

"I'm sorry, Erin. She's really, really torn. You two kinda came together like colliding comets. She said she fell hard. But part of this *is* my fault. She feels really betrayed. And that *is* on me, because I asked you specifically not to tell her what we were doing so you didn't blow the article. And I apologized for that." Nat played with the spoon at her place setting, and Erin could tell by the way her body was moving that she was bouncing her knee beneath the table. She hated to be the cause of anxiety for Nat, but it touched her.

The waiter brought their plates, but she pushed hers away. Nat did, too.

"Look at me," Nat said.

Erin finally did.

"She was really glad I called. I filled her in on everything she didn't know, and she gave me some stuff for the article. There was less crazy emotion, so she could hear me out, and she understood why we were doing the article."

"I don't care about the article!"

Nat cocked her head and gave her what she called her stink-eye.

"Okay, I *do* care, just not now, not here."

"Thanks, asshole. She told me she misses you. Like, bad, awful misses you."

"What?" Erin was elated.

"But she can't be with you right now."

Erin put her head in her hands, crushed. She hated roller coasters.

"I told her why you did what you did, I told her that I pushed you. I told her you didn't want to when you realized you'd fallen for her. And I told her that your loyalty to me, and what you did to bring this article to life, had to count for something."

"Nothing counts for anything without her."

Nat twisted the button on her shirt, hard. "Erin, she left the door open. She told me she's coming back Friday night. Late. But I don't know what late means." Nat pulled her plate in and bit into her cheeseburger.

With that one bit of information, Erin was back on the roller coaster, a euphoria rising within her, hurtling her toward the top. She reached out and touched Nat's arm. "I'm sorry I almost screwed this up."

Nat wiped ketchup from her lips. "Who knew you were going to fall in love?"

Erin hoped there would be no cresting on the roller coaster this time, no ride down.

Chapter Twenty-three

Erin lay in bed watching the hands of the little clock on her nightstand tick past midnight. It was now officially Saturday. Catherine would be home. And, according to Kendra's plan, which Nat had seconded, she *hadn't* been there to meet her at her door and help her with her suitcases. The wisdom of what Kendra had proposed was irrefutable. But Erin had spent the day refuting it in her head anyway.

Let Catherine come to you. It was a sound plan. Give her the space she'd told Nat she needed, but let her know she was indelibly on Erin's mind. To that end, Erin had sent flowers to arrive in the afternoon. The card simply read "Erin." At the last minute, she'd slipped in a sketch she'd done of Catherine as she sat on the edge of the bed the morning after they'd first made love. Her back was to Erin, and she'd put her hair up in a bun. She'd turned to Erin ever so slightly, everything about her glowing, and Erin thought she'd never seen any woman so beautiful.

She sat up in bed. If sleep was elusive, she might as well get up and work. She went to the bathroom to splash cold water on her face and caught a look at herself in the mirror: she'd lost weight and her eyes had that hollow cast to them. Just as the hamster in her brain was climbing into his wheel for his nightly run, her phone dinged with an incoming text message.

Nat: *I know yr up. Kendra says come spend the day. bring those phone msgs about yr stupid painting, let's do something w/them*

It was a comfort to know that Nat was still up, too.

That stupid painting. And those damn phone messages. She wondered what life would've been like for the Impressionists if they'd had to deal with phone messages from dealers and buyers, the salons and hangers-on. Her sketchbook was leaning against the desk, and she flipped it open to a clean page and began roughing out a number of those ubiquitous pink forms that came on the small pads people used to use to write down messages.

Some of them she made to look like they were tacked to the drawing, some paper-clipped to it, or crumpled up on the bottom border but legible. Most lay haphazardly across the page, corners and partial phone numbers visible. The first message she made out to Monet from the Royal Academy. "We don't want your paintings, but thank you for taking the time to bring them in." One from Degas to Cezanne read, "The Impressionists are disbanding. Let's have dinner to discuss." The one at the center was from Le Figaro to Mary Cassatt thanking her for the free advertising of their paper in her painting and suggesting she let them make posters of it to put up around Paris. "We can give you one percent of our advertising revenue in exchange," the message concluded, "which is probably more than you'll get for the painting."

Erin worked until dawn, bringing out her colored pencils, giving depth, shade, and nuance to the slips of paper and the messages. There had been no vestiges of the usual fear or self-pity as she worked. And no thought of Catherine.

Erin rang Nat's buzzer at eight o'clock. The peephole opened a minute later.

"Jesus," Nat said, flipping the locks.

"No, just me. Go back to bed. I'm making pancakes and bacon and sausages for breakfast." Erin held up the grocery bags. "And for dinner, pulled pork, collard greens, and potato salad. Kendra said it would be okay, and I'm using her grandma's recipe from when her grandma taught me how to do this last summer. Slow cooker still in the bottom cupboard?"

"Yup."

"Good. This'll take a while to prep. Breakfast around ten. Don't worry, you can still make love to Kendra. I won't hear you over the mixer."

Nat snorted. "Too late, asshole. I rocked her world half an hour ago. She was just falling asleep in my arms."

"Oops. Sorry. Get back there, cowgirl. I'll call you when breakfast is served."

"You forgot to tell me what's on the menu for lunch." Nat leaned on the open door, a smirk on her face.

Erin rolled her eyes. "Warm turkey sandwiches with thin slices of cranberry jelly on a ciabatta with watercress and orange slice salad, and a panoply of fromages and grapes for dessert."

"Wow. You really *are* in pain."

"Fromage. French for stinky cheeses Nat won't like. All the more for you and me, Erin." Kendra appeared over Nat's shoulder, draping her arm over it and kissing Nat's ear. "You were out here so long I thought an encyclopedia salesman had gotten hold of you. Let her in."

Nat stepped aside and Erin swung the grocery bags through the door.

"Good God, did you buy out all of Whole Foods?"

"You two go back to the bedroom and let an artist take over your kitchen for the day."

Kendra grabbed Nat's hand. "Don't have to ask me twice."

Erin unpacked the groceries and put everything away, riffling the cupboards for the ingredients she'd need for the pulled pork. She got out the slow cooker, sliced up a Vidalia onion and some garlic, and spread the slices around the bottom of the pot. As she worked, her mind wandered and bumped right into Marquita. Nat had finally told her she'd been let go from Sumter Realty that next morning. Apparently, the boss had called it a cost-cutting necessity. She felt guilty and wondered if there wasn't something she and Nat could do to make it right.

"Not our fault," Nat had said. "She knew the risks."

But in a way, it was their fault. She cut deep slices into the pork butt and shoved slivers of garlic into them.

Erin found the bourbon on the shelf above the refrigerator, poured a cup into a large Ziploc bag, and dropped the meat in and massaged it for a couple of minutes, rolling the bag over and over to work the liquid in. Nat must know someone who could at least give Marquita a temp job. She loaded the brown sugar, mustard, ketchup, cider vinegar, and barbecue sauce over the onions and garlic in the pot and concocted the rub from among Nat's spices.

After patting the rub onto the wet pork, she put it in the cooker, poured some of the bourbon around it, and put it on low.

There was a half-full pot of coffee sitting on the coffee maker. Erin touched it. Cold. She poured it into a small saucepan and put it on a burner. She and Nat were probably the only two people left in New York who didn't own microwaves. And that suited her just fine. She wasn't a tin-hat nut job; she simply didn't like them. There was something so much nicer about the aroma of slowly warming food on a stove.

Washing the dishes to make room for cooking breakfast next, she thought of Catherine giving her popcorn pot a quick scrubbing the night they'd watched the movie together. That seemed like a lifetime ago. Erin had wanted to curl that ponytail around her hand and kiss her hard. She wanted to do that now, wanted to tell her that opening herself up had laid something bare in her, sliced right through the veneer of her canvas to get at the heart of her, touched those feelings she'd buried under meaningless relationships, leaving her vulnerable and wanting. Bracing her hands on the sink, Erin fought the tears. This feeling of desolation wasn't one she wore well. She wanted to walk right out of here and go to her.

Instead, she poured the coffee into a mug, took a cotton rag from an old nightshirt out of her back pocket and wet it down, and squeezed it nearly dry. Then she picked up a small bag from the Blick art supply store that she'd left inside one of the grocery bags and went to the little room she used as a studio. There were several different-sized cast-off canvases leaning against the walls, all of them dusty. She chose a small one, dusted it, wiped it with the damp cloth and searched around until she found an old piece of fine sandpaper. It didn't take long to smooth the canvas over. Particles of old paint speckled the floor in the process; she hadn't thought to put down a tarp. Luckily, she still had the doormat in the corner of the room. She never wanted to track anything through the apartment. She wiped the canvas again, put it on the easel, and opened the gesso primer. She reached into the bag for a new wide brush. When she was finished, she put a small fan on the canvas. It would need a second coat of primer, but this painting couldn't wait.

Back in the kitchen, she set up the coffee maker for a fresh pot, mixed the pancake batter and got to work. When she was setting the table, Nat and Kendra appeared.

"Do I smell paint?" Kendra asked.

"God, I hope not," Nat said. "I don't want a side of that with my pancakes."

"Sorry. I just primed a canvas. The windows in there are open, though, and I have a fan on it."

"Oh." Kendra and Nat looked at each other.

When they'd finished breakfast, Erin told them to go do whatever they wanted, but to leave the kitchen to her. She cleaned up and went back to the studio. The canvas was dry, so she very gently sanded it, grateful that sandpaper never went bad. She'd spent more at the art store than she could really afford. Money was a worry that she had to face again. She had one more paycheck coming from the website and one more week with Nat and Kendra. She'd been able to set aside some money, and was considering asking Nat what she thought about approaching Red for something more permanent. But when it came to art supplies, she still bought only the best. The second coat of primer went on quickly and she sat next to the fan as it blew on it. *I am literally watching paint dry. I have hit a new low.*

She hadn't thought to bring the speaker for her phone and she hated how tinny it sounded without amplification, so she went in search of Nat's boom box. The shelves by her old stereo unit had a ton of music on them, nothing conducive to the feelings she was wrestling with. Until she came across Vivaldi's *Four Seasons.* She could hardly believe Nat had the one piece of classical music that had been haunting her for days. Catherine had played it as they'd driven through Westchester and into New York City that Sunday night.

Although she hardly needed to make a thumbnail sketch of what she was going to paint, she had to occupy herself while she waited for the second coat of primer to dry. She took out her large sketchbook and set about penciling the spare lines that would make up Catherine's back and head. When she'd finished that, she pulled her small book out of her back pocket, turned to the drawing of the funny-looking guy she'd made in the Met several weeks ago, and began translating that to the large paper. By the time she was satisfied with how it looked, the canvas was dry. She sanded it once more, wiped it clean, picked up the fan to move around on it for a minute or so, and then picked up a long, thin charcoal to begin bringing Catherine to life. She had done this drawing so many times now that her hand flowed over the canvas, through the curves and the dips and the circles, leaving off in mid-stroke for the strands of hair, or the hint of muscle, as though her hands were gliding over Catherine's body like they had the first night she made love to her.

She picked up the tube of black oil paint and squeezed a large splotch of it onto the piece of wood she used as a palette, then drew the palette knife through it to smooth it out. Lining up the new linseed oil, turpentine, and resin bottles made her feel good, a little like being back in the haven of her favorite art studio at school. The last thing in the bag was the new set of red sable brushes, each a different size. She dribbled some linseed oil into the black paint and dragged the knife through it like she was icing a cake, mixing it until it had just the right elasticity and pull, and dipped her brush in it. She drew it over the sketchbook paper first before daring to touch it to the canvas. Her first stroke, a broad one, didn't please her. She opened the turpentine and shook a few drops into the black paint to thin it. Several more strokes, and it felt right, so she followed the charcoal map until Catherine was there. Then she mixed the resin into the paint. It had been a long time since she'd mixed that into any color, but it was muscle memory. As soon as she brushed it on, the ethereal shine she was looking for that appeared in certain light and at certain angles gleamed in the sunlight.

She was completely lost in her work until the cell phone alarm went off. She silenced it, working until she knew she had what she wanted. Then she cleaned her brushes and was sealing all the bottles when Kendra knocked. "Do you want me to take care of lunch while you work?

"No, I was just coming out to the kitchen."

"Can I take a look?"

Erin stepped aside and Kendra came around the easel to see the painting in the light. A long moment passed while she considered it. "It's beautiful. Very spare. You've never done anything like this."

Erin wiped off her brushes. "I don't think I've ever felt anything like what I'm feeling now."

Kendra hugged her. "I think it's going to be okay."

"I'll go make lunch," Erin said. "Then I'm gonna go home and feed Lincoln. I'll be back later."

Kendra put her hand on Erin's shoulder, but she was looking at the drawing of all the pink phone messages Erin had tacked to the wall. "Oh my God, when did you do this?"

"Last night. I think I was pissed off."

"It's perfect. Can I have it? Oh, wait, that's rude. Are you making a painting of it?"

"It's yours. Are you kidding me? For everything you guys have done for me? I'll give you the painting, too, when I do it. And I can change it for you. You know, a message from Martha Graham to Agnes De Mille saying *Oklahoma* was inspired, or from Mother Russia to Isadora Duncan telling her it's time to come home."

Kendra snorted a laugh. "No, I like this. It came from the heart, didn't it?"

It had come from the heart, it was true. Lately, it seemed like her best work came from moments of unguarded emotion.

When Erin got home, there was a message on her landline from Daniel. He wanted to buy the "stupid painting," as she and Nat were now calling the ruined canvas from the Biennial, for Nikki's birthday. She'd not had any time to talk to Nat about the research she'd already done, contacting all the gallery owners who'd called her, fielding offers, talking about their collectors who were suddenly interested in the work that had once spelled her demise in the art world. She knew she wanted to sell it to Daniel because she liked him. But she knew she ought to do it through a gallery owner who was going to be her ally as she embarked on this new path she'd discovered with her line drawings. Gallerists tended to be more hands-on with an artist's career trajectory because they were also invested in it. While she was a pretty good judge of people, Nat was better. She wanted her to meet them with her, talk with them, use her no-nonsense interviewing skills to drive to the heart of which one would be the most supportive.

Over dinner that night, Erin proposed her plan to Nat. Of course Nat said she'd help her choose the right person to represent her work. They laughed about the legend of the "stupid painting," but in truth, Erin saw it as her Everest. She knew selling the canvas to Daniel had been the right thing to do. He'd wanted it. But she still felt raw, finally letting it go. People would see it in his home. People of consequence. Would they laugh behind his back? Or would they think he knew something they didn't? Either way, it would be a vindication. It would finally signal her worth, if only to herself. And that would be like summiting the mountain and planting her flag. A lightheadedness hit her, like she imagined mountain climbers felt when they reached a certain point of ascension and needed oxygen. She floated on it as they continued to talk.

Sunday morning, Erin was back in Nat's kitchen. But she came early to work on the canvas of the guy in the Met first, spending several hours with it, touching up the soft dark lines, widening them here, thinning them there, honing his laser eyes. She stood back at one point and stared at it critically. Something was missing. She picked up her charcoal pencil, drew a soft line from his pencil to his sketchbook, and drew in the figure he'd been drawing as though it was reaching out of his book to touch his pencil. She knew it was clichéd, but for now, she would let it sit and think about it. It amused her, spoke to her.

Nat, Kendra, and Erin sat over a brunch of French toast and another watercress salad talking about the success of Kendra's show, and Nat's worries about her series of articles. It would hit the website Monday, just after midnight.

"Nobody's going to read it. Or if they do, they won't pay attention to it. It'll come and go, with no reaction." Nat shook her head.

"I don't think so," Kendra said.

But Erin was elsewhere. Something had come together in her in the last few days. She felt the edges of peace spilling in like the infusion of sun through the clouds in Monet's *Houses of Parliament* paintings. She felt strength just picking up her brushes, a renewal with each brushstroke. And in the background the whole time, Catherine, like the heartbeat that kept her alive.

Chapter Twenty-four

Erin pushed her cart through Fairway taking in all the mounds of fruit, the barrels of olives, endless cases of cheeses from everywhere in the world, and bins of potatoes. It was at once an assault on the senses and a thing of beauty, soft-core grocery porn. Her particular favorite was the wall of olive oils. There were tasting cups in front of each bottle that had been selected from a particular shelf in the wall. Little plastic boxes of bread pieces were placed every foot or so for dipping and tasting. Usually, Erin had to taste a few of them. It would be rude not to.

But tonight, she wasn't interested. She didn't even feel like swiping any pieces of baguette to chew on as she rolled up and down the aisles. She loved this store, and never got used to the sight of such bounty, no matter how often she stopped here each week. At eleven o'clock on a Sunday night, she had the place to herself and usually loved taking her time wandering around looking at things, having no idea what to do with half of them, but not tonight. Kendra had asked her to stay on for another week while she came down from the month at the Joyce, and she wanted to get the shopping done and get home. She picked up a jar of Moroccan preserved lemons, read the ingredients and put it back. No idea.

With the recipe for a vegetable gratin casserole that she and Kendra had come up with in her hand, she made her way to the produce section and began picking through the zucchini looking for the best ones. There were so many vegetables in this dish that she figured she'd be here a while, but marketing was her favorite errand, so it wouldn't be a hardship by any means. It always took her mind off everything. Maybe she'd forget about the last two weeks while she picked through mushrooms, green beans, and tomatoes.

The last item, a small eggplant, was in her hand when she looked up to see Catherine staring at her from across the pyramid of beefsteak tomatoes.

When the blood singing in her ears finally waned, she put the eggplant in her cart and braced herself for a hurricane.

"Hi," Catherine said.

No hurricane. Not even any gale-force winds. "Hi."

"That's a lot of vegetables."

"I'm cooking for Nat and Kendra again." She noticed the basket over Catherine's arm contained a bottle of red wine, a small box of crackers, and one lonely piece of what looked like smoked Gouda cheese in its brown wax lining. "I hope that's not tomorrow night's dinner."

Catherine looked at the basket. "I'm not really eating a lot lately."

They looked at each other over the tomatoes. Those blue eyes seemed to hold a question Erin didn't want to guess at, but she knew she had to answer it with something before Catherine decided to leave. She had never desired someone so much in her life. "Why don't we get some baby Swiss, some bacon and," she picked up a big fat, squat tomato, "and I'll make you a grilled cheese, bacon, and tomato sandwich."

"You would?"

"I'd like to."

Catherine looked down at the floor.

"We will never figure this out if we don't talk," Erin said quietly.

"We did a lot of talking, as I recall." Catherine finally looked up at Erin. "Even with everything that Nat told me, I still feel like you took me apart."

So that was it. Deep melancholy following the hurricane she'd been at the office. Erin understood melancholy. "You took me apart, too."

"I did?"

Erin rolled her cart a little closer to Catherine, hopeful. "I didn't expect to find a woman who understood me, who was willing to take a chance on me, and who gave me all of herself when I held out my hand."

"I think it was more that white teddy that you wore. You were irresistible in it."

Erin inched her cart forward again. "Everything about you is irresistible to me. I didn't expect to fall in love with you, but I did. I can't undo that."

"Then, why?"

"I had a responsibility to Nat. And to the series she's doing. But you have to know, what I did to you? It killed me."

Neither of them moved.

"Look, the first article comes out at midnight tonight. You should read it."

Catherine made no move, so Erin turned her cart to go. A hurricane would've been so much more humane than this knife Catherine seemed to be slowly slipping between her ribs.

"What if I *had* been one of them?"

Erin turned to look at her. "But you weren't. And I knew it, really, but I had to bring proof to Nat. One way or another."

"It still hurts that you couldn't trust me. I thought we knew each other."

"Catherine, I couldn't have trusted my own mother in this case."

"Then Nat was right."

"About what?"

"Your loyalty."

"I would do anything for her."

"Yes, she said that. She also said that eventually that would change. That one day, you would choose me over her."

Erin's stomach dropped several flights. Why would Nat say such a thing?

"I don't have any bread in the apartment," Catherine said. "You can't make grilled cheese without it." She took a few tentative steps around the pyramid.

"We should go to the bakery."

They headed up the aisle together, glancing at each other.

"Sourdough," Erin said as they stood looking at all the different breads. "It will support the smoke of the Gouda."

"I'll trust you." Catherine looked at her solemnly.

Erin met her gaze. *It's a start.* Everything behind the counters smelled wonderful, rich, yeasty, and she realized that for the first time in days, something appealed to her.

At the register, Catherine put her four items on the conveyor belt and then began unloading Erin's cart.

"Wait. Put up that little divider thingie."

Catherine shook her head. "I'm buying."

"No, I have money from Nat. These are really her groceries."

Catherine shook her head again. "I have to thank her. So I'm buying."

"Thank her for what?" Erin thought she saw a ghost of a smile.

"For calling me last week."

She decided not to fight it. Whatever Catherine wanted, she'd get.

Neither of them said anything as they walked down West 93rd Street, Erin rolling her little marketing cart behind her. As Catherine unlocked her apartment door, Erin couldn't resist touching the trompe l'oeil beach roses, half-expecting to smell their sweet fragrance. They brought her right back to those few nights in paradise. Would she and Catherine make it back to that emotional place? Or was Catherine just bringing her here to kiss her off instead? Catherine offered to put some of Erin's things in the refrigerator.

"It's just grilled cheese. I won't be here that long. That stuff will be fine."

She got out everything Erin would need to cook, including a bottle of water for each of them, and sat down to watch. "You like to cook."

Erin chopped up two slices of bacon and put them in the small cast iron skillet. "It's a creative process. Like painting. Or selling."

"Selling isn't creative. It's just hustling."

"Have you forgotten the washer/dryer?" She caught Catherine's blush as she sliced through the fat center of the tomato and cut eight tissue-thin slices from it, piling them on the corner of the cutting board.

"I haven't forgotten anything." Catherine's voice was low, soft.

"I haven't either." Erin took a small piece of bacon out of the skillet, blew on it to cool it, and put it in Catherine's mouth. Her surprise was evident; she caught Erin's hand, and held it a moment longer than she needed to, and it was Erin who reluctantly broke the moment, turning to open both cheeses, carving thin slivers from them to arrange on each half of each slice of bread, layering and mixing Swiss with Gouda.

"What are we going to do?" Catherine asked.

"For starters," Erin said, looking at Catherine's wall clock, "we're going to read Nat's first article." She lay the halves of the sandwich into the big pan that sizzled with butter, tossed the tomatoes on top of each half, and sprinkled the bacon pieces all over them. She opened the small bottle of thyme she'd found on Catherine's spice shelf and put a smattering on the sandwich. Then she cut two small pieces of Swiss and Gouda, and put those into Catherine's mouth, her face so close to hers this time that she could've kissed her. Erin's hand was on Catherine's thigh, and Catherine covered it with hers. Erin wanted to stand there forever. Instead, she handed her the bottle of wine.

"We'll read the article. And then we'll talk." Erin set a slice of tomato in front of her. "I think you want to try again as much as I do, or you wouldn't have waited for me to notice you." Erin saw that question again in her eyes, the one she'd seen in the market. Since she was now standing in Catherine's kitchen, she hoped she'd answered it. But here it was again, and it puzzled her.

The cheeses bubbled on the sourdough, the kitchen smelling of them and the bacon, so Erin plated the sandwich and put it in front of Catherine.

"Oh, my God, where did you learn to make this?" Cheese dripped out the sandwich onto her plate after she bit into it, and a crumb of bacon stuck at the corner of her mouth.

Erin dabbed the crumb away with her thumb. "Girlfriend number twenty-four was a chef."

"I had no idea I'd taken on Casanova. Didn't you say Nat's article is out now? Let's go get my laptop and read it on that."

They hunched over the counter looking at the screen. Catherine put the sandwich down as they read. "I still can't believe what I'm reading. Or that I chose to believe Jack and some of those other junior agents." She pointed at the screen.

"So you did suspect."

"I knew they were up to something, but I thought it had to do with commissions, not this. So I was out there trying to outsell them."

"I got the sense you weren't in the office a lot. And we think by your not being part of it, it's your boss's legal out. If everyone wasn't in on it, it wasn't fixed. I have to take a bite of that sandwich."

Catherine handed her the other half and they read some more.

"Marquita really brought this to you?"

"Yes. She's a friend of Nat and Kendra's. She overheard everything in a meeting one afternoon when the guys asked her to bring in coffee. So she went through the files and called Nat a couple days later."

Catherine looked right at her. "Marquita is just a friend?"

Erin closed her eyes. "I thought I had a thing for her. We had a one-night stand. The thing was cured."

"When?"

"Way before you. And the morning after, when it was apparent we didn't really mean anything to each other, it was over for me."

"But maybe not for her."

"It was over," Erin said quietly. Catherine looked away and Erin panicked. Had she lost her before she had her back?

"She was fired the next day."

"Nat told me." Erin prepared for the hurricane that hadn't happened in the market because Catherine was going to unleash it here instead. Then she felt those familiar fingers in her hair.

"Not your fault."

"Yeah, it kind of is."

"No. Don't even think twice about it."

Catherine's voice was gentle and soft, but Erin detected that this might be that cold side of Catherine that Marquita had talked of, that even Jack Hobbes had spoken to Nat about in the interview. She grasped Catherine's hand. "Okay, that bothers me. That's not you. At least, not the you I think I got to know."

"You mean the me you thought was a racist?" Catherine's gaze leveled her.

"No! I didn't think that!"

"I'm yanking your chain here. But you shouldn't think twice about it."

"How can you tell me that when Marquita lost her job for blowing a whistle on something that was terribly wrong?"

"It's business, Erin. I know that sounds cold and that it's a little hard for you to believe because you live in a different world, I think. But it's always business. You had a job to do and you did it. Nat did hers, you did yours."

"And Marquita gets chewed up in the process."

"It happens. And she knew it could happen. Sometimes you pay a price you didn't see at the bottom of the tab. So you have to be careful about what you choose to do. It can be hard to pay the piper. But for what it's worth, I absolutely think she did the right thing."

"Would you have done what she did?"

"Honestly? I don't know what I would've done. Left for another company? I don't know. I do know that what she did was pretty damn brave. And that she was lucky to have friends like you and Nat."

Erin drummed her fingers on the counter. "Friends who wrecked her life."

"No. You underestimate her. She's a very smart girl, you know. She'd good with numbers. She's good with people. She's fast on her feet. Intuitive, adaptable, likable. She's going to land on her feet."

"You sound so certain."

"I sent her to Nikki."

"What?

"Not for Nikki to hire. I'm sorry, but I couldn't go there after finding out you two slept together. But Nikki knows everyone in this city. So, a couple of days after I quit, I called Marquita. And I apologized."

"What?"

"We talked. I realized what dire straits she was in, and I called Nikki. Marquita will be okay."

Erin had to sit down on the other stool at the counter. She hadn't seen this coming at all. And she wanted to grab Catherine's face in her hands and kiss her.

"I'm not a racist. And I'm not the cold-hearted bitch the men at the office think I am," Catherine said. "I have to be a good fencer and a locomotive to do what I do every day, to achieve the kind of sales I do and fend off the men I work with who want to take it away from me. So, not very many people know who I really am because I can't always let them see that. But you…" Catherine put her hand on Erin's arm. "You saw right through all of that. From the very first day. You came out of left field and you walked away with everything I had to give." She shut the computer. "I'm not sure I can read the rest of this right now. But I do want to read it. And I want to read it with you. Only I have to go to the bathroom right now and I suspect you want to go home with all your vegetables."

Erin wanted to say no, she didn't, she didn't want to do anything of the sort, she wanted to talk some more, but Catherine had already walked out of the kitchen. So she turned to the dirty dishes. Her head swam as she wrapped up the cheeses and bacon, going over everything that had just happened in the last several hours. Putting the dishes in the sink with soapy water, she didn't know if she should kill Nat or thank her tomorrow. She reached for the dish towel to start drying the ones in the drain board. What could be taking Catherine so long? Out of the corner of her eye she caught something and turned to see her standing in the doorway, an open navy blue lace robe barely skimming her knees. Her breath caught. There was nothing underneath the robe and Erin almost dropped the plate in her hand.

"I don't want you to go home with all your vegetables."

Erin shook her head. "I don't want to go home with them, either."

Catherine came around her, opened the refrigerator, and lifted the large bags into it. "Good thing I didn't have much of anything in here."

Erin, rooted to the spot, simply nodded.

Catherine took her hand and led her down the long hallway she'd seen the night they watched the movie, the hallway she'd wanted to take Catherine down that night. When they reached the bedroom, Erin saw the candles, smelled the bayberry, and realized the covers of the bed were drawn back. Catherine reached for the hem of her polo shirt, and this time, she undressed Erin. And like that first night, when her hands had measured Catherine's body like she was putting her on a canvas, Catherine's hands lingered in places on Erin's body that set her on fire. She wanted to touch Catherine back, but sensed she should wait.

When Erin was completely naked, she pushed the robe off Catherine's shoulders, watched it pool at her feet, and then lay down on her bed. Catherine lay next to her and caressed every inch of skin she could reach. Erin grasped the bars of the Mission oak headboard behind her to steady herself and give Catherine access to whatever she wanted. And she took it, with her lips, with her hands, with her tongue. Erin trembled, on the verge of an orgasm, her skin cruelly teased by the cool night air coming in the window.

"Are you cold?"

Erin nodded, Catherine drew the covers up and disappeared beneath them. Moments later, Erin could've flung them off for the heat that suddenly shot through her body and shook her. She wasn't sure if she intoned a need for God or Catherine, but Catherine materialized beside her, took her into her arms, and kissed her. Everything that had gone wrong in the last several weeks seemed to fall away in that instant, and release flooded through her body. Erin felt tears, and realized they were hers.

Catherine kissed them. "No tears, my love."

"I thought I'd lost you."

"I thought the same."

"That I'd lost you?"

"That *I'd* lost *you*."

"We were both right."

"And I was wrong. I should've let you explain. Nat told me you wanted to tell me while we were on the Cape."

Erin turned to look at her. "She did?"

Catherine brushed the hair from her forehead that had matted there in the sheen of sweat from their lovemaking. "Yes."

"What else did Nat tell you?"

"That you'd be at Fairway tonight at about eleven."

"What the—"

"She called me when you left her apartment." Catherine slid both hands down Erin's back, grasping her bottom, pulling her as close as she possibly could. Erin closed her eyes, that luscious sensation of Catherine's soft warm skin on hers and her breasts pressing into her overwhelming her. "Had a heck of a time explaining to the manager at Fairway that I wasn't shoplifting but waiting for a friend."

"No, you didn't."

"I did." Catherine rubbed her nose to Erin's. "After half an hour, wouldn't you be suspicious of someone walking around with three items in their basket? I mean, the store's big but it's not that big on a dead Sunday night."

Erin caressed Catherine's cheek. "I can't believe you did that."

"So you see why I bought Nat's groceries tonight."

"We *could* take her and Kendra out to dinner, you know."

"We will. When we get back from Key West."

"What?"

"I'd like to take you away for a couple of days. I think we still have some healing to do, some more talking."

"I think you did some pretty good talking just now, under the covers." Erin ran a finger over her lips.

Catherine chuckled, but then Erin's hand found one of her nipples and the sound became a short moan.

"Now it's my turn to talk," Erin said. She kissed Catherine, and then slid under the covers.

Chapter Twenty-five

Erin heard her phone ringing in her shorts pocket and threw back the covers. She turned to see Catherine just waking up, stretching, such a sensuous sight that she almost rolled over on top of her.

"You'd better get that. It's not the first time this morning that it's rung."

"Why didn't you wake me up?"

"You looked too peaceful. And we both needed more sleep."

Erin looked at the clock on the nightstand. Eleven o'clock. The last time she'd noticed it, Catherine had just surprised her by handing her a gel dildo and a tube of warming lubricant from that same nightstand drawer. It was four o'clock, the midnight black fading to dark gray, and she was pretty sure they played for another hour while she learned what pleased Catherine with the soft, pliable cock.

Erin grabbed her phone, which had stopped ringing, and checked the calls and her messages. They were all from Nat, all of them in the last hour, and she panicked as she quickly pressed the phone icon that connected her.

"Hey! Are you okay? Is Kendra okay?"

"Where are you? I called your apartment, I called your cell, like, ten times—"

"Are you *okay*?"

"Yeah! Turn on your TV. The Manhattan DA is talking about the arrests he made at Sumter Realty a couple of hours ago with the *FBI.* They called Red at seven o'clock this morning about my article. They wanted my notes and everything."

"That's way fast!" She mouthed to Catherine to turn on the TV.

"Apparently the guy who owns it is on their wanted list, and when his name popped up in my articles in their computer system, it kicked the door open to getting him."

"You're on the map!"

"I just hope the shit he had in play doesn't get buried under the other stuff. It needs to be seen because it was more than just him."

"It will be. You have three more articles coming. And I bet the story will be picked up by all the media outlets."

"Well, it already blew up this morning when the broadcast stories hit the air, but it's all been about him. His racist tactics at Sumter are turning out to be secondary."

Erin thought for a moment and remembered what Catherine had said last night about how she had to be to get what she wanted. "Then find out who at the *Times* and the *Washington Post* and the *Chicago Tribune* and the other big papers reports on race relations and send them a link to your article. It's going on in their cities, too, don't you think? It has to be. Blow the whole damn real estate market open and let's see what's underneath. Link to the magazines with big online presences. And what about other journalists? Will they just pick it up or do you have to flag them?"

"I think I have to talk to Red. He'll know the best direction to take. He already texted that we're beating out the financial section of the site today on numbers, so he's very happy. Hey, where are you, anyway? Why didn't you answer when I called earlier?"

Catherine, now in a fluffy white terry robe tied at the waist, kissed the back of Erin's neck. "If that's Nat, tell her I said hello. I'm going to make breakfast since we now have bacon to go with the eggs in my fridge, and that incredible sourdough bread." She walked out of the bedroom trailing a scent of cherries and sex.

"You're not!" Nat said.

"I am," Erin replied.

Nat laughed. "It worked!"

"Yes, it worked, you little weasel. So, thank you."

"Well, Kendra told me I needed to make it right. And as usual, she knew best."

"She always knows best. You scored, marrying her, my friend." Erin opened Catherine's closet door looking for a robe to wear.

"I think you have, too."

"Let's not jinx it. But hey, I need to know if you can take care of Lincoln again in a few days."

"Where you goin'?"

"Catherine wants to go to Key West." Erin ran her hand over the suits and shirts in the closet.

Nat chuckled. "That's not just a score, cowgirl. I think you busted the filly."

"Shut up."

"Yes, I can hang out with your cat. You still coming down for dinner tonight, considering you have all my groceries?"

"Yes, I'll be there around four. And I'm bringing a guest."

Nat was still laughing when they hung up.

Erin found a large oversized white shirt, and put it on. It came to her knees and she had to roll up the sleeves several times. The smell of bacon drew her out to the kitchen. "I didn't know you once dated Paul Bunyan," she said, holding her arms out to show the sleeves flopping over her fingertips.

Catherine laughed. "Aren't you a sight for sore eyes."

"Considering how little sleep we got, our eyes should be sore." She plunked down on a stool and Catherine set breakfast in front of them and poured mugs of coffee.

"This should help."

Erin breathed it in and then took a tiny sip as they watched the news together.

They ate in silence. Erin could see the TV from where she sat and watched again the new footage of the FBI takedown of Catherine's boss. It was surreal, knowing she'd played a part in it with Nat. That Nat had turned to her, needed her, and trusted her to do this with her said volumes about who and what they were to each other. It hadn't been easy for either one of them on many occasions. And it had been hard for Erin to come face-to-face with the casual discrimination Nat experienced in many situations that she either didn't see or didn't even recognize. It made her feel bereft that anyone would do that to another person, much less someone she loved.

Catherine got up to refill their coffee mugs and she watched her, almost in wonder. This moment, this woman, never would've happened to her if all of these circumstances hadn't come together around Nat's articles.

Catherine turned to her. "Can I ask you a delicate question?"

Erin wasn't sure she liked this. But she had to trust what was coming if they were building again. And she was pretty sure that's what they'd started doing last night. She nodded.

"When can I see your new paintings?"

Nat must've told her. Good Lord, telegraph, telephone, teleNat. What happened to keeping secrets, keeping silent for the sake of her article? Erin took in a deep breath. "How is tonight?"

"But aren't you going down to Nat's?"

"Yes. And guess who's coming to dinner?"

"Are you sure?"

"You wanted to thank her in person."

Catherine nodded, a shy smile appearing. "Yes, I did. I do."

Erin stood a little behind Catherine as she looked at the canvas of the young artist from the Met, all fluid black lines and waves, not a straight edge in sight. "I remember this, from your sketchbook. Yet, something is different. I can't put my finger on it."

"Well, that reviewer said I probably couldn't draw a straight line with a ruler. So I thought maybe I should prove her right."

"No, that's not it. There's a life here that wasn't in your original drawing."

"Oh." Erin reconsidered the canvas but wasn't sure she could be objective about it anymore.

"I like it." Catherine inhaled, held her breath a moment, and exhaled. "You should definitely show it to Nikki. You know she dabbles in managing."

"I found a gallery downtown. The owner is pretty well known and respected. She's going to put up a show of my work as soon as I have enough ready. And I think she'll be a good agent on my behalf."

Catherine nodded. "That's really good. Smart." She gazed at the picture again. "Well, we should get back out to the kitchen. They'll wonder what we're doing."

"No, they won't. There's something else I want you to see." Erin moved the painting off the easel and replaced it with the small one she'd done of Catherine. The sound she emitted was barely audible, but Erin heard it. She studied Catherine's face, her reaction, almost not wanting to know what she thought, but needing to know.

"You are not selling this one."

Erin didn't realize she'd been holding her breath until she let it out.

Catherine drew her fingers over the painting, tracing the lines, and Erin thought of her own hands learning Catherine's body that first night, the pure joy of exploring it last night when she thought she might never know it again.

Catherine tracked her finger over Erin's signature at the bottom of the canvas. "To think that I know the artist."

"Hey!" Nat called down the hall. "The oven just dinged!"

"I think she's calling for the chef." Catherine gazed at the painting again, and then put her arm around Erin's waist and led her out of the room. "Did Jasper Johns really like your painting on Anika's Instagram account?"

"The morning of Daniel's wedding. That's what her email was about. Well, one of the things her email was about." They walked down the hall. "He's how I found the gallery. He sent me a message on Instagram." Erin smiled at the thought. "I have to figure out a way to print it out and frame it. And are you really going to work for your competition?"

"Mama's got to put bread on the table until you can buy us that house in Provincetown."

Back in the kitchen, Kendra handed Catherine the bottle of wine and the corkscrew. Erin took the casserole out of the oven as Nat put the finishing touches on a bowl of salad and everything was dished out. When they were gathered around the table, Kendra insisted on joining hands and saying grace. With Nat's hand in one of hers and Catherine's in the other, Erin realized she had so much to be grateful for. A few months ago, life had been bleak, and she wasn't sure where she was going to turn, or if she had any kind of a future. Her best friend reaching out had changed that. Nat's need had been her lifeline. And in the process, she'd found herself again, connected with the touchstone of her creativity, able to finally move beyond the enormous rut she'd burrowed into. But the gift above all of that was Catherine. She'd suspected this woman would change her world. She just had no idea how profound it would be. Looking around at these three women, she knew she was home.

About the Author

Mary Burns is a long-time resident of New York City. She received a master of fine arts in playwriting from Columbia University in 1991. After a twenty-year stint as an executive assistant, she took a sabbatical to write a play and ended up with a novel instead. *Forging a Desire Line* was published by Bold Strokes Books in 2020.

She has also published short stories in Cleis Press's *Best Lesbian Erotica, vol. 4* (Dec. 2019), under the pseudonym Catherine Collinsworth and *vol. 5* (Dec. 2020), both edited by Sinclair Sexsmith.

She and her wife of twenty years used to go to theaters, cabarets, museums, and on vacations all the time prior to the pandemic. Now they enjoy bingeing Netflix and Amazon Prime and discovered they can attend live cabaret and Broadway shows online. Perhaps a YouTube vacation is next. You can reach her at maryburns11C@gmail.com and www.marypburns.com.

Books Available from Bold Strokes Books

A Different Man by Andrew L. Huerta. This diverse collection of stories chronicling the challenges of gay life at various ages shines a light on the progress made and the progress still to come. (978-1-63555-977-4)

All That Remains by Sheri Lewis Wohl. Johnnie and Shantel might have to risk their lives—and their love—to stop a werewolf intent on killing. (978-1-63555-949-1)

Beginner's Bet by Fiona Riley. Phenom luxury Realtor Ellison Gamble has everything, except a family to share it with, so when a mix-up brings youthful Katie Crawford into her life, she bets the house on love. (978-1-63555-733-6)

Dangerous Without You by Lexus Grey. Throughout their senior year in high school, Aspen, Remington, Denna, and Raleigh face challenges in life and romance that they never expect. (978-1-63555-947-7)

Desiring More by Raven Sky. In this collection of steamy stories, a rich variety of lovers find themselves desiring more, more from a lover, more from themselves, and more from life. (978-1-63679-037-4)

Jordan's Kiss by Nanisi Barrett D'Arnuck. After losing everything in a fire, Jordan Phelps joins a small lounge band and meets pianist Morgan Sparks, who lights another blaze, this time in Jordan's heart. (978-1-63555-980-4)

Late City Summer by Jeanette Bears. Forced together for her wedding, Emily Stanton and Kate Alessi navigate their lingering passion for one another against the backdrop of New York City and World War II, and a summer romance they left behind. (978-1-63555-968-2)

Love and Lotus Blossoms by Anne Shade. On her path to self-acceptance and true passion, Janesse will risk everything—and possibly everyone—she loves. (978-1-63555-985-9)

Love in the Limelight by Ashley Moore. Marion Hargreaves, the finest actress of her generation, and Jessica Carmichael, the world's biggest pop star, rediscover each other twenty years after an ill-fated affair. (978-1-63679-051-0)

Suspecting Her by Mary P. Burns. Complications ensue when Erin O'Connor falls for top real estate saleswoman Catherine Williams while investigating racism in the real estate industry; the fallout could end their chance at happiness. (978-1-63555-960-6)

Two Winters by Lauren Emily Whalen. A modern YA retelling of Shakespeare's *The Winter's Tale* about birth, death, Catholic school, improv comedy, and the healing nature of time. (978-1-63679-019-0)

Busy Ain't the Half of It by Frederick Smith and Chaz Lamar Cruz. Elijah and Justin seek happily-ever-afters in LA, but are they too busy to notice happiness when it's there? (978-1-63555-944-6)

Calumet by Ali Vali. Jaxon Lavigne and Iris Long had a forbidden small-town romance that didn't last, and the consequences of that love will be uncovered fifteen years later at their high school reunion. (978-1-63555-900-2)

Her Countess to Cherish by Jane Walsh. London Society's material girl realizes there is more to life than diamonds when she falls in love with a non-binary bluestocking. (978-1-63555-902-6)

Hot Days, Heated Nights by Renee Roman. When Cole and Lee meet, instant attraction quickly flares into uncontrollable passion, but their connection might be short lived as Lee's identity is tied to her life in the city. (978-1-63555-888-3)

Never Be the Same by MA Binfield. Casey meets Olivia and sparks fly in this opposites attract romance that proves love can be found in the unlikeliest places. (978-1-63555-938-5)

Quiet Village by Eden Darry. Something not quite human is stalking Collie and her niece, and she'll be forced to work with undercover reporter Emily Lassiter if they want to get out of Hyam alive. (978-1-63555-898-2)

Shaken or Stirred by Georgia Beers. Bar owner Julia Martini and home health aide Savannah McNally attempt to weather the storms brought on by a mysterious blogger trashing the bar, family feuds they knew nothing about, and way too much advice from way too many relatives. (978-1-63555-928-6)

The Fiend in the Fog by Jess Faraday. Can four people on different trajectories work together to save the vulnerable residents of East London from the terrifying fiend in the fog before it's too late? (978-1-63555-514-1)

The Marriage Masquerade by Toni Logan. A no strings attached marriage scheme to inherit a Maui B&B uncovers unexpected attractions and a dark family secret. (978-1-63555-914-9)

Flight SQA016 by Amanda Radley. Fastidious airline passenger Olivia Lewis is used to things being a certain way. When her routine is changed by a new, attractive member of the staff, sparks fly. (978-1-63679-045-9)

Home Is Where the Heart Is by Jenny Frame. Can Archie make the countryside her home and give Ash the fairytale romance she desires? Or will the countryside and small village life all be too much for her? (978-1-63555-922-4)

Moving Forward by PJ Trebelhorn. The last person Shelby Ryan expects to be attracted to is Iris Calhoun, the sister of the man who killed her wife four years and three thousand miles ago. (978-1-63555-953-8)

Poison Pen by Jean Copeland. Debut author Kendra Blake is finally living her best life until a nasty book review and exposed secrets threaten her promising new romance with aspiring journalist Alison Chatterley. (978-1-63555-849-4)

Seasons for Change by KC Richardson. Love, laughter, and trust develop for Shawn and Morgan throughout the changing seasons of Lake Tahoe. (978-1-63555-882-1)

Summer Lovin' by Julie Cannon. Three different women, three exotic locations, one unforgettable summer. What do you think will happen? (978-1-63555-920-0)

Unbridled by D. Jackson Leigh. A visit to a local stable turns into more than riding lessons between a novel writer and an equestrian with a taste for power play. (978-1-63555-847-0)

VIP by Jackie D. In a town where relationships are forged and shattered by perception, sometimes even love can't change who you really are. (978-1-63555-908-8)

Yearning by Gun Brooke. The sleepy town of Dennamore has an irresistible pull on those who've moved away. The mystery Darian Benson and Samantha Pike uncover will change them forever, but the love they find along the way just might be the key to saving themselves. (978-1-63555-757-2)

A Turn of Fate by Ronica Black. Will Nev and Kinsley finally face their painful past and relent to their powerful, forbidden attraction? Or will facing their past be too much to fight through? (978-1-63555-930-9)

Desires After Dark by MJ Williamz. When her human lover falls deathly ill, Alex, a vampire, must decide which is worse, letting her go or condemning her to everlasting life. (978-1-63555-940-8)

Her Consigliere by Carsen Taite. FBI agent Royal Scott swore an oath to uphold the law, and criminal defense attorney Siobhan Collins pledged her loyalty to the only family she's ever known, but will their love be stronger than the bonds they've vowed to others, or will their competing allegiances tear them apart? (978-1-63555-924-8)

In Our Words: Queer Stories from Black, Indigenous, and People of Color Writers. Stories selected by Anne Shade and edited by Victoria Villaseñor. Comprising both the renowned and emerging voices of Black, Indigenous, and People of Color authors, this thoughtfully curated collection of short stories explores the intersection of racial and queer identity. (978-1-63555-936-1)

Measure of Devotion by CF Frizzell. Disguised as her late twin brother, Catherine Samson enters the Civil War to defend the Constitution as a Union soldier, never expecting her life to be altered by a Gettysburg farmer's daughter. (978-1-63555-951-4)

Not Guilty by Brit Ryder. Claire Weaver and Emery Pearson's day jobs clash, even as their desire for each other burns, and a discreet sex-only arrangement is the only option. (978-1-63555-896-8)

Opposites Attract: Butch/Femme Romances by Meghan O'Brien, Aurora Rey, Angie Williams. Sometimes opposites really do attract. Fall in love with these butch/femme romance novellas. (978-1-63555-784-8)

Swift Vengeance by Jean Copeland, Jackie D, Erin Zak. A journalist becomes the subject of her own investigation when sudden strange, violent visions summon her to a summer retreat and into the arms of a killer's possible next victim. (978-1-63555-880-7)

Under Her Influence by Amanda Radley. On their path to #truelove, will Beth and Jemma discover that reality is even better than illusion? (978-1-63555-963-7)

Wasteland by Kristin Keppler & Allisa Bahney. Danielle Clark is fighting against the National Armed Forces and finds peace as a scavenger, until the NAF general's daughter, Katelyn Turner, shows up on her doorstep and brings the fight right back to her. (978-1-63555-935-4)

When in Doubt by VK Powell. Police officer Jeri Wylder thinks she committed a crime in the line of duty but can't remember, until details emerge pointing to a cover-up by those close to her. (978-1-63555-955-2)

A Woman to Treasure by Ali Vali. An ancient scroll isn't the only treasure Levi Montbard finds as she starts her hunt for the truth—all she has to do is prove to Yasmine Hassani that there's more to her than an adventurous soul. (978-1-63555-890-6)

Before. After. Always. by Morgan Lee Miller. Still reeling from her tragic past, Eliza Walsh has sworn off taking risks, until Blake Navarro turns her world right-side up, making her question if falling in love again is worth it. (978-1-63555-845-6)

Bet the Farm by Fiona Riley. Lauren Calloway's luxury real estate sale of the century comes to a screeching halt when dairy farm heiress, and one-night stand, Thea Boudreaux calls her bluff. (978-1-63555-731-2)

Cowgirl by Nance Sparks. The last thing Aren expects is to fall for Carol. Sharing her home is one thing, but sharing her heart means sharing the demons in her past and risking everything to keep Carol safe. (978-1-63555-877-7)

Give In to Me by Elle Spencer. Gabriela Talbot never expected to sleep with her favorite author—certainly not after the scathing review she'd given Whitney Ainsworth's latest book. (978-1-63555-910-1)

Hidden Dreams by Shelley Thrasher. A lethal virus and its resulting vision send Texan Barbara Allan and her lovely guide, Dara, on a journey up Cambodia's Mekong River in search of Barbara's mother's mystifying past. (978-1-63555-856-2)

In the Spotlight by Lesley Davis. For actresses Cole Calder and Eris Whyte, their chance at love runs out fast when a fan's adoration turns to obsession. (978-1-63555-926-2)

Origins by Jen Jensen. Jamis Bachman is pulled into a dangerous mystery that becomes personal when she learns the truth of her origins as a ghost hunter. (978-1-63555-837-1)

Pursuit: A Victorian Entertainment by Felice Picano. An intelligent, handsome, ruthlessly ambitious young man who rose from the slums to become the right-hand man of the Lord Exchequer of England will stop at nothing as he pursues his Lord's vanished wife across Continental Europe. (978-1-63555-870-8)

Unrivaled by Radclyffe. Zoey Cohen will never accept second place in matters of the heart, even when her rival is a career, and Declan Black has nothing left to give of herself or her heart. (978-1-63679-013-8)